FORGED BY FROST

Forged By Frost

Illusions of Ingilaef

JOHNNY LEE CHAPMAN III

For Tammy G. Chapman

"Be You!"

Illusions of Ingilaef

It lies not in the swarming wood
Nor the peak of glacial summits,
Its existence is doubtful, I admit
Yet, if veritable, find it, I would.

To this task my end of days I commit
For the risk is worth the rewards
And, as pens birth noble words,
So, too, shall I uncover the residence.

By chance, the odd path occurred
When life channeled my course to lost
Longingly, I wandered the forgotten frost
Seeking an invitation to another world.

A place where time does not cost,
Borders diminish between those alive
And the dead who dance and thrive
Can share a path to be crossed.

However, when I did inevitably arrive
And the mist dispersed the illusion
In the end, I came to an honest resolution:
I discarded all reasons to stay alive...

Until I sipped the wondrous potion
Erasing all doubts, fears, and grief
Granting a second chance at peace,
This tonic rewrote my initial conclusion.

Find the cordial where orchards curl like reefs,
And offer yourself to the watery trickster,
If you wish to drink the blessed elixir,
And earn a new existence in Ingilaef.

~Cain

ACT I

Sleeper Agent

"We are but gods trapped within golems. We are but gods trapped within golems. Ahem, we are but gods trapped within golems."

The final page of the printed script turned over as polka-dot boxers ruffled next to a porcelain toilet. A young man shifted to the sink to wash his hands. He dismantled his du-rag, revealing a miniature curly fro. With an electric toothbrush pointed at the reflection, he shouted with a voice stretched two pitches too high.

"I am the blaze that burned the world, the shadow that gave birth to light. I am the myth that men whisper about with envy. *I am Baudelaire! I am Baudelaire. I AM BAUDE-LAIRE!*"

"Yo, June! What gives? Cafe meatloaf got you dropping bricks again?" An interrupting voice vibrated through the doorway, dispelling the young man's fantasy.

Right, you're not Baudelaire.

Shoulders dropped as June stared into the oil-stained mirror. Almond eyes were widely spaced along his thin brow, and a rounded nose dipped to the left at the bridge. His mustache finally thickened over this winter break, so he was no longer offered the kid's menu at Golden Panda.

June flicked off the bathroom light and re-entered his bedroom, throwing a sock atop the second bunk. "My dude, it's ten-fifteen. We've got history in like an hour, but I'm hitting the cafe first. You trying to pull up with me?"

"Negative, Ghost Rider. Why go to class when you're about to? I'll just copy your notes."

"Lance, is this gonna become a habit? This is already the second class you missed this semester."

"So?" groaned Lance.

"The semester just started last week!" exclaimed June.

"And you've been in class every day, which means I've been in class every day, too. I need to sleep in a bit longer. Last night was a movie."

"You came back at like four in the morning, smelling like a pound of that *fuego*."

Drool from Lance's paper-thin lips curled along a bare chin as he descended the lofted bed. June watched him scratch his back, remove the twelve-volt battery from the charger, and load it into a digital camera. Standing, he and June were similar in height and weight; the main physical difference between the boys was their complexion and hair texture.

"I wasn't planning on staying out that late, but the match took longer than expected. And turning down a session invitation is inconsiderate," Lance yawned.

"Such a nobleman," June joked.

Lance patted the jacket he wore yesterday, locating his wallet, a lighter, and another object. "Like Scoobert, I think we have a problem."

"...Don't tell me? Not this again," June said.

"I don't know why this is becoming a habit."

"Apparently, the sixth commandment means nothing to you."

"I told you, this is what happens when I get crossfaded. It makes me scrap my morality."

"Is that *a coffee mug*?" Embedded on the perimeter of the pilfered mug was a comical image of Lady Liberty getting loose on a pole made from her torch. "Odd choice of design, but it's New York. Anything goes here."

"Another addition to the collection," said Lance. The collection included a blue traffic cone, a small picture frame with the Hudson River, a pair of cream high heels, six garden decorations including two gnomes, and a wind chime with metallic images of the school mascot.

"Better slow it down, or I'll have to intervene with a TLC camera crew. Do you at least know why you do it?" June asked.

"I'm Clark Klepto, and substances are my phone booth. One minute, I'm docile; the next, I'm tucking household objects into my socks like I'm smuggling dope across the border. I don't do this sober; I promise."

"That's why it's so fascinating, Lance. You're a specimen worth studying," said June.

"A specimen with a serious hangover," Lance added.

"You might as well put Lady Liberty to use. I can smell last night's sins from here." After excavating the top cabinet of the dresser, June removed a sweater with a stitched graphic that read MSU.

"What was with all the shouting in the bathroom?" Lance inquired.

"Ummm...I was rehearsing."

"That's right! Today is the day, isn't it? You better go out there and *Macbeth* the stage. Right?"

June palmed his forehead. "Dude, what the hell? Don't say that!"

"Why not?"

"It's like an ill omen to refer to that play as the title."

"Well, that's just stupid. Why title something and not call it that? Plus, I thought that's what you said instead of 'break a leg' or whatever."

"No, bro. We say break a leg so we can get *in the cast.*"

"More stupidity. Why wish injury on your friends?"

"Oh lovely, now I have to deal with being cursed," June sighed.

Hope you're ready to bomb today's audition, June. Totally going to blow it; seriously, how stupid are you to think this is possible? Absolutely stupid. You're gonna choke again. That's all you can do!

"I should just give up on this; it's so stupid..." June muttered.

"Stop! Gimme that neck!" Lance hopped from the futon, and June turned to face the wall. *SWIPE!* Warm fingers ran across the back of June's neck.

"Shit, not so rough, dude. Why did we ever agree to this stupid deal anyway?"

"I enjoy helping my best friend become a shining light of joy."

"My neck seems to think otherwise."

"I wouldn't have to do it if you stopped being an Anxious Alex! Don't worry; we will change that *tonight.* I hope you're prepared for our voyage," Lance said as he tiptoed into the bathroom with his boxers halfway down.

June went to his desk to collect his belongings. Atop the desk was a laptop with a wireless mouse, a Broadway souvenir cup containing various writing utensils, Denzel

Washington's signed biography, and an overly complicated printer. Checking the time on his laptop, June pulled his bag from the wooden bunk bed and carefully packed it.

"Okay, June, today's the day. Let's go do our best!"

You'll probably blow it like you've blown everything else. Don't tell me you believe you can get the part. There are so many others better than you. You're a nobody, even on the stage. Nobody remembers any of your performances except when you choke!

A mischievous laugh accompanied by a foul stench emanated from the bathroom. "Oooh, that's a ripe one. It looks like Mt. Rushmore."

"The narration is not necessary, Lance."

"As an artist, I needed to paint a visual for you. Don't forget to send me twenty so I can pick up supplies for our voyage."

"Will do. I'll see you later tonight, bro," said June. He tapped his pockets. "Cell phone? Keys? Wallet? Check!" Then, he scanned the desk. "Script? Check!" he said as he tucked the binder underneath his right arm. June slipped out of the dorm room, and the door locked behind him.

"Ughhhh! Damn it, June!" shouted Lance. "You used the last of the tissue. Can you grab me a roll from the lounge bathroom, June? Wait, June! Bro, you out there? Aye, June, c'mon, man, don't leave me like this. I'm going to use your sock. You're gonna have *asslete's foot*. Juneeee!"

In 1951, Morrison Straight University received funding to convert the Brachman Gymnasium for Court Athletics into the Brachman Café to accommodate the influx of students after World War II. Wooden floors stretched from the kitchen in the far west wing to the smoothie shop near the front of the building. A buffet-style diner where various entrees were served daily was added, and a lounge-style seating area was incorporated into the second floor.

Today, June decided on quesadillas, sticky jasmine rice, fried fish, and a cran-grape soda to wash it down. He'd taken up seating in his usual position near the window overlooking the Washington Student Union.

As he ate, he observed the cosmos of his college campus: students orbiting the academic stations, professors probing into professional lives with other faculty, custodians and parking officers congregating near the utility lot, construction crew members navigating the work zone around the Clock Tower, and the occasional university admin migrating to meetings.

While nibbling on his fish, June saw a group of students exit the Union. The crowd outside the common area split like the Red Sea as the strange group strolled across the yard. Something about them transfixed him. Then, June felt eyes stalking him. He couldn't figure out who or where, but instinct told him something marked his presence. Glancing around, he didn't catch anyone's stare, but his apprehension convinced him to move seats.

Relocated in a quieter area, he bit into his quesadilla. As the cheese strung from his mouth to his chin, a heavy-set student with a British boy band bowl cut placed his tray beside him. The boy's plate was packed, sampling nearly every station's signature dish. Instead of eating, he whipped out his cell phone and played some cheap puzzle game purchased from an internet-based app store. After finishing the game, the boy began gnawing at his meal. June tried to ignore the lack of manners, but the droplets were getting closer to his space.

Suddenly, the student choked on the meatloaf he'd been scarfing down while tapping the screen. He banged the table thrice and motioned for help. Panicked, June tried to talk him through the ordeal, but words were useless. The boy reached for June's soda and washed down the bolus, finishing with a refreshing "Ahh." Before June could scold him, he noticed the source of the Brit's near-death experience.

Ascending the escalators was the same pack of students he observed outside. Everybody stayed their distance, and even the kitchen staff stopped serving to stare. Childlike envy swelled within June. How easily the masses respected this group. *If only I could make others see me like that.* However, June failed to realize that they weren't just commanding respect. In that instant, the Brachman Cafe shared a collective silence, as a village would do if visited by a royal caravan or an execution squad.

Leading the squad was a bearded man who resembled an Alaskan mountaineer, followed by a fashion icon rocking a flashy yellow Adidas warm-up suit, a goth girl wearing an anime-inspired cat mask, and an olive-skinned beauty with a medical brace around her ankle.

Within the limits of June's peripheral appeared the final member: a young man wearing a pair of glossy spectacles. Although he drifted towards the strange party's rear, he moved as if commanding from the stern. June's gaze lingered on the stranger's face for a second too long, and a streak of light hit his eyes.

A sharp auditory stimulation caused him to wince, but it had already started to fade by the time he registered the sensation. Then, he noticed the young man in the rear peering at him. Heart palpitations increased, and June's thoughts imploded into dust, yet he couldn't turn away from the stare. It reminded him of the moment Caesar met Brutus on the Ides of March.

Finally, after making uncomfortable eye contact, the double doors of the dining hall flapped open, and the squad exited, carrying with them a thick cloud of ominous apprehension.

"Oy...I'm glad they're gone," said June's neighbor, startling him.

"Who are they?" June asked.

"You a student here, mate? And you ain't never heard of them?" He asked with a loud Cockney accent.

"Can't say I have."

Fear welled in the bullhorn's face. "That's the *Lemurian Order*. They, well, they one of them secret societies. The ones we don't speak of."

"And yet, here we are speaking of it. What was it you called them again? The Lemarian..."

"Lemurian Order," he repeated.

June downed a spoonful of rice. "What's so secretive about them?"

"It's less a secret and more word of mouth, you know. Rumors and such to scare first-years. And the adjunct professors. Probably the provost, too."

"Must've missed the seminar on university rumors."

"You ain't heard not one peep? You might be a *sleeper agent*."

"Or maybe I'm not a conspiracy theorist. Still, why would they be here in the Cafe if they're so elite?"

"Well, there's word on the streets *they're recruiting* since some of their members are seniors."

"Recruiting?"

"Yeah, I heard you must be invited to join the Lemurian Order and then sacrifice someone—a close someone. Or a pet. Maybe it's someone else's pet that has to die."

"Clearly rumors. They would've been brought to justice by now," June said.

"Justice doesn't mean shit compared to status."

"You really think they can get away with killing someone?"

"*I bet they've done it.* Probably a few times," the Brit responded.

June imagined the flashy students coming together under the shadow of night to prey on a vulnerable stranger. Would they strip their victim bare before stabbing a dagger into an unsuspecting back like the senators did Caesar?

"Aye, don't believe me? Let's get another opinion then."

The Brit shifted his attention to the booth behind them. "Hate to interrupt your readin. Got a quick question that I need you to answer for me and my mate. Be a deciding factor in our discussion."

June covered his face out of sheer embarrassment. He leaned over the booth railing to better see the target of the Brit's explosive vocals—a woman with a fabric wrapped around her head. Not a hijab, but a satin scarf for fresh locs. Freckles populated her cheeks, and a finely chiseled nose rested on the midline. However, the features were masked by a weathered book held close to the face, instructing others to keep their distance.

"Oy. Hard of hearing, are ye?" the loudmouth chattered.

"*A baptism of ash awaited me at the end of my life...*" June delicately recited. The woman stopped reading, folded a slight crease on the corner of the page, and shut the book. He felt her inquisitive eyes dissecting him to determine whether an interaction was warranted. "I'm sorry, that's a line from—"

"*...And the flames lick the crystals of my soul, providing a light to call my own,*" she replied.

Both boys were astonished to hear her respond, but the Brit interjected again since it wasn't to his question. "So, you do know English, yea?"

"I do, but I'm not sure you understand anything under a hundred decibels."

"Got ourselves a talking dictionary here. Now that I've got your attention—"

"Quiet, blowhorn. You," She pointed to June and then to the book on the table. "You've read this?"

"Yeah! That's *Foglands*, the latest collection of poems by Xavier. I didn't know anybody on campus was hip to him. He's not...well-received in some spheres."

The young woman smirked, "That's an assumed statement; here I am, reading him, receiving him well. How versed are you, though? What's your favorite Xavier line?"

She handed him the book. "Ah, uh, favorite line? I mean, there are so many, but if I have to choose one..." June took a moment to flip through the pages until he discovered the target. After reading it twice, he set the book beside his tray and cleared his throat.

"*The moments of life dashed against the prismatic surface; water wished to be more than a reflection as I wished the chance to change the portrait in the cerulean canvas.*"

"*Temporal Tangent.* I wouldn't necessarily consider it his defining work, but it does represent many of his ideologies."

"We have ourselves a critic. What would you consider his best?" June asked.

"We wait on those who exist to take a risk...On the belief that life is beyond suffering, even though we will be forgotten...like foam on the shores of absolution."

"I've never read that one," June said.

"It's an older poem from Xavier's blogging days."

"Why that one?"

"I like it because the closing stanza highlights the process of compartmentalizing grief. Regardless of what ordeals we may face here, there will be a point when all becomes nothing."

"Sounds deep," June commented.

"It's no surprise you think *Temporal Tangent* is his best. You've only seen the surface level. If you want to know Xavier–and maybe yourself–you should go deep."

June's cheeks flushed at the statement while the Brit placed his silverware in the clear plastic cup and threw his bag around his shoulder. "This is bollocks; all you two are sayin is fairy gibberish. I'm late for class anyway. Be seeing you around, Sleeper Agent."

"Sleeper Agent?" she asked, expecting an elaborate story to follow.

"Ignore him. Are you reading the book for a class?" June asked.

"No, this is strictly for pleasure. Although, I'm not sure how pleasing Xavier's poetry can be considered."

"It's heavy stuff. I had to take it in spurts, and sometimes I had to read it repeatedly before I could understand my feelings."

"That's Xavier for ya. I believe that confusion stems from his personification of emotions. His adoration for sorrow is almost an act of rebellion, and the way he heralds melancholic laments as creative boons rather than spirit-crushing obstacles. Such an authentic take on reclamation and well-versed when you think about word selection and format."

"He's also a unique voice, able to cover a diverse range of topics without feeling too performative or false. Haven't run across many writers like him."

"Because there are none like him. Xavier created his style by blending elements of the Romantic bards with a pessimistic philosophy he developed as a response to modern culture. But, in my opinion, he tainted the entire concoction when he tried to speak about hope, ultimately creating poems that are both potions and poisons. And here I am rambling now…" She hid her face in embarrassment.

"Please, rambling is good for the soul. I'm impressed that you've taken the time to understand him. I get what you mean about the sorrow, too. He's so unafraid of expressing his internal workings to the world, and I think it takes real courage to show vulnerability."

"It does, and even more to publish it," she added.

"Strange though, I haven't read any new pieces lately. His social accounts have also been quiet since last year," June said.

"Artists often venture on a pilgrimage to recollect themselves after navigating the exhausting routes of society. I wouldn't be surprised if he were on a temporary hiatus."

"Maybe he's working on a new manuscript or something?" June asked.

"Doubtful. I'd wager that Xavier's absence is self-inflicted."

June rubbed his neck. "Self-inflicted? How do you figure?"

"*A writer's life is reflected in their work.* We both agree that Xavier's greatest theme for his poetry is sorrow. So, it's easy to assume someone like him could never be happy. And that sadness is what caused him to disappear."

"Hmm, now that's an assumed statement," June countered.

The woman stopped packing her bag and stared at him. "This is an unexpected rebuttal. Then, let me pose a question: Do you believe that people can recreate something they've never experienced before? Can they embody an emotion that is foreign to them?"

"Um, yeah...yeah, I do," said June.

"How so?"

"Actors do it all the time, embodying the lives and experiences of another. They become characters by embracing the set objectives and adhering to necessary exposition."

"Agreed. But a character is nothing more than an agent. A created vessel whose sole duty is to cause a change in a plot. They work for television shows and novels, but poetry is different. Authentic expression stems from authentic experience, and I don't think true poetry can be created by anything other than authenticity. And since experience breeds emotion, the poet has to become a voyeur to the emotions that inspire verses, including hardship and trauma."

Her bag zipped, and she left the booth to meet him.

"So you think he's taken his life?" June asked.

"Perhaps not his actual life, but his artist life? Yes."

"Why would he do that when he's so good?"

"Since Xavier's poetry is full of suffering, we can infer his life has been full of sorrowful experiences. Point in case, no matter how objectively good he is, he is bound to suffer. Perhaps he reached a breaking point and decided to put to rest his social existence. I cannot fault him; I've also been known to disappear when drained. But given your response, I suspect you've yet to experience such a hardship," she said.

"You don't know what I've been through. It might just surprise you what's stored in my soul."

"If you say so. But what I do know is I can't be late for lab. This has been rather entertaining. Perhaps our paths will cross again, Sleeper Agent."

The young woman disembarked from the conversation and headed toward the disposal center. She never looked back at him, even though he remained glued to her.

After finishing his meal, June pulled the napkin out of the container to remove the crumbs, but he accidentally knocked down the salt shaker. Translucent crystals spilled from the stainless-steel cap, spreading across the table like scattered marbles.

"Great, as if I needed any more bad luck today." He cleaned up the salt on the floor and caught sight of an object next to the tray. "Some avid fan. She makes all that smart talk but forgets her book." Fingers peeled open the worn cover to find initials sketched in the top corner. "Hmm, MP. Military Police. Wouldn't mind our paths crossing again."

Once packed up, June checked the time on his phone and hustled toward the cleaning station. On his way down the stairs, he bumped the to-go box out of an approaching student's hand, spilling their meal. Apologies rang from the arched limestones of the Brachman Cafe as June raced across the main yard of Morrison Straight University.

The lecture-style classroom within Nielson Hall contained eight rows of desks curved around the center podium. Behind the podium was a large black chalkboard covered in scribblings. The room could seat sixty-four students, but this history course only had twenty-nine registered attendants. Out of the twenty-nine who showed, five students assembled in the front while the rest remained behind the fourth row.

June removed his book bag and sat in the second row with the other overachievers. While he waited for his professor to arrive, he flipped through his agenda.

Can't believe I'm back in school again. I swear winter break just started yesterday. January 21st: First quiz so soon? That's technically still syllabus week. Leave it to Mr. Ray not to follow proper educational etiquette. January 23rd: Eye doctor appointment. I hope my sight hasn't changed, but reading that long-ass script over and over might've messed something up. January 26th: Bible study...I should start going. Maybe, but there's always next week. Lance wants me to hit that concert with him that night.

And then there's today. His index finger parked on Friday, January 18th, 2019. In bold letters was the word: **Spring Audition**.

Mint and lavender aromas filled the hallway as his Old-World History professor arrived. Scurrying feet entered, and a lunchbox and briefcase were set beside the podium. The woman dashed and erased the old notes, leaving fingerprints on the board. Using the chalk, she wrote a single word in bold, dramatically swiping to fill the characters. Stepping back, she slapped her hand thrice, clearing the dust.

LEGACY

"My apologies for the delay! I had to wrestle my bag from my roommate this morning, and if you've ever had to go toe to toe with a corgi, you know what I'm talking about," she said with a Midwestern accent. "But now that I'm here, let us begin our lesson."

Binders were opened, and pens clicked as Kelly Liam's ginger hair was assembled in a messy bun. The newly hired professor's way of talking about complex subjects made her seem wise beyond her years, even though she was only thirty-two. Her pescatarian diet and hot yoga obsession allowed her to maintain stamina for a highly entertaining lecture style.

"Often, history assimilates ancient archives into one source because advanced classification systems didn't exist. So, unfortunately, the information becomes altered or misplaced. For example, Persia was a nation with plenty of positive interactions with the esteemed Greeks despite the eventual conflicts. It's believed that many of the great minds of antiquity adopted certain beliefs from this empire and other African civilizations and incorporated them into their culture. Some customs even exist today, and we can trace the roots back to the origin of the legacy."

"So, here's your first question of the day. Does anybody remember the name of the Greek physician who attended the court of King Artaxes?"

"It was Aristotle," announced a voice from the back.

The answer is Ctesias, June thought.

"Aristotle did interact with the Persians, but that came in later years."

"Was it Imhotep?" another cried with more inquiry than confidence.

"Incorrect. Imhotep was associated with Egypt, although he is considered a father of modern medicine," she stated.

"C'mon, it's Ctesias. Nobody else read the section? The answer was right there in the third paragraph," he whispered.

Ms. Liam snagged June's wandering eyes. "June...care to give it a go?"

"Oh, right. Um...should I stand?"

"Why not? That's a good idea. From now on, we'll stand when speaking. Helps with projection." The class vocalized their complaint with random groans and grunts. Ms. Liam smiled as June rose and adjusted his pants. "Now, do you know..."

"Ctesias of Cnidos, author of *Indica*. He was there during the fourth century," June answered.

"Correct, June. Glad to know that some of you are being proactive," Ms. Liam said. She returned to the desk and powered on the overhead projector.

"While in the royal court for seven years and two kings, Ctesias documented everything. His interactions with diplomatic Persians, astrological readings from the magi, and medical reports; he was, after all, a trained physician. In his work *Indica*, Ctesias describes the autopsy of real and phantasmal creatures coinciding with legends from the surrounding cultures. Through Ctesias's autobiographical writing, we get an outsider's point of view on Persia, gaining an intimate knowledge of the system that governed one of the strongest empires. However, much of this information has been lost due to poor record-keeping. Who knows what ancient rites were removed from history, what infernal truths are forgotten to time?"

The benefit of being called early was that June could coast the rest of the class after he earned his participation grade. Reclining in his chair, he opened the black binder. As the class discussion continued, June drifted from ancient history to the fantastical world inside the words, reciting the lines of the script under his breath in anticipation of today's audition.

Conspiratorial

Our researchers on *Precursors of the Past* believe throughout human history, enlightened beings from alternate planes of existence traversed to our world through interdimensional portals caused by the appearance of *Yol's Comet.* Upon entering our world, these entities, known as Precursors, required human hosts so they could commune with our species. These hosts were chosen based on astrological data, and a series of rituals would be conducted to prepare their vessel. Many of these rituals included rhythmic chanting, physical movement, sacred objects, and the occasional hallucinogen. Once linked to the human, the Precursor granted the host access to the Precursor's collective unconscious, which spanned thousands of eons. Theoretically, those blessed liaisons exposed to the universal wisdom have often served as catalysts for humanity's progress as an intelligent species. In ancient times, the liaisons were called shamans, seers, and druids; today, they may be known as empaths, geniuses, and energy healers."

The television flashed blue to orange, illuminating Lance's face like a false sunset. Since he'd already missed history and his photography course, Lance decided to take the rest of the Friday off and catch up on his extracurricular activities. Those activities included watching documentaries while editing images.

He finished the photographic revisions by adjusting the brightness, adding a mask layer of highlight, and bumping the saturation bar up by five percent. Then, he compared the original to the edit and nodded. The cursor clicked on Export, and Lance leaned back to glance at the television.

"This is clear evidence of ancient humanity's direct interaction with interdimensional beings known as the *Precursors*!" shouted the show host with trembling hands.

His cell phone rang, and he muted the program. "Ah, what's up, bro? Good looks on the connect. Yeah, I was still looking to pick something up. Yeah, I'll be near South Campus this evening. Okay, meet by Ellis Laboratory? Cool. How much do I owe? $70?" Lance checked his wallet, counting the cash. "I'll have it ready. And you're sure an eighth should be enough for two people? Okay, thought so. Dope, I'll hit you up later."

Lance hung up and deleted any traces of the call. Then, a calendar notification appeared on his screen. "Shit. Shit. Shit, I knew I was forgetting something." He stumbled off the futon, snatched a weatherproof hoodie and black boots, and connected his wireless headphones before dashing out of the room. In the elevator, he loaded up an episode of *Found Dead By The Lake,* one of his favorite local true crime podcasts.

The episode he chose investigated the furtive land occupied by Morrison Straight University. With over 1200 undergraduate and graduate students and an additional 100+ staff and faculty employed, Morrison Straight University often ranked as one of the best private universities in the Northeast. It had a national champion lacrosse team and prestigious campus organizations. However, the departments that shined on this campus were the Arts and Biology departments, both receiving international attention due to the accolades of alumni and current students.

Regardless of the radiant record, there were some, like the hosts of the podcast, who recognized the shadow of MSU. According to the local history, the area was settled and founded by Morrison Straight in 1795, a Connecticut colony Catholic who migrated to the new world to spread the good word. While there, Morrison and his family aided in charting the Adirondack mountains and were honored with a land grant for their contributions. Straight settled the land, beginning one of many religious communes established in the Northeast.

The development of the private institute was completed in 1868, and it officially received its charter in 1869. Seven buildings were part of the original blueprint, and over the next century, another fourteen were added. However, this expansion was also the direct cause of strife on campus. Although the Straights were no longer present during the 20th century, the conservative-based nature of the surrounding area shunned away many who wished to attend, particularly people of color. Post-segregation changed this, but at a snail's pace; the first black student attended MSU in 1965—a startling fact if one considers the fifteen-year gap between *Brown vs. Board of Education* and her arrival. However, a greater controversy surrounded the eventual disappearance of that student.

Historically, the secluded community was known throughout the Northeast for having a high percentage of missing persons. The podcast host reviewed possible explanations for mass disappearance: the development of a supernatural beacon or conduit in the area, which emitted a frequency unfamiliar to the human mind. These frequencies could indoctrinate and eventually command a listener to do anything. More radical theories claimed that hidden in the mountains, underneath the hamlet grounds, was a gateway to a demon world, and the Straight's had formed a contract with the devil, granting them fortune in a time of famine for the exchange of a human soul.

Lance stepped out of the Brachman Cafe coffee shop with two teas in hand and half a dozen donuts tucked in his satchel. Then, he continued hustling to his destination. Folger Hall, housed on the southeastern section of campus, was dedicated to the Journalism and Mass Media department. Aspiring news anchors, reporters, editors, and freelance photographers constantly revolved around this hub of communication and content. He headed up a flight of stairs before reaching a set of double doors underneath a massive maroon and silver banner.

THE TRUTH IS PRESERVED IN PRINT.

The Morrison Moment's office was filled with the scent of printed newspapers, freshly poured gossip, and palpable ambition. Four of the six workspaces were already occupied by the volunteer staff compiling articles for tomorrow's magazine.

Upon reaching his desk covered in prints, Lance placed his messenger bag in the cubby and headed straight for the eastern wing with steaming cups. He stood in front of a frosted glass window, preventing voyeuristic intrusions. With a light tap, he knocked until a breathless voice welcomed him. He said no word but placed the tea next to the plaque that read *Senior Editor.*

A pursed mouth drank from the steaming cup, followed by a disappointed sigh. "I asked for the honey-ginseng-chamomile tea, not the honey-ginseng-cinnamon," said his boss.

"Hold up. You said you wanted cinnamon because it was cold today and needed to spice up," said Lance.

A gold hoop nose ring gleamed, and the four bangles upon the boss's wrist clinked as a finger pointed at him. "Uh, uh. Don't try to tell me that I'm wrong, not after you missed another meeting!"

"You're right, Anjali. It's my fault; I'll do better," Lance replied.

"I know you will," said Anjali.

The five-foot-two, sun-kissed junior lifted her eyes from the scattered stack of documents and set them upon her late arrival. Lance clocked her attire: a black blouse, gray jacket, and maroon pants cuffed at her ankles. "Here, give me that," Anjali commanded as she reached for the cup in Lance's hand. Her fingers traced the bridge of his wrist before taking hold of his drink. She then downed a hearty gulp and returned a pleased grin. "I'll be taking this from you."

An indirect kiss?! Lance melted. Relieved, he dropped his shoulders, and his blood flow returned to the rest of his body. "I also got some donuts. OG glazed for that *gangsta flava,*" he joked. However, the comedic attempt failed as a soft grunt came behind him.

The guest removed their helmet to release a set of freshly twisted braids. "We culture-appropriating *again?*" George asked, his scowl as sharp as his eyebrows.

Embarrassed, Lance tried to look at Anjali for some response, but she sipped her tea loudly. "Uhhh...my fault, George. You weren't supposed to hear that."

"Maybe that's because you weren't supposed to say it. Now, if you're done flirting, I'd like to get to work," George said. He brushed past Lance and placed something in front of Anjali. "I'm about to make your day a whole lot better. Got some shots from the Greek Life Council service event and an interview with the vice secretary. About eight minutes of footage, but I assume we'll use only a few. Gotta warn you; this isn't the most entertaining interview. This should at least help get your creative juices flowing," said George.

Anjali rubbed his hand with joy, "Great work, George. Load the files and send them to me. We can at least use them as reference points to build the template. You got time now?"

"I have a shoot in the library I've gotta run to, then I'm covering a faculty dinner in the Hamlin Engineering Workshop. Probably won't be free until about 10 or so. But I'll be up late this evening, so feel free to call. If we're gonna work now, I need to eat, though. I was about to head to the Cafe for a snack." George returned to his original pose on the wall, smirking. "Hey, Lance? Mind splitting those donuts? You know, those 'gangsta-flava' ones."

"Technically, I bought them for...well...I wasn't planning on sharing," admitted Lance.

"But you announced it as if you were willing to part with them. Didn't he, Anjali?"

Anjali raised her endearing eyes to Lance. "Do you mind? I plan on being here until midnight, if not later, and a sugary snack right now would go well with the tea."

"Sure...I'll be right back," Lance groaned.

"How about microwaving them, too? A good twenty-two seconds can make a donut into a dream."

"But the microwave is on the other side of Folger Hall. MSU has all these funds, but why do media organizations have to share one microwave? Do you know how many warm snacks are eaten by journalists? And, at this time of day, too?"

"Hot donuts will compensate for you being late," Anjali said.

"Late again, Lance? You take CP time to a new level. What held you up this time? You get the wrong drink order?" teased George.

"You know he did!" exclaimed Anjali. "Showed up late and with the wrong tea."

"We fixed the order. And I was late because I was...sorting through some of the shots from yesterday's event," Lance lied.

George chuckled, "It took you that long to edit photos of a *chess competition*?"

"I'm curious to see the emotion you captured," added Anjali.

Lance raised both hands, mimicking the *Precursors of the Past* host. "Whoa, now! No need to gang up on me. I will get the donuts; I just wanted to know what I missed in the meeting–in a sentence or less."

"We are electing a new Senior Editor at the end of this semester," she added.

"Wait, what!? Why? You've got one year left of your term."

"Because I want to enjoy my victory lap. I've given three years of my college career to the MM and have been Senior

Editor for two; I don't want to think about it next year. I'll still be around but in a less involved capacity. So, I'm passing the torch at the end of this semester."

"That's a big announcement," said Lance. "Senior Editor...how do I apply for that?!"

"You can start by fetching those donuts," George laughed.

"Slow down, cowboy," Anjali said to George. "You missed the meeting, too, even if you were on assignment."

"I just figured you'd fill me in later this evening," George responded.

"Right now, both of you are in the same position. And if either of you are interested in taking the top spot, then as a formality, I need to brief you on everything regarding the competition."

The two photographers looked at each other and then back at Anjali. "*Competition?*" asked Lance.

"Yes. We are going to decide our next Senior Editor with a competition. The applicant who presents the best editorial will be elected to serve the next term. They must show dedication, capacity to handle the workload, and innovative direction."

"What's the editorial topic?" asked Lance.

"Greek Life."

"This should be interesting," said George.

"More details to come, but it is probably good to start brainstorming ideas, as you'll need my approval before committing to a cause. Now," Anjali turned to George, "about this template."

"Lance, donuts, please?"

Ready to commence his errand with shame, Lance gripped the door handle when Anjali caught his attention. "If you're seriously considering the role, then I encourage you to do your best. Don't forget, Lance, you're the MM's eyes. The world will see whatever you snap, *so be prepared to show them the truth!"*

Casting Call

In 1974, during a stage production of *The Picture of Dorian Grey*, Albert Thompson, a three-time Tony Award recipient for Best Actor, was mid-monologue when he suffered a pulmonary embolism—his final moment occurred during the play's climax when Grey turned on the hideous portrait. The scene was laden with so much drama the audience applauded a full minute before a front-row guest realized the actor had yet to move from his fallen position.

Thompson died and left behind a widow and a lump fortune. Knowing that her late husband's true passion was the theater, his wife dedicated a moderate sum to Morrison Straight University, where Thompson completed his undergraduate studies and served as adjunct faculty in the Theater department. The institution used the money to fund a new architectural project dedicated to uplifting thespian culture. After fourteen months of construction, the Thompson Theater was erected in '76, looming like a final bastion for the performing artists.

An afternoon glow appeared over a grove of decayed trees that separated the weathered establishment from the rest of campus. Dead branches raked as June knelt beside a dried root in the surrounding woods. He finished an intimate meeting between his index finger and gag reflex, causing anxiety and quesadilla bits to geyser from his stomach.

After clearing his throat, June shook the nerves from his muscles. "C'mon, it's only an audition. This is doable. You've been reciting the lines since New Year's."

And they're hard as shit. The ecstasy of eternity? My heart turned to obsidian in your arms. He was liberated from whirlwind regret. Whoever wrote this clearly needs to have a normal conversation; some of this sounds like Lord of the Rings fanfiction.

"I can do this...I think," June muttered.

You idiot, this is impossible, and you know it. What about the last time you were on stage? Huh? Do you really want to repeat that?

"Right..." he rubbed his neck. "I'm so stupid. There's no way I'm cut out for this. I should leave before-"

The loading door swung open, startling him. "Daniel Elliott, please report to the stage," said a voice behind him. An invisible muzzle bound June's mouth despite the beckoning bohemian accent. He eventually shuffled out of the woods like a reanimated corpse. "Umm...Daniel? Are you okay?" she asked.

"I'm cursed," he said with a hollow stare. "I can't do it."

"Are you quitting then?"

"No? Maybe? Should I? I don't know what I'm doing. Why am I here?"

"You did sign up for our spring audition, did you not?" He blinked to confirm. "Then, *audition.* I'll tell you something. You'd rather be known as the actor who bombed on stage than the one who never stepped foot on the stage. If you're not willing to get on stage now, then I suggest you find a seat in the audience and enjoy from there."

No response for a minute. "You're right. I've come this far; I guess it's poetic to die in the spotlight," he said. The stagehand opened the door, and he entered the darkened corridor. June's mind raced as he navigated his way backstage.

Let's get this over with. You dug your grave, now lay in it. You're just filling the space until he shows up. Even though he didn't put his name on the list, if Timothy wants the spot, he'll get it.

"But, maybe, just maybe, he's not interested in this production. Maybe the lines are too somber, or he's on a hiatus. Yeah, an artist hiatus."

You're bold to be hopeful.

June exhaled and examined the stage before him. Stone columns stretched towards the heavens, and dual arches served as side entry ports. Instead of a traditional proscenium, the theater was fashioned in a semi-circle. A set of hatches were placed at the center stage, pinpointing the location of the grave trap. The roof above him was currently clamped down, but in the warmer months, the ceiling often remained retracted, adding a dramatic backdrop to the scenery.

Insignificance permeated his skin as he walked upstage into the spotlight. Glancing at the new light fixtures, his neck flared. The shadow currently belonging to him stretched to nearly seven feet, even though he stood at five feet, seven inches. He reached out his hand to shield his eyes from the intense glow, and that's when he saw them.

Four silhouettes were positioned in the front row. "State your name, please?" bellowed a baritone voice.

"Daniel Elliott Junior, but the streets call me June."

Did you really say that out loud? Fucking idiot.

"June," a second, squeakier voice filed into the discussion.

"Can you confirm what role you will audition for?" asked the original voice.

"Ahem, Baudelaire."

A drowsy Southern drawl joined the conversation. "You are aware this role requires utmost commitment?" June nodded. "If chosen, we ask that individuals refrain from undertaking any unnecessary extracurricular activities until the production is wrapped. Are you willing to comply with this request if considered?"

June agreed—more scribbling.

"Following standard procedure, I will have our Stage Manager share a few words."

The person at the far end lifted a script from the table. "Do I have to read all of this again?" The voice whispered. Someone answered the question, and the complaining ended.

"The protagonist of this tale is Baudelaire, a master sculptor. Baudelaire is known to be narcissistic, engaging only in his self-constructed opinions rather than entertaining the banal cries of the world. He is also an artistic soul with a natural craving for creation...and destruction. A man who pursues his desires relentlessly and never exchanges his time with others unless their company is more valuable than the minutes exchanged. Above all else, for better or worse, Baudelaire is an individual. Whenever his interests conflict with others, Baudelaire stands firm on his beliefs, heralding his ego at the peak of pantheons."

The speaker sighed and decided to rush through the next section.

"Our tale begins when Baudelaire, at age 47, is adrift in a misery of unknown origin. In the twenty-nine years he worked in his trade, Baudelaire has fashioned grand sculptures revered as 'golems of the genius' by the known world. However, his desire to exist has long been exhausted due to the exploitation of his craft, and he dreams of ways to escape this cycle without sacrificing his life. At his last exhibition, while wallowing in self-pity, he's approached by a man in a metal mask. The stranger gifts him a cherry blossom petal and informs him, through a cryptic poem, of a mythical place that contains an elixir that can 'rewrite an existence.' With only this information, Baudelaire begins a perilous journey into the wilderness."

The orator sat down, and the original speaker continued. "Thank you for the enriching education. Before we begin your audition, Mr. Elliot, let me introduce the production team. We will be your potential overlords for the momentous occasion."

The stagehand dimmed the overhead lights, granting June a view of the mysterious silhouettes, one at a time. He first recognized the one sitting cross-legged with the patterned ascot. "You know me as your drama professor, Emi Ray, and I'll serve as the sensational Stage Director."

Sitting to the right of Mr. Ray was an older gentleman wearing a steamed button-down with silver cufflinks. "Next to me is Mr. Griswald Tendleton, an award-winning charismatic costume designer and our eclectic Executive Producer."

"You speak too highly of me; I'm just a fan of drama. Call me Gris," he said with a modest twang. "I'll be handling some behind-the-scenes tasks to ensure the efficiency of the production. Oh boy, Emi's alliteration is rubbing off on me."

"We'll be of one mind before it's time to present our production, Gris."

The two grown men shared a laugh interrupted by the figure on the far right who complained about the character description. He had an Andy Warhol-style haircut and a bright yellow shirt that screamed *Notice Me!*

"You might be acquainted with Oscar Mercado, the persevering President of MSU's Theater Troupe. He's decided to step back from acting this semester and serve instead as the Stage Manager. And, at the far end of the table, our dose of divinity and drama." The woman donning a head scarf met June's stare with a victorious smile. "Allow me to introduce our passionate playwright, Michaela Patterson!"

Wait, the cafe critic is the playwright? Oh shit.

Mr. Ray sipped from his silver coffee mug. "Now that we all know each other, I believe it's time to see some acting. Miss Dobson?" The tech who beckoned June appeared from stage left. "Can you summon the Theater Troupe's successful Secretary, please?"

She nodded and headed backstage, leaving June alone. He mouthed the words Military Police as the team talked amongst themselves. They refused to acknowledge him any further, although he did notice stray glances being sent from Michaela.

A second shadow appeared next to June's as a pair of loafers appeared on stage. The brown-skinned stranger wore a burgundy crewneck, olive chinos, and a low-cut fade atop his head. If one stared long enough, they could see Michelangelo's *David* in his face. Vintage glasses covered his eyes. His hand extended and gripped June's, the firmness of his palm only matched by the rhythm of his shake.

"Parker Galician, a pleasure to meet you."

"Oh wow, Parker. I'm honored. I'm June. I've been a fan since *The Nightmare Before Christmas.* Your portrayal of the Mayor was impressive; my favorite role, hands down."

"My reputation precedes me. Yes, last spring was quite the semester for multiple reasons. Challenging, but I do enjoy roles that exhibit duality. What night did you attend?"

June coughed to avoid his embarrassment. "I was...in the production. We never met because I had a minor role."

"Wait," Parker adjusted his glasses, "June is not your real name, is it?"

He shook his head, "It's Daniel. Daniel Elliot Junior."

"That's right! Daniel, you were cast as the..." Parker tapped his cheek.

"I was part of the vampire chorus, so I never really had a name."

"If I'm not mistaken," Parker continued, "you *stole the spotlight* on our final showing."

"I...uh, you could call it that. But I'm not going to mess up like that again. I'm determined to do better."

"Correcting mistakes is man's natural duty if he seeks progress. And you are correcting yours by auditioning for the lead, no?"

"Mhm, I've been trying to approach this role differently. I want to understand Baudelaire's convictions, motives, and reason for rebelling against life itself. I don't know; I find myself gravitating toward his ideals, so I'm here today hoping to earn the chance to embody him."

"Embodiment, huh? A difficult task even for seasoned actors."

"You're not lying. But I've done some legit work since the last time I touched the stage."

"That's an ideal start, but remember: The real work begins *once the role is yours*," Parker advised.

June considered many possibilities for the audition, but he'd not anticipated performing with another actor, especially a talented one like Parker.

"Are we about ready?" Parker asked the production team, wiping his glasses with a handkerchief.

Mr. Ray flipped through his play copy. "Team, any final words?"

"Don't try too hard," said the Stage Manager.

"Leave it all on the stage," said the Executive Producer.

"Hm, I'm curious to see if June can grasp the depth of this character and convey authentic emotions. Can he exhibit the necessary sorrow and eventual madness that Baudelaire will express?" Michaela asked. June's face fell flat. Was she still pressed about that conversation?

"We'll start with the introduction of Baudelaire and Gi, which is on page 14," said Oscar.

The tech extended copies of the script to both actors. Parker declined, "I believe I have the lines ready."

Is he seriously not using a script? I'm so out of my league. June accepted his and began flipping to find the page. Once he located it, he looked at Mr. Ray for approval.

"The spotlight is on you, Mr. Elliott."

June's throat bulged as he swallowed the uneasiness and regurgitated quesadilla. The burn on his neck intensified as he looked at the newly installed rafters. Sweat pooled from his temple, brow, mustache, and arms. Even with the script in his hand, June couldn't process the next move. Meanwhile, his bladder relayed to his brain that it could expel any moment. Soon, he'd turn this stage into a watery grave.

And then there were the overlords looming like theater ghosts. They were asking him to display his essence for their entertainment.

Someone started whispering—a series of scribbles happened.

Look at you; you just had to come over here and embarrass yourself. You knew better, too. Have you not had an entire year to learn that this is a waste of time? You're not an actor! All you can do is choke. That's it! I doubt you'd even be able to play a tree, so why keep this up? Get off the stage, June. You don't belong here; you are a failure. Brittney was right; it's time you let that dream die...and maybe you too. That's right; instead of trying this again, you should try ending it one more time. This time, I can make sure you succeed at suic—

"Daniel, a word?" Parker's interruption caused June's muscles to constrict, effectively freezing his vessel. His co-star held his shoulder. Looking into Parker's lavender pupils, June felt a sense of courage funnel into his spirit.

"It's all mental," said Parker.

The words quelled the raging hurricane in June's head. He chuckled and glanced at the stage lights, wiping sweat from his palms. "All mental...that's right," June said. "The voice in my head isn't my voice."

Parker removed his hand from June and assumed his position. "Exactly. Let them hear from the real you."

Role-Playing

Soaked earth squirmed underneath weathered boots navigating the uncharted wilderness. Dense fog enshrouded the land as the next band of showers rolled over the sky, concealing all sunlight. Brambles snatched at the coattails of a wanderer's garb as they pushed through the thicket. Traversing these conditions would strain even the most seasoned survivalists, but being lost in these conditions risks death.

A blur of wind peeling through the canopy dislodged one of the decaying branches. On its descent, it cracked a dozen others, attempting to warn the wanderer below. They dodged to the right, successfully avoiding the falling hazard. However, the ground beneath them sank under their weight. A mudslide cascaded down the cliff, taking the wanderer for the ride. Down and down they rolled before entering a death pit of loose mud and roots. A puddle forming at the trench basin stopped their nose from cracking against the ground.

For a moment, nothing but untethered pain existed in the wilderness. The wanderer gently lifted their face and held out their hand. Two fingers on the left hand flaring at unnatural angles. Judging by the vignette of blackness around their vision, there was a high percentage they'd also sustained a concussion. Tears pushed out of weary eyes as the mist enveloped the world in a docile silence. Time swept over all the land, except it bypassed the space within the pit. A life full of splendor, expression, and eventual disappointment flashed. This was as far as they could go. To die here alone, a nobody in a world of nothingness.

Before the wanderer crossed the final border, something other than rain tickled their faces. Their eyes peeled open to find a sole sprite of color in this monotonous wilderness. A sakura petal floated just above the nose, suspended in the air like a puppet.

Muscles pulled forth a reckless smile. Then, the wanderer's right hand jutted into the sky, and a howl broke the vacuum. Shrieks for life echoed across the expanse, circling back to the one who shouted. The wanderer struggled to their knees and faced the cliff that had nearly ended them. Feet dug into the root formations, retaining traction as they climbed. The chisel in the right hand penetrated the vertical surface and supported the survivalist. After repeating the effort over thirty times, with almost two fatal slips, the exhausted wanderer reached their hand over the edge.

Pulling themselves out of the pit, they rolled over and gasped for air. The gasping turned into a burst of hysterical laughter. Pellets of humor laced with fear, acceptance, and hatred bled into the overcast sky. The sakura appeared again with a gentle warmth, tickling their cheek like a playful familiar. Although it knew no language, it somehow called the wanderer to follow. The hysteria settled, and the wanderer rose again. They pulled their injured arm to their chest before accepting the petal's invitation. Fog still covered the land, but now, with a supernatural guide, the path became clear. After an uneventful hike, the wanderer reached an archway of pink branches. Beyond the arches was a clearing. But it was more than a respite from this forgotten world; it was a destination.

The wanderer stepped over the threshold and was greeted by an exquisite orchard. Hundreds of sakura trees loomed in a near-perfect circle. Positioned within the center of this orchard was a crystal pond. And on the far side of the garden was a white shack.

The wanderer carefully removed the soggy cloak and stepped into the light. As they approached the body of water, a plume of hundreds of petals whipped around them. A kaleidoscope of fuchsia, lavender, and salmon momentarily whisked vision away. The cloud dispersed, and all the petals returned to their respective branches. Then, the shack door opened.

An elderly man wearing a straw hat stepped outside. Satin-white overalls covered his hunched torso, and no smudge was visible. His facial features were reminiscent of those in the Distant South, but the eyes were ambiguous. The man waved and motioned for the wanderer to come closer.

"Welcome, welcome," he spoke with a slow lull.

"Excuse me, sir, are you the caretaker of this orchard?" the wanderer asked.

"The orchard is *my caretaker*. But I do trim it from time to time. What brings you here?"

"I'm searching for something."

"Men are always searching for the same thing. Why do you seek death?"

Confused, the wanderer stepped back. "Why do you think I want to die?"

"That's the only reason this place welcomes visitors. It's a haven for those who have lost the will to live."

The wanderer opened their hand to let a blossom rest upon the palm. "I confess, you are partially correct. I am indeed looking to alter my state of being, but I do not wish to end my life. I am on a journey of renewal."

"And how do aim to be renewed?"

"Rumors speak of a special brew. An elixir said to have powerful rejuvenating properties."

"So, you have come to this place for a drink? Shall we have tea, then? I just set a pot."

"Although that isn't necessarily what I seek, I will take some. Anything to bring me peace. You wouldn't also happen to have a curative kit somewhere?" The wanderer asked, showing the stranger their broken fingers.

The elder entered the shack momentarily, leaving the wanderer to observe the surroundings. This was the place he'd sought, but to be here felt like a dream. The caretaker reappeared with two ceramic mugs filled with steaming water and a basket slung around his arm. He set the basket down next to the black bench and focused on the beverages. Rubbing a pinch of petals between his fingers, he ground them into indigo dust, then funneled the dust into a paper pouch and tied a string around it. Then, he gestured for the wanderer to join him.

The wanderer accepted the seat and basket. He opened it to find bandages, alcohol, and vials of various powders and potions. "Immense gratitude for this. Tell me, caretaker, has anything I've said thus far registered with you?" he asked while wrapping his fingers.

"Just that humanity loves to spin tales. These myths persist despite the eroding waves of time. If I may ask: why do you wish for renewal, stranger?"

"I am tired of what this existence entails, yet I fear I am permanently bound to this sordid reality. My life has not been wasted, but its potential has not been realized." He finished tending the hand injury, and then assessed his head. No blood, thankfully. But there was a heavy throb pulsing from the back to the front of his skull.

"Your sentiments are deeply rooted, but I'm curious. What makes you believe such a concoction exists?"

"However, when I did inevitably arrive, and the mist dispersed the illusion, in the end, I came to an honest resolution: I discarded all reasons to stay alive...Until I sipped the wondrous potion, erasing all doubts, fears, and grief, granting a second chance at peace, this tonic rewrote my initial conclusion. Find the cordial where orchards curl like reefs, and offer yourself to the watery trickster if you wish to drink the blessed elixir, and earn a new existence in Ingilaef," recited the wanderer.

"And that is...?" inquired the host.

"These are the final words written by Cain the Mystic, the one rumored to have discovered the elixir. And, this is the place he found; proof it is no mere myth."

The gardener's lips pressed against the mug's rim, and they sipped the freshly brewed tea. The wanderer exhaled and felt the lingering pain from his injuries dissipate.

"My deepest apologies, friend. I have rambled about my reasoning for intruding, and we have not even exchanged names. *I am Baudelaire.*"

"Call me Gi," responded the gardener. "Who would've thought the name Cain is still muttered in this modern age."

"Are you acquainted with him?"

"He's a paladin and prophet to some, a madman and murderer to many. His words have existed as long as I, and I've forgotten when I first set upon this place. Baudelaire, you are not the first to venture here with the intent to meet this alchemist. Men and women throughout the ages have come but leave sorely disappointed when they learn that he was only a construct of imagination."

Baudelaire smiled, "An imaginary construct is nothing more than a diluted representation of the truth. So long as the source is real, I will continue to search. I believe Cain exists, and so does the elixir he spoke of."

"You are free to adhere to any beliefs you wish. However, because you have arrived here, it is protocol that I extend an invitation."

Baudelaire nearly coughed up the tea after hearing the statement. "An invitation to meet Cain?"

Gi shook his head. "Although the author may no longer exist, the world that inspired those words remains. But, before you can be granted entry, you must first be initiated."

"Initiation? Does this trial require me to answer the Sphinx's secretive riddle?"

"STOP!"

June broke out of character as Michaela's voice dispelled the fantastical scene. "The line is, 'Does this trial require me to commit my life as a tribute and answer the sacred Sphinx's secretive riddle,' not whatever you just spat out. Baudelaire is not some chump with a village education; he is a man of sophistication."

"It's only a slight improvisation. For better delivery."

Michaela pulled a red pen behind her ear and aimed the tip at June. "Don't improvise my words. They're written for a reason."

"Seriously?!" June groaned.

Parker stepped in, "Can we take five, Mr. Ray?" The stage director responded with a thumbs-up. The actor then turned to June. "Hey, you're doing a good job. I know Baudelaire isn't easy to embody."

"I wouldn't have to improvise if she made him talk like a man, not a Tolkien character."

"That's a *wordsmith* for ya," Parker said as they observed Michaela sort through the script. "There's no dictionary definition she probably doesn't know. You'll have to cut her some slack; it's probably not easy to write something as compelling as this while juggling junior year."

June applied a pea-sized amount of lip balm to his lips. "You seem to know her well."

Maybe they're just friends, or maybe they've fu-

Parker shook his head, "Not necessarily; that's the power of *intuition*. It's taking small details and connecting the dots, trusting the so-called 'gut instinct.' Knowing is one thing, but learning how to utilize knowledge efficiently is a skill reserved for the enlightened. Follow me, Daniel."

Parker kicked his leg over the edge of the stage and walked to the refreshments table. He poured himself a cup of water and then June's. Paper rims clinked as Parker celebrated the occasion with a toast. June gulped down the liquid while his co-star continued talking.

"Let's assume her major is Creative Writing. But she probably started as a science major, like seventy percent of us do. We're told that doctors or lawyers are the only careers worth college tuition. With that in mind, we can assume she was one of the seventy percent who probably failed lab during her first year and decided to quit the science route. A bit of self-discovery due to trauma, a little change of behavior as self-care, and now she's on a new path. But her quitting has probably come back to bite her, and she's now stuck taking Biology 101 with some kid fresh out of high school who skips every day but is using their AP Bio notes to pass with perfect scores."

"How'd you know all of that?" June wondered, finishing a second cup of water.

"I don't; I'm just *connecting the dots*," said Parker. You must realize people are predictable. This world is so mundane; if you know at least ten people, there's another ten thousand with near-identical values. People fall into repetitive patterns because patterns are comforting. People feel the need to recreate an emotion or an experience, so they follow trends that society has designated as 'safe' for the masses. And we students are extremely susceptible to this cultural conformity."

"That's a fact. Too many influencers, not enough individuals."

"Right? At this age, we should be crafting our personal identities, but we're constantly bombarded by external voices that tell us to ignore our desires. To give up our dreams and labor for the passions of others."

"At what point do we have a chance to be ourselves?" asked June.

"For some of us...*never.*" Parker's animated facial features brought a second dimension to his dialogue. "The truth is that humanity is a mindless mob bent on devouring everything it loves, including the individual."

"You make it sound so hopeless."

"It's a bleak reality, yes. But that is why I, along with *chosen others*, believe in pursuing personal passions." Parker cracked his fingers and continued, "It eventually becomes a bore to entertain people unless they are individuals capable of engaging with our true selves. For example, our wordsmith is one worth entertaining, wouldn't you say?"

June noticed from a distance Michaela's script was red and bloody. "Engaging is one way to describe her. But she is in a league of her own."

"If you think she's entertaining, imagine what that says about you?"

"What about me?" June asked.

Parker removed his glasses, "That's the question I want to answer. I wonder, Daniel, what brings you out of the darkness and into the spotlight?"

Without the tortoiseshell frames blocking his face, June met Parker's eyes. Shimmering bolts of indigo sparked in the irises, backdropped by a constellation concealed in the cornea. It looked like a hundred stars exploded in his pupil, void dust clouding the sclera. The staring forced June's thoughts to lapse, but as he glanced towards the theater seating, he swore he could see an audience stretched to the back of the house. The faceless silhouettes rose in unison to applaud him. Faintly, he heard them chanting, each voice syncing with the next to create a harmonious sound.

"June...June...June...JUNE!"

"JUNE! Are you ready?" Oscar's voice bounced along the walls.

"Ah yes, I am ready!" June snapped away from the daydream just in time to see Parker placing the glasses back on his face.

"Let's not keep our fans waiting," said his grinning co-star.

~~~

"Does entry require me to commit my life as a tribute and answer the sacred Sphinx's secretive riddle?" asked Baudelaire.

The docile gardener pointed to the pool in the center of the orchard. "As I said, only the truth is present here. To be initiated, you must cast a reflection."

Baudelaire sipped the tea. "A reflection? What is so unnatural about that? All water can cast a reflection."

"Not this pool. It is unlike the young water you are used to, it comes from a much older source, and does not have the same properties."

"So, I must prove my worth to old gods. I suppose it's true this element can easily read one's essence."

"Yes, a man may be able to deceive other men, but not *nature*. Remember, it was water that offered humanity the first glimpse of itself. Perhaps a puddle after a long rain led our primitive ancestors to that marvelous sight of self. But the world has changed, and man has lost many things along the path. They have forgotten their original image."

Gi accepted the empty mug and motioned for Baudelaire to walk with him. Fear stiffened the artist's gait as he approached the mystical lake. The pool's surface resembled a pane of finely polished glass—no image of the blossoms, sun, or even the clouds overhead. Then, Gi moved his head over the water. Nothing.

At the ominous sight, dread pooled into Baudelaire's stomach. "Even you bear no image? How is this possible?"

"I told you, this is the power of water. I must warn you, if the two images do not match, you will be banned from
~~~

returning here, and no matter how long or far you search, it will remain undiscoverable."

"What must a man do to make his images match?" Baudelaire asked.

"He must not only know his self; *he must be willing to give up his self.*"

A southward gust rustled the cherry blossom petals as Baudelaire crept toward the water. Because he spent his life sculpting others, he understood the invasiveness required to craft a portrait, but being the subject of this supernatural artist unsettled him.

With eyes wide open, Baudelaire stuck his head over the unnatural pool. At first, the frame remained unchanged; however, the more Baudelaire remained fixed over the water, the more complete the image became. The sculptor admired his defining facial features: the strong forehead that contained vast knowledge, academic eyes able to analyze the most minute details, and a pair of tightly pursed lips that lived to share stories.

"I am who I am and will always be me," Baudelaire said, staring at his reflection with pride.

"You have passed the trial. Congratulations, you can now enter *Ingilaef.*"

Gi smiled and walked into the shed. He soon returned with an object in his hands: a key fashioned out of mother-of-pearl. Kneeling beside the bench, Gi rubbed his hand against the wood until he found a groove to insert the key. Baudelaire marveled as an artificial stairwell appeared in the earth next to the gardener's shack.

"What magic is this?"

"This is your proof of membership," Gi said as he handed the key to Baudelaire. "Now, you may come and go as you please."

"It is by luck alone I stumbled upon your residence. How am I supposed to return to this place?"

"The safe path through the wilderness will open for you, so long as you follow the sakura. Your key will dissolve at the end of your membership. That'll last roughly the equivalent of eighteen months. When that happens, your entry will be revoked, and all your memories and your existence will be erased."

"You mean there will be no trace of me?" Baudelaire inquired.

"And there will be no trace of us either."

"Such strange tenets. But true freedom demands tribute, and I am willing to pay," Baudelaire said.

"A final word of caution: Do not forget that you are *a temporary guest*. There is no place within purgatory for the likes of you, so do not attempt to create any permanent foundation in these foglands. And do not extend anything similar to the patrons."

"I understand. I am but a humble observer in this world. Gi, my friend, what else must I be aware of before I depart? You mentioned this is my invitation, but where? What exactly is Ingilaef?"

"You will learn everything when you arrive," Gi said. "Until next time, wanderer."

"Thank you for being a Virgil to my Dante," said Baudelaire.

A faint noise fluttered from the crypt to Baudelaire's ears, imploring him to investigate its source. Slowly, he hobbled down the dank stairwell. After reaching the tenth step, the crust above him closed, leaving the sculptor alone in the darkened corridor. He held his breath as phantoms pressed against his skin. But in the shadows, a lavender light appeared.

The key!

Baudelaire held it in front of him, illuminating the depths. And so began his journey. Descending became an ordeal, for the wood was soggy and mud-covered, making traction nearly impossible. The walk was strange as silence filled the space behind him while the noise grew louder the farther he went into the depths. He feared suffering another life-ending fall, but after moving about two hundred steps, the layout changed.

Baudelaire noticed a familiar material underneath his feet: marble. These well-crafted steps stretched to an open space lit by golden torches. The strange sounds transformed into melodies, some faintly familiar, others too unique to belong on the surface. Then, his boots touched the base.

A massive stone door loomed in front of him. Dwarfed by the size, Baudelaire stared at the entrance before touching it. Intricate etchings covered the door's surface, symbols both foreign and known. Next to it was a gargoyle carved in the shape of a man's head. From the expressionless face hung a rusted chain. His feet stepped to the mat before the tomb-like structure, and he fixed his attire.

"As always, the progress is worth the risk," said Baudelaire as he pulled the chain.

END SCENE

June rose to his feet, and Parker joined him on center stage. Together, they faced the production team. Gris clapped but retracted the gesture as the others stayed silent. Oscar remained distracted by his digital tablet, picking his teeth with an extended pinky nail. Mr. Ray had stepped aside to have a private chat with the stagehand.

"June, June, June," began Michaela, "you were auditioning for Baudelaire, correct?"

"Yes, that's correct."

"You might not know this, but Baudelaire is a genius. He's a man seeking something grander than status or even intellect. And although he may commit acts that one may find selfish, as we'll soon discover, they are valid choices according to his moral code. That sort of individualism must be so believable that one must acknowledge that he is real and not an actor playing a part."

Gris patted the table twice. "I agree with her. It may be hard to accept this feedback, but this role is not designed for those who contend with self-confidence issues."

Michaela twirled the red pen in her hand. "Exactly! To be Baudelaire, an actor must *know themselves enough to lose themselves.*"

June tucked his feet together, "I hadn't realized existential dread was a requirement for the role."

"It's always a requirement when playing an artist," Gris stated.

While the production team expressed their critiques, June noticed a disinterested Parker sitting on the edge of the stage. Had he just proven to his co-star that he was a member of the mindless mob? No! He was not just another name in the hat. He was an individual, one of one. But how to show him...?

"Wait a minute. I have to be honest about something. And I can't leave it unspoken anymore." The production team went silent, and Parker turned. "How exactly do you expect anybody to become this character when they can't even express his feelings?" asked June.

Michaela dropped her script on the table and dismissed herself from the desk. "Excuse me? Are you critiquing *my writing?*"

"It reads well, but have you tried saying this aloud?" June asked. "I'm just saying this dialogue is so esoteric that nobody will get it."

"Esoteric...? Nice word choice," Gris muttered to Mr. Ray. "The young fellow does make a valid point. Been a trend for many auditions, dialogue being difficult and all. Worth considering more revisions."

"That's because you are a hobbyist who has yet to understand the fundamentals of drama, and you're stiff on stage," Michaela responded.

"Look, your characters are complex, so why make their conversations sound like Catholic chants? A trained linguist couldn't even make sense of this."

The distance between the two combatants decreased; Michaela's red pen was now inches from his face. "Yet, you considered auditioning for a lead role with a seventh-grade reading level. I tallied twelve mispronounced words."

"Who do you think you are, George R. R. Martin? Is fluency in Valyrian another role requirement?"

"Go on, keep wagging that tongue of yours," added Michaela.

"My tongue appreciates good words," June growled.

"If that's the best comeback you've got, then you're hopeless," she said.

"Just like your story if you don't cut back on the fairy gibberish."

A third voice entered the chat. "Enough! How about you concentrate on not being petrified on stage, or do you plan to pull another twelve-second standoff? That's right, I finally remember who you are. *You're Mr. Stagefright!*" laughed Oscar. "I seriously cannot believe you're auditioning for the lead."

June dropped his argument, and his shadow shrunk; Michaela also reeled back after hearing the insult.

Mr. Ray finally interjected, "Ahem! I believe that concludes this critical conversation. Mr. Elliott, thank you for an ambitious audition. You certainly brought a sense of wonder to our world this afternoon. As today is the last audition, we will post the results on the theater's home page later this evening."

Gris looked at Michaela and Parker and then at June, who had departed from the spotlight. He then patted Mr. Ray on the back. "Emi, I believe we're going to have an *unforgettable* production."

Performance Review

When June entered the dressing room, he swatted a stack of old pamphlets. "Fuck me! Why did I have to go and open my stupid mouth?" Frustration settled into sadness, and he collected the documents scattered around the props and costumes. Looking at the front cover, he saw the graphic from last year's production, *The Nightmare Before Christmas.* He flipped through pages until he came across his name in the miscellaneous section.

June set the stack on the vanity set and examined the mirror surrounded by dozens of Polaroid photographs. Mr. Ray dubbed it *the Starlet Spotlight,* as it highlighted MSU's most accomplished actors. Since the time of the late thespian Albert Thompson, the Theater Troupe updated the Starlet Spotlight each spring. Like other student actors, he dreamed of having his image immortalized on this wall of fame, but he'd just blown that chance minutes ago on the stage.

The newest portraits added this morning belonged to the university's current theatrical wunderkinds. As he examined the image of a smiling brunette, June heard the handle turn. Startled, he shuffled back, accidentally ripping a photograph from the wall.

Inside walked the last person he wished to see. "Oh, *Timothy.* Do you need this room?" he asked.

Timothy responded, "If you don't mind, I'd like to have some time to rehearse before my audition. "

Genetically designed for the spotlight, Timothy Brooks stood just above six feet. His marbled cheeks contained serenity and sophistication, and the young man could express varying emotions at any moment with his auburn eyes. Not to mention, he also had the voice of a seraph, and his monologues were often infused with such intensity that they made the most hardened hearts melt. The senior theater arts major had been cast as the male lead in the last three productions and even held rank in Manhattan-based community theaters.

June tucked the torn photograph into his pocket and approached the door. "Who are you auditioning for?"

"Baudelaire."

"Really? I imagined you as the Tavern Master or Gi. Baudelaire isn't exactly like the modest protagonists you usually play."

Timothy smiled while blowing on his steaming cup, "That's why I want the role. He's unlike any of the other characters I've played."

"He's quite complex, isn't he? There's something courageous about sticking to one's ideals even if the world tells you otherwise. And his journey to self-understanding is full of failures, something I think we can all relate-"

"Ha, I'm not interested in any stuffy philosophy," Timothy interrupted. "Baudelaire is an antihero, and it's time for me to switch up my career so I don't get typecast. Oscar has an uncle who works as an agent with Broadway, and he said I needed to have a diverse portfolio if I wanted to make it big. So far, I only play men of noble virtue. But that's not all I wanna be. For once, I'm gonna be *the villain.*"

"We're all the villain in someone's story. Well, best of luck," said June.

"Before you go...mind running to get me a refill?" Timothy called. "It's a honey-ginseng-chamomile tea; apparently, it's supposed to help with brain activity and memory retention."

"I'm not the help..." June whispered.

"Ah, this is awkward, isn't it?" The settled actor gave June a quick up-and-down, examining everything from his posture to the wrinkled clothes. "You're not a stagehand, are you? You're auditioning?"

"Auditioned," June corrected.

"I see! Oscar mentioned that someone new was auditioning for the lead. I'm surprised a novice would wish to start their career with this character. Have you acted before?"

"Yeah, a few times. Nothing major, though. I was in the spring production last year," June said.

"Wait! I recognize you...yes! You're him! You're *Mr. Stagefright!*" There was that name again, suddenly becoming a brand seared into June's skin. "That may have been the longest pause of my entire life. You almost made me slip up my lines with that, but luckily for us, I improvised to cover your blunder."

Slurping loudly, Timothy waved a finger toward his guest. "To be honest, it'd be a disgrace for our esteemed establishment to let you become the lead. And it would be a disgrace to you. That sort of embarrassment could drive a person to dark places."

"You might be right, but things change. I've changed," said June.

"Perhaps, but this is tradition. And traditions are designed to stay the same. So, I, the newest addition to the Starlet Spotlight, will assume my role as the next guardian of the theater's legacy. Hm, that's strange," Timothy glanced at the wall. "What happened to my portrait? I thought Oscar said they added it this morning."

"I bet the Theater Troupe is running behind because of the audition. Anyway, I'm going to go now. Break a leg, Timothy."

The door closed without further comment, like the conversation. A harsh wind of reality stung June's face to the point of pain as he power-walked away from the theater. He removed Timothy's stolen photograph from its hiding place and watched the image of artistic genius morph into a portrait of Baudelaire.

"Macbeth. Macbeth. Macbeth. Macbeth! MACBETH!" June screamed. "Mr. Stagefright? Theater legacy? That's bullshit! Fuck him! That's right, fuck Timothy, fuck the Theater Troupe, and fuck anybody who laughs at that stupid nickname. Who does he think he is? He can't talk and act like that, can he?"

Suddenly, the aggression turned melancholy, and a timid tremor erupted in June's vocal cords. Sniffles caused by something other than the outdoor temperature began manifesting as he slowed his walk. "That's not the point, though. There's so much more to it. He's done no work, and I did. He didn't even sign the audition sheet, and I did. No effort was exerted, but I practiced every day. It's unfair because this is just another bullet on his resume, and to me, this is...this is...my dream! And it's going to be taken away by some pompous youth pastor."

I told you so, you shitty actor. Maybe now you'll realize this was hopeless, and you are, too. Go on, give up on your dreams. It'll solve all of this.

"No! I'm not giving up! And I'm not losing to him."

The photograph in June's hand tore from top to bottom, splitting Timothy's face into two asymmetrical halves. Once the shock cleared, a sense of euphoria washed over him after seeing the ruined portrait. The tears continued to bubble in the corner of his eyes as he shouted.

"That's right, that's right! It's my dream and reality, and I will make it happen. Only me! I should be Baudelaire, nobody else! But what can I do now...? I blew it. And he's definitely going to get the role. It's not fair...it's not. I *need* to be Baudelaire, or I will be a nobody."

A gust blew, dislodging half of the shredded photograph from June's hand, and he gave chase—an arm bearing two bracelets shot in the air and snatched the flap. "It hasn't even been a full twenty-four, and we've already got a case of theft and vandalism to the Starlet Spotlight. It looks like we'll have to up our security."

"Parker!" June came to a halt. "Uh...about that. I accidentally pulled the photograph off the wall...and when I was trying to sneeze...it might have ripped...but he needed some tea, and I...shit, are my eyes leaking too? Parker...please don't tell. Please?"

The bags on the bench were cleared as his new acquaintance allowed June to sit. "I won't tell, but I do want an explanation. What happened?"

June bit the tip of his thumbnail. *"I'm not going to be in the play."*

"Why not?"

"Because I'm a shitty actor."

"What makes you say that? By the way, I'm afraid I have to disagree with that statement 1000 percent."

"It's the truth. That audition was my first and only impression, and I blew it. You were there, you saw!"

"Tell me what I saw?" asked Parker.

"I have horrible anxiety, so I freeze in tense situations. Then, I make it worse by trying to think about it, which only fuels the anxiety, and thus, the spiral begins. It happened in high school plays, church plays, and *The Nightmare Before Christmas* last spring. You know, my *defining moment*. Apparently, because of that, I'm known as Mr. Stagefright."

"A childish name coined by childish men," said Parker.

"Because of that one mistake, I feel like the whole department is barring my progress. Talking about protecting a legacy and whatnot."

"Pure nonsense. There's no such theater legacy."

The tip of June's fingernail broke under the pressure of his teeth. "Don't even get me started on future Grammy winner Timothy Brooks, who's about to finesse his way to another lead role."

"You do realize that Grammy's are for music?" Parker chuckled.

"I didn't, but Timothy could win one of those too. He's the poster child for soft-boy Millennials who wear trendy *H&M* shirts to church."

"I have heard he's active in a campus Bible study."

June threw his hands in the air. "See! That's what I'm talking about. The guy is so picture-perfect, and people love him just because of his appearance. And his voice. And his talents. The audience is going to love him as Baudelaire, too. Even if he's lazy and doesn't give a shit about the character."

"Perhaps you underestimate yourself, Daniel."

"Uhh, were we on the same stage?"

"While he may have refined talent, you have discipline and a drive."

"Discipline doesn't mean anything compared to delivering the dialogue," June said.

"Although you lack formal training like Timothy, your poise and presence come naturally. You might be a conduit."

"*Conduit?*"

Parker rose from the bench and began pacing as he lectured. "A conduit is, essentially, when an actor lets the character overtake them—a commandeering of the constitution, if you will. A conduit gives the character a blank canvas; that canvas is your being—your body and voice and feelings as well."

"How do I do that?"

"For you, rather than immersing and embodying, *dissipate*. Leave no trace of your original self, and let the story create an appropriate vessel. I admit, you already seem capable of doing it intuitively."

"Wouldn't be the first time I've tried to disappear..." said June.

Parker leaned in close. "Between us, refined skill is Timothy's only redeeming quality as an actor. He's too committed to the script, the stage directions, the blocking, and the angles rather than thriving on the passion of the present. It's all a puppet performance, which is why it's a bore to share the stage with him," he whispered. "In my ideal setting, I'd rather act with one who adapts as the moment changes; a little bit of chaotic energy always leads to an entertaining story."

Out of nowhere, a pink frisbee beamed over the athletic field fence. Parker employed cat-like reflexes to dodge to the right. However, the flying saucer crashed into June's nose. Pain radiated through his nasal passage. Blood splattered on the ground and Parker's hand.

A young woman wearing sweatpants, gloves, a beanie, and a green windbreaker sprinted to the fence, waving her hands like an inflatable toy. "OHMYGOSH! I'm sorry. It was the seventh hole, and I tried to even the score with an underhanded wrist flick from twelve yards out, but...oh, and you're bleeding. No, I'm soooo sorry."

"It's alright, I swear. As long as my smile's intact, I'm good to go," June said, blood trickling down his chin.

Parker spent the next few seconds simultaneously calming the ultimate frisbee player and nursing June's bloody nose. Once settled, he propositioned the player. "If you want to make it up, why not attend our party tonight? It's a back-to-school bar crawl."

"I don't get done studying until ten," said the young woman.

"Perfect! Party starts at 10:00 PM and lasts until 2:00 AM. Enough time to study, draft an email to your professor, shower, and watch an episode of something before pregaming. You should come; he will be there, and you can apologize on the dance floor."

"I'll be there?" June asked. Parker nodded as if this information had been communicated months before.

Blush appeared upon the cheeks of the wide-eyed woman. "Hmm, maybe I'll have some time to step out. We'll see. Where is it?"

"The Lion's Den," Parker said.

"The Lion's Den?! As in the actual actual Lion's Den. Wait, I heard about this! It's supposed to be like the biggest function this year. Whoa! This is, like, a major move. We're totally going! 10:00 PM at the Lion's Den. Be there for sure!" The frisbee player waved at the boys as she returned to the game, coming and going into their lives like a playful nymph.

"Whoa, someone sure is excited," said June.

"It seems word has traveled about this evening's function. Bet we have Noah to thank for that. A bit concerning because you never know who might show."

"Nothing like a back-to-school function before things get too busy."

"I bet nearly half the campus will pop in at some point."

"Sounds like a classic case of 'Who all gon be there?' to me."

"That's the goal. My crew and I want to kick off this semester with a bigger bang than usual. It happens to be an important year for many things, one of them being the 150th anniversary of MSU's chartering. And I know some people will consider this another party, but it's more than that. It's our chance to commemorate a new chapter."

"Must be nice to have something worth celebrating. Meanwhile, all I've got to offer this school is a new nickname...and some new light fixtures," June muttered the last part under his breath.

Sunset passed, and the first stars aligned in the twilight while the Emergency Response terminals glowed like cemetery lanterns. A cold wind tumbled through the vacant sidewalk as a squirrel rustled in the pile of dried leaves.

The lights of an approaching vehicle bathed the black road in xenon.

Parker turned to his bench mate, "Daniel. *You want it, don't you? That role?*"

"Well...I'm not the most suited for it...and I'm still a newbie..."

"That doesn't matter; I need to know if you want it?"

"I mean, I'm not sure if I...the chances of me outdoing...and after all that stuff I said...it's just not in the cards...and I feel dumb for even trying...then there's Timothy–"

"June!" Parker snapped at him. "Do you want to be Baudelaire?!"

"YES! Yes, I do."

"*Why?*" Parker asked.

"Because I can finally show the school my acting skills."

"That can be done with any other role. You said you wouldn't be in the show if you weren't Baudelaire. Why is that? Why should it be you and not Timothy?"

June glanced at the winking stars. "He doesn't deserve it. Not this role. Because Baudelaire is so much more than an antihero, *he's a sensitive artist.* He should only be played by someone who understands him and can empathize and relate to his struggles."

"So, Baudelaire is more than a role; he's a mile marker on your journey to manhood?"

"There's something about him, how dedicated he is to preserving and progressing his soul. I envy his passion, curiosity, wonder, and even his hatred. Although the dialogue is stiff, and Michaela is a drill sergeant when respecting the script, his tale makes sense. He is a man on a voyage to discover what he's lost. The thematic elements also remind me of one of my favorite poets."

"A poet, you say? Who is it?"

"Xavier. Have you heard of him?"

Parker shook his head, "I've not heard of such a name."

"I'll have to share some work with you next time we meet. I think he's right up your alley."

"Ha, after one interaction, you believe you know me?"

"Nope, just *connecting the dots*," June said.

"A fast learner. I was right to keep my eyes on you." Parker removed his glasses, revealing the shimmering irises laden with intention. Again, June felt like something had invaded his interior world.

The once distant vehicle finally reached the sidewalk's curb, and Parker collected his things. "Daniel, it may be bold of me to say this, but *if you want it, the role can be yours.*"

"How can you be so sure?" June questioned.

Parker entered the luxurious ice-white BMW. The driver dapped him up before giving June a stealthy up-down. From the passenger seat, Parker smiled, and not just one of his saving face smiles. A genuine smirk highlighted his excitement at the thought of June's curiosity.

"All it takes is a bit of negotiation."

"What are we negotiating?"

"Where's the fun in giving you all the information at once? If you want to learn, you must earn; your next clue is already calling. You have to listen carefully..."

"A Sphinx riddle," June laughed.

Parker gave him a salute. "See you tonight, Daniel." The window rolled up, and the engine revved as the car skirted down the road, leaving June with a thousand more thoughts.

The streetlights ignited, and the engine of the occasional vehicle purred in the distance. According to the transit app, the bus connecting the Thompson Theater to the dormitory section of the campus was delayed. Yet, the delay worked in June's favor because he needed to entertain an overdue conversation.

He lifted the ringing phone to his ear. "How'd the interview go, Sweetie?" a voice on the other line of his cell phone asked.

"Mom, it's an audition, not an interview."

"Same thing, they both ask stupid questions," she said.

"Yeah, yeah, whatever. I think it went okay. I can't tell, but I tried my best. There were a few li-"

"Hold on. Your father just walked in. Dan! I've got June on the line; pick up the phone in the kitchen. Where is it...? It's by the wine rack! Did you check behind the wine rack? Yes, the wine rack! Behind it!"

When did we get a wine rack? June thought as he kicked a stone off the pavement. Seconds later, another voice entered the conversation.

"Hey, son. How'd the interview go?"

"It wasn't an interview, Dad," June said.

"It was an audition, Dan." Wendy's sarcasm plucked as if she hadn't just been informed of the same fact.

"Same thing. They still ask *stupid questions.*"

"Their questions aren't stupid," June said.

"Oh yeah, what kind of questions did they ask you?"

"You know if I could play the character and all that."

"Stupid question. Of course, you can; you're our son. You may be a little moody on Mondays, but when you put your mind to something, you get it done," his dad said.

"Sweetie, are you eating properly? What time have you been going to bed? I know how you can get when you go into your focus mode."

"Mhm, yes, Mom. I went to the dining hall and went to bed at a decent hour."

"Are you still having those strange dreams? You haven't wet the bed-"

"No, Mom! I told you that it was a one-time thing."

"But it happened a few..."

"Only because I was stressed out last spring."

June recalled the spring semester in which he developed a sleeping disorder. The staff at Campus Health couldn't identify the cause, but June only knew it as a massive headache because it led to an uncontrollable body. Nights were spent staring at the clock as the seconds counted, surfing the internet for nonsense and porn. His body would eventually shut down, but the mind would drift between sanity and the subconscious. He retained full awareness in this transitory state and could even accurately recall his dreams but couldn't find relaxation. The sleep disorder caused his grades to dwindle, not to mention it was the dagger to his struggling social life. He was forced to watch his urine-stained mattress be removed from the dorm because of his bladder.

"Got everything you need for school?" asked his father.

"I've got most of my stuff, but there are a few textbooks I need to purchase for the semester."

"I'll transfer some money to your account."

"Thanks, Dad."

Again, the streetlight malfunctioned, unsettling June. It wasn't necessarily the flickering that made him nervous but the endless buzzing traveling through the vacant station.

"Well, how did the interview go? Did you turn up for the judges?" Dan asked.

"Dad, it's not a–"

"Right, right, it's an audition! How did it go?"

"Maybe I should have gone for an easier part. I messed up a few times," June expressed with disdain.

"A mistake is just God's way of showing you how to grow," said Wendy.

Dan added, "You are qualified—probably overqualified. Don't they know you're going to be the next Denzel Washington? And they still have you interviewing for parts? Those Jon Snows, they know nothing."

"Sweetie, excuse your father; we binged the past five seasons of that *Game of Thrones* show this month, and that's all he's been saying about everything. The other day, he called the person who installed our aquarium a squire."

An aquarium too? Just what is happening now that I'm out of the house? June thought.

Suddenly, the pulsing streetlight went dark. In the darkness, something materialized. A whistle or hum. The noise was incomprehensible at first but had subtle hints of sorrow. He thought it might've been a pre-recorded audio being played from a busted stereo, for certain areas of the school had speakers hidden along pathways. But as it played, it sounded too spastic to be an audio recording.

June set his phone on the bench and stepped onto the shaded sidewalk. As the noise grew louder, animal instincts caused his hair to rise. The low frequency physically reverberated from his knees to his chest, disrupting equilibrium and pushing him to the brink of an anxiety attack. It felt like being watched, or worse.

Beckoned.

Hands raised to temples as June shook his head. Pressure built in his brow and spread down to his freshly injured nose; blood followed the sensation. Then, his mind flooded with dozens of thoughts ranging from the errors he made on stage, the blooming lust developing for Michaela, and even the frisbee beaming him.

Just as quick as the whine crept into the beds of his cochlea, it dispersed when the light returned. Wiping blood from his mustache, June collected his cell phone.

"Sweetie, are you still there? Your father is sorry for calling it an interview."

June stopped biting his cheek and retrieved his phone. "It's fine. Something just caught my attention."

"Well, well," Dan's voice pepped, "I won't stop you if you're scoping out a daughter-in-law for us."

"Oh...uh, no, that's not it. I don't have time to be dating this semester."

"A good woman will make sure you never lose focus so long as you prioritize her," said Dan.

"Wow, Dan, that was impressive. Those self-development podcasts have been helping. Hasn't he improved, Sweetie?" asked Wendy.

"I suppose."

"But seriously, I support your decision not to date. Just don't make me a grandmother before a mother-in-law. There are levels to love, and I don't need you skipping any to get your skipper wet."

"My skipper...?" June questioned.

Wendy continued, "I've heard of this thing...a dental dam. Do you have one? I read on the internet that HPV can affect men in their throats if they practice cunnilingus. Make sure you have one, just in case. You know what I say: If you're not preventing, you're planning. Get yourself some lube to protect your condoms against breaking from friction. Do we need to send you some money for safe sex?"

"Okay! Too much, Mom, too much!" June stammered.

"Oh, relax, we're all adults. What do I always tell you when it comes to sex?" Dan asked.

"*Trust nobody but myself,*" June recited.

"Exactly. A sheathed sword cannot harm, but a bare blade is dangerous if improperly wielded."

"It has been almost a year since you and Brittney ended things. How is she anyway? Her birthday is coming up, isn't it? Can I text her?"

"Terrible transition, Mom. I don't care what you do with Brittney. We're not exactly on speaking terms."

"Maybe there's still some hope? I'll help you rekindle it if you want. Dan! Remind me to text Brittney on her birthday! She's a February Aquarius, so she likes unconventional connections."

"Okay, clearly, this conversation has gone on too long. Alright, peeps, I love you, and I'll call you when I find out the results."

"I'm praying that this year is one for the glo-up and that your acting skills stay on fleek," said Dan.

"This is what I get for putting you two onto Black Twitter," June muttered. "But thanks, Dad. I'm gonna do my best."

"That's the spirit. This semester can be whatever you want because you can be anything you want, Sweetie. *So, be you.*"

Mr. Stagefright

Agua de Beber, a bossa-nova classic, played from the smart-phone plugged into an electrical outlet near the top bunk. A belch echoed in the dim room as June halted the alarm set for 8:50 PM. He swirled his tongue around his mouth, tasting salt deposits in the buccal mucosa. "Looks like I fell victim to another case of the itis thanks to the Cafe MSG."

Lying in bed, June scrolled through updates on his various social media timelines: someone swapped the audio from the *Titanic* trailer with the newest Drake visuals; a Facebook Live recording showed a two-headed dog humping a stuffed animal; and, Worldstar's highlight section included a three-minute compilation of this week's best fights.

The next video had two men scrapping with bare fists in a huddle of onlookers. Whoever was the cinematographer (if it could be called that) had no formal training and constantly commented on the action by screaming, "Beat that nigga's ass!" The shirtless boxer swung and connected a hit against the eye, but the du-rag-wearing fighter pushed him to the ground. Once there, he pummeled the other until their face blistered like a candied cherry. Then, the huddle formed into a mob of marauders intent on pulverizing the downed victim. The individual being mauled managed to break free and sprint down the lot. But his escape failed after he was tackled by a man built in the likeness of a bull. With the wind knocked out of him, the crew swarmed the fallen man again, continuing the volley of punches and kicks until the victim went unconscious. They all scattered at the sound of a police siren, and the video ended.

"200,000 views already? This world is seriously effed up," June commented.

You're one of those 200,000 now—just another member of the mindless mob. Honestly, you think you're better than them? As if!

The phone screen went black, and June buried his face into the satin pillow. He then retrieved a black binder from his backpack hanging from the lofted bunk. The binder opened to the script, and he powered on the craned lamp attached to the railing.

While a student in Mr. Ray's *Intro to Drama* course, his instructor often preached about the importance of the script. "It's the most critical piece to any production that dares to stand onstage. All characters, ambitions, and conflicts arise from the conditions set by the writer. To deny the writing is to deny the very essence of the play and, in turn, the playwright."

In June's hands was a set of sentences carefully spaced across sheets, emotions confined to parentheses and prepositions, and stage directions to instruct cast and crew. June ran his finger over the typed text, grazing the slight indent of ink on the page, wondering what possessed a girl like Michaela to write such a tale.

With the audition fresh on his mind, June dissected the sentences on the bound sheets, replacing the bedroom with the fantastical setting for the untitled stage production.

~~~

An ethereal light flickered above the massive door opposing Baudelaire. He pulled the chain hanging from the gargoyle's mouth, and suddenly, a stone shaft swung open. The shock returned him a few steps, but Baudelaire regained composure and investigated the shaft.

A crimson-colored eye appeared out of the darkness. "You're late. The show has already started."

"The show?" he asked.

"Ah, a fresh face, and...you're living? Interesting. Looks like you and every shade crawled out tonight to hear the new songstress."

A second shaft opened around waist level, and a small glass containing a blue liquid was positioned on the tray. "On the house. Cheers, mate."

"Am I supposed to drink this?" inquired Baudelaire.

"No drink, no entry," the detached voice stated.

"What is this queer concoction?" he gagged.

"A transmutation tonic. Physical bodies can't be sustained down here, so you've gotta let go of the vessel. Fear not; we will protect your vessel until you're ready to leave."

"I admit, this is questionable, but I must take the risk since I am pursuing something greater." Baudelaire tossed the shot back and gasped. A spasm started in his throat and spread throughout his body like a wildfire. Within seconds of the solution settling in his stomach, Baudelaire felt the force of gravity dissipate from his body. The lingering pain from his injuries also vanished. His soul dispersed through the permeations in his skin before reconstructing in front of the door. Then, he experienced a sensation akin to floating
~~~

in a salt-filled lagoon. As Baudelaire adjusted to his new state, he looked at the body collapsed on the ground—his worn and weathered body.

"That's...that's me?"

The eye replied, "Not exactly. That's just the container you occupy. This, what you're existing as now, is the real you. This is your *essence*."

"My essence?" he repeated.

"You'll get used to it. Now that that's done, I'd like to officially welcome you to Ingilaef!" said the doorman. "Once inside, you'll find a dressing room with our seasonal wardrobe to the left. After you're dressed, head to the bar and meet with the Tavern Master, who will help you settle in. Any questions?"

Baudelaire shook his head as the shafts closed, and the turning of a heavy lock echoed in the cryptic corridor. The door opened, and he stepped through, realizing one season would not be enough time to experience everything offered by this new world. In front of him was not a crypt or a jagged cavernous system with eerie denizens but rather an establishment of modern design—a lively tavern.

To his right was a fully stocked bar crowded with patrons all waiting to place an order. The seating area scattered with tables was positioned close to a stage on the far side. Windows did not exist; however, an intricate system of torches offered plenty of light to the underground bar. The floor was aesthetically pleasing, with mosaic imagery embedded in the marble tiles.

However, the most impressive aspect of the establishment was the stage. It had four columns growing from the roots of the cherry blossom trees above, each supporting a sparkling curtain to conceal the backstage area. The wood used to create the floor was ashen white and made a particular noise when one stepped upon it. Thirteen lanterns hung above the rafters, each containing dual flames in a colored glass jar. Four crew members controlled the lanterns, alternating between covered and visible to change the hues and luminance. Lastly, two silver sound bowls were placed at the downstage corner to enhance the acoustics.

The house band occupying the blood-colored stage played a sad rendition of *Gymnopedie I*. The lead pianist was a potbellied, square-nosed man who'd been shot to death over a family inheritance. His dreamlike melodies were accompanied by a living bassist, a headless drummer, and a masked individual who played the alto saxophone–the bar patrons were unsure if they were living or dead as they never showed face.

Sitting in a leather booth listening to the symphony of sorrow was Baudelaire. He wore a navy toga fastened by a silver laurel pin. Condensation bled down the sides of the chilled goblet as he meticulously rolled a cigarette. Once complete, he tucked it behind his ear and took another sip before joining the ovation. Shortly after settling in the speakeasy, Baudelaire learned that trivial matters such as animation status bore little importance in Ingilaef.

According to the Tavern Master who seated Baudelaire, the factor determining entry to Ingilaef, instead of an ambiguous afterlife, was the value of an individual soul. Those who exhibited authentic character were welcomed, while those who existed under false pretenses were left prattling outside. Now and then, however, a living soul would find their way to this place. Like him, they were welcome, but they never became residents. The local patrons were far from phantasms and hollow shades but nearly corporeal figures who could interact with the world.

Despite the grandeur of the experience, Baudelaire found it difficult to determine where he ended and the world began. Now, he belonged somewhere between death and a dream, not entirely forgotten nor real. Instead of shirking away from the unfamiliarity, he embraced it; after all, was this not what he sought?

The band concluded their final song with a haunting melody, bringing the audience to tears. Black silk curtains folded over the primitive wiring as crew members attached and collected instruments. Baudelaire's empty glass twirled in his hands as a new audio amplification machine was set up on the center stage. The Tavern Master stepped out from behind the counter, carrying a polished mug in the shape of a skull. He whistled to the lantern operator, and then a unified hush fell over the indigo house as his hand raised.

"Alright, you deathless denizens, it's time for the main course! As you know, we here at Ingilaef are all about creating a space for expression after existence. Those whose talents were not fully realized in life are granted a second chance. Tonight, I'd like to introduce you all to the newest member of our troupe. You know what that means, don't you, Ingilaef?"

The audience chanted like ritual conductors. "Re-sur-rection! Re-sur-rection! Re-sur-rection!"

"Indeed, and what do we do during a resurrection?"

"The spectators stay silent!"

"Look at you all knowing the rules. So, let's settle into our seats as a siren from the far reaches of a snowy land whisks us away with her songs."

From the ebony curtains emerged the physical embodiment of the ocean. Aquamarine fabrics flowed across the whiteboards as a woman trotted across the stage. Once she reached the center, the lantern crew adjusted the lighting to bathe her face in silver. Round, crimson eyes with the power to generate childhood memories in amnesiacs shined in the low light.

Her glossed lips pressed against the tip of the mic. "Um...hello...I've got a song, and...well, I...I'll sing it."

Everything except the stage was shrouded in darkness, turning the strange audience into a crowd of silhouettes. A solitary beam projected onto the siren nearly caused her to cry whenever she looked up. Her frail hand wiped her eye, leaving black globules across her pale skin. Shock registered on her face as the singer realized her current state of affairs.

Baudelaire tapped his cigarette on the table while stray whispers inched their way from his adjacent neighbors. "Now that's fresh meat," said the guest.

"Ya mate, you can see it all in her eyes. The poor thing's probably terrified."

"Wouldn't you be if you died and the first thing you saw was the Tavern Master's ugly mug?"

"True; at least she's been given a performer's contract. Afterlife can't be too bad for her since they'll care for her."

"*If* she can carry a tune. If she's not worth the entertainment, she's just lost her opportunity to rest in peace."

The Tavern Master snapped his finger, and a brute with a charred right arm lumbered toward the talking table. He said not a word, but steam flared out of his nose. The whispering patrons cowered in their seats and bowed at the bouncer. "Apologies, Sorex. You'll not hear another peep from us. Promise." The venue then went quiet enough to hear the boards of the stage creak under the singer's trembling legs.

Unaware of what to do, the songstress peered into the crowd, seeking someone in the audience to transfer the emotions she was about to express with her tongue. Yet, all were shadows and wisps of smoke and ectoplasm glimmering like mirages.

Tension rose as the silence lingered, and some audience members began tapping and rattling small objects. The performer stepped away from the microphone, causing the Tavern Master to hold up a skull-shaped mug. Its hollow eyes began flaring a greenish smoke. She turned back to the microphone, anxious.

Baudelaire struck the match, producing a faint light in the dark. He lit the cigarette and took a swelling inhale before focusing his attention on the silent songstress. Unknown to him, that subtle glimmer of light was all it took to begin the show.

From the songstress's point of view, there was one person who retained a definite shape. One who stood out from the crowd of the faceless audience. At this moment, she decided he would be her anchor. His gaze was dominant yet compassionate, how it could hold tight to her stare even though she invaded his presence without invitation. And because her eyes did not part from his, Baudelaire accepted his role as muse.

I am a crystal comet,
Seeking a home for one,
And the moment we first met,
Our doom was set in stone.

Magic and flesh form,
As glances are exchanged,
Room for hope being born,
Only to be sadly slain.

Love forever doomed
To a dusken daydream
Lost in a tomb
Grave for goodbyes.

A baptism of fire awaits
The soul who dares to try,
But dear, I hope it's not too late,
For us to still fly.

And if our spirits can
Burden this weight...
Then here, my dear...

We shall run away
Leaving ourselves behind,
Forever unbound to fate.

Baudelaire rarely experienced alterations to his emotional state, yet the siren's voice replaced the cornerstone of his foundation. Somehow, this woman understood the melodies of angels, her notes desperately clinging to remnants of her fading humanity. The second verse lulled and entered pores like the haze from Baudelaire's cigarette, rendering him devoid of any thoughts except those surrounding their connection: singer and receiver, artist and muse, vessel and anchor...living and dead.

Once the chorus repeated a final time and she dragged out the word "fate," her lips pulled away from the audio device. The floorboards whispered as black tears drizzled from her crimson eyes. Thunderous applause followed the performance, causing the songstress to curl back. The Tavern Master reappeared behind the curtain, signaling her to speak.

"Thank you. My name is...um...I think my name is....wait, what is my name?"

"And there you have it, Ingilaef! Meet Rochelle!" interrupted the Tavern Master before her confusion soured the moment.

"Rochelle...? I am Rochelle?"

The Tavern Master whispered something to her, and she bowed to the audience before her coral gown, glistening like a mermaid's tail, disappeared behind the curtains. "What do you think? A true siren, no? She'll be sharing her talents with us. And now, let's take an intermission. After the break, we'll hear from the Constellation Quartet, who have rehearsed a new set inspired by a famous drowning."

Baudelaire plucked the cigarette, now cooled to ash, and placed it in the calcium tray next to the candle. "Rochelle, Rochelle. I fear even Cain the Mystic could not transcribe the immensity of this current sensation. You have impressed me, no, *inspired* me. Although unknown to us, I believe our paths are destined to cross. But this cannot be left up to the universe's randomness; instead, I will make it so that our *temporal tangents* intersect."

Baudelaire rose from the table and carried his glass to the bar. Already, shades were lining up to greet the singer. The tavern hand refilled his glass, and he sipped slowly, ignoring the crowd. From the backstage area appeared Rochelle, now dressed in a traditional toga attire. Baudelaire watched the mob overwhelm her. But he couldn't save her, not unless she acknowledged him. Yet, he couldn't erase the image of her under the spotlight. Finally, after giving her hand to many guests to kiss, she looked at him. Baudelaire tipped his glass to her, sending a subtle invitation. She accepted, parting the crowd like a boat did the waves, the two souls beginning their exploration of the tragic romance between stone and song.

The alarm on June's cell phone blared again—9:00 PM. He tucked the black binder into his book bag. While sorting through the contents, he glanced at Michaela's poetry book. The binding and cover art were worn from constant bending, multiple pages had dog ears, and there were scribbles and highlights. He set it on the shelf, classifying it as the newest addition to their collection of miscellaneous objects.

"How did I not notice the temporal tangent line? And the baptism of fire, too? She's a low-key Xavier groupie, but it's kinda cool how she wove all that into the story. Michaela, who are you exactly? I need to get this part so I can get to know her, and maybe…"

So, she can downplay you? Tell you about yourself? How you're a shitty actor? What do you have to offer someone like her? You can't even say the lines in her script right! Don't forget you dissed her dialogue, too. Gibberish? Valyrian? Seriously? Stop hyping yourself and take that L with pride, you failure.

When he reached his desk, June opened the laptop and started the internet browser. His fingers typed on the keypad. "I can do this. I am a conduit. I can become Baudelaire; no, I will let Baudelaire *live through me.*"

That's right, June. Have a little hope. Please have a little hope so it can be crushed. Get hurt so bad you'll never want to do some dumb shit like act ever again.

With the story still unraveling in his mind, June charged himself to face the consequences with confidence. "If he is a man for himself, I, too, will become a man for myself." The school's theater department website loaded with a new link.

Ingilaef Casting.

Baudelaire: Timothy Brooks.

June continued to scroll down the page, seeking his name.

Tavern Master: Daniel Elliott Junior.

"No...I thought...I thought I could do it. I did my best...No, no, this isn't right...this isn't how it's supposed to go!" He reloaded the page three more times, hoping the results would change. But the decision had already been made. "I was...I was supposed to be Baudelaire, not Tavern Master," June cried.

More like Master of Failure. See, why would anyone want to put a loser in the spotlight? I told you, you're a nobody—a runt with big-boy dreams. You're easily forgotten, and people will only remember that you failed. Isn't that right, Mr. Stage-fright?! The best thing you can do now is stop failing. And the only way for someone like you to do that is to stop living!

Oath of Ophelia

The dormitory door opened, and Lance crept into his darkened room. A vague piano melody hummed from the speakers, and its presence tipped off the exhausted photographer. Underneath the soundtrack were sniffles echoing from somewhere in the shadows.

"*To Zanarkand*, really? This is a code omega breakdown," Lance said, dropping his belongings and turning on the light.

Curled on the futon, with his face covered by a du-rag and pillow, was his roommate, June. White streaks stretched from the corner of his eyes to the point of his chin. An oversized cardigan hung off his shoulders, the puffy sleeves resembling elephant trunks.

"You can swipe my neck all you want. I don't care anymore. It was stupid to think that I could play that part."

"Whoa now, I don't wanna attack you while you're down, but that's at least *three* necks. I'll be saving those for later." Lance muted the speaker, "Safe to assume you didn't get the lead? Did you at least get a part?"

"Yeah, the Tavern Master."

"How many scenes?"

"He's in over half the production, but still..."

"Half the production?! Dude, that's a major win! You finally have a real role, and it's even got its own name. Talk about a glo-up!"

"But it's not what I want."

"When does life give us what we want? If it did, I'd be spending my days stoned in a bathrobe watching documentaries on doomsday cults with my harem."

"That's really what you want out of life, Lance?"

He shrugged, "More or less. Still not sold on the robe. That's beside the point. What I'm trying to say is you may not have gotten what you wanted, but you still got something—experience points. That's what counts, right?"

"It seems like a lot of wasted effort," said June.

Lance removed his jacket and shirt, grabbing a hoodie from his closet. He also swapped his boots for a pair of wool slippers. Now comfortable, he turned to his roommate. "I have a loaded question: Do you want to be the lead, *or do you want to be seen?*"

"What do you mean by seen?"

"I can understand wanting some clout on this campus. To be known and recognized goes a long way here. But maybe there are other ways to do it without the added responsibility of leadership. We're just sophomores, after all. We should be focused on living our lives, not asking the world to watch our every move. I'm not saying I doubt that you're lead material, but..."

"But I'm a shitty actor compared to Timothy Brooks, right?"

"No, June. You know that's not what I meant."

"Actually, I don't even need to compare myself to anybody; that's how shitty an actor I am."

"Bro..."

"I'm a failure who will only be remembered for my failures."

"You're doing it again..."

"There's only one thing I can do now. I'm going to quit. If I quit now, then I don't have to worry about embarrassing myself again because that's all I do these days. I'm just a joke, a waste, a thing to be laughed at until it's time to die. How easy it would be to just..."

"JUNE, CHILL!" Lance shouted, halting June's morose rambling. "Bring it back, bro, bring it back up."

They took a collective breath together. "I'm sorry."

"You're not a sorry person. You're just anxious. Now listen to me because what I'm about to say is important. If you quit, *then you ain't shit*. Like, you did get a part. A better part than last time, and you want to quit?"

"If only you understood why I wanted this role. I need to be Baudelaire."

"And why do you need to be him, specifically?" Lance asked.

"He's the embodiment of everything a man should be. Determined but understanding, creative yet courageous, compassionate but aware of his worth."

"It sounds like you have a crush on him," Lance joked.

"You don't get it, Lance. You don't need to imitate somebody because you already are *a somebody*. You get high with the chess team, snap photos of the deans, and get free admission to almost all events. A pervy conspiracy theorist, but also a skilled photographer who works for the Morrison Moment."

Lance rolled his eyes and placed his camera next to scattered copies of the Morrison Moment. "I am not a conspiracy theorist; I prefer the term devout skeptic."

June halted his growing smile. "Me though? I'm just another face on campus. Just a GPA waiting to be inserted into a database. A nobody. What's my legacy? What have I done to make a statement aside from the pissy mattress?"

"You're an actor."

"The highlight of my theatrical career is my blunder on stage last spring. Do you know what they call me in the theater?"

"What?" Lance asked.

"Mr. Stagefright!"

"Like Mr. Brightside? Damn, that's kinda good," Lance snickered.

"Ugh, name-calling, it's so middle school. The insults don't bother me; what hurts is knowing that's who I am to this community. I'm a mistake, not June. Do you see it now? Baudelaire was my chance to be somebody."

"Then, use this as a chance to be yourself, not some imaginary character. Where's the guy who wants to be the next Denzel Washington? Isn't that biography signed by him? Shouldn't that make you want to, like, do better or something?"

"I was going to start that with this part," June said.

"You're forgetting something. Denzel doesn't model himself after his characters; he *models his characters after himself*. That's why he's so good at what he does; the roles represent the best of him. Even you should know that. And June, you are *somebody*. You're a theater geek seeking perfection, but you're also motivated. An empath, pretty smart, and an overall good dude."

"You sound like you have a crush on me," June responded.

"Because you're my best friend. You inspire me the way you go after what you want. Even if it's way out of your reach." Lance let the words marinate in his friend's mind before patting him on the back. "Just be you, June. No matter who that is, be you."

More tears formed, these coming from a source of acceptance and joy. "Ha, exactly what my mom said earlier," said June.

"That's because your mom's cool as hell, and she's right."

"I got caught up in the character, not the production. Just because I'm not him doesn't mean I can't give a great performance."

Lance dapped him up: "For sure, dude. Learn some new things along the way for the future. One day, I need you to give a dope monologue so that we can hit a Grammy's after-party. Then we can get the ladies to throw panties at you. Or do they throw corsets in the theater?"

"Shut up, fool. And Grammy's are for music," June laughed, drying the streaks on his cheeks. Once he caught his breath, he acknowledged his roommate with a smile. "Thanks, Lance. I mean it. I could feel myself beginning to spiral, but you saved me before it got worse."

"No need to say that; it's what I'm here to do. Aren't you glad I threw up in your laundry bin last year? Look at us now."

"I had to get rid of my favorite shirt because of that."

"What's one favorite shirt compared to meeting a new best friend? Like I told you that night, I'm here to help you become a more positive person. Speaking of positivity..." Grinning, Lance raised his hands and started rubbing them to produce friction. "How about we get these out of the way?"

June granted Lance's open palm access to the back of his neck. Three swipes followed, and he fanned the heated patch of skin. "Now that we're done with that, can we drown out our sorrows?" June asked.

"*Our sorrows*? Pssh, I had a solid day today," said Lance.

"Word? Anjali finally let you get your balls back?"

"Haha," he mocked. "If she had 'em, I'd tell her to treat 'em like Curry. Double dribble them thangs, girl."

"Oh, shut up," June said, rotating the metallic chair towards the futon. So, if your love wasn't reciprocated, what made today so solid?"

Lance lifted his camera and mimicked snapping a photograph. "I've found my next calling."

"Your calling? Is it to be a reclusive reporter who infiltrates a futurist cult worshipping an artificial intelligence? Or a porn director?" June teased.

"Nope, but I may come back to those later in life. I'm talking about applying for the position of Senior Editor, the highest position at the Morrison Moment. Anjali Purohit is currently occupying the spot, but it will be held by her future baby daddy, Lance Xiao, next year."

June shook his head in disappointment. "Damn, you're not even gonna wife her? Just put a baby in her and leave after that? I thought you were a better man, Lance."

"You're missing the point here," Lance rolled his eyes. "I've got big goals to chase, just like you. The difference between us is that I'm not in competition with myself. I have a *Ri-Dol* I need to destroy if I want the position."

Confusion clouded June's face. "You have a...what to destroy?"

"Ri-dol. It's a new thing, and I'm trying to make it stick."

"It sounds like a discount brand of period medicine. What does it mean?"

"It's someone who is both your rival and idol. Like Goku and Vegeta. No matter how much he envied him, a part of Vegeta respected Goku because Goku accomplished everything he wanted to do."

"But you're not Goku; you're more like Yamcha."

"The disrespect. I'm at least Krillin."

"Lemme guess, George is the Ri-Dol?"

Lance nodded to confirm. "He's a major annoying Type A dick, and he's always doing lame shit. Like, after fetching donuts for him and Anjali, he decided not to eat more than three bites, claiming he was avoiding unnecessary sugar that could cause cavities. Not to mention, George is a pervert. He's only doing this photography thing to get girls. He's so thirsty for Anjali, too; it's so wack."

"Oh? He's a pervert, and you're a what?" asked June.

"A connoisseur of erotic excursions."

"So a bougie pervert?"

"Again, missing the point. George is a dweeb, but there's part of him I respect: His artistry. Dude's images are always crisp and composed with the utmost precision; edits are subtle yet add a larger-than-life aura to his subjects. I can't deny that his work is dope. Like dope enough that he's been featured on digital streetwear blogs, local investigative articles, and in one of those fancy middle-aged lifestyle zines they sell at the bookstore. Instagram even shared one of his posts on their global account."

"Bro's nice like that, huh?"

"So nice that his creativity kinda makes up for all the wack shit he does. Kinda," Lance emphasized.

"And that makes him your rival and idol...a Ri-Dol."

"Exactly. You should get one. They say nobody grows you like a rival, and it might as well be someone you admire. Could even be someone on the cast with you."

"Maybe I will, but we're talking about you," said June. "How exactly will you take down this formidable foe?"

"Documenting Greek life."

"Like snapbacks and Air Max bros who all have 'one black friend' who is 'cool' with them saying the N-word? This should be entertaining," June said.

"Yeah, that's them. The assignment is meant to highlight organizations, but I'm looking for more than keg stands kings and molly mistresses. This could be a chance to expose some *secrets*." Lance revealed a conniving smile and rubbed his hands together. "Because sensational secrets make sensational stories."

"What kind of secrets do you want to uncover about the Greek life on our docile little campus, Lance?"

Lance rose from the futon and moved to his desk to begin flipping through older editions of the MM. "I don't know, sacred rituals involving animal sacrifices, blood pacts between university officials and unnamed magicians, maybe people chanting and dancing naked around the Clock Tower?"

"These sound like conspiracy theories," June laughed.

"To be fair, I'd also be cool with learning which fraternity has ties to drug operations because someone has to supply all these trust fund dealers."

"Shit, I'd rather you uncover a ritual than a cartel circuit. You will end up angry and alone chasing theories, but if you expose a kingpin, someone will put a hit on you because you know too much."

"I'd rather die for the truth than live a lie," Lance proudly stated. Then, he deflated his chest with a chuckle. "Sounds like the opening of my memoir, you know, because I will totally get a book deal one day. And it will happen because I will create the most exposing editorial ever!"

"Who are you gonna cover then?"

"Honestly, I don't even know. There's Smoke and Toke Sigma Tau, Lusty Ass Lambda Delta Kappa, the coke boys known as Mu Nu, the ultra-conservative daughters of Chi Xi Chi, or the geeks in Gamma Zeta Omega. George will probably focus on a Black organization, which already gives him points for diversity."

"You could always do the same?"

"And culture appropriate for my benefit? No way, bro. I'm above that," Lance stated.

"What exactly makes a good editorial?" June said.

"Not sure on the specifics yet, but knowing Anjali, it's gonna boil down to a compelling narrative and style. If I choose an org with some serious dirt, that will get me points. But if I want to get that position, I'll need to incorporate more than photographs and taglines; I'll need facts, data points, and maybe even a chart. I already know George is gathering his info through interviews, which is smart because it can be uploaded to the digital cloud. So, I need something so innovative that those ladies throwing corsets at you will toss whatever's left in my direction."

June dismissed Lance's banter by opening his laptop. He connected to the speaker and started playing music from his library. Meanwhile, Lance placed his camera bag and a kit of electronic cleaning supplies on his desk. He began tinkering with the device with deft hands, opening latches and lining up his lenses in order of focus distance.

The Smiths came on fourth in rotation, and June turned to his roommate in his desk chair. "Yo, Lance. You ever heard of something called the Lemarind Order?"

Lance stopped polishing the 85mm lens. "You mean the *Lemurian Order*? Duh! Who hasn't heard of them?"

"What do you know about them?"

"They're only MSU's most prestigious organization. They give me cult vibes though."

"How so?" June inquired.

Lance toyed with his camera, "For starters, they don't associate with anybody outside their crew unless the agenda calls for it. And when they do, they operate as if the rest of us are *inferior*. But we might be according to their standards. The Lemurian Order is only for the elite of the elite. Their alumni include militant capital moguls who now sit at the top of Wall Street, innovative scientists advancing synthetic biology, and avant-garde artists with works exhibited across the globe."

"I didn't realize they were so next level," said June.

"Bro, they are the pinnacle. The podcast I listen to has referenced them several times in this latest series. Apparently, everything they touch is golden. But behind all that glam is something...dark."

"Organizations can be grand and not be involved with sketchy shit," June argued.

"Sketchy? No, they're probably tapped in with something sinister. I mean, have you seen *their eyes*?" His roommate nodded slowly as if recounting some recent experience. Lance continued, "Answer me this: why would a reclusive group of elite college students wear the same *colored contacts* unless they're a devil-worshipping cult?

"How do you know they worship the devil?"

"Satan is also known as Saturn. Saturn is the seventh planet; it's a sphere surrounded by silver rings. Sega Saturn's graphic was a purple sphere with a silver lining, like their eyes. Sega also released the Genesis system. Genesis is the Bible's first book, where Adam and Eve are tempted with forbidden knowledge. Who tempts the humans but the serpent? And what's that serpent's name? Satan, or Saturn. Boom!" Lance gestured as if he'd dropped a mini-nuke in his lap.

"I can see the headlines now: Secret Satanic Sega Fraternity Sacrifices Serpents for Saturn," June announced. Sharing the laugh. Lance's cheeks felt the warmth of camaraderie. "How do you know all of this anyway? Aside from your weird programs?" asked June.

"I work in the media. My job revolves around investigating any and all rumors. Plenty of articles have passed by my desk mentioning their names, and I read them all. The Lemurian Order isn't a 'secret' society by traditional standards; they're quite open about their accolades. But they're definitely sharing their successes to conceal their shit. A hundred years' worth of shit, at least."

"Sounds like they are the perfect group to use for the editorial, yeah?" said June.

"Theoretically, yes. However, as much as I'd love to uncover their connection to the hidden demon realm gateway, realistically, it's too great a risk."

"Lance playing it safe? This is new," June said.

Lance set the cleaning supplies down and leaned back in his desk chair. "If I show up with something too obscure to prove, Anjali will promote George. And then I'll have to fetch donuts for him to stick his dick in for an entire year."

"Gives another meaning to the term glazed donut," said June.

"I can't let George ruin my time at the MM. So the most rational decision is playing it safe and spilling tea on a frat or sorority."

"Interesting. Even though the opportunity of your college career might be breathing down your back?"

"That's why I can't chase the rumors; I need something real."

"But isn't that who you are?"

"What do you mean?"

June pointed at the lost and found collection forming in the corner. "Lance, you're not exactly the best at direct interactions. You're much better at uncovering what's hidden. Didn't you tell me to be myself? Well, I'm doing the same. Why not be the best Scoobert Doobert and solve the grand mystery?"

"And what's the mystery?" Lance inquired.

"Expose the Lemurian Order."

"Believe me, that web runs too deep, June. If I start yanking at that, I could pull the whole rug from underneath MSU. But I'm awaiting the day I can conduct a full report."

"That day is just not today, huh? And here I thought you wanted to be sensational."

"I do, but I want something I can wrap up by April. Exposing a cabal of elite masterminds who have kept their name clean for a century? Impossible."

"No, it's not."

"Why are *you* so interested in this?" Lance asked.

"I'm just upholding my end of our friendship. Didn't you just say I inspire you to go after what you want, including things that seem out of reach? So, go after it." There was more to June's reasoning, but Lance let it slide. "Hear me out: You're a history minor. Instead of finding new information, use what already exists. An organization that old has to have slipped up somewhere."

Lance looked around his desk, noticing the date of one of the articles. "There are the MM Archives, and that's been around since the campus's founding. I'm sure their HQ has to have records too."

"See, a blend of past research and present investigation. This sounds exactly like the story that would bag you what you want. It could be your *big break*."

"I mean, you do have a point. They still fall under the fraternity category, and now might be the perfect time to open a case against them since it hasn't been done before."

"Not to mention, this could go viral. You'd appear as a guest on various podcasts and shows; hell, you could even host your own."

"I could, yeah! I've always wanted to be a guest on *Found Dead By The Lake* so I can talk about the concept of portal technology."

"A lot of people would know who you are," added June.

"Status would help finance some of my future endeavors, and I can't go wrong having a couple of millionaires on speed dial."

"And you know..." June grinned, "this editorial would immortalize the current employees at the Morrison Moment. You'd be part of the campus legacy, as would Anjali, because the editorial was her idea. In a way, you'd be making her dreams come true. I can only imagine how she'd thank you for that."

Like a cartoon, Lance felt his heart thump out of his eyes. He touched his wrist, remembering the subtle graze from earlier when Anjali accepted his drink. Then, the indirect kiss…

"Fuck it, I'm sold!" Lance's excitement dissipated as the reality of his assignment dawned on him. "But now I have to figure out who I could interview. I doubt I can pull up to a member and ask for them to air out their dirty laundry. Plus, I don't personally know any of the current members."

June scratched the fuzz forming on his face. "I…I might have a connect."

"Wait! You're *friends* with someone in the Lemurian Order?! Talk about sensational secrets. You need to hook me up with them ASAP!"

"But I barely know him myself. He's just a fellow cast member I met during today's audition."

"Do you know his name?"

"Yeah, Parker Galician," June said.

"Parker…Parker…hmm? Don't know him, must be a newer member. Sounds like a bougie pervert, though." Lance raised his camera, "But a name is all we need for an introduction."

"You can't just bombard him with this request!" stammered June.

"Then, I'll have you request it for me."

"He probably doesn't even remember me."

Lance's face flashed to confusion, "Why not? You just said you auditioned together."

"But…" June began.

"I know you may not understand it, June, but I have to seek out all opportunities if I want to progress. Especially the smaller ones. If I don't, what's gonna happen when the big gig falls on my plate? You know what I want to do, right?"

Lance guided June's eyes over to his desk. Above the workstation was a shelf filled with countless yellow-bound publications.

"Nat Geo. I know," June said. "Sorry, I'm being difficult. I don't know him well and don't want him to think I'm using him to climb a social ladder or something. But I'll talk to him next time I see him."

A wide smile appeared on Lance's face, and he returned his camera to the bag and packed up the cleaning supplies. "You do this for me, and I'll never neck swipe you again."

"Deal!" shouted June.

"Ha! Check me out. Morrison Moment Senior Editor and the first investigator to expose the secret satanic cult known as the Lemurian Order. Not to mention Baby Daddy of Anjali Purohit. The legend of Lance is growing!"

"Oh, please, man. The only thing growing is your ego."

"That is precisely why I am excited about tonight. I shall put this ego to death and begin my pursuit with renewed drive!"

"Wait, you got *them*?" June asked with childlike curiosity.

A mischievous grin appeared as Lance removed a folded plastic bag from the depths of his camera bag. Resting inside were five pencil-length mushroom stalks connected to dried caps.

"Tonight, we shall voyage as psychonauts into the realm beyond reality! Our destination: the astral plane!"

Psychonauts

The pungent odor of the dried mushrooms caused June to gag and pinch his nose. He zipped the bag and threw it back to Lance, who reminisced on his first experience with psychedelics. The story involved a Brooklyn-based funk concert, and he and his friends being kicked out of the bar for collectively licking someone's tattooed kneecap.

"I'm not an expert or anything, but the person who sold them to me said they were legit," Lance said as he removed one of the mushroom stalks. "I'm thinking we split the eighth and ride the wave."

"I'm following your lead. And yes, I'm nervous as shit." June stated.

"No surprise there, Anxious Alex. Don't let pop culture fool you, though. I doubt there will be any wild hallucinations with this dosage. Best case, you feel happy as shit, music sounds amazing, and the world is a big ass sandbox that you can't wait to build."

"And the worst?" June inquired.

"You have a bad trip, tweak out, and die because you jumped off the roof thinking the floor was snakes, and you were Indiana Jones."

June's fear cut the humor short. Wouldn't be the first time I've almost lost my life on this campus, he thought.

Lance lifted one of the mushrooms to the desk light, inspecting it like a rare specimen. "Dude, relax; some of the world's greatest people experimented with mind-altering substances: Steve Jobs, one of those guys who discovered DNA, Tim O'Leary, and even Mike Tyson. And I'm sure some of your favorite actors are all about taking psychedelic adventures to expand their emotional capacity. Who knows, *this trip might unlock your potential,*" concluded Lance.

June accepted the stalk from Lance. The cap was shriveled and covered in pink microscopic furs. "What are they called?" June asked.

"Umm...shrooms? Caps? Cow-perales? Do you want the scientific name?"

"I'd like to know what I'm about to get myself into, that's all. I'll Google it," June checked his phone. After a few minutes of web browsing, he found a picture that resembled the mushroom in his hand. Then, he read the article.

"*Ophiocordyceps unilateralis.* The street name for this strain is Ophelia. Users report an illusory, out-of-body sensation that coincides with mood swings, cognitive dissonance, euphoria, bouts of hysteria, and tears. Some even claim to experience a stasis resembling death. Hell no, man! I'm not taking that."

"Can't trust everything on Wikipedia; that's fake news," Lance affirmed.

"Lance, I'm reading from the Drug Enforcement Administration page."

"You'd rather trust the government over Wikipedia? I'm ashamed. What I know about these mushrooms is that this little cap will be eaten tonight. And this one, and this one too, oh and that one there."

"Why are we doing this anyway?" June asked.

Lance rationed out two and a half mushrooms to June. "We need to celebrate our accomplishments! You're cast in a play! And I've got a new assignment!"

"We could easily celebrate with a shot or a smoke."

"We talked about tripping together before things got too crazy with school. And there's no better time than now."

"Why do you make me do these risky things?" groaned June.

"Oh no, don't make it sound like you're being forced. I may create the opportunity, but *you choose to join me*. So, will you?"

"Why the hell not? It's a new semester, and you're right. We've got some good wins so far."

Two solo cups were retrieved from behind the four-foot mini-refrigerator. The sink faucet shouted as the water filled each of the cups. With the drink now in his right hand and the shrooms in his left, June buried his rational thought and prepared his stomach for the sacrifice.

"Damn, we're really doing this. This is like a milestone in our friendship. We need to toast."

"What are we toasting to?" June inquired.

Lance raised the cup towards the ceiling, "What we always toast to on the first shot."

"Bro, we can't keep making this a trend. If someone finds out we say this, then they'll judge us. It's kinda messed up, lowkey."

"Unless we're in a court of law, I don't care who judges me. Plus, doesn't it just rile up your bones when you say it?" Lance tapped the bottom of his friend's cup until it lifted in the air. "Our goal tonight is the same as every night we turn up: to get some consenting coitus!"

June rolled his eyes, "Dude, just promise to take my phone away if I get too lit? I don't want to make any mistakes like last time."

"You mean you don't want to drunkenly confess to Brittney how you two are star-crossed lovers lost in lines of a sonnet?"

"You read that?" June's jaw nearly popped out of its hinge.

"All seven paragraphs of your poetically crafted texts? Hell no. Just the highlights, but I've saved at least three screenshots on my phone just in case folk wanna pop off."

"Not even gonna ask how you got access to those texts. You're an asshole, you know that?"

"Asshole is such a harsh word. I prefer investigative journalist. It's all good, though; we all get in our feelings now and then. You happen to express them through cell phone stanzas sent from *Marvin's Room*."

June laughed, "And you commit larceny because you can't get your royal jewels back from your crush."

"Aye, good one! I'm wondering what tonight's trophy could be—there's no telling what I will swipe when I'm on these. Oh, the last thing," Lance glanced at his cell phone. The current time is 10:11. Remember that."

"Why?"

"The trip should only last four or five hours. No matter what happens, we should be ready to crash by three."

"Five hours, huh? Sounds like a work-study shift," June said.

"Best to think of this as training for a new reality. Now, are you ready, my fellow psychonaut? To the beyond we go!"

The shrooms were stuffed into their mouths, chewed and ground by coated teeth, and swallowed with tepid water. Both faces morphed into disgust as the earthen flavor spread through their mouths—a gag here, a cough there, followed by more water.

"Gross, oh my god. So gross."

"Don't think about it. Just chew. Ugh."

"I'm gonna EARL," said June.

"If you start EARLing, then I'm gonna EARL too."

Eventually, the bolus descended throats, and the boys gasped for relief. June finished another cup and coughed. "Shit. I can't believe I ate that; it tastes like sponges soaked in hot dog water. How long does it take?"

"Patience, my apprentice, you'll know when it hits." Lance reclined back on the futon, hooked his phone up to the speakers, and started playing *Let It Happen* by Tame Impala.

"What's this grand master plan of ours when it does hit?" asked June.

"I heard there's a new *Planet Earth* documentary where they go to the depths of the sea and uncover some new organisms. We can also vibe out to some tunes."

The television booted up, and within minutes, the two boys were piloting a submersible capable of reaching abysmal depths. The speakers continued to play alternative beats while the screen showed blips of bizarre fish and aquatic biology still unknown to modern society. After the forty-eight-minute documentary, June patted his belly.

"Do you feel anything yet? Honestly...?" he asked Lance.

His roommate shook his head and then sniffed the empty plastic bag. "Just wait on it, I think."

"I keep waiting for *it* to happen, but it's not coming. I'm not even sure what's supposed to happen. You think they're duds?" June questioned as he used the remote to power down the television.

The black screen revealed June's reflection, and another replaced his image. A figure with lanky arms and a slender torso also bared the curves of his cheeks and the furrow of his brow that arched like a ravine. Instead of finding the same almond-colored eyes at the ravine's base, he saw a lustrous amethyst accented by a silvery glow. They resembled Parker's glaring eyes. Then, the image dissipated, causing June to pace around like an expectant father in a waiting room.

"Lance, let's get out of here."

"Ummm...I don't think that's a solid move, bro. This is your first time tripping, and they say you shouldn't switch your surroundings to an unfamiliar setting."

"But we're not tripping! If we were, we'd be bouncing on the walls or having a mad tea party. We're doing the same thing we did every weekend last year. Sitting on the futon, with empty stomachs and *empty beds*."

Lance stared at the red cup as if the answer to his conspiracies were at the bottom. Meanwhile, June snatched a package of chocolate chip cookies and pivoted in place, stuffing the snacks in his mouth. "We need to jump some bones tonight! Didn't we toast to that?"

"Jump...some bones? What's gotten into you? Plus, where are we even gonna go to talk to girls?"

"The mall! A bus ride! The Student Union! Anywhere but here! There has to be somewhere we can go. Somewhere there will be a lot of babes."

Lance motioned for some cookies. Instead of passing them, June threw a handful like a trainer rewarding a pet seal. However, the package went faster than both anticipated, and the bridge of Lance's nose became a target. "Ow, damn, dude. Don't throw it so hard. You taking up ultimate frisbee or something?"

"I've got it!" June snapped, dancing in place. "There's a car brawl being thrown tonight!"

"A car brawl? Like *Transformers*?"

"No, ha, no, haha, not car brawl. Bar crawl."

"Impossible. How do you know about a party before me? Who is hosting it?" Lance asked.

"*The Ormelian Lerders.*"

"The Ormelian Lerders are throwing a car brawl? You mean the Lemurian Order is hosting a bar crawl? Now, I know you're tripping; they sure as hell aren't throwing a function."

"I'm serious; that guy I told you about in the Lemurian Order, that guy Parker invited me after I got hit with this frisbee, and this girl came over to apologize, but she really only apologized once and then started flirting with Parker while my nose was bleeding, but then Parker said she could make it up to me by coming to the party because I'd be there, and then she smiled and said that she'd bring her girls and before she left she winked at me, so technically..."

"Technically, that's an invitation to a party. But do I want to spend my Friday evening at a frat party full of kids who have no friends except their therapist, drug dealer, and designer pet? Why are they even having a party?" inquired Lance with a mouth full of chocolate.

"Who knows, but maybe this is a chance for that introduction..." And this is a chance to get information from Parker about that negotiation he mentioned, June thought.

Lance whistled, "As tempting as making out in the dark and investigating blood sacrifices sounds, I still don't think we should leave. Not gonna lie; I'm starting to feel something in my teeth."

"I don't, and I'm tired of crying in *Marvin's Room*. I'm tired of simping about my shortcomings. Tired of being a lil punk and not taking risks, damn it! Well, today, I took a risk. Today, I went out of my element and did something I wanted to do. I auditioned for the role, the lead! That's right, I went big, and because of that, today is a glorious day! A day that shall hold reverence when gazing back on our college days. Today is the day I, Daniel Elliott Junior, became a real actor. No more Mr. Stagefright from this point on!" June marched around the room, using his hands to form each word of the sentence. "No more Mr. Stagefright. No more Mr. Stagefright! That's right! I risked it, and I got some damn results! And because of that, I want to stick my tongue down a cutie's throat."

The curtain covering June's closet slung back, and he tore through his outfits. Scrappy hipster with patterned chucks and a flannel? No, perhaps casual socialite with ripped denim jeans and a bubble vest atop a sweater? Too bland. Or sensitive and suave with a black turtleneck and chain? Too business casual.

Behind the shirts hung according to their color scheme sat a simple black button-down with a mandarin collar that June eventually chose. To accent the outfit, he threw a gray wool sweater as outerwear and a pair of jeans with rips at the knees. Then, he removed a pair of white sneakers from the shelf.

"What are you going to do?" June looked at Lance, still sitting on the futon. "Watch another documentary on how aliens left subliminal instructions for space travel in *The Lion King*?"

"Like, Scoobert, I think this is a crazy idea, but I can't let you do it *alone*," Lance exclaimed, jumping toward his dresser. Seconds later, he wore denim jeans and a black hoodie with a stereotypical alien passing a bong to Bigfoot.

"Aye! My guy!" June's temperament was that of a child waiting to open presents on Christmas. "We have a problem, though...I don't know where it is.

"Dude, what? Then how are we gonna jump any bones?"

"Well, it's at a place called The Lion's Den, but I've never heard of that venue," he confessed while tending to his clothes.

"So, we need to locate The Lion's Den? Say less." After munching on nearly half the rack of cookies, Lance attacked a container of trail mix belonging to his roommate. June yelled at him to stop, and Lance apologetically bowed. "My bad," Lance apologized. "I'm just starving. I didn't get a chance to eat earlier because half my donuts were wasted on my Ri-dol."

"All good, all good." June reached behind him and removed a package of ramen noodles.

Lance poured the seasoning into the bag and slapped the dried noodles against the edge of the bunk bed until they were in pieces. He then retrieved his phone from his pocket and sorted his contacts while June observed this new culinary dish.

"What the hell are you making?

"*Dinner.*"

"Are you going to put that in any water?"

"This?" Lance pointed towards the bag, "Oh ho, not at all. My meal is already complete."

"Bro," June's laughter slowed, "you've done some off-the-wall things, but this right here is the weirdest. The weirdest. I've never seen anybody eat dry ramen!"

"Don't you want to get to the party to start scheming? The microwave takes five minutes. Five minutes, bro."

"You microwave your noodles for FIVE MINUTES? Bro, it only takes two. It only takes two, bro."

Laughter turned to squealing as June, tickled by the scenario, teased his friend to the point that the neighbors banged on the wall for them to quiet. Lance crunched on another piece, "Laugh all you want, but you'd be here all night if it weren't for me."

"What do you mean?"

"Look up *56 Alabaster Court.*"

June turned back to his roommate, "56 Alabaster Court? Is that the Lion's Den? How did you get that so fast?"

"I told you, knowing the unknowable is my job."

Silhouettes drifted along the television as the duo packed all nightly essentials into Lance's satchel. Once the zipper closed, he collected the ramen and continued munching on the chips. Tripping or not, June couldn't fathom how dried noodles were remotely enjoyable.

"I gotta say, June, you've grown. I mean, I did catch you drowning in your feels by listening to that sad-ass music, but at least you didn't pee your bed like last time. I'm proud that you're tackling misfortune head-on."

"Don't get it confused; I'm still in pain. I just need to own up to it and move forward. You ready, Lance? I can get us there; your job is to get us back in one piece," said June.

"We'll be back here before you know it, and we won't be alone!"

"Hell yeah, let's get get get it!"

June's cheeks formed a goofy smile as the requested rideshare appeared on the map. That smile came from the graphic on the device: the car had been replaced with a black rat, and his location pin became a block of cheese. It started at the Mongrel Complex, skimmed past the Thompson Theater and athletic fields, doubled back by the Washington Student Union and Hamlin Workshop, scurried by the detoured Clock Tower, cut through Nielson, Folger, and Malta Hall, pressed on beyond Ellis Laboratory, turned at the Keel Rare Book Library, and swung around the Brachman Cafe before the digital vermin appeared in front of Derringer Dormitory.

Lance pulled his black coat out of the closet and threw it over his shoulder. "Hey, don't you wish you could teleport? Like, if I just clicked my heels and said, 'I wish I were at the party,' we'd just arrive without any delay? Like Dorothy did in that one movie?"

"Dorothy could only teleport when she was in trouble," said June.

"And we are, too; we're in trouble of not getting our meats rolled," Lance claimed. "So, we might as well try it."

Fueled by the psychedelics, June closed his eyes, clicked his heels, recited a phrase...and awoke inside a gloomy corridor with blood leaking from a throbbing knee.

ACT II

The Car Brawl

Housed at the base of 56 Alabaster Court, obscured by a dense thicket of bare maple and pine, sat a massive structure known as the Lion's Den. As the destination came into view, Lance relayed information he had learned from an episode of his favorite true crime podcast, *Found Dead By The Lake*. The aged establishment once operated as the hub of spiritual gatherings for Catholics in the Adirondack mountain range. Constructed in 1810, the foundation resembled the Gothic edifices of European cathedrals but had a distinct post-colonial approach to architecture. Various stones from the neighboring cliffs and timber from the surrounding forests were used in the construction.

For nearly fifty years after its creation, the cathedral served as a place of reverence; however, during its operation, the temple gained a certain notoriety. History stated on multiple occasions, the congregation suffered from what could be described as mass hysteria. Individuals claim to have witnessed hours of uncontrollable dancing and erratic behavior reminiscent of creatures found in primordial jungles. There were claims of "communal coitus" occurring upon a particular altar. Despite the varied reactions, all hysterical events had a common factor: the deranged believers claimed to bear witness to the "voice of God."

Naturally, rumors of a curse spread through the commune. Some blamed the malevolence on the men for colonizing and chasing out the indigenous populations, while others considered it a punishment for their neighbors fleeing from Christian values to practice paganism. Numbers dwindled, and the dust accumulated along the pews as individuals aged and passed. With heavy hearts, the clergy and community agreed to close the cathedral's doors in 1866.

Years later, the structure came to the attention of Norman Washington III, a pioneer in the bioengineering field who'd recently relocated his workstation from the South Pacific to the secluded mountains. Under his care, the building received multiple renovations over fifteen years, including electricity. The cathedral became Washington's research station, and while this site was active, he created various pharmaceutical advancements that improved the lives of many. When the professor ended his tenure at MSU in 1955, he passed the cathedral deed to an alumni association. The foundation then received another development, converting the research station into the living quarters for the Lemurian Order.

"And tonight, for the first time since 1866, the building currently known as Lion's Den is opening its doors to the public," Lance said as the boys exited the car.

June tightened his jacket and stared at the looming spires. Who knew a castle had been this close to campus? After stumbling and giggling down the driveway, the two psychonauts reached the cathedral entrance. A line of guests wound around a set of marble lion gargoyles positioned at the start of the main stairwell. Flashes of mauve splintered across the horizon, and suddenly, a shrill buzzing formed in June's ear. The noise increased the more he moved, but it wasn't until he peered upward at something in the window of the tallest tower that he confirmed it. It was faint, but a quaint hum drifted around the Lion's Den as if inviting him to enter.

"Yo, June. You good?" asked Lance, patting him on the shoulder.

June reacted, turning quickly to his friend. "Yeah, I think I'm starting to feel it."

"Hell yeah, brother! Buckle up for the ride! Oh yeah, if shit starts to get too weird, meet at the first-floor bathroom. Always a safe place to regroup."

"What do you mean by too weird?"

"You'll just have to wait and see. Now, let's get inside; I'm ready to groove!"

As they waited in line, June looked up again to find a darkened tower window, and the odd sound faded into the night. Too weird.

The duo eventually reached the check-in table and were greeted by a bouncer wearing a black snapback with "National Champions" stitched in gold. A knotted brown beard burst from his chin and concealed most of his mouth. The rest of his face was hardened, and the skin pulled tight over bold cheekbones. For the party, he rocked a two-piece athletic warm-up suit, much like the windbreaker fits from the 90s.

The bouncer patted them down and instructed the boys to wait at the station beside him. On the table, a complex philter resembled the mechanisms found in graduate chemistry labs. Green liquid sloshed in the slowly rotating flasks. A young woman wearing black gloves, black jeans, a pink and silver polyester jacket, and a face mask shaped like an anime cat operated the philter.

When June turned to enter, the goth server handed him a cup of the solution. June tried to turn down the shot, claiming he didn't feel safe accepting a drink from strangers. The bouncer rationalized with him until the person registering patrons at the final station overheard the complaint.

The receptionist was a boy with a broad nose and a brow resembling a mountain goat's forehead. He wore a beige designer shirt with the words *Love is Free, Sex is a Luxury* printed across the chest and a pair of pleated patterned joggers. White Balenciaga sneakers decked out his enlarged feet. A peculiar stench surrounded him; June deduced the smell came from the blunt behind his ear.

He rose from the chair, grabbed the next prepared cup, and thrust it into June's face. "No drink, no entry," said the receptionist.

Lance eyeballed the young man and snapped his finger thrice. "Yo, my man, it's me, Lance. Remember, I just picked up those caps? Quality stuff bro. Quality stuff."

"Ayo, chill out," he whispered. "You making the block too hot."

"Oh right, right. My bad. So, what's happening here?"

"Like I told ya mans, no drink, no entry."

June then asked his roommate if he wanted to go, and Lance would've said not really, but something drew his attention. Lance saw a young woman exit the glass door and perch beside the gargoyle. A small bowl was brought to her mouth, and she lit the tip. The photographer caught her eyes, and she greeted him with a signature peace sign pose, showcasing dual tongue piercings.

"And there she is...Timia with the tongue piercings." Immediately, Lance snatched the cup, threw the shot back, and moved to the final station of the registration desk. He encouraged June not to think about tomorrow and take the risk. And before June could respond, Lance dashed up the stairs to hug the woman. He hit the bowl and accepted her hand as she led him inside the party.

Left alone, the shrooms made their presence known to June by enticing his anxieties. The marble lion's mane flowed with the thump of the stereo system, and its eyes seemed to show signs of awakening from the stone slumber. June felt something bump his chest. It was the receptionist again, handing him a cup.

"Look, take the damn shot or leave, yo! You're holding shit up."

"Noah, easy. He already looks pretty turnt." The bouncer's soothing tone provided much-needed comfort.

"That doesn't mean shit. We don't make exceptions for plebs. If he wants in, he's gotta do like all the rest." Unaware of what to do, June accepted the cup. He was about to swallow when something caught his attention. Noah's eyes. They were cosmic and full of mystery, just like Parker's.

"You're one of *them*," June muttered.

"Enough of this. Big Fella, help me get this pleb off our doorstep!" Noah commanded. He pushed June in the chest, causing the boy to flinch and drop the cup. The party juice spilled on Noah's white shoes, and a collective breath was held by the patrons who witnessed the act. "Are you serious right now? Yo, my man, these are Balenciaga. Balenciaga!" shouted Noah.

"I'm so...I'm so sorry. Wait, I can clean them. I'll fix it; I just had a panic attack from all the yelling, noise, and colors. I just need a minute. Please..."

"Fuck this, and fuck your anxiety!" Noah pressed forward with a balled fist until the bouncer calmed him. The bouncer then instructed the aggressor to take a smoke break. On his way out, Noah snatched another cup and tossed the contents down the hatch, watching June the entire time. "You see that," Noah pointed, "face don't change, baby. The face don't change," he repeated before flicking the empty cup in June's face as he walked away with a lighter.

The bouncer offered some dap as he led June to the registration table. "Sorry about that, bro. Noah gets pretty rowdy when things don't go according to plan, but he means well. Don't worry about the shot, either. If anything, we'll say Noah covered your entry. Got your ID?"

June patted himself for his wallet but immediately realized his pockets had been empty since they left the car. "Shit. Um...uh...My roommate...uh...it's with him." Both looked into the party and then back at each other, unsure of the following action. At this point, the guests behind June verbally expressed their disdain for the situation. It was cold and dark outside, and they were missing out on the first party held at the Lion's Den.

"Damn, no drink and no name? I don't know. It's not like I can just let that part slide. We do have to have some documentation or proof you were here. What do you think, Kimi?"

"Rules are in place for a reason. That is because we can't be held liable if something happens to you," chimed the goth behind the philter.

Hands trembled, and June felt the bladder attempting to dispel fears through fluids. *Of course, you failed to get into the party. You're so useless!*

"You're right, I'm useless. I'll just...I don't know. Wait? Walk home? I'm not sure...what to do...and I'm not really in a good space...I...don't know..."

A person whose presence caused whispers among the impatient guests appeared from a pathway left of the lion statue. Mitch and Kimi saluted the stranger before they huddled at the registration table. June watched the bouncer explain the situation to the stranger, and after brief deliberations, each nodded in agreement. Before the urine could streak down his leg, the stranger greeted him with a smile and handshake.

"You must be Daniel Elliott Junior? A mutual friend asked me to keep an eye out for you." The calm stranger then led him past the registration table. "I apologize for the inconvenience; I should've relayed to them that you were on the list."

"I'm on the list?" June asked. The crowd murmured, wondering why this nobody was receiving VIP treatment from the school's student body president.

"That you are. Now, allow me to officially welcome you to *the Lion's Den.*"

* * *

Two centuries ago, the Congregation Hall housed religious processions. Now, it has been transformed into a fully functional party venue. Colorful neon flares shot around the walls as modern Hip-Hop and Pop blasted out of the six-foot stereo speakers. Contrasting the millennial decorations were suits of armor and family crests on the western wing, ancient Sanskrit paintings, and feudal Chinese calligraphy portraits towards the north.

Some people danced, allowing their sweaty bodies to rub and be rubbed; others opted for conversations around an extended table where drinking games were being played. One person removed their shirt and slung it in the air, shouting "North Carolina!" following the current song lyrics, and, the cups flowed. Cups of the PJ continued to be poured as the back-to-school bash reached the end of the second hour.

Lance's thirst for womanly attention carried him through at least four different introduction scenarios–three were surprisingly successful, and he ended up walking away with a social media profile. Lust finally dwindled after exchanging info with the musician by the windows, and he finally registered his roommate's absence. So, he began a journey to the rendezvous location.

Lance cut through the line at the drink station and then wound around a single row of pews at the front of the Congregation Hall before arriving at the bathroom. He scanned the line twice before patrolling the area. No June, but a couple of yards to the left of the bathroom was a curtain-covered corridor monitored by a silent security guard. Headphones covered the guard's ear, and a handheld gaming console occupied his attention.

"Now, if I were a secret fraternity, where would I hide my secrets? Oh, well, of course, behind the suspiciously guarded doorway," said Lance. "The question is...how do I get past you? A distraction? But what kind?" He sighed and leaned next to the window.

"Well, well, well, how did a plebian like you manage to get invited here?" Lance looked to the windowsill on his left and groaned. Perched on the edge was a woman wearing a black blouse, a gold sequin skirt, and two cups in her hands. On either side of the young woman were two burly athletes who looked thirstier than desert wanderers. Painted lips parted like a freshwater clam as she addressed Lance. "Are you not going to speak?"

"To be honest, I didn't see you there. You're just so *transparent*." Unaware of the sarcasm, the woman jumped from behind the two dudes and ran to embrace Lance. His arms flopped to his sides as she constricted him like a python. "Brittney...Melrose...hi...okay, I can't...breathe."

"Oh, haha, HA! Lancey! Is that crying I hear? You missed me that much?" sang Brittney.

As if commanded by her thick East Harlem accent and the chemicals from the caps, Lance's lacrimal glands prepped for secretion. "No...I'm like...seriously dying...the tunnel of light...there it is. It's real. I'm moving to it...wait. I can't die now; I've so much left to do...so many women to..." Brittney released her grip, and Lance loosened his collar. He noticed her makeup left a smear on his hoodie—still over-powdering her face. She bounced offbeat, liquid sloshing out of red cups as the music blared in the Congregation Hall.

"It's good to see you, Lancey. What's new with you?"

"Oh, nothing. Things are good. Very good. So good right now. Not on drugs or anything."

"Uh, I guess that's a good thing. Maybe. At least you're here. Where's Danny? I always figured you two were attached at the hip. Then again, this isn't his scene. And it's not really yours either..."

"I'm here on assignment. Personal thing. As far as June goes, he's on a trip. Yes, a long trip! To see...um...a prophet.

Yeah, that's right. A prophet in the toilet. He went to the restroom. Break the seal."

She turned to the line and stared. "You sure? I haven't seen him, and I've been here all night."

"Positive. He's gotta be here, or he's lost," admitted Lance.

"It's probably best if you find him ASAP. Drunk Danny is not the business. The last time he was like this, he sent me some messages."

"Messages? What'd he say?"

"Long story short, Danny's going through it. He said he...well, that's not proper party talk."

"Neither is talking about past relationships, but here we are."

"I'm glad I ran into you, Lancey. Now you can do it for me."

"Do what?" he asked.

"Make sure he doesn't do anything stupid. Does he seem okay these days? When we talked that night, he said he's tired. That he's tired of being him...whatever that means. He wished he could be someone else. *Or forgotten altogether.*"

"That sounds like him, but what makes this any different than before?"

"He confessed that after the last showing of *The Nightmare Before Christmas*...he went back to the theater that night...and well, he tried to...he attempted..."

"*June tried to kill himself?!* No, no, that's not right. Why would you say that?"

The secretions in Lance's eyes began to swell, starting as micelles before forming into droplets. Brittney stepped forward and placed a hand on Lance's shoulder. "It's tough to hear, but it's true. And if he tried it once, he might try again..."

Unable to control the ocular floodgates, the boy allowed the tears to cascade down his chin into the empty cup. "I'm worried about June," cried Lance. "I don't want to admit it, but things may be getting worse. And I'm the one to blame; I don't show him enough attention and let him know how awesome he is. He's my bro for life, and I want what's best for him. It's just tough because shit doesn't always work out for him. And he tries hard. So hard!"

Those around the bathroom focused on Lance kneeling on the ground. Brittney's palm remained in his hands, serving as an absorbent for his mucus drainage. One of the beefcakes laughed but was elbowed by the other fellow, who seemed genuinely invested in the confession.

"I hear you, Lance. I do," Brittney said.

"That shit sucks, you know. He's so passionate and brilliant, but nobody sees it. Yeah, he goofs up sometimes and is in his head often, but that doesn't mean he's not amazing. That he's not one of the best people born on this damn planet. Seriously, if I was a girl...*I'd fuck June.* At least give him a handy. I'd love him too. He's probably better at that, but *you* wouldn't know, would you?"

"Look, you think you know everything, but you don't." Brittney brushed her bang to the side, "What happened is in the past now."

"You don't think it's a coincidence that the night you broke his heart, he tried to kill himself?"

"I never meant for that to happen, honest. I do care about Danny, but I couldn't keep ignoring my feelings. I may have made some mistakes during our relationship, but never lied to him." Brittney gulped a quarter of her drink. "Can *you* say the same?"

Although tears were still streaming, Lance sniffed like a tiny pug with an attitude. "Got something you need to get off your chest?"

"You know what I mean. I've been watching Danny blow it on stage since middle school, and nothing's changed. How do you fuck up three lines and go silent?"

"A silence you caused."

"Like I said, I'm not proud of what happened, but that doesn't change the fact that he sucks at acting."

"It's not easy to stay in character after hearing your high-school girlfriend tell you she wants to break up and see other people. Right before getting on stage," said Lance.

"The timing could've been better, but I couldn't keep lying to him or to myself. Danny wasn't meeting my needs. So, that's why I told him the truth. My question to you, Lance, is when are *you* going to tell him the truth?"

"What truth?"

"That he needs to stop fucking dreaming. The next Denzel? C'mon, that's not possible. Danny doesn't know who he is." She scoffed, "I'd rather drive *a fucking spike* through my eyes than watch another performance by Danny. Or June, or whatever he's calling himself this year. If you're his friend, you'll tell him he needs to give up on that dream because it hurts him too much when he fails. And he always fails."

"Of course, I'll pass on your enlightening message," Lance said, tears drying. "But what did you expect? He's not exactly simple like those fuckboys whose dorms you're dashing between."

"Don't get rude with me! I'll shut that mouth quick. As a matter of fact, just stop. Stop talking about things you don't understand, Lance. I came to give you information you might need, yet you turn me into the villain."

"You crushed the heart of someone who loved you. That makes you a villain. He really felt something for you. I don't know what it was, but he swore it was real. This guy used to keep me up at night talking about how he'd always had a crush on you since seventh grade, and it was destined to be. He even introduced you to his folks. That's like legit legit, even more legit than posting someone on your social media. I'm not bringing anybody around my parents unless I'm thinking of marriage and mortgages." Lance's knuckles whitened, "He was going to be the man you wanted him to be, and what did you do? You stopped believing in him. And then, you killed his chances of happiness and almost got him to kill himself."

"Bullshit, I finally decided to choose my own happiness! Does that make me wrong?"

"Did you have to do it at the expense of pushing him over the edge? Couldn't wait another day, or were you so eager for new dick it didn't matter what happened to him?"

"I'm not going to even go there with you."

"That's right because you're a coward. You crushed him in a moment when he needed your support. You might as well as held the knife."

"Shut the hell up, Lance. I never wanted him dead. *Never.* What right do you have to say that?"

"Because I'm watching my best friend rebuild himself after you tore down everything he loved. So, stop this. Don't act like you fake care because you don't. If you did, you never would've tried to change who he was, and you wouldn't have strung him along all this time. And I don't care if it's two days or almost a year since the break-up, fuck linear time, and fuck you."

Fed up with the fussing, Brittney flung her drink. Lance ducked as if granted foresight by the psilocybin. Instead, the cup hit two partygoers waiting to enter the bathroom together. Droplets of green liquid covered the floor as the two women approached Brittney and her crew. An altercation began, starting with accusations and finger-pointing that eventually led to pushing. The security guard blocking the curtain rose from his station to assist before the confrontation escalated into a brawl.

Once they were separated and tensions cooled, Brittney showered the young woman with apologies, blaming an accidental reaction on some creep talking to her. However, when it came time to identify the culprit, Lance was nowhere to be found.

Daniel & The Lion's Den

What the...where am I? How the hell did I get here? Why does my head hurt? That guy took me around back, and then...I did...what did I do? Did we go inside the party? I don't remember. What was his name again? Fred...Frank...Fish? I don't know, but I followed him. Then that guy...Frannie maybe? He walked with me. A long walk, and we talked, but about what? Then...something...something happened. And now, I'm lost.

Why can't I move? Am I dead? Or am I dreaming? It feels like...lucid dreaming. Am I asleep? Are my eyes closed? The eyes, yes! I remember the eyes. They shined like fire. Like stage lights. Where are the lights now? Oil lamps? Kerosene? I smell it. Gas. I hope I don't pass gas. Hm. Smells gross. Like a crypt.

Where's Parker?

Ah, it feels like I'm floating. Floating down, can one float down? Frown. No, that's drown. But there's no water, only brick. Brick. Lots of brick. Brick by brick by brick by brick. On the walls, maybe on the floor, too. What kind of brick? Held with cement. Same color, only cooler. And wet. Moist brick.

Moist. Music. Makes sense. Where's the music? Why can't I hear the music anymore? I thought I was at the party.

Why am I here? Need to find Parker...and ask him about the roll. No, the role. There's nothing to roll here, only rock. Everywhere. The ceiling. Is this the basement? Or is this a prison? Am I a prisoner? Why here, though? And who imprisoned me, was it Filly? I can't be a prisoner. I can't be alone.

I'm not alone. I hear something. Noises...? A voice?

Parker might be behind the noises...we need to talk. I want that role. I don't care how I get it. Timothy took my spot on the stage. He's in my place. I need to tell Parker I want the role.

I hear something again. Should I get up? Wait, I can get up. My legs are back. And so are my arms. I'm not dreaming. I'm not dead. It's dark, very dark, but at least I can leave. That's good—I'm not a prisoner.

A gust of stagnant air filled June's lungs as he snapped back into his body. He gently flexed and pinched and rotated his appendages, confirming everything still belonged to him. The atmosphere was so tart his eyes stung from prolonged exposure. Using the wall as support, he stumbled out of the cramped cell.

Two lanterns hung on the wall, tending flames barely illuminating anything. Looking around the room, June noticed seven other cell-like structures were carved into the wall. The cells were closed, however, each door was adorned with a particular symbol. Across from him, in the darkest part of the room, a ninth door existed; this gateway was much larger and more weathered than the others. Situated near the ninth gate was a waist-high pillar.

June continued to wander through the eerie basement until he heard a noise. Except it didn't enter through his ears but through some vestigial organ long dormant in humans. The ominous ambiance of the crypt faded, enhancing the melody's echo in his being. It resembled the notes of a flute played in a Middle Eastern bazaar. June's surroundings blurred as he sought to escape from the chamber. However, the incredible acoustics radiating from the shadows prevented him from moving. He felt safer enveloped by the sound and stench than anywhere on campus.

Thinking it belonged to the party, June followed the sounds, eventually reaching the massive door. He traced the mythic indents with his fingers as one did constellations in the night sky. It reminded him of the marble door that led Baudelaire to Ingilaef. However, when he reached for what he assumed to be the chain handle, the melody halted. June heard a sudden rattle mimicking the clanking of rusted iron.

The massive stone gate shook twice, kicking off dust and sediments. A puddle of ooze drooled from a crack between the base of the door and the floor. Although dark, the liquid appeared gelatinous and flowed like coagulated blood. The tip of June's finger dipped into the foul liquid, and pain radiated through his forearm as if icicles were jammed under his fingernails. The humming returned and dulled the pain; soon, he only experienced bliss or, rather, a silence of the mind that established a new equilibrium.

June considered testing the sample again, but the sound behind the stone altered a third time. Unlike the other sonic sensations, this one had a degree of sentience. As if it belonged to a being capable of respiration. Then, all noises halted as wood creaked on the opposing side of the room.

"He...hello?" His hesitant question was made visible by the chill in the crypt. Something shot out of the darkness and latched onto his shoulder. A cry escaped his lips but failed to materialize because his mouth was covered.

"*Jenkies!*" Lance dapped him up, "Damn, June. How the hell did you get here? I was expecting to be surprised by what I found, but this is mad different."

"Parker...I thought I...saw Parker. Why are you here, Lance?"

"I was looking for you, then I found this guarded walkway and decided that there had to be a sensational secret at the end of it. So, I went down the steps, a lot of steps, and ended up here. This place smells gross AF too. Where are we anyway? Wait, look! Are those prison cells? Cages? And look at the symmetry of the torches, the walls, and rooms." The flash of a smartphone discharged multiple times as Lance snagged images of the location from various angles.

"Lance, careful. I think there's someone here."

"Nobody's home, bro. I would've seen them on my way down. Unless they're trapped in those cells...?" Both boys looked at the doors, conjuring images of enslaved individuals forced to live in these conditions. How close was he to becoming one of them, June wondered.

Their examination ended at the largest cell. Something about the sheer difference in size and design intricacy triggered apprehension. The photographer snapped another image and then turned back to June. "Altar site...human-sized cells...a large doorway. Is this the demonic portal? We all knew it existed, but to see it in person? Fascinating. I have to contact *Found Dead By The Lake*!"

Lance touched the door, and suddenly a loud shrill pierced June's ears. "Don't you hear that?" June asked, pressing into his temples to alleviate the pressure.

"Just the sound of my bank account blowing up thanks to this discovery."

"Seriously, you don't hear that screeching? It's so loud!"

"Dude, it's quiet as balls down here. I know what it is; you're just *peaking*."

"Peaking?"

"You're probably coming to the height of your trip experience. It's like hour two, and that's when it all hits. I say we get out of here before you tweak out."

June nodded, following Lance to the exit. As the duo crept out of the ritual room and into the dim stairwell, June paused his roommate. "Wait...I hear voices...again."

"June, I told you there's nobody here."

June covered his friend's mouth with his fingers, "Voices...definitely real voices. Coming...from above us."

Footsteps and minimal chatter echoed from the top of the corridor, accompanied by an intensifying light. Recognizing this, the boys began to scramble. "Oh shit. You're right. Shit, shit. There's nowhere to hide. If we're caught down here, we'll be sacrificed by the magicians who want to open this demonic portal. I can't die tonight; I still haven't made out with Timia!"

Lucidity returned to June's speech as he bared a scheming smile. "We're not dead yet. Follow my lead."

***

The green liquid swirled in the glass cup as Parker conducted his scheduled perimeter sweep of the basement. Wrapped around his arm was a young woman donning a medical boot on her right foot. Once the couple reached the base of the lengthy corridor, the woman slid a hand behind

Parker's neck and the second on his ass. Lips connected, and tongues swirled as they explored each other's mouths.

Their intimate moment halted when they noticed something different about the wooden door. "*The Oracle Chamber is open*," he said curiously.

Parker instructed his partner to wait outside, and he gripped the iron doorknob. Stepping inside, he activated the light source, however, the circuitry frazzled, leaving him with minimal illumination. Still, it was enough to complete a scan. From his initial glance, everything seemed in place until he noticed a shadow moving in one of the cells.

"Come on out. I know you're here." A figure crouching in the corner came into the light. "What are you doing down here? This area is restricted. And how did you even get in here?" Parker said.

"I'm so so sorry, but my friend is past his limits and insisted on finding a bathroom before meeting EARL." The guilty party pointed to a second individual dry heaving on the ground.

"Don't you think this is too far to be traveling for the bathroom?"

"Of course, but knowing his weak stomach, he'd take at least twenty minutes. I'd hate to have people waiting that long to take a quick leak, which doesn't even include the clean-up time."

"And now, we must clean up a restricted area. Your logic is undeniable. I'd prefer we resolve this quietly, as I'd much rather let security have a calm night. I can help transport your friend upstairs, but you must leave the party once we're there. Understood?"

"Will do. I'll be out of here as soon as my friend gets help."

Parker then stepped forward to get a glimpse of the sick individual. "Daniel, how'd you end up down here?"

"I...looking for you," mumbled June.

"My apologies," Parker extended a hand to Lance. "I didn't mean to come off so harsh. Parker Galician. Had I known you were a friend of Daniel's, I would've approached the interaction differently."

"It's all good, Parker. I'm Lance Xiao, his roommate. And we should be the ones apologizing. We weren't thinking; I just wanted to ensure he didn't embarrass himself upstairs by blowing chunks on the dance floor. Wouldn't do good for his reputation, seeing as it's only the first full week back from break."

"Agreed, it's important to maintain an image that matches one's identity. Well, I hope our mixture didn't do that to him. I asked Noah not to make too strong of a batch. "

"No, he barely had a sip. That honor is reserved for Ophelia," answered Lance.

"Ophelia? Is that the name of his partner?" asked Parker.

"Oh no, but she's a great time."

"Mush...rooms are like the pimples of the earth if the pimples were like filled with good stuff," June said before hugging his stomach.

"Daniel, I had no idea you were a connoisseur of mind-altering substances. It's refreshing to know that some of us are willing to devote our lives to developing *the higher self*."

"Or those who want to trip balls with their bros before the semester gets real," Lance joked.

The young men aided June to his feet. "My room is on the top floor; why don't you two join us? We were just about to start a session after making the rounds," said Parker.

"It'd be rude to turn down your invitation. Lead the way," stated Lance.

"Let's go on an adventure," said June. His shirt had specks of stomach acid, but it didn't matter because this was precisely the situation he desired. They left the Oracle Chamber one by one. Despite the door being closed, the bizarre notes continued to reverberate within June's body, producing a jumbled collection of phonetics that he swore sounded like an alarm.

The Interrogation

Lance stayed close to June as they followed their relaxed guides out of the corridor, heading toward the lights and sounds projecting from the function. Instead of stopping at the main floor, Parker led them through a secondary corridor, avoiding the Congregation Hall altogether. Although the party had already peaked, a tangible vibrancy radiated from the dance floor. At least another two hundred had to be present; the DJ was going strong, and there were still at least two containers sloshing with PJ.

On the ascent to the tower, Parker introduced the woman accompanying them as his partner, Delilah Hawthorne. A curled brown bob rested atop her shoulders, and she dressed in a black knee-length skirt and fishnets with an accenting red blouse that made her look more like a countess than a student. The tattoo on her left arm read "DEATH LIVES IN THE VERSE." To complete the ensemble, she rocked a pair of gold-tinted aviator shades as if channeling the spirit of fabulous rockstars of the past. However, the medical boot wrapped tightly around her right foot clashed with her aesthetic.

As they climbed, Delilah explained to the guests how she sustained the injury over the course of winter break.

"Decided to run at my old high-school athletic park to prepare for the season. Coach has been pressuring us to stay in shape, claiming we're destined for states even though half the sprinters can't hit 100m in under 15 seconds. But I did my part, even hit a few two-a-days."

"Delilah's the closest thing we have to Allyson Felix," Parker stated.

"Because I'm a winner. I'm not like my team; I'm running toward victory while they run around. I hurdle, and I win, and that's all that matters to me."

"So you run and jump? You must be in crazy shape."

"Moving forward isn't fun unless a couple obstacles block the path," she smiled. "And usually, I overcome the obstacles. Now, I cleared the hurdles flawlessly, but I took a spill on my final lap. The landing was shit. Fell right on my ankle and bought myself a season ticket to ride the bench."

June instinctively reached for his foot. "Sheesh, did it hurt?"

"I cried my ass off for about two minutes. But after that, no more tears. Even when the doctor said it was a severe sprain."

"I'm impressed you can even make it up these stairs," Lance said.

"Hurt, pain, discomfort, that stuff is *all mental*. Control your mind, and you control your reality. Control your reality, and you can do anything you fucking want. And right now, I wanna get blazed. Couldn't get high like I wanted while on the team, but now, I'm free."

The four finally reached the top floor. As they headed through the lit corridor, Lance counted three rooms. Looking inside, he saw a bed—living quarters. Parker led them to a door at the end of the hallway. He removed a key fob and flashed it against the electronic lock. The door opened, and he hit the lights before welcoming his guests.

Lance had frequented plenty of dorm rooms around campus but had yet to lay eyes on an immaculate setup like Parker's. A stained-glass window offered a full view of the nocturnal horizon. The room also included a queen-sized bed with a pressed checkered comforter, a couch able to sit three, hand-crafted dressers for his clothes, a functioning bathroom with a standing shower, and a forty-inch television and stereo set connected to a gaming console.

The most alluring feature of the room had to be the library surrounding Parker's desk. The hardwood shelves were embedded into the brick foundation, as if the initial building plans had designated this space for contemplation. Carved marble lion heads with perfectly chiseled fangs sat on the end of each shelf to prevent the books from tilting.

Parker watched Lance and June's amazement flourish as they examined the bindings of the various texts. Starting from the bottom shelf were the famed stories from poets active during antiquity (Homer, Socrates, Plato, Aeschylus) and the complete works of William Shakespeare on the second shelf (his copy of *Hamlet* was lying in front of the other books). The third shelf contained various collections of philosophers (Hegel, Kant, Machiavelli, Nietzsche), a special edition of the *Tibetan Book of the Dead,* a printed and stapled guide on *Astral Projection Principles and Application,* and three volumes of work by Aleister Crowley.

The top shelf, however, was vacant. "Why the empty shelf?" June asked.

"Ha, it's somewhat childish to admit this, but I plan to fill an entire shelf with my words."

"You're a writer, too? You're like the coolest art major," a wobbly June complimented.

"Actually, I'm majoring in philosophy to develop my concepts, but I plan to get a Master of Arts in Creative Writing."

"What will you write?" inquired Lance.

"And why do you write?" June followed up.

"An interrogation session?" Parker joked. "I'm interested; let us get comfortable before we officially begin."

He removed his boots, setting them on the shoe rack before he took a seat on the couch. He invited the boys to do the same while Delilah perched on the edge of the bed. She reached for a book titled *Virtues* and opened it. Lance sniffed the air and peered at the woman's hands. She made a cryptic gesture, but Lance understood it.

Time to roll up.

"I'll start by saying this," Parker began: " Communication is difficult. It requires translation, transcription, and understanding. Even if we can hear and listen to someone, it doesn't mean we can accurately interpret their thoughts. This is because words are symbols that represent a definition, and yet, each definition is different for an individual."

"Which leads to miscommunication," said Lance.

"Exactly, and it also alters the impact of the communicated idea. Consider when one reads the daily news or a technical document. They only inform, not *inspire*, for words without rhythm and reason have little power. But when certain universal symbols are structured together and assisted by a rhythm, they implore the reader to interpret the image immortalized on the page. And this medium of using words to create imagery is called poetry."

"Dude, I love poetry. So cool, so expressive," said June, his words slurring.

"Why poetry?" Lance asked.

"I believe only poetry can encourage the restructuring of human communication on a universal scale. It's the basis of all language and even memory. Poetry is also important because of its often abstract nature. Since the author rarely gives a clear definition, it's left to individual interpretation, and there are no wrong answers when you discover them yourself."

"Parker here thinks a bit of Shel Silverstein can help us connect when SnapChat just dropped new filters. I think it's cute how he wants to be a pre-internet human," teased Delilah.

"I do, and it's wise not to underestimate the power of words, my friends. We all hold some poetry in our hearts. Prayers, chants, mantras, odes, lyrics, and creeds are all rooted in poetry. In ten years, nobody will remember that you sent a selfie of you looking like a forest fauna. But they may remember that haiku when grieving heartbreak or worse, saying goodbye to a loved one."

"Xavier's poetry helped me get over Brittney," commented June.

"Brittney, who?" asked Delilah.

"Melrose." Lance noticed Delilah and Parker nodding in recognition. It seemed her name had even reached them, but how and why?

"That's my point exactly. Poetry intrinsically speaks to what makes us human. Some of the greatest manifestos, revolutions, love stories, betrayals, and even inhuman atrocities happened because of these tiny symbols. Tell me, can you imagine having the opportunity to change perspective with phrases alone?"

Lance cleared his throat, "You make a solid argument—pen versus sword and all that. Another question: If I can ask, feel free to speak how much or how little you'd like." Parker consented with a nod. "Have you thought about writing for the Morrison Moment? We've got open positions this spring."

"It crossed my mind, but I doubt I'll have additional time to contribute."

"A busy semester, huh? Junior year, acting, relationship, and running a fraternity?" Lance recorded a suspicious shift in Delilah's gaze. "Speaking of, what's it like being a member of the Lemurian Order, one of MSU's most celebrated organizations?"

"An honor and a privilege that I am grateful to have."

"So, they've been that instrumental in your college experience?"

"Certainly."

"What makes it so special? Why the reverence?"

"I wouldn't be who I am today without the Lemurian Order."

"But there's gotta be more to it, yeah?"

"What do you mean?"

"Like there's only a handful of you, but you make waves across this campus. And have been for decades."

"We pride ourselves on our commitment to our community and ourselves."

"And how could such an organization accept one?"

"I'm afraid that information is reserved for prospective members. However, one can visit our website and learn more about our efforts."

"Oh, Parker, why you giving me the automated media response? C'mon, you can tell me, is there like some secret rite of passage or metaphorical inner *portal* one has to explore to achieve greatness?"

Parker's gaze flittered to June. Lance took the break in eye contact as a sign. He was about to press further until he heard the ignition of a lighter. "Hate to interrupt the profound discourse, but who's ready to smoke? Damn, it feels good to ask that," said Delilah as she sauntered across the bedroom, sitting next to Parker.

The lighter sparked the blunt, and the room filled with the scent of marijuana as crooning vocals hummed in the background. With each rotation, the barriers between physical and astral blurred. Once the ashtray collected enough sacrificial embers, the four entered the space where time dispersed, and all became unified.

"Sounds like the party's dying down," said Delilah. She then began to rub on the back of Parker's neck.

Lance dropped the interrogation to save face, knowing he'd collected plenty of information. His gut instincts also told him it was time to leave now that the atmosphere was thick with lust and suspicion. He yawned, stretching his arms out to tap his roommate on the shoulder.

"Yo, June. You about ready to dip? I think our hosts have other plans that don't involve us, bro," Lance said.

"I'm baked, bro. I don't think...I'm ahhh...whew," June tilted to the left, leaning against the couch.

"Did you two drive?" Parker asked.

"Caught a ride and plan on catching one back," Lance stated as he rose. "June, you got everything? Go ahead and get your stomach right before we get in the car. I don't have time to drop $150 on a cleaning fee because you had to meet with EARL."

Although they conversed as if all were coherent, June began to mutter while Lance checked his belongings. "This feels weird—like floating—floating out in nowhere. Like arms are clouds or waves. There are no ripples, just small ones that won't disturb any reflections. Like the reflection pool. If that's the pool, then am I Baudelaire?"

Lance opened the rideshare application on his phone when Parker raised his head from Delilah's thigh. He gave her a peck, and she excused herself to the bathroom, probably preparing for the personal after-party. "There's no need for that," said Parker. "I'll text one of the guys downstairs to give you two a ride back."

"You don't have to go out of your way. I promise," Lance responded.

"I insist. I want Daniel to be ready for his big debut."

"On that, we can agree. He's been freaking out about the audition since the flyer appeared in the union."

"That was posted before we left for winter break," Parker said.

"That's Anxious Alex for ya. Sometimes, he gets worried about little things, so you can imagine what he does when the big events come around."

"Still floating. Except the water is still. Maybe I'm frozen in anxiety. Because I have anxiety. I have anxiety about being frozen, floating then frozen, and being frozen on stage," June muttered.

"Past all that inherent anxiety probably lies a fearless individual. I bet he's unaware of his potential," Parker said to Lance.

"I sure hope so, too. I was bummed out about him not getting the lead role. He's been practicing nonstop. Even when he's dropping a load before the day begins," Lance chuckled.

"I see, so Daniel did not earn the lead role? I didn't have time to check the results with all the party prep."

"Nah, think his assigned character is some tavern guy or S&M master?"

"Characters are agents. Agents of change. Sleeper Agent. Shakespeare. Macbeth. Hamlet. Ophelia...Floating like Ophelia. Dead like Ophelia. Is this death? No, but that role. It's mine. I want to be Baudelaire. That's...right." June raised his voice, "I want to...I want...I am...Baudelaire."

Parker smiled, "That you are, Daniel."

"Ladies and gentlemen, our protagonist," Lance said as his chest flashed. Glancing at his cell phone, he licked his lips and cleared his nose of crusted residue. "Excuse me for a second," he said.

"Who...is it?" June asked. Lance stretched his arm to show the name of the caller. "Oh, shoooooot. Nuhh...what did workkk baeee wa-want?"

"Maybe the same thing any babe wants when she hits you up past midnight." Lance stepped out into the hallway and answered the call. "Oh, hey, Anjali. What's up?"

"Where are you?"

"About to leave the Lion's Den. You?"

"Leaving the double M now. Lance, can you come over? Like now?"

"Ab-absolutely. I gotta get my roommate back safe, then I'll..."

"Never mind then."

"Wait, wait, wait...what is it?"

"I was hoping you'd have time for me. Although, I don't plan on staying up much longer. So if you've gotta take him back then..."

"I think," Lance peered into the room at June. "I think he should be good on his own. I'm about to leave right now, okay? Wait up for me!"

"Text me when you're outside."

Lance hung up the phone, tapped his chest twice in celebration, and then readjusted his boxers. Excited, he returned to the bedroom and leaned into June's ear. "Soooooo, she invited me over."

"Uhhh, you gonna go...bump jones?"

"I should, shouldn't I? I mean, this is it. The moment of truth! But...there's a problem."

"What?" June gurgled,

"She's not gonna wait much longer and told me to come straight to her. But I don't want to leave you like this. It's almost two, and you know what that means."

"Crash. Crash. Crash. Yah. But I'm where...I need to be. I need...I have to...talk to...Parker. Trust me; I'm okay."

"You sure? I mean, really sure? I'll decline her invite if you need me."

"Yes, I'm sure. You go bump jones," he smiled.

With that confirmation, Lance immediately went into departure mode. "We'll recap in the morning, June. Here, take your stuff back. Phone's on like 40%, so you should be good. Parker, thank you for your time. I know this is an odd request, but is it okay to leave June in your hands? He trusts you, and I need to do something right now."

"Absolutely," Parker said.

"Sometime soon, I'd like to catch up and continue our interrogation session." They shook hands, and Parker's gleaming eyes peered deep into Lance's.

"Perhaps next time I'll put you in the hot seat." Although it was playfully stated, the photographer felt a twinge of intimidation.

"Oh yeah, can you make sure he texts me when he gets back in? And his hair is wrapped, and he uses the bathroom before bed because accidents happen. Haha, he comes with so many instructions; he's like a pet!"

"Fear not. Daniel is in good hands with *us*." Parker grinned as the bedroom door closed. As he descended, Lance contemplated his choices, wondering if he'd just sacrificed his best friend to the secret satanic cult for a booty call...

Liberatus

A chill from the vacant hallway crept into the bedroom as June stared at the rotating ceiling fan. Rumblings in his stomach pressured him to sprint to the toilet, but Delilah had yet to exit the shower. Downstairs, the last thumps of the party's heartbeat ceased, and his world went mute.

Like the party, Parker was also silent. It felt like he'd been conversing most of the time since their initial encounter in the basement. With him no longer speaking, June hoped this was his chance to ask him about the production, but the thought slipped his mind like most other thoughts.

"Daniel," Parker's voice flickered in the dim room. "How are you feeling? Are you still on your voyage?"

June tried to nod, but gravity kept his head down. "Too much...I shouldn't have...drank and smoked and...I need my bed. Crashing...hard."

Parker rose and walked to his bookshelf. "It's a tragedy that we're slaves to these sensations. Don't you wish you could sometimes go beyond the limits of this faulty vessel we call a body? Perhaps gain sobriety without having to sit through another hangover? Or live free from the constraints that plague our mind?"

"I want to live...free."

"The mind is mankind's key to liberation. It is the sole thing that separates us from the feral mongrels, yet the use of the mind has been ridiculed in today's culture. Reduced to a fraction of its original capacity, and that's because society has squandered its importance. However, there are blessed ones able to conquer consciousness and unlock the secrets of the soul."

Reaching into his pocket, Parker retrieved a small, golden vial. He swirled it thrice to mix the contents and uncapped the bottle. The curious actor approached June. "What say you then? Do you believe yourself worthy of upholding the *absolute truth?*"

"Um...I don't know what's true?"

"Then, let me show you. Open your mouth, Daniel."

"What...is that?"

"Consider it your entry fee."

"...I shouldn't."

"No drink, no entry," recited Parker. "And remember, Baudelaire, to progress..."

"*I must take the risk,*" finished June.

Parker's indigo eyes shone through the haze as he ordered the young man. "Good boy, now drink."

June tilted his head and propped open his lips as instructed. A sole droplet fell from the vial's rim to the tip of his tongue. Instinctively, he swallowed, but what followed next was a prickling in his pharynx. The solution slid down his throat, exciting every nerve on the voyage to the stomach. Gagging and coughing resounded louder than the EDM tracks playing earlier in the night. Fingers clawed at his neck, and June was about to gnaw off his tongue when the ceiling fan stopped spinning. All sound dissolved, and he felt the force of gravity disperse.

For a second, he existed not as a human or himself, merely a mote of pure consciousness free from any restrictions. June lifted his hands to his eyes. No more trembling, fatigue, or hallucinations, and the pain in his stomach subsided. "What's happening?"

"You are finally *awake*."

"Awake?" June noticed his speech no longer slurred.

"Yes, welcome to *reality*. The world we experience is a poor representation of true reality, and our weathered bodies are to blame for this shortcoming. But," he presented the vial, "this is a blessing bestowed upon those brave enough to carry the burden of the absolute truth. With this, one can merge the physical and astral, thereby gaining total control of their reality. Control the mind to control reality. Control reality..."

"And you can do whatever the fuck you want," June repeated Delilah's phrase.

It was hardly believable, yet the zen established at this late hour could not be explained. Minutes ago, he'd been stumbling and on the verge of vomiting, but now he felt normal. No, refreshed. Energized. *Superior*. June rose to his feet, surprised at his agility. He glanced around the room, observing every detail with the perception of a researcher at his microscope. It felt as if he'd opened his eyes for the first time. However, the silence within his mind marveled him the most; the anxious voice that persisted within him was all but eradicated.

Light refracted off the golden vial as Parker held it to the ceiling. June stared at the swirling liquid. "What exactly did you give to me?"

"It's less about what I did and more about who you are. You may have drank the potion, but the reason you are awakening is because *you are compatible.*"

"And what does that mean?" June asked.

"All I can reveal at this time is you've got an opportunity to ascend and become who you want to be. Baudelaire, Daniel, June, or any character you wish."

"It feels like I'm tapping into the other 90% of my brain or something like that," June said.

"It is powerful, no? It worked wonders for me, and I'm convinced that a proper dose could permanently cure your anxiety. Imagine how it would feel to stand on the stage as Baudelaire and proclaim your truth to the masses without a single error?"

"Like a dream come true, but it's impossible now, even with this buff potion. The part has already been given to fake ass Timothy Brooks," June recalled.

"My dear Daniel," Parker's grin twisted, "only death is ever set in stone. If the role is what you desire, you will receive the role."

"What about Timothy?"

"What about him?"

"How will you make him give up the role?" June asked.

"We have our methods."

"*We...?*"

Parker closed his fist into a palm and faced the young man, his shadow extending to the wall. "I beseech thee, Daniel Elliott Junior. What I am about to offer will dictate the direction of your life. If you deny it, I will act as if this invitation was never extended. But, if you accept, you will begin a rite of passage that will redefine your earthly existence."

Parker's voice imbued June with a desire to salute as he listened to the address. "I am offering you *a choice!* Either you remain asleep as a mindless mongrel with no sense of the inner self, or you confront the challenge and awaken the higher being by accepting the invitation offered only by *the Lemurian Order.*"

June rubbed his temples as the pressure swelled in his skull. The room started to revolve around the stable fan, and the corners of his peripheral vision dimmed. "Ungh, my head. What's happening...to me?"

"The dose is but a sample. I cannot give you the blessings of my brotherhood when you are not one of us. *If you were to join*, you would receive the true blessing," Parker's eyes flashed.

"No, don't take it away. I...I want this feeling. I want more."

"And there is so much more to give. But to receive it, you must overcome the trials. What say you, June? Will you accept the invitation?"

"I...I get to be Baudelaire...right?" June asked, pressing into his forehead.

"Yes. You will be him and so much more."

"Good, I need to be Baudelaire so I can be a better me. So...yes! *I accept.*"

"Excellent. Your first task is to arrive at the Clock Tower tomorrow night at precisely 9:19. A stranger will approach you, and when asked, 'What is forever?' you will reply, 'A fragment of the future.' Understood?"

"A fragment...of the future?" June attempted to commit the phrases to memory by repeating them six times, but the words became jumbled. As he recited the seventh time, the mushrooms initiated the crash sequence. Seconds later, the source powering his consciousness shut down, and he blacked out. The last thing he saw before his body collapsed on the floor was Parker's shimmering eyes.

Once he confirmed the boy was unconscious, Parker dialed a number on his phone. "You were correct; he's compatible. I agree that we should include him, but before we recruit him, we must eliminate a minor obstacle. His name is *Timothy Brooks*. Understood, I'll leave that to you. Also, how shall we handle his initiation? The others will object. Right, right, we shall explain everything in the Conclave. *Absolute is the truth*." The phone call ended a moment later, and the bathroom door opened.

"You think it was him, don't you?" Delilah asked Parker, staring at the young man passed out on the couch.

"Daniel is an unexpected development and may not have been in our initial plans, but we cannot ignore his potential. So much potential. The way he adapted to the sample was unlike any I've seen before. I bet we could've *linked to each* other without proper training. It's interesting finding one like him. I imagine what he will become when he crosses to the other side."

"*If* he crosses to the other side. How did you know he'd be so compatible? Did you stick him in the Oracle Chamber as a test?"

"No, I was just as surprised as you were to find him down there. That was the work of our fearless leader. You know Fitz; he won't leave anything to chance."

"True. Still, doesn't it freak you out a bit?" she asked.

"What, babe?" Parker guided her to his lap, rubbing the back of her neck.

"How did one lost lamb startle *the Hierophant*?"

Bump Jones

Lance reached the base of the stairwell and stared into the apocalyptic remains of the Congregation Hall. Crushed cups, dirty napkins, lost clothing, shoes, bags, and all manner of streamers and confetti saturated the floor, one notable piece being a bottle of Ace of Spades. A few stragglers remained at the hall's front entrance, awaiting a ride back to campus. One of the remnants was Timia, who huddled with a crew near the speakers. She winked and stuck her tongue out, showcasing the fabled piercings. The sight of the pink and metal halted Lance, and he nearly disengaged from his mission. But then he recalled Anjali's hand touching him.

"This story better get me laid..." he muttered before merging with the shadows.

Although Lance had no set destination, he knew intuition would take him exactly where he needed to go. But before he moved anywhere, Lance spun around in place, yawning. Eyes scanned the corners. "Two visible cameras, so assume at least four hidden around this place." Entering his imagination, he tried to materialize a layout of the place topographically.

As a child, Lance occasionally spent afternoons with his dad, where he worked as a security guard at a private parking lot in Manhattan. From his father's career, he learned that the average range of CCTV cameras reached 40 feet. Most footage captured high-traffic locations, such as stairways and corridors. But unless someone actively monitored them, they wouldn't raise an alarm or come looking, he assumed.

"Goal here is try not to get seen, and if so, at least avoid identity detection." Blessed by the psychedelics, mental pieces came together to sketch a route. Lance opened his eyes. The path was clear.

While still outside the camera range, Lance removed his hoodie and shirt. The black jacket was flipped inside out, hiding the recognizable cryptid graphics. The shirt was wound and wrapped around the bridge of his nose like a bandana concealing his face. Lastly, Lance threw on the hood, becoming nothing more than a humanoid shape.

He held his phone by his side and crouched, adopting a stealth archer pose, as he entered the Hall. His camera recorded the entire first floor with a surprising level of steadiness. In the dark, the Congregation Hall was hardly different from a warehouse. Although the party seemed packed, they only used 60% of the available space.

"Over half of MSU could fit in here," remarked Lance.

The trail brought him to finely crafted double doors enhanced with silver doorknobs. A gentle turn and nudge granted him entry with minimal sound. Upon first glance, Lance assumed he'd entered the dining room based on the placement of the regal table. However, the cabinets looked more like those in the MM archives. Big tables often mean big decisions.

"Their meeting room," he muttered before closing the door behind him. A perimeter sweep showed no camera placement. Wasting no time, Lance skipped toward the cabinets and examined them. All of them had locks installed into the drawers. Lance tried several handles, each refusing to give up their position. At the third one, he pulled, and the drawer screeched.

Immediately, his lungs imprisoned his breath, so he hurried back from the object. Then he crouched, lowering himself to the level of the table. A minute of silence passed, and Lance crept to the door. He exited as quietly as he entered, vowing to return with the right gear.

Back in the main corridor, he plotted a course to return to the stairway leading to the lower level. On his way, he reached the bathroom again. On the other side of the hall hung the curtain and his ticket downstairs. Before crossing, Lance took cover behind the wall next to it. One camera with its eye on the curtain. No other way to get down without getting seen. Weighing his options, Lance tightened the hoodie, becoming a shadow.

A giggle came from behind him, and he rushed into the bathroom, leaving the door ajar. Peering through the gap, he watched a woman run through the hallway. Seconds later, a man went chasing after her. Her back pressed against a wall, and he pinned her. They kissed and laughed before the man pulled something out of his pocket.

A small tincture. He opened his mouth and released a single drop into it. Then, he held it out over her and dabbed two on her tongue. "This is some of my special shit, will take you straight to heaven. Cooked it myself. Got a couple hits of K and some diluted Ophelia mixed in. Won't last more than 15 minutes, but you'll feel like it's been forever," said the man.

"So we've got 15 minutes then?" she asked.

"Just about. And I know how I want to spend it."

A ringtone broke up the scene. Lance sunk to the floor, converting into a cornered rat. The man reached into his pocket. "Hell do you want, Fitz? High-priority assignment? Alright, what you need, yo? And what are you gonna do with that? You, of all people, know serum's nothing to fuck with. Yeah, whatever, I'll get you some if it's that important. Alright, bet. You owe me, you hear that."

He hung up and caressed the woman's chin. "Gotta go handle some shit." She pouted and bratted. "C'mon Brittney, wait for me. For real, just wait in my room, yo."

"We've only got 13 more minutes, Noah. Take too long, and the moment will be gone," Brittney sang. "Your time starts now." She kissed him again and broke free from the pin before running farther into the Lion's Den.

Noah threw back the curtain and hustled into the depths. Lance waited another six minutes, passing the time by replaying the footage from his initial walk. But he couldn't fully appreciate the work while in this position. Finally, Noah reappeared from behind the curtain. The young man leaned against the wall, panting heavily while wiping away sweat. "I'm coming...Brittney. I'm...I still got another seven minutes," He looked at his watch before racing off into the dark.

Once alone again, Lance made his way to the curtain. He slipped into it and ran down the corridor. Deep enough inside, he activated the flashlight on his smartphone. Time passed, and he reached the base. The door he found June behind called to him again. Entering the ritual site, he heard only the echo of creeping wind. The lack of noise inherently put him on edge. He found nothing new or noteworthy in the cells or around the perimeter.

Lance stopped at the altar, which had changed since his previous visit. A new addition, a uniquely carved box with jewels embedded in its design, sat atop it. The amateur sleuth grinned. "What do we have here?" Quickly, his hands shuffled into his pockets, and he found his phone vibrating—a text message.

"WRU??!"

"Fuck, Lance. You're supposed to be getting your meat rubbed, not dungeon crawling." He replied, "OTW still," before re-examining the strange cells and the massive stone tablet. Torn between desire and duty, he closed the camera app and retreated. Lance ascended the stairs with a heightened sense of fear and ecstasy. A chuckle even weaseled out of his nose as he neared the curtain. The hoodie was re-adjusted, and Lance stepped into the central corridor again. Then, he rushed toward the door. Nobody was present, and yet, he felt observed. But he couldn't concern himself with that now, seeing as the rideshare app notified him of the driver's arrival. He gave one last push, breaking out of the home and racing up the driveway.

Eventually, he crawled into the backseat of the requested vehicle, panting. "Hell of a night?" asked the driver.

"My friend, I live a hell of a life. But tonight, I'm about to go to heaven," replied Lance. The car departed from the Lion's Den, and Lance watched the ominous spires dissolve into the darkness.

Walking to the townhouse's door, Lance noticed an oddly familiar cobalt electric scooter parked outside. He removed his phone to fix his face, and then Lance called Anjali. Seconds later, she flew out of the darkness, her gray and silver robe floating behind her like a wispy tail. She held her index finger to her mouth, gesturing for him to remain quiet. Then, Anjali reached for his hand and guided him through the darkened apartment.

They reached the second floor, and a light was on at the end of the hallway—her room. Lance played a thousand scenarios in his head about how to begin the passionate liaison.

A shadow flickered along the bedroom wall. He paid it no mind, instead preparing his lips for their first kiss. Anjali invited him inside, and all the passion Lance had stored in his tank vanished. Sitting at the cluttered desk was his Ri-Dol. Something about George's casual demeanor infuriated Lance. Anjali excused herself for a moment to grab another chair.

"Why are you here?" whispered Lance.

"I could ask you the same thing."

"I didn't know she was into this kind of thing. I mean, I wish the other guy wasn't you, but...if this is how it happens..."

"Ohhhh, I see what's going on here. You thought she hit you up to *get some,* huh? As if."

"Whatever, George," he responded.

"This your late-night link fit?"

"Sure, maybe. Style is individual," said Lance.

"Don't know what you were up to, but I'd switch up the styles right quick if you want to stay in the competition."

Lance accepted the advice and fixed his hoodie. "Thanks, George," he said.

"Naturally, I have to invest in my future subordinate. You'll be representing me next year when I'm Senior Editor, so it's best to groom you now."

"Fuck you, I'm gonna be the one running shit," he said.

Anjali returned and offered Lance the third seat. "Why the hell were you so late, Lance?" she asked.

"It took me forever to find a ride," he lied.

"You should've told me; I would've had George come pick you up. Either way, now that you're both here. Let's talk Senior Editor."

Anjali covered everything from the dedication required for the role to the importance of reviewing and revising all articles that came by the desk to topics worth highlighting and overlooking, facilitating interviews and publication dates, the payment schedule, and assigning and hiring new employees. Few questions were asked mainly because she explained the requirements in great detail.

The impromptu meeting lasted twenty-four minutes, and once it adjourned, both boys were escorted to the exit. Her last order was for George to give Lance a ride back to campus, which he grudgingly accepted.

The duo hopped on the back of the electric scooter, and Lance awkwardly wrapped his arms around his Ri-Dol. "Don't enjoy this too much," George said before they rode into the winter night. Although George was a dick in his eyes, he did look out for Lance. He even dropped him off at the entrance of Derringer Dormitory. Lance thanked him, but he still stuck out his middle finger as the scooter drove away.

Entry into the dorm was gained after Lance swiped his metallic fob across the keypad. While he waited for the elevator, he thought about how to apologize to June. Although the two had never officially stated "bros before hoes," it was an assumed understanding. Yet, he couldn't erase the shitty feeling after voluntarily leaving his best friend alone with strangers during a moment of genuine vulnerability.

Not just strangers, *cultists*!

Droplets of rain started tapping the window as Lance entered the dark room. Given his inebriated condition, he threw shoes on the ground, unclamped the satchel, pulled off his hoodie, and grabbed the blanket from his bunk as quietly as he could manage. He peeked at his roommate's bed. June was probably knocked out by now. What a funny recap they would have in the morning. Like a creature of habit, Lance curled up on the futon and allowed the sleep to take him without a second thought.

Wordsmithing

The eighty-four-page manuscript rested on a circular table housed within an office in the Thompson Theater. The cover page contained two crucial bits of information: the production title (UNTITLED) and the author's name. Its creator, Michaela Patterson, was sitting alone at the desk.

She avoided the morning rain but anticipated the eventual downpour by wearing a gray jacket and black weatherproof boots with multiple laces around the ankle. Her locs were tucked into a head wrap to prevent them from soaking up water. Her patterned umbrella sat in the corner.

The office was chilled and smelled like theater kids, which is to say it smelled too pompous and sweet for her taste. Hopefully, she would only have to be here briefly; today, Saturday, she planned to revise the story. Although it was technically finished in terms of content, the script needed to transform from words to production, and some details could only be changed in real time after seeing them unveiled in front of her on stage.

While waiting for the rest of the production crew to arrive, Michaela thumbed through the document with her red pen. As she skimmed her script, listening to the patter of droplets tapping against the window, she thought about a unique statement Xavier made on the acknowledgments page of *Foglands*, his latest poetry collection.

Writing has been described as many things: obsessive, addictive, draining, expressive, honest, deceptive, and fulfilling. And writing is all these things, but it is so much worse. Writing is a parasite.

First, it begins with an idea, most likely a question that comes in a hot flash of passion. It becomes a pleasurable experience to toy with the budding idea, and a script often requires one to sweat and squirm. Over time, that infiltrating idea develops into a full-blown imagination infection. Sentences swell into stanzas, and you begin to nourish the parasite of passion without understanding what it siphons from you. Eventually, you'll reach a point where the parasite latches to your soul. It drains you of energy and time, and your attention shifts from the run-of-the-mill bullshit to this strange entity that has chosen you as host. It's a bizarre relationship, how both you and the idea share the same vessel, and yet, only one of you can remain in control. And as long as a pen is in your hand, the parasite will always prevail. That is why we must bring our tales to completion; if not, how can we ever cure ourselves of this metaphorical malady? But the truth is, we only cleanse our system to prepare for the next parasite.

Michaela lifted the result of her passion parasite, stared at the title, and then looked out the window. Haze, rain, and day coalesced to form an illusory climate. Glancing deeper into the gray, memories flooded Michaela's cranium, recalling the moment the idea infected her imagination.

Michaela ended the second semester of her sophomore year with tears. Frustrated after failing Biology lab again–

the rest of her grades were a mix of A's and B's–Michaela went through a brief but potent period of depression. The drowning lasted only a week, but within that time, she contemplated her past, present, and future. Her initial dream of following her father's footsteps into healthcare proved to be more of a burden than a boon. In the midst of grieving her grades, she happened upon an old journal entry that reminded her of a childhood fantasy. The record served as a reminder that before she was interested in human bodies, she was interested in human emotions. And her way of expressing and experimenting with emotions was through words. So, with a heavy but hopeful heart, she decided to change majors, diving headfirst into creative writing. To confirm her choice, she set out to write a story that summarized her struggles and successes. Initially, she wasn't sure what it meant to pursue her passion; however, she wasn't concerned about the final product. All that mattered was she started the journey. And to start that journey, like all heroes, she needed to leave home.

On the last day before summer break, when her parents were moving her out, she presented her plans to them. She'd already consulted with her academic advisor on how to stay on course to graduate on time while simultaneously completing credits for her new major. They took the news well; however, when she explained to Phillip and Callie that she'd be "on sabbatical" the following week and would miss their annual beach trip, they flipped their lids.

And a desk.

Michaela's father had been carrying her desk from the storage truck when she decided to break the news, which led to the breaking of her father's big toe. The injury granted him a temporary break from the dental office and a week with his daughter, who showered him with enough genuine affection (and homemade meals) to convince him to let her go. However, Phillip was the easygoing parent; it was her mother, a senior-level financial officer at a biotechnology company, whom she had to convince.

After returning home from the hospital, Michaela's mom conducted a thorough interrogation regarding her summer plans. "I still don't see why you can't stay here with us?" Callie asked.

"This has nothing to do with you or Daddy. I just need to write; I need to heal."

"Then, go to therapy. I don't see how staying in the city will change your mood."

"Because *writing is my therapy*. And I need space to express these feelings freely."

Her mother twisted her finger, "Didn't you beg us to buy you that desk for your birthday so you could write? You even put down half the price for it; I was impressed. But now you're about to waste your extra savings this summer?"

"We just reviewed my budget, and you said I could do this because I had cushion change."

"Ahem, I said it would be less of a financial burden because you have a cushion; it doesn't mean you should add unnecessary stress to your purse."

"It's not unnecessary. This is money I earned from my work study. I saved it by not going to the mall every weekend to buy a black dress for a lame party that I also probably had to buy a ticket for since I'm not sleeping with the bouncer, the manager, or the party promoter. So, instead of following the route others have taken, I decided to set up a personal fund—money that is strictly for my pleasure."

A thick striped maroon sweater was snatched from the laundry hamper and thrown on Michaela's bed. The cotton on the sleeves was snagged, and a tear formed in the collar. Callie rolled her eyes. "I support you trying to embrace the bohemian, hipster, creative life, but please don't dress like *that*."

"Like what?" Michaela held the sweater over her torso.

"Like someone who begs outside the bodega."

"This is my writing sweater, though. I can breathe in it, unlike those stuffy suits you wear."

"I'm gonna be honest. I've thought about tossing it into a dumpster fire. It's hideous, and I think you wear it to irritate me. But I won't stop you from being who you are. Just promise me you won't wear it outside of the apartment. Or outside of your room. I'd hate for your host to see you like this."

"Mother, I only wear this when I'm writing, and since writing is all I'll be doing this summer...*it's the only thing I'm packing*." Her astonished mother was about to respond until Michaela broke her stone face. "Joking. Only joking."

"I hope you're not writing comedies because that wasn't funny."

The desk chair squeaked as Michaela sat, the smile dissolving like fog hit by sunlight. "The story that I'm going to write in this sweater will be a tragic tale."

"Why does everything have to be so moody with your generation?"

"Because we have to reconcile with being ordinary after a childhood of being told we're special. I should've done better this semester. I wanted to improve but lost who I was along the way."

"I understand what happened the first time, but I thought you said you had it, though? What got you? The final?"

"I bombed it. Badly. Now, I'm screwed. I need to earn my science credit this year because my senior year's schedule will be dedicated to taking the last Creative Writing courses I need to major. But they don't offer this biology course in the fall, so I've got to wait. Next spring is my last chance if I want to graduate on time," said Michaela.

"I get it. My senior year, I failed a damn drama class and had to retake it the summer I graduated."

Michaela furrowed her brow, unaware of her mother's failure. She assumed her parents were naturally intelligent since they held high-ranking positions in their respective fields.

Callie closed her eyes, "Before I took the class, though, I went to the Dominican Republic for ten days. Let me tell you, nothing recharges a spirit like Mama Juana and dancing." Her mother's thoughts drifted to a past life full of late-night bachata and toes digging in the sand under the ivory moon.

"But, when summer session started, I went straight to work. I realized that I wasn't going to pass it on my own, so I enlisted the aid of a tutor. It was embarrassing to admit my shortcomings and ask for help, but it saved me. I passed with an A, thanks to my classmate. Shame, I don't even remember her name. Julia or Juliette? I don't know. But I know I wouldn't be where I am now if I didn't let someone in."

"Ew, letting someone in? Why?"

"Gross, right? Being independent is a natural skill for us Patterson women, but it can sometimes hinder our progress if we become too isolated."

"Nobody cares about me or what I want."

"Michaela, I know it's hard to trust people after everything that's happened, but you can't let that stop you."

"But they won't get me like Maxwell."

"You don't know that. Nobody can replace your brother, but some people may be equally compatible in their own way. I genuinely believe someone will come along; ensure you're open to receiving."

"Yeah, yeah. You're right or whatever."

"So, I'll let you have this solo sabbatical if you promise to be open to receiving help come spring."

Michaela accepted her mother's proposition with a warming kiss on her forehead. "I'll see if your father wants to go shopping this weekend. You know him; he won't send you anywhere without ensuring you're set with new shoes."

Nine days later, after a short but traffic-packed drive to Manhattan, the Patterson family arrived at Michaela's designated creative cabin: A quaint two-story apartment nestled in Spanish Harlem. It had been advertised as a respite, and the reviews all affirmed the description. Michaela knew the hermitage would be memorable after the host started the welcoming tour by pouring them tea. The host, Tyler Xi, was a half-man, half-machine elder with sunburned cheeks and chicken legs that wobbled with each fifth step.

First stop on the tour was the kitchen. It contained vintage utensils and a dining room table able to seat six individuals comfortably. Michaela loved the canary yellow electric kettle and collection of handcrafted mugs. Opposite the kitchen was a study containing an enormous shelf of leafy green plants. A large square window was near the study desk; natural light bathed the wooden floors and foliage. Her bedroom was nothing special, and this is what she preferred. This space was purely utility, understanding that she came here to write, not relax. She would only occupy the room when it was time to sleep, shit, and shower.

Outside was a courtyard with a fountain in the center. According to Mr. Xi, the plumbing had yet to be fixed, explaining why the water did not gush on command. Since the apartments surrounded the square, little to no wind penetrated the fortress, and the pond's surface remained steady. However, the miniature pool was well-kept by the dutiful host; he never allowed debris to sit in the pool longer than an afternoon.

Lastly, a full-sized parlor stocked with wine and spirits from multiple generations resided underneath the establishment. The cabinets were freshly polished, and the scent of pine filled the basement level; apparently, this was a meeting place for tenants who used to thrive here before the building was repurposed. After discovering this location, she vowed to spend her evenings unwinding with wine and Xavier's words.

Once the tour finished and the Patterson parents said farewell to their daughter, Mr. Xi surprised his guest by inviting her to the parlor for dinner. He prepared lamb, charred asparagus, buttered rice, and wine samples.

During that dinner, Michaela learned about the life of this stoic groundskeeper. As a young boy, Mr. Xi had been diagnosed with a rare disease that required him to receive stents in his kidneys. He broke his kneecap in a factory accident and had the patella bone plated back together at twenty-two. Near the end of his first marriage, his ex-wife "accidentally" knocked him down a flight of stairs and blew out his shoulder; treatment consisted of a ball and socket joint being installed in his arm. At sixty-one, Mr. Xi almost stroked out during water aerobics at the local YMCA; the doctors placed a shielded pacemaker in his chest to regulate his circulation. From these extensive injuries, Mr. Xi was eligible to apply for a medical marijuana license. Now, he spent most of his days stoned on the stoop like a boulder in Arizona.

After stuffing her face full of food and inspiration, Michaela prepared to retire to her room until Mr. Xi offered advice and a fresh bowl pack.

"Isolation may give rise to the imagination, but not relations. I have lived here alone since my second wife passed, and although I've become my best friend, I've also become my warden. I've imprisoned myself within my comfort because I lack the courage to discover anybody else but me. And I'm telling you this because I see similarities in you. Don't let complacency turn you into a coward, and don't let cowardice keep you from experiencing genuine connection."

After that admission, they shared a smoke and a few words, both preferring to sort through their minds rather than explore each other. In this instance, a mutual understanding was formed, and Mr. Xi clarified that he'd be available to her anytime she needed him but not to expect him otherwise. She agreed, saying she planned on interfering with his life as little as possible. At that point, the two departed, and Michaela acclimated to the new creation chamber.

Later that night, Michaela sat in the study, slightly buzzed and emotionally charged. She experienced a sensation that had gripped her on numerous occasions in her youth, especially in times of ecstasy or anxiety. When she opened her notebook, Michaela's sense of self-awareness dulled, and the only thoughts flowing through the stream of consciousness were related to the story. Then came the scribbling.

She was "wordsmithing," a term her brother, Maxwell, coined. A self-prescribed superpower, wordsmithing happened whenever the lines of reality blurred, and her somatic response was to write without regard for the mind's instructions. At first, she only produced gibberish, but over the years, as she leaned into the talent more and more, the results became more coherent.

Although wordsmithing was a creative boon, it always left her a stranger to herself. It never sat right with her that she could generate grand ideas only while on the edge of consciousness, but she also recognized that it was more of an ego problem than anything.

During the brainstorming phase, Michaela generated at least twelve ideas for a script; that number was reduced to two, ultimately one. The other plot she toyed with for a stint was about a group of four siblings who unsealed an evil entity at their new foster home in Washington state, and they'd have to band with a few "degenerates with decent hearts" to save the world from certain doom. But Michaela equated this too much to every other modern teen mystery and went with her original idea despite how convoluted it seemed on her storyboards.

The initial draft required nearly six days of uninterrupted critical thinking. Michaela spent so little time asleep that she wasn't even sure about the date, the hour, or the weather. Instead, her mind was infected with ideas like: "Will I create a love triangle? Rectangle? How can I show my character's declining state of sanity without making it seem melodramatic? Who is going to die? Who is going to kill them if they do die, and how? Because how someone dies is just as important as how one falls in love."

Completing the draft took less time than expected, but that's because her wordsmithing ran wild in this residence. And how she wrote, crafting over seventy pages in eleven days. Her hands cramped, and she swore she'd make an appointment to check on her carpal tunnel syndrome, but it didn't matter about the state of her body as long as the idea was conceived.

A brief rest period followed her initial drafting. For those three days, although she explored the city's vintage stores, museums, curio shops, niche galleries, and hole-in-the-wall restaurants that served cultural dishes made by first-generation hands, Michaela couldn't tear her thoughts away from the tale. It was like Xavier had said: the parasite and she became one entity.

She returned to the study, ready to begin the next phase: revision. This process required less creative brainpower but more effort and critical thought, and she had to question every word while being assaulted by self-doubt. At one point, after recognizing a significant plot hole, she considered scrapping the entire concept and starting over with her foster sibling's idea (the evil entity would've been their possessed father, who unexpectedly returned). Still, persistence proved her most significant asset, and her revisions were soon complete.

On her final weekend of the six-week sabbatical, Mr. Xi treated Michaela to another meal. After sharing a farewell bowl pack, he provided another nugget of wisdom that became the glue for her tale.

"In the end, life's not about the choices or the consequences; it's about the ones who gave us the courage to dream when it's the darkest. Hell is already here on Earth, which also means we can find Heaven too. Sometimes, it takes looking into a mirror, but remember, *every mirror is a window.* So, think about who's looking at you when you're looking at yourself."

As the dawn of the final day pushed through the study's windows, Michaela placed the last period of the epilogue. Before departing the respite, she requested Mr. Xi to print the script. Then, she fell asleep. Awakening in the early afternoon, she found the old man sitting on the stoop, reading the tale. Initially, she thought about snatching it, but then he wiped his eyes. He was invested in her story, her world, her truth. She left him alone to finish it and decided to pack her belongings instead. Later, after he completed the impromptu reading, he placed it on the doorstep of her bedroom. Mr. Xi left for the day, never sharing his thoughts about the story. However, He asked her to invite him to the play when it was completed. She agreed and said farewell to her summer sabbatical, returning to her world with a new creation: a script.

Closing the script once again, Michaela stared out the window of the Thompson Theater office, observing the patterns of rain falling against the glass. The spring semester was off to a frigid start, and the challenges were only beginning. However, in her mind, she was miles and miles away from the world of electricity, required reading, and pompous theater kids. No, she was in the sakura orchard that enshrouded the mythical reflection pool.

There to tend to the blossoms was Gi. Although he'd been modeled after her dear caretaker, Gi was more than a gentle gardener; he was her favorite character. His role would be realized when the time came, but until then, she kept him a docile green thumb who wore stainless white overalls. That is until he met a particular sculptor.

For this story to succeed, she needed a main character not to be a Boy Scout with a badge. So, she created the egotistical artist Baudelaire, who eventually rose to the protagonist role. Although he was a challenge to construct, she grew to relate to this character in surprising ways. His hands would be stained in blood and choice; that was the only way Michaela could thematically represent the duality of human existence. How humanity is maddening flame and darkness ready to thrash and consume, and simultaneously parallel sheets of frost measured and structured to the utmost precision. Despite wavering between logic and passion, Baudelaire never lost his balance...until *love* was invited to his world, and its presence led to his demise.

But it was more than the character arc that made the author suspicious of Baudelaire. Michaela disliked him because he represented the qualities she wished to deny in herself. The sculptor was her if she dared to be authentic at all times. And when faced with such a reflection, it's hard not to cower and be disgusted. Yet, for her to learn anything further from this character required Baudelaire to become real; he could only do that through the stage. And even though the production team had chosen the most successful and talented actor to play Baudelaire, the same intuition that led her to wordsmith informed Michaela of a blaring truth.

Taking the red pen in hand again, Michaela flipped to the list of characters and scratched out a name. "It's not him," she whispered. "Timothy's not my Baudelaire..."

Stranger Danger

June's consciousness resided within the darkness of a slumbering mind. The boy's frail essence embraced the silent comfort until a spark of light ignited and fought for presence against the imposing dark matter. It flickered like a beating heart on the verge of collapsing; each shimmer of the cosmic glimmer represented an ego death—dying like the spotlight during his bout of stage fright, dying like his dream of becoming an actor, dying like his body dangling from the theater's rafters.

Materializing from the darkness was an empty stage. June found himself behind the backstage curtain, staring at the vacant space. He wore nothing, and yet, the sight of his naked body did not register as odd. Perhaps his worries were absent due to the presence of a mask on his face. He did not know its shape or design, but it was enough to conceal his true face. Looking into the crowd, he saw an empty audience. No, one individual was positioned at the back of the house, nearly concealed by the darkness.

Although the luminous spotlights and judgmental eyes waited for the actor to enter the light and begin the play, he stayed behind the curtain. A crippling anxiety attempted to hold him in place, preventing the progression of his character arc. However, a quaint whine, echoing from the direction of the audience member, beckoned him to leave the shadows. The noise fluttered into his ear like a migrating butterfly resting on cherry blossom petals, and as wings beat to the spasms of tangible notes, June answered the call.

He stepped from behind the curtain into the blazing beam, highlighting center stage. Finally entering the spotlight, he bared his soul to the hidden audience. Subject to such exposure, he questioned if he would release his ambitions and lofty goals, his fears of being inadequate, or the contents of his stomach and bladder. However, what would be left inside his vessel if he spilled it all on stage? And, if left vacant, he feared something would take refuge. Something sinister that transcribed curses into the chorus, something ancient enough to remember the Earth when the infernal children of Echidna and Typhon roamed. Something like the forgotten patron of a world lost to time, like Lemuria.

Suddenly, the noises hit a crescendo, and the stage boards began to leak fluid. At first, he thought it was blood, but the liquid was too thin. The solution rose to his ankles, and the cool temperature settled any remaining anxiety. The spotlight above morphed into brilliant rays of sun. Moving closer downstage and the sole audience member watching his performance, June felt the crisp heat of sand between his toes. Looking down, he was no longer in the Thompson Theater but on an uncharted beach. The silent spectator was gone when he looked back up, dissolved with the rest of the house. Something splashed in the water below him, the mask. Before he could examine it, the cries of gulls and lulls of water lapping upon itself caught his attention. And then, a familiar melody broke through the maritime illusion, a gentle bossa nova jazz that tickled the inner lining of his physical ears.

Agua de Beber.

June sprang from the pillow, confronting a radiant light above him. Swells of sensations crashed against the shores of his consciousness as his physical body calibrated to the sight. Lying there, peering into the intense glow, he tried to close his eyes and return to the comfort of the dark world that had just dissolved. But this illumination wouldn't allow him another chance at slumber.

He'd awakened.

Yet June could not remember when he'd returned to his dorm. And why was the ceiling so far away from his bed? To his shock, his shirt was missing. He was also wearing basketball pants that, for some reason, hung way off his waist. He attempted to recall the night's events, but more was unknown than expected, terrifying him. Confusion swirled as June stretched, and his legs poked out of the blanket, which felt too textured for his sensitive skin. He touched his hair and wept, for his du-rag was missing. Had he been so lit that he even forgot to wrap his hair, an action he'd performed consistently for the last three years?

All questions were immediately answered as June rolled on his right side to locate his blaring phone. Next to him in bed was a warm body. At first, he made no movements and stared at the figure—a woman. Her skin was pale, like the sheets wrapped around her delicate shoulders, and her hair curled down a scalloped neck. Nails kissed the edge of the pillow like a low tide on that same Brazilian beach conjured in his mind. A checkered comforter covered everything else, but he knew how her body looked.

The bossa nova ringtone croaked again, alarming his bed-mate. The young woman smacked her lips twice and jutted her arms across the mahogany headboard, knocking him in the chin. She then released a deep yawn that sounded like the cries of a young wolverine, and a cloud of morning breath penetrated the atmosphere, spoiling the serenity of lavender and sage.

"Oh my God, Dannyyyy. If you don't turn that shit off, I'm going to break it in half."

He thought of things to say but became muddled by the lingering stupor. When he did not react, she swung her arm underneath the pillow and pushed the phone off the bed. The device hit the floor with a resounding clang. June's jaw clenched while he watched her face beam like a dog awaiting the praise of its master. "Jeez, Danny, get with the times. You're the only person still using elevator music as their ringtone."

"I think you're missing the point here, *Brittney*." Saying her name made him shudder; how foreign and furtive it flowed like forbidden language.

"It didn't seem like you were going to pick up the phone."

"...You shouldn't be handling my phone."

"And you shouldn't be sleeping in my bed anymore, yet we're both here," Brittney said almost accusingly.

"Which brings me to even more missed points. How the hell did I get here? When did we even meet? And," he lifted the covers and glanced underneath, "Am I wearing another dude's pants?"

"I forgot you get tipsy off sparkling water. How much did you drink last night, Danny?" she teased.

"Um, I only had one cup." It was true. The alcohol had been a minor contributing factor to his condition; Ophelia is what led to his eventual crash, but he chose to retain this information. The last thing he needed was his ex trying to pick his mind. As if there was anything to pick right now, his little astral voyage resulted in the worst migraine of his life.

She shifted a little, and the covers slipped from her body. "You really can't remember anything?"

"I'm not sure. Just fill me in, please. Because I cannot understand why I am here."

"Danny...*you had nobody else but me*. Although the party ended, I was hanging out with some friends when one got a call to handle something important—decided to peace out shortly after. Stepped outside and found you being fireman lifted downstairs. Don't know what they were gonna do, but I offered to take care of you. Mitch threw you in the back of his Jeep and drove us back to my place. Oh yeah, you pissed yourself too."

"I did what!?"

"Not a lot, but you did. Nobody knew at the time. I only found out when I saw the stain on your pants."

"So, the reason my pants are missing?"

"Is because I didn't want your bodily fluids in my bed. Although that wouldn't be the first time, would it? What? You thought we...?" June nodded. Brittney cackled, "I prefer consensual coitus. I was only taking care of you because I saw you needed it. I'm glad I did because it only worsened when we returned. To think, they would've had to handle all *that*."

"All of what?" he asked, even though something urged him not.

"Like, I thought you were dying or something. At least that's what it sounded like to my suitemates."

"Dying? What are you talking about?"

"Danny, you just about woke up half the dorm at dawn. You were screaming, but it didn't sound painful. More primal, like you were possessed. The RA even checked on us because they received a noise complaint. I explained that you were experiencing PTSD and that it'd pass. Somehow, she bought it because she didn't even ask if you'd been drinking. Right after she left is when you started rambling."

"What did I say?"

"You went to Shakespeare again, going on about ideas, society, and artistry, and kept repeating a particular line. Forever is a factor of the feature...or Future is Drake's best feature. I don't know; I was half-asleep when all this went down. Oh yeah, you were calling yourself Baudelaire; that was weird."

Suddenly, as if he exited lightspeed and the blurred surroundings became normal, June remembered the end of his evening: the hazy lyrics crooning as Delilah twisted the blunt, his abandonment by Lance, Noah's excessive barking, and, he also remembered his negotiation with Parker. How naive he'd been at the time, agreeing to something as trivial as the opportunity to play Baudelaire. Had Parker taken him on a ruse while inebriated, teased him with the idea of success only to snatch it away like a vengeful deity retracting a blessing?

But what of *the elixir*? How alive and fluid he'd felt when a droplet of the mysterious potion landed on his tongue. Perhaps it wasn't just a fragment of his imagination.

"Any of this ringing a bell for you yet, Danny?" Brittney asked.

"Oh, uh, it's all hazy, but I believe you. Thank you for taking care of me; I appreciate it."

He threw his legs out of her bed and landed on the floor, the baggy warm-up pants slipping to his ankles. He raised them around his waist and retrieved his shirt and sweater. "Who do these belong to? Your new boyfriend?" he asked.

"They're Noah's, but he's not my boyfriend." Brittney rested her hand against her stomach, "I like to sleep in loose clothing when it's shark week. Why do you think I always wore your Camel Crusher hoodie in high school? Felt like being snuggled by a bear," she said. "Speaking of snuggles, this is the perfect Saturday to spend in bed. Why don't you stick around and sober up some more?"

A pearly smile peeked from her lips, but June stayed his distance, fearing what could happen if he entertained this glimmer of hope. "I really should get going," he said.

"*Can we talk?*" Brittney's voice cracked like a mishandled firework. "I've only got a few things to say; honestly, it won't be long."

In theory, he wished he could ignore an admission like this, but June felt he owed her. At least for the hospitality for the previous evening. "What is it, Brittney?"

"Danny, have you been taking care of yourself? Last time we talked, you said some heavy things."

"Ignore all that; I was drunk. I'm much better now."

"Yeah, what changed?"

"I did. Finally plan on doing therapy things, too. I'm just ready to start the new semester. Also, I'm going by June now."

"Danny's been put to death, huh? I liked him, though."

Funny you say that when you were the one who called for his execution. "Yeah, it's time for me to grow up; leaving things behind is part of that process."

"Well, some things that get left behind find a way to come around again. If they matter," Brittney said.

"If they matter..."

However gentle her concern sounded, June knew no time could be spared for drawn-out responses. This was her plan, initiating deeply emotional conversations where she would erode his defenses with pleasantries until he lacked any protection. And then, she would make her point. That part of the argument usually consisted of baleful shouting and the occasional physical threat ("Sometimes I just want to choke you, Danny."). However, this wasn't the worst part of their talks; it usually occurred right after the screaming match.

It happened like clockwork: Brittney's intense staring, the excessive flirtatious touching, and increasingly exposed skin. And just like a defenseless slave, June would melt into her, allowing his body to be used as her toy. They'd hooked up at least four times since they stopped officially dating, leaving June more confused each time. Maybe this time was another repeat; perhaps he was forever bound to Brittney as if she were *the one* like his parents often claimed. But what if he finally broke free from the cycle of self-sabotage? What, indeed, would his future resemble without fear of falling backward?

June sat on the edge of the bed and looked at the vanity set in Brittney's corner. In the mirror, he could once again see his figure. Much to his dismay, his curls were already sloped to one side, but the interesting detail was his eyes. Had they always looked *so vibrant?*

"I heard you're still acting?" Brittney asked, bringing his attention back to her.

"I am. I was just cast in the spring play. I'll be in a couple of scenes this time, and I'm going to use this chance to get better."

"You're still serious about it, aren't you?"

"As serious as what you said at the end of last year's production."

"How long are you going to hold that over my head? I told you I was joking when I said that," she said.

"You did, and I heard you."

"Then, why can't you let it go?" Brittney asked.

"Why can't you just apologize?"

"Why do you need an apology?"

June watched her sharp, willful eyes metamorphose to the sclera, cornea, and dry pupils. He rose from the edge of the bed, somewhat disgusted at himself for even entertaining this nonsense. "You almost ruined my acting career. It was hard enough that you broke up right before my show, but did you have to shove it in my face like that?"

"I told you I wished I would've kept that to myself."

"But the truth is you didn't. You said it out loud, and I listened to you. Like I always do."

"You over-reacted, Danny. Do you know how much it hurt me to hear that you almost killed yourself?"

"How much *you* were hurt? Did you even consider how much I suffered?"

"I did, and that's why I've been trying to make amends. That's why you should stay with me now," she admitted. "I know I wasn't the best for you back then, but Danny, you need me."

"I refuse to entertain this, Brittney. You're not going to mess with my head anymore. It's been nothing but hell every time we've hooked up. Last time, you went a month without saying anything to me. How is that best for me?"

"I can explain. Just hear me out, like you used to."

"Why, Brittney? Why should I care about anything you have to say? All your words do is cut me."

"Here you go again, still accusing me of ruining your life. It's not my fault you couldn't handle a little friendly criticism."

"*Friendly criticism*? You call telling someone they're *a shitty actor* friendly!? Or *Mr. Stagefright?* Yeah, that's right. That's all people call me now; I'm just a failure in their eyes. And it's your fault. Why can't you at least feel fake guilty?" he asked.

"Because that would make me a liar, and if there's one thing I'm gonna do, it's tell the truth. Even if it sucks to hear," she said.

"Oh, you want the truth then, huh? You want to go there? Well, the truth is, I think you're a hateful person."

"And I think you're too sensitive!"

"Well, you didn't care enough! You know what else I think? I think you're lonely and have finally realized what you lost when you let me go. And I told you, I told you this would happen. That you would try to come back, didn't I?"

"You're full of it. I'm not lonely, and I don't need you. I'm just trying to be a friend."

"Why? What could you still want from me? I've given you my heart, my body, and my dreams. What more do you want?"

"I just want to know that you're okay."

"But you don't get that privilege anymore. You don't get to know about me or my life unless I want you to."

"Is that what you want, Danny? You just want us to become strangers again? What about all of our time together?"

"It doesn't matter anymore. It's in the past. You chose to end this, so you must also live with the consequences. I don't need you to rescue me anymore. "

"You say that now, but did you really want to be there with *them* last night?"

"Them? You mean the Lemurian Order? I bet they would've treated me better than you."

"We both know that's not true. Who knows what would've happened if you stayed there?" She sighed, "Tell me, what happened that made you hate me so much? This isn't like you."

Strange sensations wormed from the corners of June's eyes to the center of his forehead—a thick pressure built behind the frontal lobe. "No, that's the problem. This is me, and for too long, I've been hiding myself from you. Been cowering and protecting what little peace I have. I was naive, thinking we had a chance to salvage our relationship. But ever since you severed our connection, we've been unable to get it back. All it's turned into is you using me as a fix for your loneliness."

"That's not true. I admit, I've been doing some thinking about how I handled things. And I do miss you...even though I shouldn't. But I can't help it. Don't you see, Danny? This is us; this is who we've been. Can you say you don't miss me? Miss us?"

Brittney closed the distance with a clumsy three-step. Violet-colored booty shorts defined the arches of her waist. Frozen, June felt the arm slither around his nape while her tongue readied to caress his left ear lobe. "You remember what happened the last time we argued...c'mon, don't you wanna stop all this fussing and get right to it? Let's just kiss and make up and go back to bed. I'll even do that thing with my tongue you like..." Brittney brushed her lips across his cheek before pulling him close to her wet lips.

Suddenly, June felt a pang in his gut—the shrooms. He pushed her out of the way, lurched forward, grabbing his stomach, and a hot burp seeped out of his mouth. Brittney, disgusted by his actions, raised her hand. An open palm splashed across his cheek, and an arresting ringing echoed in his ear. They remained stagnant, waiting for the director of life to provide instructions. The squirming behind his eyes intensified as he stared at her. Finally, his hand rose to rub the site of impact. Doing so, he felt a tear begin to form.

"Danny...I'm sor...I didn't mean to. Let me make it up to you...I'll fix this, I promise."

Before they flooded down his cheeks, June snatched his phone, jacket, and shoes. He made his way to the exit, but Brittney reached for him. Her hand latched to his shoulder, face wide with concern. June shot a deathly stare in her direction, and a searing pain erupted behind his eyes. At the sight, she cowered away from him, even retracting her hand back to her chest.

"No, there's nothing more to fix. *We are broken.*" Further apologies rained like droplets outside their window, but June shielded his face and kicked the door with his right shoe as he departed from the dungeon.

Plebians

Three black gallon trash bags lined the first step of the cathedral's entrance as icy precipitate soaked the spires of the Lion's Den. From inside the home blasted 80's electro-Pop, echoing into the grove of pine and maple. A large man exited the house and threw a fourth trash bag next to the pile. His letterman jacket had a giant letter C stitched next to a graphic depicting the school mascot, the mighty Mongrel. After completing his task, signaled by wiping his hands, Mitch Battle sat down on the steps, removed a lacrosse ball from his pocket, and tossed it in the air. Suddenly, the ball was snatched by a second pair of hands. The unexpected catcher twirled the prize in his palm as the gold veneer on his canine shimmered. Noble luster glinted against a black Fendi jacket as Noah dropped an unwrapped trash bag beside Mitch.

"Yo, Big Fella, you're a smart guy. Answer me this: Why are people so fuckin messy, yo?"

"Avoiding mess is inevitable. We all accepted the risk when we opened our doors to a bunch of private school students. The way I look at it, the more mess means the more people that showed. And you know what that means."

"True, we did what we set out to do. But still, yo. Ain't no reason I, a grown-ass man..." Mitch scratched his beard, "should be wiping a stranger's vomit off the back patio."

"People get drunk and lose their sense of self, Noah. At least you didn't have to collect used condoms in the parking lot."

"Fucking plebeians have *no fuckin respect.*"

"Respect for what?" Mitch grabbed his ball back from Noah.

"For us."

"How should they respect us more then? By not getting wasted on the liquor we provide at the party we throw? It was a bar crawl. This is what happens."

Noah leaned against the lion statue, nudging Mitch's shoulder with his shoe. "I'm just saying they should know not to disrespect us. Every day, it seems like the plebs of MSU forget who *we* are!"

"Who are we, then?"

A voice behind the lion startled Noah, causing him to lose his footing. On his way down, he scuffed his shoe against the concrete steps, tipping the garbage bag and releasing its contents. Dozens of cups, some crushed and others with lipstick tattoed around their rims, fell from the trash. Three used condoms also drooled out of the gallon bag.

Behind the lion's mane arose a fair-skinned goth with her right temple shaved; the rest of her jet-black hair fell to her shoulders. Her make-up consisted of a foundation two shades too dark, and her neck and head looked like two pieces hastily sewn together. The assumed haziness around the crest of her cheekbones emaciated her face. She walked towards the duo, glanced at the trash, and back at them. "People are so fucking messy," she said.

Noah blocked her ascent up the steps. "Cut the shit, *Kimi.*" What the hell were you doing behind there anyway, you stalker?"

Kimi's eyes flickered with annoyance. *"Preliminary calculations.* The statue's dimensions are ideal measurements and will help me with my current project. "

"Slow down there, Android 17. I don't care what kind of Bill Nye bullshit you're cooking, but you'll apologize before anything."

"Negative. I've made no fault, so I have no obligation to apologize, " Kimi responded.

"Your fault is that you made me scuff my shoes with your lil interruption."

"Failing to see my role in your lack of balance."

"You have a lot of shit to say today, huh? Saying everything but what I want to hear."

"Then I'll adhere to a no-talking policy for you," said Kimi, earning a grin from Mitch.

In retaliation for being ignored, Noah kicked a cup full of PJ, and the droplets landed inches away from Kimi's white canvas sneakers.

"Oh c'mon, Noah," groaned Mitch while searching for a napkin. "Can you just be chill for one morning? Kimi didn't mean it."

"Nah, here's where she got me fucked up, yo. I'm not asking her to apologize; I'm telling her she needs to beg for forgiveness before I have to punish her."

The echoes of a car parking in the rear garage reached Mitch's ears. When the rest of them arrive in a few minutes, this escalating confrontation will be concluded, just like all the previous fights between Noah and Kimi. However,

Mitch knew them well enough to know there was still time for irreversible actions to occur.

Kimi tiptoed across the leaking garbage before reaching the marble lion on the opposing side of the entrance. She pulled measuring tape from her jacket and spread it, gathering data on the length and width.

"Aye, Kimi! You think we're done yet? You see these," Noah held up his ankle, modeling the designs as if paparazzi cameras were voyeuristically snapping in the bushes. "These are custom Yeezy 350 Boost. I got these from the Adidas store in Paris, where Kanye West shops. That means he might've tried these on because we wear the same size. You scuffed them, have yet to apologize, and are ignoring me. I don't know who you think I am, but *I'm a Casca.*"

"So...?"

"See, Big Fella. This is a perfect example of what I'm talking about. Fucking disrespectful people. If we let this shit slide internally, then we're not shit. But not me; I address shit immediately because I have *zero tolerance* for disrespect. Whether it's from these wack-ass students tearing up our crib. Or this spooky bitch who keeps trying my last nerve."

Noah's pupils converted from dark indigo to lustrous lavender. He snatched the napkin from Mitch's hand. "Bro, too far!" shouted Mitch.

The napkin flew from Noah's hands. It dislodged like a space shuttle rocket, and the condom defied gravity, flying towards Kimi's neck. As it flew, the contents of the latex vessel leaked along the stairs.

Kimi glanced into the five-panel glass entrance to witness the semen salvo soaring at her. Reflexively, she pushed off the step and crashed into the garbage Mitch had collected.

Her ass hurt, and she could feel scrapes on her palm, not to mention her right knee dipped into the puddle of purple PJ.

The condom slapped against the front windowpane. The present three stared at the impact site, but none said a word as a figure appeared on the opposing side of the glass. Noah's once prideful glare devolved into a guilty scowl as the door opened.

Out walked a slender young man wearing a custom-tailored suit cut right above his ankles. His brown hair was firmly slicked back, and a freshly groomed goatee hung around his tight lips. The wooden soles of his loafers clicked against the concrete as he approached Kimi.

"Let's get you up." He spoke with an empathetic yet firm tone. Kimi clasped his palm and was hoisted back on her feet. He then brushed her shoulders, taking care to remove any blemishes. Slowly, the lavender in her eyes cooled to cobalt again.

"Ah, thank you, Fitzroy."

Fitz pressed his hands on her cheeks. "Finally went and shaved the hair. This is an excellent look for you." Turning her head to the side, he gleamed with joy. "A woman who lives by her code. That is why I respect you, Kimi Wilkshire. However..."

Fitz glanced at the condom, leaving a trail of lubricant and semen along the glass pane. He walked down the steps, patting Mitch on the shoulder as the captain hustled to collect the condom.

"My father often claimed those who lacked respect for anything were among the greatest failures, for they lacked respect for themselves." Fitz continued, "Pity, I'd expect one who shared his blood to share his values, but you never listened to father back then, did you, *brother*?"

Fitz flashed a cocaine-white smile shining brighter than Noah's lusterless gold grill. The smile concealed a seething irritation. "What's going on here, Noah? Do you understand how utterly disgusting that is? You decided to throw a stranger's used condom on our front entrance!"

"But Kimi wouldn't apolo-"

Fitz bit his thumb. "Don't tell me you just interrupted me. You, of all people, should know how I feel about being interrupted. I'm not asking you to talk; I'm *telling you to listen.*"

Low-hanging tufts of mist collected around the Lion's Den as the Fitz turned toward the members. Delilah and Parker lingered at the entrance while Mitch cleaned the window, and Kimi occupied the step below them. At the base stood the Casca siblings.

A rain droplet ended against the leather glove on Fitz's right hand. He opened his blazer, looked up at the sky, and then at the present members.

"I will address this now because we have no time for distractions during today's *Conclave.* We are a brotherhood. A sisterhood. A fraternity. *A family.* I'm aware that where people gather, conflict will follow. And families often quarrel more frequently than friends or foes. But that must stop. Greater dynasties have been destroyed because of internal division. We have a loaded schedule this semester, and we must come together to accomplish all required tasks. So, we're going to eliminate all nonsense. Now!"

Although these words were for all, they were primarily for Noah, the youngest of the crew. Fitz lowered the volume of his voice but maintained the same intensity, his eyes never breaking contact with his brother.

"Only when we respect each other will we gain the respect of the campus. And we need them to accept us more than ever this year. So, right now, we are going to lay it all out. Now's your chance to speak if you've got a grievance against one another. Address it now. If not, then leave your ego on this side of the door. Once we walk inside and sit at that table, we're no longer individuals but *the Lemurian Order*."

Upon the conclusion of the address, anonymous birds chirped, and the vermin rustling through the dried leaves added to the natural ambiance. Then, a band of icy rain cascaded from the overcast sky, washing away the liquid residue from the garbage.

To avoid the deluge, everybody dashed up the stairs under the awning. Fitz opted to scale two steps simultaneously, trying to keep his suit as dry as possible. However, his loafers slipped on the last step, and he landed straight on his ass, splitting his suit down the pant leg.

Unable to hold a steadfast face, Mitch burst into howling laughter. Noah joined, stating they should pull the footage from their camera records so they could go viral. Even Kimi's smile appeared like a faint light peeking through the sheets of gray clouds.

Noah stepped forward and offered his brother a hand. An expert at poise and composure, Fitz accepted the help, wiped the sediments from his pants, and did his best to free himself from further embarrassment by ignoring the tear.

"Now that everybody's lightened up, why don't we head inside and have lunch? I'm sure we'll all feel better with a full belly." The mood shifted from humorous to austere as Fitz lowered his gleaming eyes. "Heed my words, though. I will not tolerate any further quarreling. It's tasteless, and we have an example to set for the campus and our initiates."

The members accepted the dismissal and marched into the Lion's Den, leaving Fitz and Mitch to bring up the rear. Both individuals gazed into the vast horizon. While observing Fitz in action for the last two years, Mitch learned that many wanted the status of being a leader, but only a few truly wanted the responsibility of leadership. Fitz was a rare breed, one who was destined to sit in the high castle. And Mitch enjoyed being the genius's bodyguard.

The thick wool of Mitch's beard tickled his lips as he discarded the condom again. "Glad you came and defused that situation," he said.

"I only did what you were about to do. I know you. Always keeping my little brother in check." Fitz removed the leather glove and stuck his hand in the storm. "Sometimes, you do a better job than me."

They peered through the glass wall into the Lion's Den, watching Noah roast Parker as they walked through the Congregation Hall.

"Bullshit. Not only are you *El Jefe*, but you're also his older brother. That's a bond I'll never be able to share with him. Or anyone."

"Lately, though, Noah seems different. Frustrated? Depressed? Sexually deprived? Maybe all three? I don't know."

"He told me about this girl he's been crushing on for a minute, but I think she's more interested in the supply than the supplier."

"Perhaps that's the cause for concern. Or I could just be acting over-protective," admitted Fitz.

"I think you're acting like an older brother."

"Hey Mitch, do me a favor, please? Keep a close eye on him. Make sure he doesn't get into too much trouble. Last thing I need this semester is Noah causing a scene. You know, he just got cleared of probation."

"I'll be your brother's keeper if you promise not to over-extend yourself," said Mitch.

"Ha, if only. I need everything to be planned now so we can execute our tasks efficiently. There are so many meetings, dates, and activities, not to mention the art installation, my commencement speech, recruitment, and my father hovering everywhere. And there are other things."

Mitch frazzled the young man's hair. "Fitzroy, you don't need to explain yourself; I understand. Everybody in this crib is here to help you. *Everybody, including Noah.* He'll find his place within our family. Just don't think you have to be the hero all the time. Remember: *heroes die first.*

"I'm no hero, just a mediator."

"And it's my job as the muscle to make sure you make it through."

"How can you be so sure I won't break?" asked Fitz.

"Because *we are blessed.*"

"I sometimes forget because it's become so normal now. Hard to believe it's been two years since our ascending."

"And now, we have an opportunity to offer the same blessing to others one last time. It's time to welcome a new generation of the Lemurian Order. But first, let's get you some new pants, Prez."

Fitz laughed with his shoulders and patted his friend on the back before opening the door for him. Although it went unstated, Mitch realized Noah wasn't the only Casca he kept in check.

Reversal of Fortune

What are we going to do about Baudelaire? Would they even listen to me if I suggested something? What am I suggesting anyway? Who would play him if not Timothy?" Frustrated, Michaela closed the binder containing her script and leaned back in her chair. Glancing out the window at the transforming sky, doubt collected like clouds, shielding her eyes from a hopeful outcome.

The silver handle toggled, and the office door opened. Mr. Ray hung his moist jacket on the coat hanger and set his stainless-steel coffee mug on the table. "Ms. Patterson, a superfluous Saturday to you. I hope we haven't kept you waiting too long. Dreadful downpour out there today, and everybody decided to drive like they ordered the double espresso."

Gris entered behind the theater director, setting a plastic-wrapped umbrella in the rack. Some of the rain had touched his shoulders, but for the most part, he remained dry, unlike Mr. Ray, whose hair was slick with a touch of brooding artist. Once settled in a seat, the older man peered at the cover page and then at the writer. "Fret not; the best ideas are born when things seem bleak. And titles are often the last piece of the production."

As Michaela cleared space on the table, the last production team member, wearing tinted shades, strolled inside. Oscar slammed the door, and a string of irregular language fell from his mouth, landing just shy of Gris's umbrella. After apologizing for the noise, Oscar joined the team at the table and removed the digital tablet from the tan messenger bag.

"Has your fame finally become too bright a burden? What I mean to say is, do you mind removing your sunglasses?" asked Mr. Ray. Annoyed, Oscar removed the shades, revealing bloodshot eyes. Michaela mouthed the words "*got damn*," and Gris coughed to conceal his shock.

Seats were taken, and an exhausted Oscar was about to open the notes tab when Mr. Ray motioned with his hand. "That won't be necessary. We have but one thing to address today." He swallowed two gulps from his coffee mug and waited for everybody to settle before addressing them. "I assure you, there is a rational reason I requested this mandatory meeting. We have an emergency regarding the progression of our production, and I require your responses. This morning, while I was enjoying a Cary Grant marathon on Turner Classic Movies..."

"Cary Grant? Oh, what phenomenal acting. Which movies?" Gris cheekily asked.

"A sophisticated selection: I caught the last half of *Charade*; then they had *An Affair to Remember* on deck, and *Arsenic and the Old Lace* is scheduled for later tonight."

"What classics. His constant identity-swapping in *Charade* is priceless. And, I especially love Peter Lorre's portrayal of that bizarre doctor in Arsenic," chimed Gris.

"Gentlemen," Oscar interrupted, "do you think we can return to the subject? I didn't crawl out of my room to reminisce about the good ol days of cinema."

Mr. Ray nodded his head, "My apologies. However, this may be an ideal transition. It seems tragedy has already struck our stage as if someone muttered the name of the ill Scottish play."

"What happened, Mr. Ray?" asked Oscar.

"*Mr. Timothy Brooks* has succumbed to some unfortunate malady and is now presenting as a patient at Vera Grace Memorial."

Oscar straightened his slouch, "Wait, Timothy's in the hospital? He was just fine last night."

"I'm not sure about the full report, but it seems his roommate found him in an injured state on the bathroom floor."

Oscar's lungs flattened as he tried not to dissociate from this latest development. "Timothy, why?"

"His roommate claimed Mr. Brooks returned home from meeting someone for an early breakfast and seemed more tense than usual. Then, out of nowhere, Mr. Brooks started acting belligerent, tearing at furniture and making bizarre noises. The roommate eventually left, but when he returned, he discovered the aftermath of the strange behavior. Mr. Brooks was found with jagged wounds around his neck. He was taken to Campus Health, but his injuries are too severe for their skill level."

An image flashed into the production team's collective imagination as if they were receiving transmissions from a universal beacon. There, inside the sterile walls of Vera Grace Memorial hospital, was Timothy. His body stiff, swarmed with plastic dream killers jammed into his veins. Bandages wrapped around his neck, the flesh underneath the gauze meaty and raw, torn with no precision. Like he'd been mangled.

"What could cause such a horrific episode?" asked Gris.

"The staff believes it to be self-inflicted. Potentially a combination of intoxication and an acute response to a traumatic incident. I believe that is why the hospital transfer was necessary," relayed Mr. Ray.

"...Are you sure they properly diagnosed him? How do they know he was intoxicated?" Oscar muttered.

"I'm only relaying what was told to me by the campus Health staff who checked him in. They immediately informed me as his academic advisor." Mr. Ray swirled the cap of his coffee mug around the table, "Why do you ask, Mr. Mercado?"

"*Timothy doesn't drink,*" Oscar said.

The production team cocked their heads. "Mr. Mercado, what are you saying?"

"I'm saying that I know Timothy has not tasted a drop of liquor; he won't even use alcohol-based mouthwash. As an executive member of the campus Bible study group, he practices abstinence of all temptations."

"Then, how'd he get intoxicated?" Michaela asked.

"Apparently, he went to a house party the night before." Mr. Ray downed another gulp.

"Should we investigate?" questioned Gris. "Potentially discover who the denizens behind this domestic dance club were?"

"The Lemurian Order hosted the party," said Oscar.

"*The Lemurian Order?*" Both Gris and Mr. Ray shook their heads in confusion. At the mention of their name, the red pen in Michaela's hand began tapping against the table.

"None of you have heard of them? They're an old fraternity on campus—the best of the best. Trailblazers and wavemakers. Parker's a member," Oscar said.

"Well, these wavemakers are trying to sink our production before we started surfing," Gris said.

"I highly doubt this is Parker's fault. To me, it seems like Timothy got a lil too excited about his role, overestimated his limits, and became another victim of unhealthy frat culture," said Michaela.

"Just because he was there doesn't mean he had to drink anything. *Someone could've drugged him*," defended Oscar.

"Who would want to drug the vice president of the Theater Troupe?" responded Michaela.

"The doctor's report stated Timothy was intoxicated. You can say he doesn't drink, but he might've last night," added Gris.

Panic accumulated in Oscar's throat. "But he didn't!"

Michaela pointed her red pen at him. "How do you know what he did? Unless *you* were with him?"

The tone in her voice was like a mother punishing her child after the school principal called her out of work. Like the guilty child being scolded, Oscar's lip quivered as he spoke. "I wasn't...with him...all night. We did show up together, and I drank his entry fee for him, but we split ways afterward, and then he texted me saying he was leaving early. Said he wasn't in the headspace for all the stimulation. And he was sober, just like he always is." Each pondered the revelation in silence. "I know Timothy, and Timothy is not someone to turn his back on us," Oscar pleaded.

Michaela noticed the minute crack in his foundation, so she struck again. "What if Timothy was interested in joining said fraternity? Maybe he acted out to impress them? Show them that he could, I don't know, hang?"

"What...? No, he's not interested in that. Why would he throw away his future for coked-up math majors fucking their professors?"

"But you said the Lemurian Order isn't like that. They're the cream of the crop. Someone like Timothy might find that appealing."

"Not appealing enough to destroy his dreams. He'd already accepted the lead role and was set to meet with a Broadway talent manager this month. So, I can't understand why he would do something as irrational as get wasted. Oh, that's right, he wouldn't because Timothy is responsible."

"Unless you don't really know Timothy like you think you do. He is an actor, after all; all this camaraderie you speak of could be a front."

"Lies, I know Timothy better than any of you."

Michaela continued to load her artillery, making more accusations regarding Timothy and wearing Oscar's defenses down. Each statement sent him into a deeper burrow, and he tightened his fists. But his clenched fists weren't for her. They were for himself and what he'd done at the house party last night. He had to defend Timothy, though; Oscar owed it to him because there was a chance he was *at fault* for his condition.

Outside, ice and rain continued to tap against the glass. The landscape was doused in a dismal gray fog familiar to the northeastern region of the United States. Despite the soothing sounds of perpetual downpour, it did little to ease the growing tension between Michaela and Oscar. Perched along the sidelines were Mr. Ray and Gris, both waiting for the argument to end naturally. However, they shuddered to consider what conclusion awaited this conflict.

"And now, thanks to your boyfriend's episode, we have to play damage control," said Michaela.

Oscar jumped from his chair, slamming his tablet like a plastic tray on the table. "He's not my boyfriend!"

"Oh, my apologies. Is he your ex or your next? We all know you're a little gay for each other."

"Shut the hell up, you condescending cunt! Don't you dare say anything else about him; I mean it."

"Mr. Mercado! Have you no decency?" Mr. Ray shouted. All present members held their breath as the normally docile man's voice boomed. "I will not tolerate such crude commentary, especially from my assistant. And you, Ms. Patterson, please refrain from assembling any further accusations towards Mr. Brooks' character. Must I remind you that his condition may not be critical, but it is cautionary."

Oscar propped his elbows on the edge and used his fist to cover the frown stitched to his face. "I...I apologize, Michaela. I didn't mean..."

"It's whatever. But don't you dare call me out of my name again. Or I'll *wreck* your shit, you hear me, Oscar?" He nodded and flipped over his tablet to find it shattered.

Finally, Gris regained the floor. "Glad to know it's water under the bridge, but that still doesn't fix our pressing problem: *We are down a lead.*"

"Thankfully, Timothy's condition is only a temporary setback, requiring a temporary solution," said Mr. Ray. "If the doctor's report is correct, our starlet should return on his feet in the next three weeks after some physical and psychiatric therapy."

"Three weeks!? Rehearsal begins Monday," said Michaela. "There's no way we can throw away three weeks while he recovers."

"Precisely why we are meeting today, Ms. Patterson. It's our job to search for an alternative solution."

"A re-audition?" she asked.

After salvaging his pride, Oscar returned to the conversation. "A re-audition would cost us valuable time, and we will require ample amounts to succeed. What if we don't use Baudelaire during rehearsal?"

"Impossible. He's the most important character. Without him, the story is incomplete," responded Michaela.

"Agreed, we need someone to be him. Even if only temporary," said Gris.

"I'd like to suggest we have someone *substitute* for Timothy. Give someone the responsibility of being our rebellious protagonist for the time being?" said Mr. Ray.

"How do we choose our stand-in?" Michaela pressed.

"How about that Parker fellow? He seemed seasoned enough to take on that task," said Gris.

"Naturally, that was my first suggestion, so I rang him. Unfortunately, he declined, stating he's already memorized most of his lines and started adapting character profiles," informed Mr. Ray.

"And, it'd be somewhat risky to make him swap given the unique circumstances regarding his role," Michaela added. "It looks like we need someone with little responsibility regarding their role, and yet, someone with enough talent and time to command the stage." Oscar suggested other actors, but Michaela found reasons why they wouldn't work. Eventually, they exhausted their options, once again feeling helpless and confused.

"Ahem..." the production team directed their attention to Mr. Ray, who had an accomplished smile. "Parker did leave me *a name.* Someone he personally vouched for."

"Someone already on the cast?" Gris inquired.

Like the rest of the team, Michaela sat through the entire audition process, an ordeal that lasted five days. Most had been straightforward, a recitation followed by the cold reading. Some were rather notable for their lack of talent. One such case was a young woman who desired the role of Rochelle. To audition for the songstress, one had to showcase their vocal range, and the woman chose to perform an "operatic re-re-remix" of *Bodak Yellow.* Michaela burst into delusional laughter as the first lyrics crooned through her tenor tone. In her head, at least, for she remained stalwart throughout the entire screeching. Aside from this audition, there were few memorable performances. Only one stuck out now as she perused through her memory bank.

"*Mr. Daniel Elliott Junior,*" said Mr. Ray.

"The sleeper agent," Michaela muttered. Again, hysterical laughter erupted in her head, yet Michaela, physically unfazed, tapped her pen twice.

"What role did we assign him?" asked Gris.

"He is currently serving as our Tavern Master."

"That means he's got time to donate."

"Could be a solid option. What do you think, Michaela?" asked Mr. Ray.

"He's still somewhat of an amateur actor, but I think he could fit the bill. I'd be curious to hear his thoughts about this opportunity."

Oscar's voice broke through the calmness. "Daniel...Daniel...? Wait! You mean Mr. Stagefright? That's who you're talking about? We want to bump him up to one of our *leading actors*? Ha! A foolish move, if you ask me. I mean, I barely remember his audition."

"He did seem well composed and read with vigor; I also appreciated his audacious attitude regarding Michaela's character critiques," said Mr. Ray

"There's something to be said about someone who can adapt to directions that quick," added Gris.

Oscar threw his two cents into the conversation. "He was a bore, and letting him assume the lead role, even for rehearsals, is reckless."

"What other option do we have, Mr. Mercado?"

Oscar's thumb uncurled from his balled fist and pointed at himself, *"Cast me."*

"No can do. This is your first production as a Stage Manager. Your hands will be tied until the day of the show. It may seem slow now, but everything will ramp up very soon."

"Mr. Ray is correct. Without a dedicated manager, our production will truly sink. I'm sure nobody wants that, especially us in this room," said Gris.

"So, our best option is Mr. Stagefright?" the red-eyed Oscar huffed. "I'm sure we all remember that awkward silence during his solo last spring. He only had three lines and couldn't even do those right."

Gris responded with a lighthearted smile, "Only a simple case of the nerves; remember, the spotlights often blind the first time one stands under them. If given the stage again, I'd imagine he'd take it without fear."

"Agreed, he's a diligent student too. Always comes prepared to class. Having him for two semesters, going on three, I've watched Mr. Elliott dramatically develop, and I believe he could handle this responsibility."

"If he does not live up to this said potential and fails at this, then we're *fucked*." Oscar glanced at Michaela. "You'd want your protagonist to be portrayed how it was written, right? What chance does this nobody have of living up to that task we designated for Timothy?"

"Let me correct you. I did not write this role for Timothy. Based on auditions, he was chosen, but it's not his role," Michaela said.

"You realize Daniel's gotta know your story almost as good as you. And even if he knows it, he probably won't be able to say anything on stage without screwing up. Didn't you stop his audition to correct him?"

"I did, and I remember him making the necessary corrections."

"Even though he talked bad about your script?"

"I've concluded that his opinions hold a certain degree of truth. What I learned from that critique is my dialogue is difficult. I didn't realize it before because I've yet to see two skilled actors speak my words out loud. June's audition made it clear. On the other hand, Timothy didn't need correction, but that's because he's trained for theater."

The thudding against the roof intensified as rain bands trailed across the campus. Mr. Ray finished his coffee and popped all ten of his fingers. He nodded at Gris, acknowledging the elder to provide his wisdom. "I'll level with you, Oscar. As far as June goes, we won't know what he's capable of unless we give him a chance. Regarding Timothy, though, as great an actor as he may be, given the circumstances, we might have to consider having him sit out this entire production. Recovering from this malady may be one thing...but returning to the stage after a mental break is another journey."

"Shit, you're *Team Stagefright* too?" Oscar's hands massaged his temples, and the red eyes reminded the staff that the boy was still recovering from the previous evening.

Gris placed his fingerpads together, "I'm not on anybody's team, but the truth is, Oscar, we cannot rely on Timothy at this moment. Three weeks is a long time to miss rehearsal. And even if he were to catch up, could he portray this individual? Possibly, yes, but we have to consider that he might be in a fragile state, and the last thing we need is for him to be triggered for the sake of entertaining others. Whether it's the result of his actions or an accident, Timothy is absent. So, we must keep our options open."

Michaela said nothing as the men debated amongst themselves.

"I refuse to write off Timothy that quick. You don't know what he's capable of doing. When he's back on his feet, I'm telling you that he'll want to get right on stage. And if we don't have a place for him to return, that will trigger him. To be abandoned by those in his time of need...is that truly what we want to do to our most respected actor?" said Oscar.

"I agree with you, Mr. Mercado. It's still too soon to talk of permanently replacing him; however, we must make a radical adjustment to prepare for our present." Mr. Ray added, "I believe if we make this trainee thespian our temporary lead, Mr. Elliott will rise to the opportunistic occasion and guide us on the path to greatness. And then, Timothy, upon a successful recovery, can carry us to the conclusion."

"I like the sound of that," stated Gris.

"Trust me, Timothy will be back," added Oscar.

"It's almost better that June's not an advanced actor; he's got room to evolve. With Timothy set to graduate this year, it may be time for the Theater Troupe to consider who will take over when you all are gone. Letting someone younger get this experience now could help with that transition and preserve this theater's legacy," said Mr. Ray.

"Rightly so. We should cultivate the creativity of not only the present but also the future," commented Gris.

"With that being said, Ms. Patterson, might I charge you with an additional task?" Mr. Ray asked.

Michaela snapped out of her daydream. "Sure, what is it?"

"As we've mentioned, the dialogue is complex and may need to change over time depending on our actor's abilities. You know what you want to say, but perhaps it's not as easily spoken as read. Given the circumstances and your budding revisionary *relationship* with Mr. Elliott, I think working with him will improve your ability to fabricate flowing dialogue. He can also develop his ability to deliver diction to improve his stage presence. So, what I'm asking for is a creative coupling of sorts. Will you collaborate with him?"

"I'll do anything if that's what it takes to bring the production to life," said Michaela.

"By using him as a template, we can build the idealized version of Baudelaire. That way, when Timothy returns, he can adapt to the changes that have already been suggested."

"So you want June to do all the work and then let Timothy get the spotlight? *Is that really fair?*" she asked.

"It may not be necessarily fair, but it is equitable. We provide a newbie with an intensive mentorship program while also fulfilling the needs of our production. It's a win for everyone," said Mr. Ray.

"I'd honestly say this is the best-case scenario for us," stated Gris, who finished the statement by coughing into his elbow.

Mr. Ray placed both hands on the table. "It seems we have devised a fix to our current circumstance. Once Mr. Brooks recovers, Mr. Elliott will resume his role as Tavern Master, but until then, we shall have him become our Baudelaire. Any objections to this decision?" Michaela generated additional responses to these claims but ultimately held her tongue. What chance did she have of convincing them now that they'd reached a solution? Even if that solution didn't solve the "real" Baudelaire problem. A unified hush fell as the production team consented to the new standard. "Then, I say we inform Mr. Elliott of his status. Whew, I am relieved we could address this situation before it spiraled. We are one step closer to bringing this powerful production to life. Now, Mr. Tendleton and I have to prep some things for a special guest arriving tomorrow, so unless you all need anything, I believe we are done."

"Lucky for us, this happened before we kickstarted things," Michaela concluded.

Oscar packed away his tablet, jaw clenched. "How lucky indeed. I'm gonna be a real friend and visit Timothy at Vera Grace to support my people instead of turning my back on them." The door slammed against the steel column as Oscar left, knocking down the umbrella stand again.

"Someone is quite the sourpuss this Saturday," commented Gris.

"Again, I am deeply apologetic for Mr. Mercado's harsh words. I try to prioritize creating a safe space, but I can't always be vigilant. However, I do empathize with poor Mr. Mercado. He and Mr. Brooks are a dashing duo, so I understand his grief. It's horrific how quickly things happened. Just a day ago, Mr. Brooks was on our stage, and now he's..."

"Let us only grant this grief a moment, for we have an entire production to oversee. And it starts tomorrow at the casting meeting," Gris said.

"Where is it at again?" Michaela inquired.

"Albert Thompson's old estate, not too far from campus. The plan is to open doors around six, and I expect to finish the reading by eight, allowing dinner to be served immediately afterward. We will email the meeting details to all cast and crew before this afternoon. Gris, mind giving her the address?" asked Mr. Ray.

Michaela handed Gris her red pen, and he removed a sheet from his spiral notebook. Gris's hand trembled as he wrote the address down; some of his letters deformed from the shakes. After accepting the sheet, she packed away her untitled script and fixed her jacket. The binder disappeared into her bag, and she headed toward the door.

"Thank you again for meeting on such short notice, Ms. Patterson. You stay safe out there, okay?" announced Mr. Ray. "Just like Mr. Brooks and Mr. Elliott, you are an essential element of our production, and we can't afford to lose any more of you."

Walk of Fame

Dark clouds layered the horizon as June completed the daring escape from the dungeon tower disguised as Brittney's dormitory. The borrowed basketball pants were a bright shade of blue, and the moisture turned his sweater charcoal. Meanwhile, the students out at this hour were draped in darkly colored trench coats or weatherproof jackets complimented by umbrellas. Naturally, the stares and whispers began as this wacky-tacky day reject walked shamefully in front of the Washington Student Union.

As he held his face toward the sky, Daniel Elliott Junior experienced a moment. Maybe it was the calming sound of the frosty rain in the distance or the occasional racing of tires along the slick streets that caused his eyes to swell. Whatever sensation triggered his thoughts, it mattered not, for June finally accepted his fate. Soft ground welcomed his knees as he began to cry. Tears winked from swollen eyes, the cold glaciers eroding his cheeks. With each breath, he released another thought or feeling that had once been his foundation, gasping until he had nothing left to expire. And in that negative space appeared an unnamed emotion.

A delirious laugh poured from June's mouth, ringing throughout campus. The laughter had no end or beginning, no limits in its rhythm or volume either. He howled like a turned werebeast, then alternated to cackling like an imp. The laughter pulled him into mild hysteria, and he flung his arms into the sky before pressing his head into the frost-covered earth. Then, as quick as it overcame him, the insanity dispersed, leaving him confused and cold. June sneezed and suddenly became aware of his surroundings. He stumbled and tried to relocate to the bus station to avoid further public embarrassment.

"Well, well, if it isn't the *Sleeper Agent,*" said a familiar voice.

Glancing over his shoulder, he met a hooded stranger. They removed the cover, revealing a face glowing like the sun on this gray day. Michaela. The slope of her nose dipped into a crested ravine containing eyes bubbling like geysers. Bands of mist graced her cheeks even though she had a headwrap covering her mane of locs. A parka buttoned to her lips concealed the rest of her attire, and her black pants made her legs look like two charred logs.

Eyeing his attire, Michaela asked, "Forget to check the weather before the workout?"

"Oh, uh...I'm training. For one of those...decathlons where you run in the mud...and test yourself against nature...No, actually...there was a sale at the bookstore, and I...needed a book for class..." Their eyes met, and he glanced at the sagging basketball pants. "Okay, okay...I'm not an athlete nor a star student. I can't even run a mile without my knees swelling. The truth is, I had a rough night," he admitted.

"And a rough morning, too. It's nearly four o'clock. Was it that bad?"

"Sadly, yes. I needed to be babysat. My friend was taking care of me."

"Ah, and now you're up taking a walk of fame."

"You know me, the awkward star of the MSU show." They both stepped closer to each other, reaching an intimate distance. June cleared his throat, "Hey, uhh...I wanted to apologize for what I said during the audition. I was frustrated and let my emotions get the best of me."

"Don't apologize. The George R. R. Martin comparison was lowkey a compliment. And sometimes, it's good to let passion overthrow logic, as logic is not always the answer."

"I see you, Xavier. Speaking of, I've got your *Foglands* book back at my dorm. You left it at the cafe."

"Looks like I still haven't broken my habit of losing valuables. Thank you for retrieving that."

"I'll bring it to rehearsal. Anyway, I need to get my life together. And looks like you're already doing that, so I won't hold you up..."

"Wait, June. *Can we talk?*" she asked. "I have something I'd like to discuss with you. Walk with me to the library?" June crumbled the goodbye he was drafting and accepted her invitation without hesitation.

Large specks of snow drifted from the gray, formless heavens, and June pulled his arms close to his chest. Winter gusts descended from the dormitory rooftops to the sidewalk and swept through fabric and flesh alike. Peering above, he saw the endless platoons of swollen clouds, all determined to release their entire payload on the campus. However, the frigid precipitation did not touch him. Above his head was Michaela's umbrella.

"The last thing I need is for our rising starlet to get sick," she said as she welcomed him underneath the umbrella. June crept towards the handle as another burst of wind jutted through the brick establishments. Hypothermia gnawed at his neck, yet the faint heat she radiated was enough to warm him until the embers of his own emotions erupted.

As they walked through campus, their conversation drifted with each new pathway. Whatever slight hesitation the two were experiencing dwindled when they turned to the topics of expression and creation. It didn't matter if the two had only known each other for two days or that they'd butted heads on opinions; what proved to be true was their connection. A sort of chemical bond that neither could visibly locate or confirm, yet both were aware of the attraction. The first sparks crackled in the dark as the flame of passion sought a pyre to blaze uninterrupted. Still, fears of rejection prevented any admittance of the romance kindling between them.

After chatting for an extended period, June began to understand the depth of her imagination. This woman brought forth the mystical world of Ingilaef, the one who birthed the being known as Baudelaire and did it all while a student. Unsurprisingly, he'd be whisked away into her world by listening to her. She handled every word like a caregiver watching a nursery of newborns, momentarily pausing on sentences that required more thought to express. Each statement, quote, and phrase wasn't just a placeholder for the silence; Michaela's words were her truth.

And she was sharing them with him.

The entire time they conversed, June's teeth never stopped chittering like cicadas in the summer; however, it wasn't just the cold that affected him. The swirling of his stomach transferred to his throat, causing a sensation similar to acid reflux. Occasionally, he had to resist gagging while talking, and because of that, his responses became more distant. However, while immersed in the discussion,

June also learned something else about Michaela. *She was single.* The anecdote was briefly mentioned when the two discussed how Xavier's poetry highlighted the erotic qualities of nature. At this time, the information was minor, but perhaps one day. For now, he merely stored the data like the other one thousand facts Michaela had dropped on him on their campus tour.

Once underneath the awning of the Keel Rare Book Library, Michaela finally explained to him the results of the production meeting, omitting specific details about Timothy's condition. June nearly threw up after learning he'd have a chance to play Baudelaire in rehearsal. "It wasn't my decision alone. The production team voted," she stammered.

"Then, that means you agreed to it too! So, I do have you to thank." The smile plastered on his face was telling. And then, as if his day hadn't already been full of risk-taking, June hugged her. It was a simple reaction lasting a fleeting second, but it felt like his soul had spent an eternity in that shared embrace. Her fingers curled and gripped his back, fleeing only after touching a wet spot.

She readjusted herself and coughed. "Yes, well, that may be true. Anyway, I need something from you this semester."

"Of course, I'll give you anything. What do you need?" June asked.

"*I need you.*"

"What for?"

"I'm a realist, meaning I believe in approaching life head-on rather than dealing with recreated perceptions and falsified values. I also say that I am worried."

"Worried about what?"

"If we made the right choice about Baudelaire," she admitted.

"I understand I'm just a fill-in, but I will do my best until Timothy..."

"That's the thing: *Timothy is not my Baudelaire.* Sure, he has a flawless reputation, is objectively handsome, and is the supposed best actor on this campus. But..." Michaela looked at the snow fluttering in the gust. "He's missing something. And that is the one thing required for this role."

"He's not willing *to lose himself*," June stated.

"YES!" Michaela cheered. "You remembered."

"Like I'd forget the grilling you gave me at the audition."

"Only because we were dealing with my art, and I don't play when it comes to that."

"Which is why you're questioning the Timothy decision? Because it involves your art?"

"Exactly. When he auditioned, he nailed all the parts we needed, but I couldn't see him. I couldn't see Baudelaire in his image. But none of that matters now."

"Why not?"

"Because it is not my decision alone. I'm realizing how challenging it is to work with a team because every member has their own opinion and responsibility. Mr. Ray and Oscar are dead set on Timothy staying Baudelaire; maybe Gris could be swayed. But I'm not entirely sure where his allegiances lie."

June tapped his chin, "Have you shared your thoughts with them?"

"It's hard to speak up when everybody else has more expertise than you, and I still don't know what to do. Not to mention, I'm the only woman in the room; I'm not sure how much they'd be willing to listen to my ideas. I'm at a confusing crossroads," Michaela said.

"Looks like Mr. Ray's tongue-twisting tirades are finally affecting you too. And I can't speak about being a woman, but I believe they will listen to you. You know why? *You're the writer.*" June watched his words slip through the back door of her imagination, causing her to halt all movement and stare at him. "I mean, you're the creator of the realm we are about to call reality for the rest of the semester, the one giving all of us roles, including the team. If anything, you should have the first and last word about the production."

"Aren't we full of wisdom," she said, causing June to blush. "You know, I believe we butted heads yesterday because *we are who we are.*"

"Who are we?"

"Authentic, wildly individualistic, and innovative. Innately brave yet a constant victim of circumstantial cowardice. Passionate and equally unstable due to the immeasurable pillars of our personality."

"You make us sound like Baudelaire, Michaela."

"*Because, like Baudelaire, we are artists.* And artists are complex. Always creating in a state of flux," she smiled.

"Possibility comes from that lack of stability. And you never know what you'll discover when you start desiring."

"Another line by Xavier. Who are you exactly, Mr. Elliott?"

"Shouldn't it be easy to tell?" His hand broke into the air, nearly severing all droplets that fell in its path. The palm opened toward the concealed sun, and he clamped his fingers down. Bringing the closed fist to his chest, June looked at Michaela with eyes reinforced with something more than ambition and anxiety.

"I am the myth that men whisper about with envy—the prophet of passion born with no purpose, the wanderer who would walk the edge of existence. I am Baudelaire! Well...at least for the next few weeks."

"No, June. I think you should be him. Only you."

"You do? What makes you think that?"

"Right now, I just decided. Actually, I decided when I saw you break down outside the student union."

"You saw that?" He meekly replied.

"Indeed, what a sight to behold. That ability to crumble into nothing and then have the courage to rise in the face of sorrow—that's what makes Baudelaire a legend. And you can become him if you trust me."

"Michaela, do you know what you're saying?" June asked.

"Yes. *I can only see Baudelaire in you.* It won't be easy, and there will be times when stress overtakes my sanity, but I believe the solution to my anxiety is you. I will fight to make that happen...if you want it to happen."

"I do. I absolutely do."

"Then, *fight with me.* Let's work together if this is something we both want."

"You shall have my sword," said June, mimicking a knightly bow.

"That's what I want to hear. We will do it, you and me. We'll bring him to life together because he deserves to live." Michaela nodded, "Tomorrow, at the production meeting, I'll try to plant the seed with the team. Things are still tense because of the sudden role change, but I think they'll at least offer an ear to my suggestion. To ensure we make a good impression, you must arrive on time. And you need to impress them in the reading. You need to read like the lead! So practice, practice, practice. Don't stop rehearsing until it's time for the reading. The others all keep talking about your potential, but if you want the role, it's time for you to show them what's *possible.*"

"I'll be ready," he said, allowing their eyes to meet again before officially departing for the afternoon.

"I know you will." She extended her hand, and he accepted. The shake ended prematurely, but the way fingers traced across palms warranted a deeper investigation. Yet neither could follow through right now.

Chimes echoed from the Clock Tower as June approached the bus station near the library's entrance. Sheets of collecting snow blanketed the foundations around campus, the entire establishment taking on an ephemeral glow like an arctic castle. Unknown to Michaela then, the glacier that imprisoned his emotions finally suffered a crack. How often he wished to have someone who could engage his mind and not simply act like a sponge. No, he wanted feedback, responses, and dialogue. He wanted connection. And no matter how fantastical or scattered they may have been, Michaela kept up with his every idea.

"Sleeper Agent, one last thing!" she shouted from the library entrance. "Make sure to thank Parker!"

The elation June experienced since the start of their walk dissipated at the mention of this name. "Parker? What for?"

"He *personally recommended* you to replace Timothy. Looks like he sees something in you, too." Michaela waved one last time and then entered the library for a day of revision.

The bus arrived, and June sat beside the window, staring but not registering the wintry sights. No, his mind revolved around a singular thought that would continue to erode his foundations for the duration of the ride. *Join us, and you can become Baudelaire.* That was all nonsense, right? There's no way...and yet, the role had come to him, in a way. Despite all his grandiose speeches, Parker fulfilled his end of the bargain. But how did Parker get the university's most talented actor to give June a chance? Money? Social capital? A recommendation letter? Or had something happened to Timothy?

Once inside Derringer dormitory, the violent bubbling in his stomach forced June to stop at the hallway bathroom. The door locked, and he went straight to the toilet, allowing the gags he'd resisted to be released. The throat tightness subsided after vomiting, but now he could feel the burning behind his breastplate. He tore off the wet sweater and oversized athletic pants, stripping to his boxers. Sweat collected on his face, and he writhed at the knees of the porcelain deity as he flushed the remaining contents of his stomach. He came up for air every few seconds, dabbing sweat from his forehead, but the flashing lights dazed him; this was no ordinary hangover. With only actual organs left to expel, June's body couldn't sustain its maintenance. His heart rate slowed, and his skin clammed before his joints lost all tension. The boy collapsed on the floor, his head barely missing the toilet rim.

Lying naked on the cold tiles, he heard that distant whine that welcomed him into the shadow realm within his mind. Again, that sound sparked something behind his closed eyes. Then came the attempted severing of his spirit and vessel, or at least that's what it felt like. Fingers clawed at the skin surrounding his neck, tearing the tissue that connected his consciousness to this carbon construct. He feared he'd open his eyes to find his bloody body on the floor and his point of view miles above, somewhere in the endless void.

The mental strain from this particular pain did more than overload thoughts; it demolished all previous foundations of logic and understanding, leaving June without words or even the notion of awareness. Shadows crept from the peripherals to the center of his point of view, creating a violent vignette. And then, the illumination born from his slumbering mind imploded. As the interior world welcomed darkness again, a harrowing fear flooded June's mind: *He was indebted to the Lemurian Order.*

ACT III

Legacy of the Lemurian Order

Noah Casca shifted in the antique chair, the age of the wood revealing itself with each squeak, but as always, he never truly found comfort in this position. Unlike the rest of the members, his chair had been reupholstered twice, resembling an amalgamation of materials rather than the uniform. Although a minor detail, whenever they gathered in the Basilisk Room, and he had to take this seat, it nevertheless made him feel like an outcast amongst the Lemurian Order.

Initially serving as the cathedral's papal chambers and then a senior researcher boardroom for the laboratory, the Basilisk Room now operated as the meeting hall for the Lemurian Order. A regal banner flanked each of the eight chairs occupied by the eight members. Above the table hung a glass chandelier hoisted on a metal chain with over eighty prismatic bulbs hanging from four branches. Other notable decorations included five Romantic-style portraits of past members whose accolades earned eternal glory. Their eyes bore a similar purple hue despite no relation between them.

As Noah waited for his fellow fraternity members to settle, he locked eyes with his brother, who stood between the octagonal table and the crackling fireplace. Flames warped his brother's shadow into a larger-than-life figure that could swallow those afraid of the dark. However, Fitz offered a reassuring smile to his sibling, and for a moment, Noah felt seen. But then, he extended the same smile to Kimi, Parker, Delilah, Mitch, and the others; what was once his special gesture became a common tool to silence the group.

A unified hush fell over the Basilisk Room as Fitz greeted them with a firm salute. "As *Augur* of the Lemurian Order, I welcome you all once again to the table and thank you for gathering for today's Conclave. Now that we are all present let us begin. We have but two main objectives on our agenda, and I'd like to begin by offering the floor to Kimi Wilkshire."

Noah scratched at his palms as the annoying goth rose and bowed at Fitz. Then, Kimi pulled forth a strange cylinder from a rectangular case borrowed from the Hamlin Engineering Workshop. She rotated the gear attached to the object in her hand and ignited sparks. The odd device continued to sputter embers until luminous blue flames burst forth, surprising all. A frigid chill overcame Basilisk Room, contrasting with the fireplace's warmth.

"I have been working on a new invention, a torch near identical to the ones used by our predecessors."

"Why do we need new gear?" asked Mitch.

"Unfortunately, the old torches have all ceased to function due to natural weathering. So, with Augur's permission, I crafted a prototype."

"And why a torch, for that matter? Seems like we've got enough lights around the house, yo," said Noah.

"Because this is no normal flame, is it, Kimi? Did you...you actually created it?" she said.

"Indeed, it is similar to the one incorporated in the rituals."

Fitz said, "I'm sure those who aided in last year's initiation process remember when the torches diminished halfway during the Leo Trial." Noah watched the senior members nod in unison. He'd been there too but was an initiate at the time, so he had little understanding of the ritual. When the lights went out during his Trial, he merely thought it was part of the process. "With that in mind, I tasked Kimi with this duty as a means of providing us with extra security during the Trials."

Delilah's face radiated as fire wisps swam in the dim room. "*An endothermic flame*," she said.

"Back up, yo. Endothermic? That's scientifically impossible. Fire is a result of combustion, but you mean to tell me this...absorbs heat?"

Kimi nodded. "Even after running tests, I cannot identify the initial source, but I suspect a unique reaction occurs between the serum's active chemical components and nitrate, the principal ingredient in the wick of the old torches."

"I find it hard to believe a biofuel could do this," said Noah.

"And yet, when used in your concoctions, you don't question this biofuel's mental-enhancing properties. Why is it so hard to believe it can also do this?"

Stumped, Noah retreated into his seat. Mitch substituted for him in the conversation. "Kimi, you said you ran some initial tests. How does this fare in comparison to the old-school lanterns? I mean, the flame is the same color from what I remember, but this shape is new. Is it as effective?"

"First, I tried repairing an older model, but that failed. So, I salvaged what I could and made this..." Kimi raised the torch above her head. "What our predecessors left behind served as a great reference point, but most of their schematics are nonsense now, for we exist in the modern world, and the technology of that time is obsolete. I did make a few alterations to the base engineering, adding flint pistons to improve the ignitor and bolstering the torch range with an adjustable sphincter. As far as its effectiveness? That remains to be seen."

"I appreciate your efforts, Kimi. Although we may not have been able to preserve the original relics, your invention will ensure the next generation has illumination along their path," said Fitz.

"Again, it has not been fully tested, which worries me because it is almost time for *the Hierophant* to awaken."

The patchwork chair squealed as Noah squirmed in his seat. "Hell did you just say, Kimi? Yo, you're telling me it's awakening?" questioned Noah.

"That's correct," responded Fitz.

Noah glanced around the table and wondered who else was left in the dark about this. "Why am I just now finding out about this? When were you going to tell us?"

"I am informing you now because it is relevant to now."

"And yet, Kimi acts like she's known for weeks."

"I told Kimi because I needed her to work on the prototype."

"But you didn't think to tell the one person who's been in the same space with the fucking thing? I was just down there yesterday. The hell, yo?"

"I didn't want to alarm you."

"Great fucking job, Fitz."

"Listen, I understand your frustration, brother, but that is why we are taking measures to protect ourselves."

"Maybe I'm the only one thinking this, maybe because I'm the only one who's been to the Den in a minute, but how the hell do we expect a little blue flame to keep that *fucking mongrel* contained, yo?"

"Language, brother. This is our guardian you are addressing," Fitz said from the head of the table."

"It's a monster about to wake up with a real attitude problem. Ha, you're nuts if you think I'm going back down there."

"You would shirk away from your duty, then?" Parker inquired.

"If it meant living for another day, fuck yeah. *I'd ditch you all* before fucking with that thing."

"Where is your loyalty, Noah? You have an essential role to fulfill. You are *the Alchemist,*" Parker said.

"Easy for you to say, *Paladin.* All you gotta worry about is throwing little house parties and flirting with new people. What the fuck do you know of duty? Of serving the Lemurian Order?"

"I assure you I execute my duties without any hesitation. Can you say the same?"

"Bro, I'm the fucking plug. None of this superhuman shit happens without my product."

"And yet, you are useless without a steady supply," said Parker. He continued, addressing the table this time. "Have we not all communed with the Hierophant? Did it not choose to bless us? So, I imagine it will react with contempt as its liaisons."

"Aye, boy genius, you ever seen the Hierophant? Any of you?" Noah grimly asked. Only one head nodded, Andrew, the former Alchemist.

"Your point, Noah?" Parker asked.

"My point is don't speak on things you're ignorant of. You can go in the Den acting all buddy-buddy; see how long you last."

The cryptic statement raised hairs, and azure flames shimmered as freezing rain clapped against the cathedral roof. Noah's spine sunk further into his seat, creaking with each anxious twitch. Fitz and Mitch locked eyes, aware that Noah was correct. Yet fear was the last thing they needed at this moment.

"Brother, we might not know our guardian as you do, but we will be prepared for its awakening, thanks to Kimi."

"That's where you're wrong, Fitzroy. I know what that imprisoned bitch can do. I know all too well because I've handled my shit. Whenever my services were requested, I entered that Den extracted the serum without question and cooked our concoctions. And, I get that it is still asleep, but have any of you given any serious thought as to what will happen if it awakens and finds itself as a prisoner and not a guardian?" Noah opened his arms to the rest of the members. "We're gonna go in there with our glow sticks and get fucking offed. So, until we have some legit safety precautions, I'm not fucking with the Den anymore. I'm sorry, that's just how it is."

"Which is why you will not go *alone*," Fitz said. "You make a valid point, and I'd like to institute that rule. As long as the Hierophant is awakened, none shall enter the Den alone. To begin, this evening, Parker and I will accompany you."

"We will?" asked Parker.

Fitz gestured towards the torch. "This might be an ideal time to conduct the necessary field-testing Kimi needs. I'd also like to get a layout of the lower foundation and see how we can potentially upgrade things. These torches should be installed, preferably in the entire corridor, but I'd focus on the Oracle Chamber and Den for now. Kimi, shall we work on the schematics later?" She grinned, elated at combining her favorite things: Fitz and engineering. With that, she doused the endothermic torch, again welcoming warmth to the Basilisk Room.

"Why's he coming, though?" Noah spoke about Parker as if talking to his brother privately rather than at an open table discussion.

Fitz addressed him, "It's vital we three have a mutual relationship with *our guardian*. You were right when you said we do not understand what it is, and maybe we never will. But we don't need to understand it. We need enough information to evaluate the situation. I dare not march our new recruits into the devil's den if I cannot guarantee their safety. Nor would I want *you* to do that." The gesture of brotherly concern softened Noah's eyes, but he remained defensive. "Then it is settled; we three shall travel to the Den, and Noah will gather enough serum to concoct a batch of Nihilixer that should last awhile—maybe even the school year," announced Fitz. "That way, you won't have to worry about entering the Den once it awakens. Is that possible, Andrew?"

Noah looked across the table and saw Andrew Winter playing with a vape in his hand. Introverted and often more observant than vocal, Andrew joined at the same time as Fitz, Mitch, and Delilah. Through his guidance as Alchemist, the Lemurian Order welcomed Noah, Parker, and Kimi into their ranks the previous spring.

"Might not be as fresh a sample toward the end of the semester, but it'll have the same qualities. Will probably be enough for the recruitment. Parker, how are the initiates holding up after their initial dose?" asked Andrew.

"All have taken to the administration well. I personally checked on them today, and each passed the Capricorn Trial," Parker reassured.

"And what of our *late addition?*" Fitz interjected.

"Late addition...?" Andrew questioned, speaking on behalf of the confused members. The fireplace crackled in the unexpected silence.

"I will now defer to Parker, who will introduce our second order of business for the Conclave. Care to explain, Paladin?" Fitz asked.

Parker rose, "I suppose I can speak on it now. This year, we are inviting an additional recruit to undertake the trials."

Calvin, the eldest member and appointed secretary, shook his head. "No...no. See, that's too far. We can't go around changing everything. We've already broken tradition by hosting a party in our home and using questionable recruiting methods. This is not how one acts as a Paladin."

Fitz raised his hand. "Calvin, you are correct. The Lemurian Order has a tradition, and this is part of it."

"I've been in this fraternity longer than any of you, and not once have I heard about this," Calvin commented.

"Like the information about the Hierophant's awakening, this update was conveyed to me by *a higher power*. I have been assured that all will be realized in due time," Fitz stated. "For now, it is imperative that we uphold the request."

"Does that mean we have to repeat the Capricorn Trial?" asked Andrew.

"It does," said Parker. "Everything should be ready. And this shouldn't take as long because it's just one person versus four."

Mitch stopped rolling his lacrosse ball, "Okay, so who is this fifth recruit then? And have they already been informed?"

Parker lifted his phone to the crowd. A profile photo of a young black man with a goofy smile appeared on his display. "His name is *Daniel Elliott Junior.* He also goes by June."

"Ah, buddy, who I had to give a ride to last night. He's something different, alright," responded Mitch.

"Ain't he, though? He was half-passed out on Parker's floor last night. Not necessarily what I'd consider Order material, but seems he's highly compatible with the Hierophant's song and serum," stated Delilah.

"Ayo, that's the little bitch who fucked up my kicks. Fuck do we want him for, yo?" Noah asked.

"Because he has the potential to be one of us," said Parker.

"He's wack as hell if you ask me."

"You hating because his merit made him a candidate? Or because he dated your new girl?" teased Mitch.

Noah sucked in his teeth, feeling the latent heat from that burn. "I don't give a shit about that. And stop putting my business in the streets."

"And they say I'm the sensitive one," Parker whispered to Delilah.

"The fuck did you say, pussy? You callin me a bitch?" Noah shouted.

"Not in the slightest; I refrain from using such vulgar language like yourself." Further infuriated, Noah slammed the table and kicked his chair back. The look in the disrespected boy's eye revealed he meant to pummel someone's face into a pulp.

Fitz slapped his silver ring on the table. "Have a seat, Noah! N*ow!*" Like a punished pup, Noah shuffled back to his post. Once seated, the tension in the room settled. "Quit bickering like children, please. I need to wrap this up. I've got an important meeting with the Morrison Moment in an hour, and I want to have time to review plans before tonight's trial."

"Shall I summarize our meeting, *Augur?*" Calvin, the graduate student and eldest member of the Order, finally broke his silence. Fitz agreed, and Calvin scrolled through his tablet, reaching the beginning of the minutes. "The Hierophant is expected to awaken, but we don't know when. This torch Kimi designed is supposed to suppress the Hierophant, but the prototype can't be proven effective until tested, and testing cannot begin until it awakens. We've also added a new initiate to the recruitment process, even though we only have four spots. In light of this, tonight, we will repeat the Capricorn Trial using a fresh batch of Nihilixer that the Alchemist will create. But to create it, he will have to enter the Den and hope the Hierophant isn't already awakened. If so, then we can begin testing. Is that correct?"

"That's it," said Fitz.

"That's a lot of unknown shit," Delilah commented.

"Indeed it is; regardless, I will relay things to you all if I learn anything more. However, if there are no final remarks, I motion that we adjourn this meeting."

"Just one," Noah raised his hand. "What exactly is the purpose of five recruits if there are only four spots, yo? Lemurian Order's always been eight members."

Burning flame and encroaching frost echoed in the Basilisk Room as voices came to a halt. Noah's chair wearily creaked as he waited for an answer.

"As I said, all will be revealed in due time," Fitz confidently responded. They all believed him, but that's because they didn't know Fitz. They hadn't grown up with him to learn his tricks. This was a lie, and what terrified Noah the most was even Fitz didn't have the answer. Diverting attention, Fitz rose from his chair. "Now, I motion to adjourn this Conclave."

"Seconded," Mitch said.

"It has been moved and properly seconded. We shall reconvene tonight to commence the Capricorn Trial. Do we all know our roles?" Everybody nodded, including Noah. The shadows of the eight present members expanded across the banners. Fitz curled his bicep across his chest, his fist pressed against his heart. "Absolute is the truth!"

The members of the Lemurian Order rose, adopted the same pose, and recited in unison! *The truth is absolute!*"

Pressing Matters

Around sunset, Lance awoke with a yellowish drool on his pillow. He groaned as he rose, calling out to his roommate. But his calling was met with silence. Lance climbed up June's bunk to find the sheets folded and the bed empty. "Shitttttttt! I can't believe I ditched him like that! Ugh! Why do you do this to me," he shouted at his dick.

A familiar vow renouncing all sin was made as Lance started to get his life together, beginning with checking his phone. No messages. He called June twice and, each time, got sent to voicemail. A hot shower followed, which included a fifteen-minute rant about his grievances. Munching on a breakfast bar and two meat sticks, Lance threw on his sweatpants and grabbed his satchel.

After the fourth failed attempt to communicate with June, Lance made another phone call. The name that appeared on his L.E.D. screen was Work Bae. "Are you at the MM? Cool, I'm on the way. Bringing some honey-ginseng-cinnamon tea."

Lance shuffled out of the elevator with shades covering his eyes, passing by a squirming student desperately knocking at the hallway bathroom. Better luck next time, he thought. Headphones went over his ears, and the hood of his jacket covered the young man's head. Black boots left the dormitory as the photographer jogged to the bus station.

Lance scrolled through his saved playlists, and soon, the downpour was drowned out by the orchestral rendition of *Adagio in G Minor*. This song was chosen for its length and because it was one of his favorite mood-setting songs. Growing up, his father played the classical station at his security job, imprinting an appreciation for symphonies on Lance. Now, he listened to these tracks whenever he needed to accomplish a task that required unwavering focus.

The bus arrived, and he squeezed his way through the packed vehicle. Along the ride, he glanced at the campus structures again. It never ceased to amaze him how old some establishments were, like the Clock Tower and the Washington Student Union. Foundations that had existed since the early days of the commune, when the land was filled with curses and inexplicable dangers. Something phenomenal once existed here, and, given his sensitivity to the forbidden, Lance agreed that phenomenon was still present.

The bus abruptly stopped in the middle of the road to allow a scooter passage, causing Lance to hit his head on the window. With three more stops, he raised the volume on his headphones and prepared to brave the cold.

As he exited the public transit system and dashed into the Brachman Cafe, Lance held a firm grip on his satchel. Stepping inside, he was embraced by the scent of roasting coffee beans, warm laughter, and soft lighting. Due to the weather, the cafe was livelier than usual, and all the staff worked like a well-oiled machine despite dealing with a surge of customers.

Lance waited in line behind a group of five friends carrying yoga mats. Reaching into his pocket, he lowered the volume on his device, allowing his ears to scan the room. Surely, there was something worth hearing, any gossip or hearsay. The patient sleuth discovered his answer when the group of yogis reached the cashier. While they ordered, one of them mentioned the bar crawl.

"Yeah, that party was dope, not gon lie! The student body president's brother personally escorted us around the Lion's Den. He also hooked us up with a little...you know...special K," the speaker sniffed loudly. "Then they even offered us a ride back when it was time to go."

"And let's not forget that elixir. I'm telling you, best PJ I've had. Couldn't even taste a drop of liq, but I sure felt like I was four shots in. Someone said it was top-shelf vodka created by some alumni."

"Maybe next time I won't have to do a wardrobe change in the middle of a party."

"Then again, that might be dope. A different fit every hour? You'd be the talk of the party."

"I already am after that shit went down at the bathroom."

"Girl, don't get me started. I still can't believe that shit happened! That bitch really threw her drink at us. Fucked up my whole fit." At the mention of this, Lance tugged at the hood, concealing his face. The chances of her recognizing him were slim, but still, the last thing his migraine needed was an altercation in the cafe. "Real talk: I was this close to shooting the hands with ol girl, but I'm not trying to be on *their* bad side."

"That's why I pulled your ass outta there. Ain't worth the time, and I want to go to the next party they host. Maybe I'll run into that boy I hit with the frisbee."

"Like you need any more simps in your inbox. Still, if I see that girl's ass around…"

"You ain't doing shit, Tiff. We are at a private institute. Your parents pay half a mortgage so you could go here. Quit acting hard and grab your oat milk latte." The group laughed and collected their beverages and baked goods before migrating to a collection of painted benches.

For a moment, Lance considered apologizing for the incident he was partially responsible for but decided against it when the cashier called him to the register. He removed his headphones and presented a smile.

"A pleasure to see you alive and well, Lance." Timia greeted him with her signature peace sign. Lance learned that all successful journalists had an ear to the streets. His ear happened to work behind the counter of the campus's only coffee shop.

"Hey you, thanks for the tip about the party. Had a hell of a time," he said.

"I already know you got up to something. Last time I saw you, you were on your dungeon-crawling shit. Learn anything good?"

"You know it, and you'll just have to wait until I release my report."

She smiled, "All I ask is for a sentence or two on the acknowledgment page. Now, what'll it be?" Lance placed the order, and Timia snickered. "Anjali still got you running errands for her?"

"This is more of a bargaining chip than an errand."

"Well, I wish you luck, Lance. And hey, although I might be your informant, I'm also down to, you know, be the subject of one of your exposés."

"Ha, I might have too many words to share about you."

"All the more reason to capture me on camera. A thousand words and all that, right?" Grinning, Timia set the two steaming cups and donuts on the side of the counter. "See you around, babe."

Securing the merchandise, Lance stepped out into the overcast day again. The rain stopped, and sunlight winked through the clouds. Instead of catching the bus, he chose to walk to the MM. On his stroll, he sipped his tea and recounted the details from eavesdropping on the chat. "Elixir, huh?" He thought about the taste but couldn't recall it, for too many sensations had been experienced the previous night. "Wonder what they're putting in the PJ to make it so good? And why is the Lemurian Order so accommodating to the students all of a sudden? What if the party wasn't about celebrating the campus but rather upholding their reputation? But why do they care what the campus thinks about them now? Unless they are recruiting. No...it's gotta be more than that. What would the most prolific organization on campus want with us? What do any cults want? More membership, sure, but what they really want is *control*."

Lance swiped his identification badge across the keypad and entered the Morrison Moment, doing his best not to spill the hot cups. Sylvester, a slick-haired Dominican-American custodian who ended every night with two fingers worth of dark rum, was vacuuming the gray carpets. When he arrived, Lance cut into a hallway leading to the Senior Editor's office instead of stopping at his desk. He was about to tap on the door when he saw three silhouettes in the windowpane.

One of them was Anjali; the other resembled George, but that couldn't be right because he never came to the office on the weekends. The third figure stood at an angle that made it difficult to interpret their form, but Lance noted they were noticeably taller than Anjali. Words were exchanged civilly, at least from what Lance deduced while pressing close to the door. Then, he knocked.

The voices quieted, and someone muttered something to Anjali. She responded with a loud "Yes," and Lance announced himself. Instead of allowing him entry and giving him a glimpse of these strangers, she instructed him to hold onto the tea until the meeting was done. Disappointed, he agreed and returned to the desk. Before he reached his workstation, Lance detoured farther down the hallway, ending his wandering at a dead end with a weathered door. He looked at the plaque fastened to the door.

ARCHIVES.

Following in the footsteps of fellow conspiracy theorists, Lance began his search for answers in the past. Although conspiracy theorists were assumed to be overly skeptical, he understood these men and women spent hours researching documents and developing their talking points. If he wished to earn Senior Editor, win Anjali's heart, and beat George, he needed a compelling editorial to capture the reader's attention. No, he needed to give them something more valuable; he needed to provide them with *a world-shattering truth*.

Large steel file cabinets guarded the perimeter, and in the middle of the Archives was a flat bench covered with scattered file folders. The air smelled older than the classical song playing in his headphones. Still, the claustrophobia was comforting; with such bland and dated decorations, one could easily remain focused on one's work in a place like this.

Lance set his satchel on the chair and inspected the modem stationed on the sole desk in the Archives. In

2003, when MSU switched to a digital leadership campus, the Journalism and Mass Media Department received seven new computers. One of the terminals was installed in the Archives, but any records prior to installation had to be manually transcribed. None of the MM staff had spear-headed such a task at this time, leaving the Archives an untouched grave of records.

If Lance wanted to tackle the case seriously, he under-stood a documentation system needed to be created. The concept of organization had been drilled into him since boyhood, which often fueled his resistance. Too much order made things boring, and the last thing Lance wanted to be was boring. Yet, he also understood that recordkeeping was the first step to an exciting life of investigative journalism.

He booted up the old computer, which sprung to life with a wheezing yawn. The faint buzzing of the fan tick-led the inside of his skull, and he raised the volume on his headphones. Once it loaded, he opened a spreadsheet document, and the notifications were cleared. Columns and rows were labeled according to the article's title, date, and synopsis.

With the document ready to receive information, Lance inspected the first folder on the chrome desk. His fingers tiptoed along the tabs of the manila folders labeled by their publication month until they abruptly stopped at June. Before he started, Lance sent another text message to June. Still no response, but this obstruction was probably caused by the lack of service in the Archives.

As he transferred the necessary details to the spread-sheet, Lance fought the urge to read the articles in detail. There simply wasn't enough time to invest in combing through every sentence during this preliminary investigation. Eventually, when he had more time later this semester, he could thoroughly excavate the historical records, but first, he had to identify sites that contained hidden gems. Any article directly mentioning the Lemurian Order was recorded in the database.

By the time he reached the last ten seconds of his classical playlist, Lance had already researched back to March 1999. Deeply engrossed in the song, he was about to open the April folder when he felt a soft tap against his back. He turned to find Anjali wearing a white top and a red skirt with black leggings.

"Sheesh, it's freezing in here. Can I have your jacket?" Lance removed his jacket from the back of the chair and rested it on her shoulders. Anjali slipped her hands through the sleeves and patted her arms. The tea had cooled, but she sipped from the cup nonetheless. "Okay, why the hell are you in the Archives, Lance?"

"Um...I'm just going through some old articles because I think that's where the proof will be."

Anjali rolled her eyes. "Proof of what? I don't see how this will help with your application."

"I've given it some thought, and I've got an idea that will make George's fraternity editorial look like a greeting card compared to an *NYT* op-ed. I need your help, though."

He rose from his seat and crept to the Archives' entrance. The old ventilation of the computer monitor cranked as Lance triple-checked the door lock like a fugitive. Once he confirmed their isolation, he reached for Anjali's hands and pulled her close.

"I want to do my report on the Lemurian Order."

"Excuse me, what?" she asked.

"You heard me."

"I did, but I don't understand. Why them?"

"Because they are the one-of-a-kind story you want. I believe they have done twisted shit, don't you? I mean, they scream 'crazy college cult' to me."

"Crazy college cult? The only thing crazy is your imagination. An interview with the brothers of Beta Mu Phi is a tangible goal we can realize this semester. Investigating an elite fraternity that has been around since the first days of MSU may take years, decades even. We could spend our whole lives chasing it, only to find out that there was nothing. No secrets, no conspiracies, nothing."

"Or maybe we discover a gateway to Hell underneath their home?"

Anjali's hands popped out of the jacket sleeves. "Lance, why do you make this so difficult when it could be so easy? Seriously, do you want to be Senior Editor or not?"

"I do!" Lance cried.

"Then how can you sit here and do *this* instead of working on a legit assignment? I'm trying to help you out here."

"Anjali, last night, you said we could choose our subject, and I chose them. And I wouldn't take on this task if I didn't think I couldn't do it."

"And how are you going to do that?"

"I plan on combining documentation from the past with information from the present. I've already started filling out a spreadsheet to organize the MM's previous articles. Once I get them in order, I'll sift through them and look for any connecting points."

"You started archiving all of this?"

Judging by her response, Lance could tell that she was impressed. But it wasn't enough to convince her yet. "As far as the present, I'll show you how serious I am."

He removed his cell phone from the jacket and opened his gallery. He held up the device and allowed her to scroll through the most recent photographs.

"I took these last night at the Lion's Den. You know, where the Lemurian Order lives. Did you know their basement is a ritual site? Cells and creepy symbols and altars, too."

"Lance."

"Here's another fun fact: have you heard the grim folktale surrounding the cathedral they call home, how people would suffer mass hysteria? Or the strange disappearance of the first Black student at MSU? I'm just saying, weird phenomena have been happening on this land for *a long time.* My favorite podcast theorized that these incidents are the result of an otherworldly conduit located somewhere near us."

"Lance..."

"And I'm not saying demon portal, but I'm also not saying demon portal."

"Enough, Lance!" shouted Anjali. "The MM is not here to give your wild conspiracies a platform. I'm looking for media, for connection, for a legit story. If you can't give me that, then maybe Senior Editor isn't for you."

"Wait! If this doesn't convince you, I'll give up and go with something simpler, like MSU's underground drug circuit." He reached under the desk and set his bag on the table. "I happened to procure this while at their party last night. Don't ask me how I got it; just know I got it."

"You *stole* from the supposed crazy college cult? What the hell, Lance?"

"I wouldn't call it thievery; it's more like an extended rental policy. I'll return it once I'm done with my investigative report—I really will. But right now, it's evidence of something strange at work."

The pouch opened, and he retrieved three objects wrapped in cloth. The first contained a small, worn spiral notebook. Lance opened the notebook. "I haven't had time to decipher this, but it seems important. I believe this is a recipe for something called the *Nihilixer Decoction*," he stated.

"A recipe for what?" Anjali snatched the notebook from Lance's hands and scanned the page. "What are they making, an acid bath? Phenol. Sulfuric Acid. Acetate. Magnesium. Diluted sanguine. This sounds like a bizarre science experiment."

"I can't make it out everything, but there's something called...I think it says *Hero*...something...*blessing* or something like that?"

"A Hero's blessing? Never seen that in the chemistry lab."

"Maybe it means the mixture needs to be blessed? Or a Hero's dose?" commented Lance.

"What's that?"

"When someone takes a lot of psychedelics at once and has an ego-death experience, we call it a hero's dose. Wonder if it could be Ophelia? They are local to this region."

"But why would anybody want to combine mushrooms and those chemicals? No way they're drinking it."

"I think they're getting it delivered straight to the veins."

"What do you mean?"

Lance reached back into the satchel, lifting the second stolen item: a golden syringe containing a vial filled with a swirling indigo liquid. At the sight of the needle, Anjali screeched like a derailed train. "NO! Put it up! Put it up! Please, please, please!"

Reacting with haste, Lance tried to stuff it away but pricked his palm. Anjali felt her eyes flutter but fought off the fainting. As she calmed herself, alternating between deep breaths and sips of the tea, Lance kept glancing at the liquid swirling in the vial. It looked unlike any previous solution he'd seen, a caustic green resembling some form of radioactive waste.

After taking a moment to ground her spirit, Anjali began her explanation. "When my parents and I immigrated to America, we had to get vaccines to obtain visas. Hoping to save a cent, my father hired a traveling doctor. Although he never traveled, we always went to his house for the operation. That should've been the first sign of trouble, but we were ready to leave."

She closed her eyes and reimagined the clinic. "I remember that day so well. It was one of our last in Mumbai. That week had been hotter than average, and we were drenched in sweat even when asleep. The rains had recently come, too, and everything was muddy, but the humidity was the worst. I'm sure my father was suffering from mild heat exhaustion when we reached our destination because the doctor had the nerve to charge us an extra fee for arriving four minutes late."

"Damn, this sounds like a scam." Lance tried to conceal his humor, aware that this tale had a tragic ending based on her aversion.

"If only that were it. Hey, do you know how many vaccines you need for a visa?"

"Twelve. My pops is from Beijing. I kinda get it."

"Right. Then you understand what it takes to get here and how our parents would do anything for our future...even if it meant putting us into uncomfortable situations." She shuddered; the all-purpose jacket barely able to keep her secure. "Anyway, that hot day in Mumbai, we each got our second round of vaccines. The doctor didn't even sterilize the needle all that well between us, probably assuming that we shared the same blood since we were family."

"I was the last to be treated. Before my injection, the doctor decided to take a quick bathroom break, bringing along an orange bottle of pills."

"Wait, he hit the pack mid-treatment? Hell no! What about your folks? What'd they do?"

"*Nothing.* They sat and watched like they didn't care. Or rather, this was another necessary sacrifice for the future. Again, a future I had no decision to choose."

"What happened next?" Lance asked.

Anjali unbuttoned her blouse and slipped her arm out the sleeve, revealing her slender shoulder and torso. Near the bicep was a circular indention. "Now, touch there. Right...here." Lance did as commanded, and when he pressed the site, his fingertip made contact with something dense. Instinctively, he reached for his own arm, unhappily imagining the feeling of dirty needles penetrating the flesh.

"The doctor's needle took a liking to my skin. So much that he broke the needle inside my arm on that injection. Tried to pull it with his bare hands but lodged it deeper."

"Anjali..." Lance said.

"I can still hear his teeth chattering as he held the broken tool. My father threatened the doctor, but I found it funny because my father had been the one who sent me to him. But everything became a blur after that; I passed out from the shock. Worst of all...I still needed to go through one more round of injections to secure my visa. Next thing I remember was awakening in my bed as if it had all been some nightmare. But reality dawned on me when I tried to move my arm."

She provided Lance with a demonstration. The left arm only extended two-thirds of the way compared to her right. "Another doctor said the needle dug its way into my muscle and struck a nerve."

"Wow, I'm so sorry, Anjali. I did not mean to trigger you."

"You're fine; it's just my baggage. We've all got something from childhood, right?"

"That we do," Lance said, staring at the headphones. "Well, while we're at it, I'm also gonna go ahead and hide any sharp pens or paper clips." Anjali chuckled and buttoned her blouse as Lance continued. "Still, have you ever seen a syringe that fancy, though? I mean, who could they be vaccinating? The Pope? And this stuff in the syringe," he flicked the tube. "Does this get injected, or is this *the extract*?"

"I'm not sure, and honestly, I'd rather not add any more stress to my plate."

"What's got you stressed? Aside from George lurking behind every corner?" Lance asked as he lowered the volume on the speakers.

"I just got done brokering a deal with the SGA."

"So that's who that was in your office earlier." She nodded. "Fitzroy Casca has left the high castle and assigned us a duty, no?"

"He informed me of a campus-wide event being planned by SGA and the Art and Engineering Departments."

"Sounds major. What is it?"

"A renowned artist will be working as an adjunct faculty, and one of the artist's requirements is the university hosts an art installation," Anjali stated.

"Interesting. When?"

"Sometime around early March is the expected deadline."

"MSU with these lavish spectacles. The university's budget is astounding."

"Ironically enough, a third party is sponsoring this exhibit. Some company called *Contre Lux*. Fitzroy personally requested our coverage for the unveiling date. That means liability contracts, release forms, and media passes, but we'll get *unlimited access*."

"I'm definitely interested in helping."

"This is next-level content, so I'm already losing sleep. I'm unsure how I will manage planning coverage for this event and creating an editorial, but I know both need to happen this semester."

Lance removed a file dated April 1999 and started to flip through the documents. "So that's the real reason you want the applicants to create articles as part of the competition? To divvy up the weight that you're carrying. I get it, but how about I do you one better? Let me be your personal assistant."

"You're kidding? You can't even order the right tea."

"That's because *I am an investigative journalist*, not an apron-wearing barista serving corporate sludge to the laborers. If you want me to do my job, *give me a job that fits my description*. Hear me out; having an extra hand will ensure you're prepped for the installation, and when I'm not helping you with that, I'll work on my contribution to the editorial. And...I'll even collaborate with others, including George, when it makes sense."

"And what do you want in return? This won't get you extra points for the competition."

"All I ask is you support my investigation into the Lemurian Order. Matter of fact, you don't even need to officially support me; just let me snoop around."

"Why should I?" Anjali asked.

"Because this is a sensational story. The photos, the party, the syringe...All signs that they are clearly up to something this semester, and that deserves to be discovered. Who else to cover them but me, the best sleuth you've got?" They also seem to be interested in June, which worries me, he thought. "I won't disappoint you; I promise. I've already proven I can get results. Don't you see it, too? There's a truth waiting to be unearthed here. The question is, will you let me dig in?"

Anjali toggled the bangles on her hand and examined Lance. Usually, he'd squirm whenever they made eye contact; however, his gaze was steeled by resolve. She set his jacket on the seat and rubbed his shoulder before making her way to the door. Smiling, she announced, "You may dig in, but don't chase ghosts all semester, then leave me with my ass in the wind, okay?! I'll never forgive you if you do!"

The Triumvirate

In the southwestern corner of MSU, across from Folger Hall and the Morrison Moment, sat Ellis Laboratory, a hub for biomedicine for the past sixty years, and on the third floor of this establishment was the gross anatomy lab. Noah entered the laboratory wearing the traditional navy medical smock, clear safety goggles, and green nitrile gloves. Aside from them and the secretary working the equipment desk, the only other individual present on this floor was a silver-haired custodian last seen around the refrigeration unit.

Noah, who aspired to be a pharmacist, tightened his goggles and stared at the desaturated eyes of the cadaver splayed out below him. As a TA for the *Intermediate Anatomy & Physiology* course, his ID badge granted him permission to access the laboratory and all the equipment after hours. The body below would serve as his study materials for the upcoming semester, as he preferred to educate himself in the chilled labs rather than the lecture halls.

The stench of the formaldehyde and prolonged death irritated his nose as Noah charted the cadaver. Starting from the crown, he marked all the blemishes and abnormalities. Medical findings were jotted on the clipboard next to the tools. After palpating the ribs of the corpse, noting the broken intercostal bones, Noah set his clipboard on the slab and opened a sterile pouch containing a stainless-steel scalpel.

The scalpel slid from the marked forehead to the chin with deft accuracy; an identical incision was made underneath each cheekbone. Dermal layers, once protecting the skull from the world's toxins, were peeled apart. The tip cut around the face, slicing tendons and tissue with grace. Noah withdrew the blade, grabbed the retractors, and placed the tool underneath the flap of flesh. A swift swipe tore the connective tissue sewn between the muscles and marrow, and the face unfolded like laundry. The right side received the same treatment, and soon, the amateur surgeon had an anatomically accurate view of his subject's hypodermic layers. According to the report, his subject suffered a fatal blow to her head, causing a severe concussion and cranial swelling. There were also several dark splotches across her chest and abdomen.

As he assessed the corpse, Noah received flashbacks of his mother; she'd also been a brunette of similar build. Nora Casca was a radiologist in the oncology ward at Vera Grace Memorial. Known around the ward for her diagnostic abilities, Nora could, given enough time and the proper scans, locate everything from early signs of metastatic activity to cells undergoing remission. On multiple occasions, she was consulted by administrators and medical professionals across the globe to provide lectures, but she preferred the intimacy of clinical work. Some residents joked that Nora's eyes were so keen that they needed lead-lined scrubs to avoid her X-ray vision.

Throughout childhood, Noah spent afternoons in her clinical office whenever his father traveled for work (usually with the older Fitz). While there, he witnessed the various defects of the human body, not only physical but psychological as well. A general hopelessness often shrouded the oncology ward, and all who entered the doors knew their life would never be the same. Only young Noah, blissfully unaware, laughed and smiled and played in such a place. The young boy occupied his hours by mixing different liquids to create "potions" for the patients. His decision to study pharmacy at MSU stemmed from following his mother's footsteps; she'd also graduated and worked as a laboratory researcher at the private university. It was also here at the university that Nora met his father.

Through his mother's efforts, many lives were saved. However, Nora's abilities would fall short of saving her own. It began with a series of recurring migraines that turned her from provider to patient after a sudden loss of consciousness at one of Noah's Little League games. The headaches were linked as symptoms of an atypical neurological disease involving tissue degeneration that morphed into a terminal illness. After two years of enduring chemotherapy, radiation treatments, and unexpected nights in the ICU, the disease claimed her soul. Nora's body was dipped into formaldehyde and donated to MSU's medical department, leaving the Casca boys alone. Noah was only nine years old.

Outside the lab, Noah heard the closing of a large door: the refrigeration unit. *Now's my chance.* Tightening his gloves, Noah stepped away from the slab and moved to the equipment cabinet. He transferred a glass beaker and two sheets of paraffin wax film to his pocket. He then collected three pre-packaged syringes from an adjacent drawer. The sterile pouch ripped, and Noah pierced the gelatinous membrane of the left eye. He pressed the tip in further, then withdrew a sample of fluid and tissue fragments. Noah removed the syringe and squirted the contents into a dropper vial in his pocket. Then, he threw the syringe away in the sharps container before sprinting across the room.

The chemical locker swung open, assaulting him with a pungent odor. Brown bottles lined the shelves, each of them properly sealed and labeled. Noah removed four Erlenmeyer flasks from the dispensary and headed to the sink with the materials. He laid out four more vials, each uncapped and ready to accept the offering. A funnel dipped into the mouth, and Noah lifted the jug of phenol, pouring roughly 125 mL. He tapped the cap back on the first bottle and returned it to where it had been. He then performed the same action with magnesium, sulfuric acid, and another liquid with a missing label.

The last droplets leaked into the fourth vial, and he cleaned the counter as if he expected his father to inspect it. With vials secured in his pockets, Noah returned to his workstation and his "mother," just as bachata blasted from the approaching janitor's handheld radio.

The amateur anatomist folded the flaps of skin over the cheeks and checked the corpse's eyes. Swollen spheres, petrified by death, stared enviously at the spark of life still within him. Noah threw the blue tarp over the preserved skin sculpture and then jogged out of the anatomy lab.

He stopped by his locker to change clothes and transferred all the stolen items into his laboratory tote. Once secure, Noah exited the Ellis Laboratory's back door and headed toward the parking lot, where Fitz was waiting in his ice-white BMW 6-series.

"Pack is secured; let's get it," Noah said to his brother.

Together, the Casca siblings drove from campus to their residence. They exchanged bits of dialogue along the drive, but nothing substantial. Plenty had been said to each other earlier during the meeting. Silence didn't faze either of them, however, recognizing that they'd both learned to tolerate silence thanks to their father.

Noah's older brother had followed closely in their father's footsteps, earning his reputation through merit and ambition. Fitz was set to graduate with a degree in macroeconomics and served as president of MSU's student body for two consecutive terms. Leadership had been instilled in him since birth, but when he joined the debate team in sixth grade, Fitz unlocked his actual skill: the ability to mediate. Immediately, their father was made aware that Fitz could chart a bridge between two opposing forces. Recognizing the talent, he began conditioning his firstborn to become king of the modern world. It was always Fitz who traveled abroad, Fitz who attended his father's lectures and exhibit openings, and Fitz who was introduced to sponsors, philanthropists, and donors. By the time Fitz entered MSU, he'd already been handpicked to be part of a regional specialty club that identified youth of excellent caliber. Not to mention, his two-year tenure as president ushered the private university into a golden age of social activism and cultural inclusion. However, his greatest achievement may have been his election to Augur and his advocacy for a new era for the Lemurian Order.

Due to this successful lifestyle, the eldest boy lived in a grand reality where he was celebrated almost everywhere they went. But it wasn't enough for them to benefit from their father's foundation; no, Fitz understood one day, he would be tasked with continuing the Casca dynasty. Noah, unlike his brother, had no significant accolades to his name. He earned a fair amount of social clout, which rewarded him with more digital likes than respect (his IG account finally reached 30K followers). Around campus, he was known as the party plug, someone who had access to designer drugs. He'd already been caught once during his first year, but instead of expulsion, he received a sentence of community service for ten days. Some say his father's influence as a distinguished alumnus persuaded the institution to overlook the transgression.

Since boyhood, Noah was aware that all the factors that gave him rank were earned by someone else: his father, his brother, his mother, and *the Lemurian Order.* Since his work was usually done in the dark, he was rarely credited for anything except enticing confrontations, but, as Mitch liked to tell him, some of the greatest heroes only received a sentence in the history books.

When the Casca brothers arrived at the fraternity house, they were greeted by Parker, who had already donned his attire for the Capricorn Trial. Noah slung the lab bag over his shoulder, checking inventory before departing. Fitz also collected the case containing the experimental torch. Once the brothers confirmed their loadout, Parker nodded and led them through the Congregation Hall. They reached the curtain, and Parker pulled the cloth to the side, revealing the entrance to a stairwell. Noah powered up the light switch on the corridor side, but the bulbs proved less than reliable and flickered rather frequently, reminding them how darkness ruled the depths.

The trio said little along the walk until they reached the halfway mark, which indicated the need for more stable lighting. From this point on, they'd rely on handheld lights. Before they traveled further, Fitz dug into the bag he'd carried from the car, connecting the three metal pieces. The golden hilt flashed as the flint was struck. The air became acidic before a white flame burst from the torch. Eventually, it condensed and cooled into the recognizable bluish hue.

Shadows scattered to the damp corners, and Fitz rallied the crew behind him in the azure glow. They reached the Oracle Chamber, and Fitz illuminated the door. Noah nodded and operated the handle, stepping into the ritual site. The lights faintly pulsed, so they relied on the torch to illuminate more of the area than the poor wattage bulbs.

Unlike the rest of the lower area, the Oracle Chamber was warm and uncharacteristically inviting. The more time one spent in the chamber, the calmer their spirit became. Kimi proposed the effect was caused by the harmonizing acoustics provided by the thousands of microscopic pores drilled into the ceiling. According to records, the pores helped establish the resonance of vibrational patterns, melding them into a single waveform that could reach the edge of the original commune perimeter. She called it a prototype surround sound system for a city square.

They crossed the dome-shaped room, and Fitz and Parker went straight to the Den's massive stone door. Seven of the eight cells were closed; the one nearest the large doorway was partially cracked. No matter how many times he laid eyes upon it, Noah couldn't shake the feeling that he stood at the gates of hell, mainly because he knew what resided on the other side of the stone. He shook off the apprehension and moved to the altar, setting his lab bag next to the column.

His light hovered over the altar, "No fucking way. Are you shitting me, yo?" he whispered. He checked around the floor, scanning the ground with his hands.

The erratic movements caught the attention of the other two. "What is it?" asked Fitz, the torch shining upon his brother.

"*The box is open*," Noah responded.

Parker scoffed, "Isn't that what a box is supposed to do?"

"I didn't open it yet," Noah peered inside. "And, there's things missing."

"You're kidding? How could you-"

Noah spat on the stones, "What, yo? You think I have something to do with this?"

"You are the only one who uses it."

Noah threw him a middle finger. "So, automatically assume that it was me? Fuck you, Parker."

"When was the last time it was used?" Parker asked.

"I made sure to lock everything after last night."

"Why were you toying with it last night?"

"Because Fitz asked me for some serum."

Lights and eyes shifted to Fitz's, which looked more suspicious than usual. "In the essence of transparency, I'll tell you. Yes, I did request a dose of serum after the party."

"What did you want with it?" Parker asked.

"I can't say."

"There he goes, dirtying his hands again," said Noah.

"Really? Because a certain actor is in the hospital," stated Parker. Fitz remained silent, the flame whipping next to his face.

"What the fuck, yo? Did you give someone the raw serum? You could've fucking killed him, yo."

"I'm fully aware of the serum's capabilities, but he's not dead. Just out of the picture. We needed a bargaining chip for our new initiate, right, Parker?" responded Fitz.

"Is it safe to assume you also brought our lost lamb down here during the party? To see if he heard the calling, no?" Parker asked. "Fitz, you know I have full confidence in your abilities, but it's risky to make big moves without telling us."

"I needed to confirm his compatibility before we moved forward with him, and I was on a time crunch. But I left him in the cell, and the kit was well hidden. That was all before Noah retrieved the serum."

"And I told you, I left it all like normal, yo."

Hesitation laced Parker's voice, "Are they missing or *stolen*?"

The three stared at each other as the flames spun and snapped. "No way, yo. The party was done by the time I used it," said Noah.

"But it doesn't mean all the guests were gone, right?"

"They would have to know this was down here, though. It's not like someone would wander to this place and specifically take these things."

"But someone did wander down here—someone who found Daniel and rescued him...What if he came back to investigate? He was left unattended..." Parker's mind materialized the name and face of a nosy rat.

"Then it's possible. Very possible." Fitz halted their speculations. "I'll have Calvin check the camera footage while we conduct the trial. For right now, let's focus on the task at hand."

"Yo, genius. I hope you realize I can't whip up shit without serum," Noah stated.

"And yet, we need a fresh Nihilixer for tonight. There has to be another way for us to get what we need. Can't we, I don't know, improvise it?" asked Parker.

"Only if you want a hole to burn through your hands," replied Noah.

Fitz tapped his chin, "it seems that altering our approach may be our only way of progressing. Brother, how much serum do you need from the Hierophant?"

"I mean, a few drops should do, but may not be as pure," said Noah.

"I've read in the records that the Alchemists of old used to extract the blessing manually—a milking of sorts," said Fitz.

"Hold up, I'm not about to fucking beat off anything."

"Fear not, brother. This is a chance for us to learn something new about our guardian. And this may be a chance to prove yourself as a capable leader," his brother smiled.

Intrigued by the prospect, Noah eased his tension. "I hear you, Fitz. I know it can be done, but still, shit would be much easier if the Hierophant wasn't about to finish its nap. Why the hell is it even waking up anyway?"

"I'm not entirely certain, but our predecessors have presented a plausible theory. You ever heard of something called *Yol's comet*?" Fitz asked.

"Yol's comet? What the hell is that? " Noah asked.

"Apparently, this celestial anomaly passes our solar system at random intervals. Nobody knows where it comes from or how long it's been doing that; it simply exists."

"And what does this mean for us?" inquired Parker.

"Our predecessors may have been primitive, but they also understood things differently. From what I learned, this anomaly enhances the emission of vibrations during its appearance, and these oscillations activate certain be-ings. It seems the Hierophant is one such being. And if the team over at NASA are correct, we believe Yol's comet is currently en route to pass Earth this spring. It's been five years since the last passing, twenty-seven for the time before that, and then fifty-four. Each passing has been accompanied by pivotal moments in the Lemurian Order's history. Moments where our fortunes shifted in grand and unpredictable ways."

The youngest Casca leaned closer to the torch to give his eyes a respite from the darkness. Pupils filled with angst and fear shone in the dim glow. "Ahh fuck, what a perfect year to be a member, huh? Awakenings, random recruits, stolen artifacts. This ain't off to a good start," said Noah.

"Which is exactly why I need us to be on the same page," said Fitz. "Alchemist, Paladin, Augur. We each hold a po-sition of power, making us *the Triumvirate*. The rest of the members and the initiates will look to us for the answers on this journey. That said, I want us to have open lines of com-munication. We tell each other when something happens, no matter how big or small it may seem. Shared, universal information may save us from failure."

"You say that, yet you've already been keeping secrets from us, Fitz. So make it make sense. Do you want our help or us to stay out of your way, yo?"

"This is me asking for your assistance."

"Then, trust us to do what's best for the Lemurian Order. You always do this, trying to do it all on your own. We're here because we're equals, so let us help. Even if you're an asshole to me, you're a Casca, and we stick together."

"I agree with Noah. Have faith in us, Fitz. We've all been blessed, which means we're chosen to continue the legacy of the Lemurian Order."

"You're both right. If we fulfill our duties together, we will succeed in creating a new foundation for the future. Still...doesn't mean I'm not scared of failure," Fitz whispered to himself.

The Triumvirate stared at the stone tablet that separated the Oracle Chamber from the Den. Noah stepped forward and pressed his ear against the cold stone as if he could hear anything other than the anxious pulsing of his heart. Then, he knelt and dipped a piece of cloth into a puddle of ooze congealed at the base of the door. "Someone's been waiting for us." At the sight of the pooling liquid, apprehension swarmed like ivies spreading from their trembling knees to their dry throats. "Fuck! We're really about to do this, aren't we?"

"It's unfortunate, brother, but it seems that's the only way. However, we will be extra cautious. Now that we know its slumber isn't so deep, we should be mindful of how we approach the Hierophant," said Fitz.

"Do you think it's awake now?" Parker asked.

Noah bit his cheek, "I don't know. It was chill the other night when I extracted the solution. But that was like five days ago before we hosted a six-hour rager in our crib."

"Awake or not, we have to go *inside*," Fitz said. "Noah, what do you need us to do to help with the extraction?"

Noah reached into the tote he'd carried from the car and donned the gloves. Then, he wrapped the wax film over the beaker and fastened it with a rubber band. He tightened the wrinkles and inspected the surface. "I think I know how to milk the serum, but it will take extra hands. All you gotta do is listen to me, and we can dip out. Once we get the juice, I think I can cook up the rest on my own," said Noah.

"A solid plan," Parker said.

"If it's asleep. But if it's awake, then what?" Noah asked again.

"Then we pray that Kimi is the genius we all believe her to be," Fitz responded, holding the torch high.

Noah pushed the lever concealed behind a rivet on the eastern wall, and the massive door shrugged. Soon, a mechanism cranked, and the tablet started to roll to the side. A sickening stench swept from the opened crypt, tempting the Triumvirate to abandon their quest, but they remained steadfast.

Soft, rhythmic hisses radiated from the shadowy crypt. The noises reverberated off the walls of the Oracle Chamber, filling the space with harmonic tones. A shimmering veil was the only obstacle between the three trembling individuals in the Oracle Chamber and their sleeping deity. As they crept into the Den, Noah held his nose. The scent of death had been in the air all afternoon, but now it smelled like he'd reached the source. Because of this smell, he feared for the next generation, for he knew there was a day when *the Hierophant* would awaken and bring death to all who disturbed its slumber.

Hero's Dose

Around seven in the evening, June opened his eyes to find the toilet bowl staring down at him. He lifted his sluggish body from the floor and pressed fingers to his throbbing temples. An insatiable desire for thirst overcame him. June stuck his mouth under the sink and drank from the faucet. Then, he raised his gaze to the mirror. "Oh, shoot, no. No, no, no! Please!" Turning his head to the side, June noticed his afro was covered in vomit. He washed the hair as best he could but couldn't bear the discomfort. All movement intensified his internal pulsing, nearly sending him back to the floor. Accepting the cosmetic travesty as the norm, June exited the hallway bathroom.

Stepping into his dorm after being gone for nearly twenty-four hours, June was surprised to see it was vacant. He took his phone from his pants pocket and dialed Lance. Lance did not respond, but he left a voicemail for his roommate. "I'm meeting the car brawlers tonight. At the Clock Tower around nine-fifteen. Make sure your camera is charged."

After concluding the message, June hopped into the shower. Each plop of the droplets on his skin caused bumps to stand as if he were in peril. The violent pulse still radiated from his head as if his mind had been overcharged with plasma. "This is just a crash, June. A really bad one," he told himself.

Once dry, he went to his desk and spent the rest of his Saturday evening attempting to get ahead on schoolwork. He tried to read for Ms. Liam's course but drifted off during a section on Sumerian astrology, and math was no better. At one point, he started using letters and not numbers to solve non-algebraic equations. Ultimately, he gave up on schoolwork and crawled onto the futon to relax.

Checking his phone, June discovered it was close to nine. Lance was still nowhere to be found, but at least the hangover had settled. Wasting no time, he dressed in black and wore his bookbag to give the impression he was en route to another location on campus. Then, he departed, preparing to meet Parker at the designated location.

As June hustled across the brick sidewalk, the anvil-shaped clouds above campus released a platoon of snow. The temperature for this particular evening set a new record for the lowest temperature, a title held since 1999. Although the jacket warded off the chills, June's body felt hot, like a smooth stone cooking in a sauna. He removed his phone from his windbreaker's pocket to check the time. "I hope I make it. But to what exactly?"

Under the second wave of snow, his footprints were lost, and the wind bit his bones, but he pressed on through Morrison Straight University. The greenway connecting the campus to the Clock Tower was currently under renovation, restricting access to the foundation. Construction set up detours to guide travelers; however, detours wouldn't take him to his destination. After finding an opening in the fence, June slid through the orange mesh and cones, reaching the other side of the plot. It hadn't crossed June's mind that he'd begun trespassing, a crime punishable by a $250 fine and a meeting with Campus Court. But, the prospect of answering the invitation outweighed his fears, so he continued.

He cut through the restricted area, keeping his footsteps and breathing to a minimum. There weren't people out here per se, but he didn't want to raise the alarm either. Minutes later, June reached the Clock Tower without incident.

June shuttered at the sight of the constructed Cyclops. As the first building on the campus grounds, the Clock Tower served as the university's silent guardian. Limestone columns held firm, and the arms had rusted to a chalky brown, resulting from enduring countless seasons. In the wintry darkness, the structure emitted a menacing glow, for only two lights were active; one aimed at the base and the other pointed at the clock's origin. The bell encased by the spire was designed to ring every fifteen minutes; however, the mechanism had sustained a malfunction that caused the bells to produce chimes at irrelevant intervals. Sometimes, an entire month would pass before it rang.

A lightning bolt skirted through the snow-ridden clouds, and the boy crawled underneath the building. "Great, I'm right under the rod. But at least I'm here. So I'll just wait, I guess?"

So, he waited...and waited...and waited until he decided to pull the black binder from his book bag. June sat with his back to one of the pillars and opened the script. Due to the poor lighting, he couldn't make out much, but he re-read Baudelaire's character description.

"An elixir that can rewrite existence? Sounds like whatever Parker gave me last night," he said. Closing the binder, he began to pack his things. "What are you doing here,

June? This is a waste, and nobody's here. This could all be a stupid prank. Frat boys having a go at you because you got too lit at their party."

Frosty droplets cackled like evil imps as they fell on the tiles. The sky filled with scattering bolts resembling exhumed roots, and the bell chimed. The ringing caused June to flinch and depart from whatever fantasy realm he'd conjured while reading. Suddenly, the chiming intensified, becoming something like a melody. It drifted through the atmosphere like falling snow before piling into his being. The soothing notes embraced him as they had done in the basement underneath the Lion's Den.

With his eyes closed, June entered his mind's realm. A thin rainbow line zipped across the peripherals. Like a sound wave, it bounced and frayed with each hummed chord. Enamored by the imaginative spectacle, June tried to interact with the mote of imaginative vibration. In response, the hum turned into something more primal, like the roaring of a monstrous kaiju. The once thin line exploded, spreading phantasmal colors and prisms across the darkened plane. Hues melted together and formed a canvas of vibrant imagery. And then, a quake ripped through his spine.

June opened his eyes and dizzily leaned on his knees for support. He breathed as if a Sisyphean boulder weighed upon his breast; each inhale attempting to break free from his lips was met with an inevitable downward spiral. He also gagged at the scent of lingering stomach acid.

Then came another noise, something June recognized as a voice. He doubled back and scanned the surroundings but saw nothing.

"From the dark emerged a mongrel who wished to become a Man. But in this age, it isn't enough to be a Man, for men are mindless and are no better than the snarling beasts that roam the damp caves. Yet, you approach us with arms outstretched, begging for liberation so you may discover what lies beyond Man."

Thunder bellowed as an enigmatic figure finally stepped forward from the shadows. They wore olive robes covered in intricate patterns. Silver chains hung around the wrists and forehead, and shimmering frills accented the areas where the joints met. Eight tendrils jutted skyward from the make-shift crown adorning its head, and each tendril resembled the bulbous tail of some prehistoric insectoid. In their right hand was a golden scepter. "

"What is going on? Who are you?" June asked.

The figure continued to approach June. "The real question is, *who are you*? We have been tasked with bestowing a blessing upon one who is worthy, but to prove your worth, you must offer something of equal value in return. What you will give is contingent upon your desire, and the more you seek, the more required. Still, we entreat thee to make a proposition worth our ears. But, before the transaction begins, you must be tested before engaging with us. So, I ask: *What is forever*?"

Another bolt illuminated the sky as June turned towards the stranger, and, in the light, he caught sight of another silhouette. No, *six silhouettes*.

More chimes from the Clock Tower rumbled above as June tried to increase the distance between them, cursing under his breath. Terrible sensations in his body prevented any movement. Barely able to stand in their presence, he leaned against the column while the circle enclosed around him.

"Stay back, seriously. I'm warning you. I'll...I'll scream!" In the distance, June located a pulsing blue bulb at the top of an electrical column—the Emergency Response System. *If I can make it there, I'll be safe. Just hit the button and keep running. That's right, all you have to do is run. Don't be a hero; be a survivor.*

Escape plans deflated as June glanced at the hulking figure guarding the exit.

"What is forever?" Again, the question rang, but it sounded as if the group shouted in unison. Then, the original figure broke through the crowd, or rather, the crowd parted to grant them entry into the malformed circle.

Suddenly, the chanting stopped. A second robed figure stepped forward, produced a pouch, and the leader reached inside.

"What the fuck..." June muttered.

The hilt of a medical syringe glimmered as the lightning cracked. Inside the cylindrical container swirled a viscous purple liquid. The leader tested the syringe, and two droplets leaked from its tip. The ground hissed, and vapors rose from the newly formed puddle.

Crackles of hot thunder echoed over the horizon, and then there was utter darkness. However, a blue glow sparked from the shadows. The azure fire gleamed against June's cold cheeks while a splatter of colors poured across his imaginary canvas. And in an instant, he heard the melody again. Although he knew it hadn't spoken language to him, he nonetheless understood the context of the message.

Run!

Muscles ignited, and nerve pathways transferred high voltage volumes through his vessel as June leaped forward. He tackled through the robed figures, barely catching his feet. Three of them dashed for him, hands clawing. One caught his bookbag, and June crashed on the concrete. The impact jarred the stomach and increased his need to expel all liquids in his body. Swiftly, he slipped out the backpack straps before the hulking figure could snatch him.

Back on his feet, June sprinted. And sprinted until his stomach had other plans. The vomit burst like a pent-up geyser, spewing acid from his nose and mouth. One pursuer shied away at the sight, but the rest charged. He wiped his mouth and continued his escape.

Oh God, if I survive this, I'm never doing shrooms again. I promise! I'll go to Bible study every week. I'll even teach the class if you want. Please, just save me!

A shadowed figure materialized on June's left and tackled him to the ground. His body rag-dolled and tumbled in the snow—sharp pain radiated from his knee, which absorbed most of the impact with the ground. A foot stomped next to June's head as he reoriented his vision. "That's for the shoes, pussy," said the tackler before spitting on the ground next to him.

"Enough, Alchemist!" shouted the crowned leader. "Now, subdue the mongrel!"

June remained in the snow, waiting for the cold grip of death to welcome him home. The blue flame appeared like a will o' wisp, and he wondered where this beacon for lost souls would tarry him when they stabbed him in the back like Julius Caesar. Wisps of divinity drifted from heaven, some landing in the streams under his eyes. *Tears?* He also experienced a sudden release of body pressure followed by a rush of warmth between his legs. Of course, he'd pissed himself.

The snow crunched as the cult members surrounded him. Then, he felt the grips of various, unnamed hands latching to his body. They pinned him, ice cutting his ears as he struggled. A set of fists bashed against his chest, then sweating palms hovered over his eyelids. The chanting quietly resumed, this time intensified by the harmonizing. It sounded like the words belonged to one terrible god rather than seven individuals.

Finally, the tendril crown and the syringe appeared again. At the sight of this, June made a last-ditch effort to escape. He kicked and flailed, but none of the captors relented. Again, they demanded an answer to their question, "What is forever?"

A gust blew, and the leader's hood fluttered, revealing a pair of shimmering irises shielded by a fine layer of glass. *"Parker, why?"* June muttered. But he knew the answer. Wasn't it Parker who helped him with his audition, assisted in caregiving after the party, and even put in a good word to the production team? Reality proved it was Parker who earned Baudelaire for June. And now, it was time for Parker to collect payment.

"What! Is! Forever!?" The cultists screamed.

"Speak, Mongrel!" hissed the one who tackled him. "Or suffer the fate of the ignorant!"

"A fragment of the future!" gasped June. *"Forever is a fragment of the future!"*

All went silent, even the melody that had occupied his head. Then, the leader knelt next to him. As he expected, underneath the hood was a proud grin. "Excellent, Daniel. We recognize your response. Prepare the mongrel to receive our blessing."

The moist fingers above his face pinched his eyes and peeled the lid open. Wind and ice stung his exposed pupil, causing cold tears to materialize. "Wait, wait, wait. Stop, no, stop. You don't have to do this..." June said. He flailed and jerked, but the multiple binds were too tight to break. The syringe appeared within his field of view, existing as a gray blur. June continued to plead, but the leader ignored all.

"Now, awaken and ascend to the realm of Man!"

The needle disappeared into June's sclera and administered the solution. The crew disengaged from his body, and June sprang from the ground. He sprinted across the Clock Tower, but his inner kindling reduced to ash, and he collapsed in the snow. Nerves set ablaze when the liquid hit June's tissue, fiery streams spewing through optical cells. A budding volcano erupted from the cones, sending lava through lacrimal canals and melting all rods. All fluids within his eyes flooded out, leaving a creek of blood, tears, and oils. The orbs felt like hollow cubes of fragile glass. His hand started clawing at his face and temples as if hundreds of fire ants were released into his cranial vessels.

"The truth is absolute!" The group shouted as it encircled him.

Parker, their leader, held the torch over June's spastic body. "We beseech thee, Daniel Elliot Junior! The Lemurian Order has accepted your invitation, and we respond by granting you the noble task of ascension. Starting tomorrow, you will no longer be a student but an initiate of the Lemurian Order. As you embark on your journey to enlightenment, you must, without fail, adhere to our tenets. They are as follows:"

Each hooded member stepped forward and recited a tenet.

"You must uphold the utmost secrecy regarding the initiation process."

"You must excel in academia, and all grades must remain above a 3.5 GPA."

"You must train your body weekly and monitor your diet, sleep, sex, and hygiene."

"You must meditate daily and journal weekly about your experiences."

"You must avoid undertaking actions that can result in a damaged reputation."

"You must always be ready to assist and answer a member should they call upon you."

Parker then brought the recitation to a close. "Failure to adhere to any or all of these will result in severe repercussions, including dismissal from the process. However, prove your loyalty, and perhaps, you will be summoned to meet our guardian." He turned to the sky, arms extended in reverence. "Now, gracious Hierophant! We call upon thee and offer this vessel to serve as your host. In return, I ask that you guide this scion. Only through you will he come to understand himself and the world. And through him, you, too, can return to our plane through his personal devotion. Do you accept our tribute?"

A deafening boom echoed through the campus, dousing all noise, including the storm's thunder. The members of the Lemurian Order crouched, then looked above in awe. Parker removed his hood and glanced at the silent mob, but Noah spoke first. "Fuck...Did you hear that? It sounded like..."

"*Like a response*," said Parker.

A flash of light illuminated the Clock Tower. Another two followed despite the lack of thunder. They stood in a circle, unaware of what to do. "Let's finish the trial and get out of here," said the largest cult member. The huddle broke, and the members wiped the scene of evidence despite the irregular flashing. Items were secured in Noah's pouch, and the torch was disassembled. Parker collected June's book-bag, noticing the open script. He scanned the page and chuckled under his breath.

Another three flashes illuminated the members. Looking up, Kimi noticed the thunder did not sync with the flashing lightning. "That's not lightning; that's *a camera*," she muttered. She then began screaming, "Pelican! Pelican! Pelican!"

When Parker heard the shouting, he threw on his hood and placed June on the stairs below the Clock Tower. Immediately, the others scattered in various directions, abandoning the foundation and the poisoned June. Seconds later, their presence was unrecognizable, save for the footprints in the snow.

With palm outstretched, the wanderer watched a cherry blossom flutter across the pond. It cast no reflection as it glided to his hand. The petal glimmered thrice before returning to the air without the aid of wind. It pulsed as if to guide him. So, he followed, heading to the crystal surface. Looking into the reflection pool, he saw nothing. No image, no reflection, not even the shade of a familiar. He crouched next to the water's edge and reached out a finger.

A furred claw broke through the shimmering surface. The darkened talons latched into the wanderer's arm. He tried to yank free, but the nails were deep in his flesh. And then, more hands rose from underneath the pool to overtake him. They swarmed his arms and shoulders before gripping his neck.

Despite his efforts to resist, the claws dragged him into the pool.

All the foundations that had taken root in his mind were washed away, sending the world into a formed blackness that, somehow, had shape, density, and matter. At first, it engulfed him, but over time, the darkness condensed into a more defined figure—something humanoid with recognizable features but somewhat perverted. In whose image was this art made?

Baudelaire?

Although unexplainable, the wanderer communicated with this shadowy homunculus. They shared a genuine unification of soul and soma, but his body was still too engrossed in pain to stabilize the connection. So, like other constructs of the unconscious mind, this one vanished, leaving a residue of light, color, and truth.

The minuscule knowledge he'd obtained over his life, now trivial, was expelled along with the remnants of his dinner. In that instant, as if tapped by great beings from the primordial past, the wanderer understood the nature of his laughable insignificance. But the lesson didn't stop at just existence; in the depths of his mind materialized transcriptions and theories inscribed on papyrus, ideologies that governed entire civilizations lost to the Great Flood, rationalizations about reality reserved only for the most enlightened, he even glimpsed into the distant future, capturing fleeting images of the farthest reaches of the Void.

When June finally regained consciousness, he felt like he'd been reborn. No pains, no trembles from the plummet in internal temperature, not even a dash of the hangover's presence. The entire surface area of his skin registered as one signal easily transcribed by the senses. Lungs filled with air and exhaled the total capacity, yet his gums were swollen like oversized balloons, and there was a taste of blood in his mouth. Ears deciphered and classified all manner of noises, both cosmic and infinitesimal. Limber arms rotated as toes and lumbar vertebrae curled.

And then, he opened his eyes to his new world. It looked the same, yet it had changed because he'd changed. Sparse glimmers of unfamiliar elements floated in the peripheral view. Lifting his head, he saw a glowing green shape ahead of him. Despite its ethereal nature, it had a definite form. Blinking thrice, the glow disappeared, replaced by two individuals before him.

"*He's awake.* Lance, hey, he's awake!" said a voice.

"Easy, bro. You're okay. You're safe."

"Lance, oh man. Lance. It's you," June responded.

"It's me, bro," Lance smiled.

June looked across the room at the young woman sitting in the office chair. "Work Bae, too?"

"Work Bae?" asked Anjali.

"Ah...haha...you mean Anjali? Yes, ah, she's here. We were getting work done in the MM when I got your text. Archives have no service, so I didn't see it until I stepped out for a breather. We went to the Clock Tower as you suggested, and I got some photos of something...strange. Was that really the car brawlers? Did they do something to you, June? You were passed out on the stairs," Lance said.

Something compelled him to keep details confidential. So, he acted. "I don't really...I'm not sure. But I remembered something...I made a deal."

"Don't tell me you made a deal with them? Why, when we know they're a secret Serpent cult?" Lance asked.

"Not the Lemurian...Order. A deal with...the production team. Lance, I'm gonna be...him."

Both journalists looked at each other. "Be who?"

June smiled, *"I am Baudelaire."*

Fallen Starlet

A black dress frilled from Michaela's hips like a dragon's tail as she rang the doorbell. Tonight, her blonde locs had been set free from their usual wrapping, hanging just below her shoulders. The combination of her signature pink hi-top canvas sneakers put the outfit somewhere between high fashion and streetwear. Charcoal and maroon were the colors chosen for her mascara and eyeliner. Unlike other business casual events, she wanted to be seen and recognized as the artist.

The door opened, and she was welcomed inside by Oscar, dressing as glam as ever with a beige suit. He skipped the tour and guided her up the winding stairwell. They reached a parlor, and Oscar offered her a seat at the granite counter. Relics of brass and ceramic decorated the walls. Across the room was a love seat and another couch that curved into an L shape, both a satin red to accent the creme walls. An aroma of aged maple filled the entire estate, adding to the regality of the atmosphere.

Mr. Ray, the interim host, waited next to Michaela. He wore a ruffled black turtleneck and dark denim slacks, continuing to identify as a brooding genius. The other person in the parlor was Gris. The older adult donned a navy three-button suit with an open collar that exposed his sagging jowls.

Michaela glanced at the lavish bottle of bourbon and then at the older man. "Always bring your own entertainment," Gris smiled as he discovered an ice cube in the freezer. "Want one?"

"Sure, is that okay, Mr. Ray?" asked Michaela. The theater director cheerily tipped his own glass in her direction.

Gris finished preparing her cocktail as Parker Galician arrived. He reached into his tweed blazer and removed a handkerchief to clean his lens. At first, she wondered why he was present, as he wasn't on the production team, but then she realized he was filling the Theater Troupe's secretary role.

As soon as the actor settled, Oscar opened his mouth to address them. However, Michaela, rising to her feet first, prompted the group to pay her attention. "I'd like to say something before we begin, if that's okay," she announced. Oscar wasn't about to cause another confrontation, so he let her take command. She scanned the faces of the men. They seemed fixed in their ways, with unchanging wrinkles and bone structure. Would they go for this shot in the dark just because she had a crush on June? Then, she had to hide her face for a second.

Seriously, a crush?

Michaela cleared her throat. "I want to start by saying thank you all for trusting me thus far. As a writer, it's often overwhelming, in a good way, to see your work come to life, especially with all sorts of great hands involved. I know we've made our decisions about the cast, and decisions are important, but they can also change if the circumstances present them. So what I think is..."

"We should recast Baudelaire," Oscar interrupted. The shock on the production team's faces was soap-opera-worthy, especially Michaela, who had to confirm he wasn't a secret telepath.

"You've had a change of heart. Because just yesterday, you said that was, and I quote, *a reckless endeavor,*" Michaela responded.

"It is!" His boyish shout echoed downstairs to the kitchen, where the catering staff was busy garnishing the dishes. "But now, it's our *only option.*"

"It seems there have been some capital changes in circumstance since our gathering yesterday. Okay then, let us open the floor for deliberation. Mr. Mercado, could you please elaborate?"

Oscar loosened his tie, "After mass this morning, I went to Vera Grace Memorial."

"How is our dear Mr. Brooks? Eager to engage with the stage, I imagine."

A weighted sigh fell from his lips. "I didn't even get to see him. *He's in a coma...*"

Gasps flittered out of the production team. "A coma? That's not what I expected to hear," Gris commented.

"Shit, I thought this was just alcohol poisoning," said Michaela.

Oscar's sadness polymerized into frustration. "I told you Timothy doesn't drink! They found *no trace* of alcohol in his system."

"If there was no alcohol involved, then what happened to Timothy?" Gris questioned.

Sniffles began to pour from Oscar as he relayed the information. "The toxicology report showed...the doctors were baffled...his parents told me they found traces of powerful neurotoxins that can...stop an adult heart in seconds. The pathologist said these chemicals are only found in venom."

"You're telling me we're dealing with a bad bite?" Mr. Ray asked.

"It was hard to determine what creature the toxins belonged to. Could be anything from a snake to a scorpion to a freaking octopus."

"That doesn't make any sense, though. Hello, we're in Upstate New York during winter! None of those creatures populate this area, right?" Michaela left a pause. She tried not to overestimate her scientific knowledge with two F's in biology.

"Perhaps a student in his dorm had one, and it escaped? And then, he was attacked and the poison got to him over time. That could explain this situation," suggested Gris, but even he recognized the idea was a stretch.

"Everybody at the hospital is confused, so they decided to stick him in that plastic box until they can get some antivenom. It might take them days to identify what they need in the first place." Parker tried to console the grieving man, but Oscar swatted his hand away. "Everything was going good between us until we went to *your stupid party.*"

"Party? Parker, did you have something to do with this?" asked Gris.

"My organization did host a back-to-school bash to commemorate the 150th year of MSU's chartering. There was alcohol involved, but it was only accessible to those with proper identification. I assure you, Oscar, I sympathize with the current scenario, but the doctors have already ruled out alcohol, so how can you continue to lay blame on us? Perhaps we should check all of Timothy's movements? Maybe backtracking will reveal a greater truth?"

"It doesn't matter now; it won't change his situation."

"But it might help you get some closure, so blame doesn't weigh you down," said Gris.

Oscar snatched Gris's drink and chased away his grief. "I don't know. It all happened so fast. And without Timothy, our production is ruined."

"But it's not ruined," Michaela said. "We have another actor; we have June. And I decided that he is the *best choice* for Baudelaire."

"Screw that. He was supposed to be a body to fill the space until Timothy returned! Any idiot could've been our stand-in."

"He might not be ready yet, but he will be by the time the curtains pull back."

"How are you so sure?"

"Because he *wants* to be the character, he will do whatever it takes to get it done," said Michaela.

"Are you that dense to believe *Mr. Stagefright* can lead this entire play?"

"Don't call him that anymore. It's crude."

"Oh, now you're defending him? What kinda plot did you two hatch? This a secret plan to get your boyfriend into the spotlight?"

"I already told you not to talk about me like that. Don't do it again. And no, he's not my boyfriend. I think it's child-ish to bully people with nicknames. Especially people who we need to succeed."

Parker raised his hand and entered the discussion. "If I may. Although I believe there are more talented actors than him, I would, once again, stake my name on Daniel. I've briefly shared the stage with him, but from our single inter-action, I recognized his potential. Like Michaela said, his desire to become a better character will aid in developing his skills and, in turn, may inspire the rest of us. Have faith in him like I do; I believe he will excel in this role."

"This is a pertinent proposal," said Mr. Ray. He scratched his chin and stared out the window. "I'm conflicted about whether we should extend this offer to the entire student body, and yet I also foresee this affecting our schedule with more re-auditions. I'm also somewhat hesitant to vouch for Mr. Elliott's long-term position as Baudelaire. Although he's been a great student, to assume the role permanently will require much. Is it fair to ask this of him?"

"I believe with an opportunity such as this, he will exceed expectations," stated Parker. "Think, would I be who I was if not given the chance? Or any of us, for that matter?"

"A valid point, Mr. Galician. What do you think, Mr. Tendleton?"

"What do we do about his current role?" he asked.

"We can bump up one of the extras," said Michaela. "I can easily write out one of the tavern patrons, thereby freeing up a position."

"Seems like a sound strategy," said Gris. He took a sip and shrugged his shoulders. "Hm, why not? Let's bet on the wild card. And if things go wrong, we'll be there to pick up the slack."

"Before we finalize this choice, for this is indeed a critical choice, are we sure?" asked Mr. Ray. "If we reach this agreement, we'll have to move forward without regret. Can we all progress from this?" Everybody nodded while Oscar finished his drink, slamming the glass on the counter. "Then, we make the announcement before we begin the group reading," said Mr. Ray. "I also believe in transparency amongst teams, so to promote a unified group, I will update the cast and crew on Mr. Brooks's unfortunate status."

"Perhaps it's best to leave some of the details out? Don't want to spread misinformation," Gris suggested.

"Agreed, we will relay all that needs to be said and nothing more. I also extend this request to the team: please refrain from revealing too much regarding Mr. Brooks. If anybody becomes too curious, feel free to send them to me. Ms. Patterson, before we break, I know you mentioned wanting to change roles. I'm assuming it was regarding Baudelaire, so I'm confirming: Does this adjustment fulfill your desires?"

"Ah, yes. Thanks for hearing me out," she said.

"Naturally, your opinion as our playwright holds significant weight here, so feel free to share it anytime. Now, if there's nothing else on the agenda, then let us prepare to welcome our passionate peers. Although hearts may be heavy, today begins the first day of production, and we will need all the pride required to progress!"

The production team exited the parlor to find a handful of the cast already settling into the lavish estate. Guests were asked to find a place of comfort and lock into that position for an undetermined amount of time. Over the next five minutes, the familiar strangers pooled into the grand home at a tremendous rate, as if half the team had arrived in a caravan.

Michaela strolled down the stairwell, scanning the crowd like a military advisor. She assumed a position on the couch and continued monitoring them. At least thirty individuals had already been seated before she noticed someone was missing. She wanted to see his face the most, his radiant eyes with a sensitive touch that exhibited the inner character. He was, however, the last person who could afford to be absent at this time. A group reading without its lead was like having a choir rehearsal without the soloist.

Mr. Ray thanked the attendees for arriving and completed a roll call. When he finished, Mr. Ray explained to the students that Timothy would be out indefinitely. He avoided using words like coma and venom, opting to leave his condition as unspecified. As Michaela expected, gasps of concern and a few questions followed the announcement. When asked who the new Baudelaire would be, Mr. Ray answered, but June's tardiness made it awkward. To save face, Mr. Ray led with some of his poor dad jokes, but when he'd exhausted his best hits, he reluctantly looked to Michaela to prepare the reading.

Michaela pulled the red pen from her binder, opened the metallic clips, and then removed the original copy of the script. She carefully placed it on her lap as if they were classified documents containing national secrets. Some students watched her with intent; others wrote her off as weird and waited for their following instructions.

"It doesn't matter who I am or what you think of me. From this point forward, all you need to focus on is who you are becoming. Understand? Now, open your scripts to page one."

Bags were unzipped, pages unfolded or rolled out, and flattened with elbows. Soon, everybody in her vicinity invited themselves into her mind. Michaela glanced at her cast, then at the cover page. The word UNTITLED struck her with a feeling of helplessness. How could she expect them to serve if they didn't even know what they were to serve? However, there was no time to consider a title now; everybody was assembled and ready to receive the story from the source.

Everybody except June.

And so Michaela, for the first time in her life, welcomed a living room full of strangers into the mystical world conjured by her imagination. Although someone fulfilled the role of narrator, she nevertheless read along silently. Each person had the chance to assume the role they'd been offered and how they adapted. Even in this simple recital, some actors, like Parker, immersed themselves in character. Others read with zero enthusiasm, but she did not hold it against them.

They had to pause the reading a few times to reconfigure a particular line or detail because Michaela found it failed to maintain flow. However, the actors' struggles to recite their lines caused other delays. Then came the critiques.

Some were positive, like the woman cast as Rochelle asking about her accent and particular phrases. In contrast, others complained he couldn't pronounce his name, like the tavern bouncer named Gnambacious Sorex. Still, the comments steadily chipped away at her with each page turn, and it wasn't until two-thirds of the way through that Michaela began to question why she even wrote such a terrible script.

A disconnect grew between her and the cast, and she feared the results of the final product if this gap wasn't mended. However, she couldn't be the one to bridge this; no, she belonged on the writer's side. To close this distance, she needed *him to be the lead*. But he was not here, so she finished the reading with a solemn attitude.

***

The final page turned, and everybody breathed a collective sigh, signifying the conclusion. A hurried five knocks followed. Gris rose to investigate the front door. He opened it and greeted the tardy individual with a smile.

"Fashionably late, just like a leading man," Gris remarked as he welcomed June into the living room. The young man, dressed as if he were preparing for rush week, adjusted the curls atop his head and straightened out his red tie and navy blazer.

Michaela's scowl quivered, and she did her best to conceal the budding grin. She couldn't show him relief until he knew how much his absence affected her.

He tried entering the corner beside her before Mr. Ray seized his arm. "Mr. Elliott, why don't you share a few words? You missed the icebreaker, so you'll have to split the glacier," he laughed at the poor joke.

All eyes were on him, including those on the portrait hanging above the mantle. There were too many eyes to count, yet he stepped forward with new confidence.

"Hey, everybody. As Mr. Ray said, my name is June...well, my real name is Daniel, but you can call me June. Or July. Or October. Just not May. Because I may not respond. I apologize for being late; it's been a rough weekend."

Many of the faces around the room had a similar expression: surprise. Some whispered about his past failure on stage, while others commented that they didn't know someone so cute was in the production. Michaela watched June's gaze wander toward the back of the living room. He exchanged a glance with Parker, who mouthed the phrase, "You're welcome."

June refocused on Mr. Ray, who had yet to finish the introduction. "Mr. Elliott was once our beloved Tavern Master, but the transcending thespians known as fate have decided to offer him the role of Baudelaire," announced Mr. Ray.

"Temporarily," June said.

"Actually, this is permanent. Mr. Elliott, *you are Baudelaire.*"

That confident shell cracked along with his voice. "Wait...you're serious? What about the stand-in? I'm...a lead? What about Timothy?"

"If you would've shown up on time like asked, you would've heard this already," Oscar mumbled behind Michaela, nursing his third cocktail.

"Circumstances outside our control have forced Mr. Brooks to withdraw indefinitely."

"What the shit?! Wow, wow, oh, wow. Well," June continued. "As your leading agent of change, I will do my best to bring your story to life. I will not fail you!" Although he faced the crowd, Michaela knew he was speaking directly to her. His determination earned a blushing smile.

Mr. Ray then assumed the floor. Pausing a moment to scan the crowd, the theater director relaxed his shoulders. "I know we are all starving, so I'll keep this short. I'm thankful to be able to share creativity and community with you all. Some may be unaware of this, but this is a tradition. It's always been customary for plays I produce to have dinner on the first and last day of production. Each of you here is now part of that tradition."

He walked around the fireplace, cup in hand. "To bring this production to life, we must work together; in a way, we must be of one mind. In the coming weeks, I will be expecting nothing but the best from each and every one of you. You've been chosen because we see the potential within you, even if you do not. By the end of this semester, I hope that potential is a thing of the past and you become the best version of yourself. Anything else to add, Gris?"

"You've said everything I would say, Emi. Now, how about a toast?" Gris raised his drink into the air. The rest of the students, including June, lifted their glasses. "To...to...oh hell, it's rather challenging to toast to a production without a title," the critic confessed.

"Hopefully, our play will have something right by the end of this semester," Oscar said.

"It will; you can't rush genius," June countered. Michaela's rosy cheeks lifted as she nodded and thanked him. "Why don't we toast to...hm? Ah, how about Ingilaef? I kind of feel we're in the tavern now," said June.

"A wonderful suggestion. On the count of three." As Gris began counting down, Michaela locked eyes with June. Time slowed as they shared a stare, neither of them blinking. Something deep within her gut welled, yet she maintained eye contact even after the countdown reached zero and the glasses clinked in celebration.

Shit, it really is a crush, she thought.

Kindred Spirits

After the toast, the ensemble broke for dinner, and June calibrated his system to the new setting. His day leading up to this event began in the dorm, with breakfast and debriefing with Lance. Then, he finally used his student ID to enter the Bradford Gymnasium. Immediately intimidated, June stored his belongings in the locker and crept to the nearest machine. After seasons of hibernation, his muscles received a maintenance check. After the gym and a shower, he visited the library with a crew of classmates from his Sociology course, diving into subjects that generated debated opinions. Twice, he even participated without the group requesting that he share. Later, he meditated in the Contemplation Corner, located in the Washington Student Union. Although he couldn't find nirvana, he did get a moment to gather his thoughts. But his self-care routine had taken double the time and left him with scraps of minutes to reach the production dinner.

And now, he was sitting next to someone with a history of ruining his reputation. "Tell me, how does it feel to go from nameless extra to the leading man?" Oscar inquired while picking his tooth with a chicken bone.

June finished the last bite of his morsel before addressing him with false cheer. "I know! I'm still processing it myself."

"Must be intimidating to have the responsibilities suddenly thrust on you like this?"

"To be honest, I was under the impression that it would be temporary. I heard Timothy was coming back."

"*Timothy's not coming back,*" Oscar muttered.

"Oh, did that Broadway thing go through?"

"No, the Broadway thing didn't go through. Ask yourself, do you think Timothy, the best actor to touch our stage since Albert Thompson, would turn down the last production of his college career? Here I thought you were going to exceed my expectations. I have too much hope in the common people; that's the Cancer in me," he said.

"What's that supposed to mean?" June asked.

"Nothing. All you need to worry about now is saying your lines. I refuse to allow you to fuck up while I'm in charge."

"Whoa, hey, I get it. Trust me, it won't happen again."

"So you say, but that's yet to be proven."

"I'll prove it to you. Just watch; I might even match Timothy's energy."

"Like you could ever do that. Timothy is a gem, and you're granite at best."

"And yet, I'm the one with the role."

"A role you didn't earn for yourself. It's only because Timothy's in a coma that you're doing anything," Oscar said.

June held his breath. "Did you say...coma? I thought he was just–"

Oscar's drunken lips loosened at the seams. "That's right. This is all fucked because Timothy was *poisoned*, and the person responsible for it is...that person is..."

"Who poisoned him, Oscar?"

"We're all complicit, one way or another."

A flush of emotions overcame Oscar, and he snatched his cup and stumbled out of the living room into the bathroom. June gave a brief chase but stopped at the kitchen. The actors were exchanging their opinions on character profiles and potential outfit ideas. Someone offered him an invitation to join the huddle. However, when June glanced at the stairwell, he saw a pair of reflective glasses that hadn't left him all weekend. He turned down the invite and bee-lined to the stairs.

"Parker, we need to talk now. What did you do to me last night? And did you hear about Timothy?"

"Silence, Daniel. You must not speak of that here. Some ears wish to know."

"Then, let's go chat somewhere private," June suggested.

Parker scanned the room, whispering, "Nothing I say will satisfy your curiosity; this lesson is best learned by listening."

"Enough of the riddles; just tell me what I need to know. Please?"

"Trust me, Daniel. All will be revealed in due time." Then, Parker strolled over to a waving Mr. Ray, shutting down any further discussion.

June, again, tried to give chase but was halted by the limp smile of Gris appearing behind Mr. Ray. "You're quite the hot commodity. Might I borrow a moment of your time?" June nodded, and Gris extended his hands to the left toward an art studio.

The studio was decorated with accents of diverse cultures: a cabinet full of Indian inks, aged Ghanaian spirits, dozens of Indigenous paintings and portraits, a floral kimono drizzled with violet cherry blossoms, and thread spools with mystifying hues. On the workspace was a giant tapestry, or at least the outline of one. Its frills dangled like the bodies of hung fruit over the edge of the desk. The design had been completed; it was now only a matter of stitching the strings together.

The gentleman pulled a plush stool from the counter and gestured for June to sit. "What's your fix?"

"Come again, sir?"

"A drink. You do drink, don't you?"

"I'm underage..." June confessed. Any more substances would surely kill his poor liver.

"And I'm senile. Now, Daniel, Mr. Elliott, or June? Which one do you prefer? You have so many names; who are you, *really*?"

"I'm still trying to figure that out."

"Maybe I'll just call you *Baudelaire*?" Gris teased.

He blushed, "June is fine, sir."

"Then, June, although I may be well off in my years, I also recognize who you are. I know that you are a man who is no stranger to alcohol, so I offer you a drink before we converse as men. Now, if I'm misinterpreting the signs and you truly are abstinent or a man of the cloth, then..." Gris started to close the glass cabinet when June politely raised his hand. The least he could do was share a glass with the man who'd voted for him to be the lead.

The elder raised a half-empty bottle containing a shimmering amber liquid. He then highlighted the country of origin, the year of origin, and the originator. Being underage meant that June's liquor knowledge was limited to whatever bottles he and Lance could score from their upperclassmen friends when they went to the store. But the bottle Gris opened was far from the cheap "gasoline" he and his room-mate guzzled.

After shaking and pouring, Gris presented the boy with a cocktail. The young man took a sip and tightened his face. "It's like that, yeah?"

"It's excellent; I can't taste any of the bourbon, which makes me worried because I saw how much you poured," he laughed.

"The secret is blackberry and a pinch of clove. Flavors can mask almost any taste," Gris smiled. "Now that we have our favors, what would you like to discuss, June?"

"Um, I'm not sure. You summoned me," he said.

"You were summoned so I could see who you were for myself. I've only briefly witnessed your acting abilities, and I must say, you have a commanding presence on stage."

"Commanding? I don't know about that."

"It's only a matter of time before they see what I do. But you have to see it in yourself first."

"Easier said than done."

"And yet, still doable, no? I mean, look at you now. Did you imagine being in this spot, say, five years ago?"

"I always dreamed of being the lead, but now that I'm it, it feels kinda surreal."

"Welcome to life, my friend. It's important that on this journey, we never forget our origins; how else can we mea-sure our progress?"

June took another sip, which allowed his mind more room to explore his thoughts. "I have a question, Gris. What's your origin story?"

"I wish there was a complex way to answer that ques-tion. However, it's quite simple: I am bound by the threads of fate. My grandmother was a seamstress during the

Reconstruction period in America. She started a family business. The skills and shop were passed down to my mother and me. Got my first sewing lessons in the middle of the Vietnam War since I was too young to enter the draft. I stitched everything from flags, fatigues, ammunition pouches, and funeral suits."

"That's so interesting. You literally helped out in a war," said June.

Gris twirled the two ice cubes in his glass. "You'd be surprised at the effect death has on the human spirit."

"What do you mean?"

"Fate granted me an opportunity to develop my artwork authentically, but only because of death's hand. When I was around twenty-four, I took over the family business. Developed my skills and started to get a bit of notoriety for my talents. And then came the open call by Gianni Versace."

"As in the Versace?"

"The very same. Nice fella, even if he was a bit of a playboy." Gris continued, "Now, at that time, everybody wanted to work with the fashion genius. And Versace was looking for the best. Compared to other artists in Dallas, I was great at what I did but not the best in the state. That title belonged to Keith Kale, a seamstress in Austin. And if anybody was going to be chosen by Versace, it was Keith Kale. However, it just so happened that the other individual was a less-than-favorable gentleman nobody had the patience to deal with."

"An asshole," June suggested.

Gris laughed, coughed twice, and wiped his mouth with the moist napkin around his glass. "Your words."

"So, what happened next?"

"I created a one-of-a-kind suit lined with genuine snake-skin. One of my greatest masterpieces to this date. But it wasn't good enough to get me in the door. Naturally, Keith Kale won the open call, and I was shortlisted. However, just before he accepted the position, tragedy struck. It seemed the reason Keith Kale was an asshole, excuse my language, was not wholly his fault. There were rumors the artist had been struggling with a mental illness. We didn't have language for these things back then, so his health went unchecked, like the rumors. Unfortunately, an incident occurred, and the fella ended his journey."

June felt the condensation of the glass kiss his sweating palms. *"Suicide...?"*

"He hung himself with fabrics from his shop. With an open vacancy, Versace contacted me to fulfill the role, and I accepted. My path was paved from then on, and I began my professional career as a fashion designer."

"How'd you end up attached to MSU?"

"After thirty years in the field, I realized there were fewer ideas to create and more information to bestow. So, I worked as an adjunct professor in the Arts Department for a time. I'm no instructor, but I did enjoy the gig while it lasted. Retired five years ago, and now I'm just an old man with exquisite taste."

"Talk about a journey," said June.

"And now, the journey has me, once again, crossing paths with the next generation of artists," Gris finished his glass after reminiscing. He motioned to the bottle to see if the young man wanted a refill, but June declined.

As Gris mixed another cocktail, June wandered around the studio space. Unique prints, weathered relics, and incomplete sculptings lined the shelves. Something next to a silver set of dentures caught his eye–A shimmering cup with emeralds intricately placed around its basin. June's fingers traced the outlines, running over the polished surface before gracing the smoothness of the embedded jewels.

"Ever used one of those?" Gris asked.

"No, what does it do?" June inquired.

"Hit it and see for yourself."

June grabbed the handle and patted it against the edge of the bowl as instructed. A low vibration bounced around the bowl before filling the room with a single, expanding note. He repeated the action, another *thummm* floating through the air. Gris then advised the boy to rub the edge while the sound echoed. This time, the noise spread through his chest rather than his cranium.

"So tranquil. Legend states that the vibrations produced from sound bowls can cure mental maladies."

"Mental maladies? Like a brain disease?"

"It's believed that an *illness of the mind is an illness of identity*, and a human being without an identity is nothing more than a husk."

"An identity illness?" June carefully placed the sound bowl on the workstation, and Gris sat with another drink. June looked at the cup and Gris's drifting pupils; the old drunk was being the old drunk, looking for any ear to spill their whiskey words. A few minutes of rambling wouldn't hurt; after all, he was one of the voters in June's succession.

Gris leaned off the couch and propped elbows on his knees. "An identity is what gives form to individual will. It is the vessel for the idea to pilot during our brief existence, the same way the brain inhabits the body. Each of us should seek an identity as long as we breathe. We live in a time when people are more interested in donning false values to appease another. Lately, it seems there is no room for the individual now that the internet has grown into what it is. And no, I do not blame you Millennials for this outcome; my generation is at fault for our lack of vision."

June nodded. "We are the guinea pigs of the digital age, though. Having social media is cool, but there are times when I can't tell what represents me, the world I live in, and if I'm even representing myself in this world. They're all mixed together."

"Exactly, June. So many are too quick to accept something in our lives as long as the person next to us says it's socially acceptable. This lack of individual thought is the fastest way to squander an existence. Too many live as drones commanded by cultural norms. But there is hope, thanks to people like you."

"People like *me*? Maybe like Parker and Michaela and Oscar, but not me. I couldn't even get the lead role without divine intervention."

"Do not downplay your...drive," Gris's burped. "Ah, you may not recognize it, but I do. We're *kindred spirits*."

"Kindred spirits?"

"Indeed, June. We're cut from the same cloth, and the threads of fate continue to weave," he said.

A light knock came to the studio, and Gris shuffled to the door. He opened it and greeted the individual. "A pleasure to finally meet your acquaintance. It's an honor to have you join us this semester, sir."

Gris stepped to the side, revealing a man whose presence filled the atmosphere with authority. His figure stretched toward the ceiling, standing at an imposing six-foot, five-inches with a wingspan to match. He bore an aquiline-shaped face, and upon his hands were two rings (one bronze and one gold with frills dashed into the perimeter) that clattered every time he touched his wine glass.

"June, allow me to introduce one of our generation's greatest artists, the production team's newest member, and the current keyholder of this exquisite establishment: *Franz Casca!*"

Franz set his wine glass on the counter, and Gris gestured for them to shake. The grip was stiff and demanded respect; June imagined this is how it felt when one met a veteran general. Staring into the icy pupils, he recognized something. He'd seen eyes just like this before and recently. Eyes that both condemned him and examined him in a closed room while music and party echoed, eyes that forced him to do...to do what...?

"So, you are *the cornerstone*?" Franz's hardened tone snatched June from the illusion.

"Come again, sir?"

"The cornerstone that will hold this play together. That's what Emi kept calling you downstairs."

"Oh, no...I'm just-"

"You're the lead, right?"

"Ye-yes, I am," June answered.

"The others won't admit it, but you have the hardest job. One minor fault in your foundation could collapse everything. A failed production because of personal imperfection." Franz swirled his wine, "One thing you need to know about me is that *I don't deal with failures.*"

What else did June know besides failure? Hadn't that been the fuel for his entire life? What about the lessons learned and the detours provided by mistakes? To a student struggling to find himself, failure meant everything. But to

Franz Casca, a man calcified by a twenty-plus-year career in high art, failure was failure.

Intuition informed June that he'd have to imitate him if he wanted to impress him. He raised his shoulders just a hair and held his chin high. "I won't fail you; just make sure you don't fail us." June's direct response cracked a slight smirk from Gris.

"Ha, a spark. Maybe you can hold it all together after all," said Franz.

"How lucky we are to have such a highly regarded talent on our team," Gris commented. I know you've just come off a long trip, but may I interest you in some designs I'm considering for the tapestry?" The artist nodded and started a solo journey into the studio.

Gris placed his hands on June's shoulder. "My friend, I believe we've exhausted our time, and I'd rather you not think of me as that senile lush who rants about the downfall of culture because of the internet. Thank you for the chance to chat; I look forward to seeing you evolve this year."

"I've enjoyed our discussion and am grateful for the opportunity to foster my foundation with your aid." All twenty-six of Gris's teeth became visible as the starlet excused himself from the room.

June stepped out of the studio and returned to the foyer in time to catch the end of a mass exodus. Half the cast and crew had departed, leaving the stragglers and the production team members. He descended the steps to join the crowd when a shriek pierced his eardrum. Balance dispersed, and he lost feeling in his knees. Gravity prepared to bash and break his body against the hardwood steps. But a hand grabbed his arm, catching him. He found additional support from the railing and steadied himself.

Michaela's blonde locs tumbled across her form-fitting black dress as she bared an accomplished smile. "Falling for me already? How cute," She teased.

All June could do was blush and attempt to salvage his pride. "Did you hear that?" he asked.

"No, what did it sound like?"

"Like a scream. A really painful one."

She shook her head, "Can't say I caught that one." A moment of lingered silence. Michaela raised her gaze to him. "So, how are you? Enjoying your stardom status?"

"Truly. Signed a few notebooks, posed for the paparazzi, and just finished an interview with Gris," he said.

"What did you two talk about? The importance of the individual and the dangers of the internet?"

"Actually...yes? How'd you know?" June questioned.

"I'm pretty sure we had the same alcohol-infused interview. A morbid tale about his rise to fame? Threads of fate and yada yada?"

"Kindred spirits?" June inquired.

"Kindred spirits!" They laughed. "Given all that went down tonight, I'd call this a somewhat successful meeting."

"Agreed. I'm hype about the play," he said. "Tomorrow, I begin my journey as Baudelaire. But tonight is all about celebration."

Michaela's glossed lips parted, "Do you have any plans after this?"

June's eyes widened with surprise. "I was just...gonna catch up...on some history reading...for next week."

"Never mind, then," she halted.

"NO! School can wait! What is it?"

She reached for his hand. "I need to tell you something, but I don't know how to put it into words yet."

"Give it a shot," he suggested.

"Promise not to overreact?"

"Promise."

"*You're not ready to be Baudelaire.*"

"What? I thought you said I was the best choice?"

He began to retract his hand, but she held firm to him. "What I mean is you're going to need mentoring if you want to become Baudelaire."

"Mentoring?"

"Mandatory one-on-one training; it's a condition on you assuming the role."

"What does that mean?"

"You'll have to meet with production team members at designated times. Each of us will work to develop your theatrical abilities."

"And when does this start?"

"Your first session is *tonight.*"

"Tonight?" he asked. "With who?"

"With me."

"We're doing this tonight?"

"We absolutely are," she said, concealing a grin.

"Why tonight?"

"Because you missed the reading! You are the last person who can afford to get behind. So I recommend we do an impromptu rehearsal back at my place."

"Your place?!" he gasped.

The parlor door opened, and Parker waved farewell to Mr. Ray before joining the couple in the foyer. Michaela gave his co-star a high-five. "Big thanks for siding with me during the meeting. I feel better knowing the role is in the right hands."

"No, thank you, Michaela. If you hadn't spoken up, I doubt they would've listened to me alone."

"I was just telling June about the mentoring."

"Yes, I'll also make myself available to assist in this process; just let me know, Daniel." Parker turned to him, his eyes shimmering behind the glasses. "I was just about to leave. Do you need a ride?"

He had a choice to make, and as many times as he weighed the options, he didn't know what to do. Go with Parker and learn more if he wanted to share, or go with Michaela and begin building Baudelaire?

June exchanged a timid smile with Michaela, who had the answer to his question written on her face. "Sorry, Parker. It seems like I owe her some of my time since I missed the reading."

"Ah, understandable. A woman worthy of time is rare; I'll leave you to it then." June held his breath. Was that disappointment in his tone? Parker exited the front door, tightening his blazer.

"Michaela, one second, please? I have to ask Parker something." She nodded, and June stepped outside. He pursued Parker to a familiar Jeep. "Before you go, tell me, did you have something to do with Timothy being out? Oscar told me he was poisoned?"

"Poisoned? That's a dangerous accusation. Are you certain you wish to believe that?" June shook his head. "Perhaps this coincidence is nothing more than the threads of fate weaving together a new design."

"Threads of fate? Wait, you got interviewed by Gris too? So much for being special," June scoffed.

"I'm growing rather fond of the old critic. We all could learn something from him. Speaking of learning," Parker put one hand on June's shoulder and pulled him close. *"Heed the call of the Hierophant."*

"The Hierophant? What's that?"

Parker unlocked the door to the Jeep and entered. "The answer to all of your questions. All you must do is listen well, Daniel." The window rolled up, and he was met with his reflection. Glassy lavender eyes stared back at him. June considered taking the ride to continue the interrogation, but it seemed the co-star was done revealing information. The car cranked, and he watched the enigma known as Parker Galician drive off into the misty night.

At the estate entrance, June and Michaela bid farewell to Mr. Ray. Behind them was Oscar, half-asleep on the front steps with a stained suit. "Mr. Elliott, I appreciate your adaptiveness. This may not be your chosen path, but it is the path that chose you. Remember this night, as this is the origin of your story, and it is from this point that progress will be measured."

"Let me guess, that's a Gris original," June asked.

"Indeed! The gentleman has phenomenal phrases, some of which I wish I could brand on a banner somewhere. You two get home safe, and I'll see you both on set tomorrow!" Mr. Ray nudged Oscar with his foot, and the drunk stirred awake. "And you, Mr. Mercado, let's get you settled. I understand this weekend has been emotionally exhausting for you, but after tonight, it's time to work. So, let's leave all the frantic feels here."

"But Timothy...he's hurt...I hurt him," Oscar groaned while the theater director guided him to a car.

"Yes, yes, we are all hurt by this sudden loss, but we shall overcome all obstacles."

All that remained outside of the mansion were June and Michaela. A frail beam of moonlight dipped across her softened cheeks, enhancing the natural beauty of her oval face. June, flustered by this look, tried to play it cool. "How long is the mentoring going to take?"

"It'll take us as long as it takes. Until I know you know the story, I can't rest. Which means you can't rest either."

"Why is this starting to sound like boot camp?"

"Because it is," Michaela said. "Do you remember what you told me yesterday? When you were on your walk of fame? You said that you were *all mine.* So, it doesn't matter if I want you at 11:30 tonight or 11:30 on February 30th; when it's my time, I expect *you* to be there."

"You surely don't give me any other choice."

"On the contrary, June, you have the choice. But you're a smart lad and know that giving me what I want is the appropriate choice. Because if I get what I want, you will get what you need."

"And what is it that I need?"

Michaela rested against the guardrail. Radiating from her smile was a subtle glow of something akin to unbridled passion. "*Me.* After all, I am the one who birthed Baudelaire."

Entanglement

After a twelve-minute car ride full of well-timed jokes, a curated playlist, and the occasional flirtatious laugh, June arrived at Michaela's residence. He followed her up the flight of stairs—on the railing in front of her door rested a clay ashtray holding burned filter tips. Michaela invited him inside, and June's imagination began to spin fantasies. There was no social furniture: no futon, no sofa, just one squeaking fold-out chair sitting under her cluttered desk.

Upon reaching junior year, MSU students who maintained a GPA above 3.0 earned the option to move into a solo studio apartment in the Morrison Complex on the southern outskirts of campus. He'd toured them once but never realized how claustrophobic the setting could be until now.

While he adjusted to his surroundings, Michaela went straight into the bathroom and changed into sweatpants and a shirt bearing the Three-eyed Raven from *Game of Thrones*. She reached into a basket next to her desk and lit two incense sticks, planting both in the soil of a potted bonsai. The aroma gently tugged at the sensuality beneath June's reserved character.

Still dressed in business casual wear, he attempted to sit in the chair, but the squeaking annoyed the host, so she tapped the corner of her bed. Cautiously, he joined her on the soft mattress, doing his best to maintain a comfortable distance. However, Michaela scooted closer, claiming they couldn't adequately rehearse if they couldn't read each other's emotions. But he feared what would happen if she read his current emotions. Maybe he was the first to be invited here; perhaps he wasn't. However, it didn't matter because he was here.

The tip of Michaela's thumb tucked between her molars, and she curled her lip while the other hand rested against her face. "Let's begin."

"So, where do you want to start?" June shifted to calm the blood rushing to his groin.

"Although the beginning seems the standard choice, I'm more interested to see how well you can *deliver diction*."

"Diction?" he repeated.

"Yes, I want to see if you can wield words like our eloquent protagonist. That said, one of Baudelaire's most defining moments is when he sculpts Rochelle. I feel like there's something so primal and dominating about this act. It's wildly impulsive, yet it's an essential experience for his character development."

"Impulsive is one way to put it," he said. "He's straight up claiming her essence."

Michaela flipped through the pages, diving into the meat of the story. "Kinda erotic, right? But think what it means for him. When we are introduced to Baudelaire, he's in the middle of an identity crisis. He's tired of the world and its uselessness, so he escapes to Ingilaef. And while he's here in this magical realm, he meets Rochelle, and she instantly entrances him. Not only because of her beauty but because of what she represents."

"And what does she represent?" asked June.

"She is proof that *second chances* exist. That we can become someone new if we are unsatisfied with who we are."

Seeing Michaela in her element intensified the connection, and while she searched for the scene, he failed to keep his attention on anything else but her. When she looked up and caught his curious eyes, June felt a star explode in his heart. And for a second, he thought he'd need to check his boxers. Her lips quivered as if expecting something, like a confession or a kiss. The couple held the moment, allowing the world around them to dissolve.

The incense tickled his nose, forcing a sneeze out of June. Like frightened felines, they jumped back to the corners of the bed, acting as if the interaction had never happened. But the lingering tension merely waited in anticipation for the next spike in passion.

"Here it is!" Michaela cleared her throat and showed June the script. He was about to take it when she snatched it away. "Whoa, now, this is the OG copy. I can't let you look at it. C'mon, you don't have your lines memorized yet?"

"The part officially came to me only four hours ago. How would I know them already?"

"Because I can tell you're serious about this role and have probably been rehearsing since it was released on the school website. June, from now on, you would do well to always keep my words with you. At the cafeteria, in your backpack, in the bathroom, hell, you should even *sleep with them*." She immediately covered her mouth as if that would retract the words. Both showed embarrassment in their cheeks, but the melanin in their skin made it nearly impossible to see the blush. "What I mean to say is you can't get caught slipping. You gotta do better, seriously. Everybody else was prepared tonight except for you. It's almost like you just rolled out of bed and said, 'eff it, this is what they get.' You can't do that if you want to be the lead; you have to be disciplined."

"It won't happen again, I promise."

"I believe you. Either way, it won't be beneficial if we keep sharing the page; that's not how dialogue flows. It must be fluid and natural. This vibrant romance between artist and muse is the beginning of the tragedy, and the authenticity of this bond has to be solidified in this fateful encounter."

"That's a lot of pressure for their first date, don't you think?"

"It has to be! If we can't get the audience to invest in their love, how can we get them to invest in the story? *This all starts with you, the initiator of their intimacy.*"

"If it starts with me, can I at least look at the page? To jog my memory?"

"I've got something better." Michaela walked to one of the dressers and pulled out a binder. She handed June the notebook and said, "I always keep a couple of copies; you never know when you'll need a spare."

While June scanned the following twelve pages, Michaela retrieved the ashtray from the front porch. A familiar herbal scent flooded the studio apartment. He tried to pay her little mind, for he was busy retaining the words, but the burning torch distracted him.

"Don't you think that will mess up the flow?"

"Hold up, are you about to tell me not to smoke my weed in my spot?"

"No...uh, not at all!" He apologetically waved his hands. "I meant that since we were...uh rehearsing, and I thought it'd be good, uh, if we had sound minds."

"I appreciate that level of dedication, but three things are wrong with your statement." Michaela lifted her index finger, exposing a small scar underneath her nail that extended to the bend. "I'm not rehearsing. *You are.* This is to help you get ready." She brought her middle finger next to the index. It was slender and longer than the rest. "Second, if you want me to have a sound mind, I suggest you let me take a hit to calm my nerves. My mind journeys at a moment's notice, and the occasional smoke break slows my thoughts; it helps the stuff in my head make more sense." She tossed her locs back and returned to his face with her ring finger raised. "Lastly, don't think I can't smell liquor on your breath. Did you drink at the party too? I know I did during the Gris interview. So, ask yourself, are you in a position to call me out on a lack of sobriety?"

"Right! Damn, I'm sorry. You know what? Just ignore what I said. I'm not thinking straight."

She inhaled and released a thick plume from her nose. "Already done, June." After taking a second hit, she placed the blunt in the ashtray and set it on the edge of the bed. "Ready?" she whispered, inching closer to June. He nodded as the embers of the blunt flared, and the two descended into the mystical world at the edge of existence.

~~~

The cherry blossoms surrounding the garden were in full bloom as Rochelle lay against the bank. An emerald sash was thrown across her torso, exposing both the right shoulder
~~~

and breast, while the lower extremities were covered by a cerulean fabric resembling a toga. Her flaming eyes looked like rubies lost in the snowy expanse of her face.

On the other side of the reflection pool was Gi, the gardener. He wore his signature set of all-white overalls with crimson threads stitched along the straps. Hanging from his arms were a pair of hedge shears and a tin bucket to collect any fractured branches.

Fingers moved across the water, yet no ripple or wave was generated. The gardener's words still echoed in Rochelle's mind. *"Only the real is reflected here."* Since she lacked a reflection, was she not real? Or did she exist as a source of entertainment for those cursed with eternity? Still, being here was better than being in the grave. Or so she thought.

Roughly two lunar cycles had passed since her first performance as the Siren. In that time, she began to learn the workings of her new existence. One of the most significant changes revolved around her freedom. Per the artist contracts, Ingilaef performers were offered access to the garden when the tavern closed, so long as the Tavern Master was satisfied with their performance. Visitors were also welcome, so long as they held invitations to Ingilaef.

As she lay on the bank's side, Rochelle considered her fate. What had she been doing before appearing underneath the spotlights? Before her eyes fell on a man tucked in the corner of the bar. Perhaps none of that mattered now because that man was standing before her with his famed tool in hand.

"I confess, I'm a tad embarrassed. I can't recall if I've ever done something like this," Rochelle said.

Baudelaire's fingers rubbed along the black block situated in his hand. He brought the carving knife down, shaving away a sliver of the wood. "What joy it is to hear that I am both the first and not the first. Although, such matters are trivial, for *I am the best.*"

"It's peculiar to know I carried out a life that I cannot hope to remember. Everything was hazy until I took the stage, and then it all came into focus. All those faces staring at my exposed self. I didn't know what to do."

"You did what was natural, reciting passionate lyrics, and what melodies you produced! Perhaps you were a songstress in your previous existence?"

Rochelle stroked her ashen-white hair as the strands obscured her crimson irises. "Perhaps. I can't explain where the lyrics came from, but they felt like mine. Comforting but distant, like I was staring at my home in a thick fog."

"Then praise be to the vastness and mystery of your mind. I have never felt such worth-"

"**Hold up!** Praise be to the vastness and mystery of your mind?" June questioned.

"What's wrong?" Michaela adjusted the fit of her shirt.

"You talk about flow and eloquence, but that's clunky dialogue. It sounds too philosophical, like a poorly prepared lecture. It lacks passion, too."

"And you're the expert on the subject?"

June rolled over on the bed, assuming a more comfortable position than the edge. "Not necessarily, but I know Baudelaire. He's an artist seeking the meaning behind his existence. Not a Shakespearean construct."

"Go on," encouraged Michaela.

"I mean, he's normally this egotistical man longing for the unknown, but that's because he has been by himself. Now, there is this woman, an unknown woman, who is rediscovering herself. So, I think Baudelaire needs to be less himself and reflect who she is at this moment. *He needs to be vulnerable."*

"Baudelaire...vulnerable?"

"Yes. It's only by being vulnerable we can witness his true strength. He's sculpting her, which is him acting on his truth, but this one tiny totem means more than the other golems he's created. It answers his current pursuit, meaning there should be pressure."

"And what do you plan to accomplish with this pressure?" Michaela inquired.

"Pressure is what fuels passion. Through carving, he's bringing his feelings to life by creating something in Rochelle's image. So, words should be decisive and uplifting. Aside from that," June shrugged, "vastness of the mind sounds like an insult. Like a fancy way of calling somebody an airhead."

Michaela tapped the script three times before pulling the red pen out of her hair. "What then, June, do you think he should say here to express vulnerability? What would you say to your muse?"

"I'd say...Hm, what would I say?" He tried to formulate a response in his mind.

Michaela added, "Consider the conditions: these two strangers are in this intimate space, and this is the first time they've had a real moment together. Baudelaire's already admitted he's found his truth in her, but now, he's got to make it real. And Rochelle's telling him that her past is like a thick fog," she said.

"Ugh, I don't know. This is hard," he said.

"Welcome to writing, June. And this is the perfect time for a smoke break." Michaela reached for the ashtray, twirled the blunt in her hand like she did her pen, and searched for the matches. "Mind giving me a light?" she asked.

June found them right next to his thigh. He struck the match and tended the fire while she leaned close to him. The flames singed the rolling paper, and the inevitable smoke appeared. The scent became earthen and natural. Both caught a glimpse of eyes navigating the vapors to scan cheeks, nose, and lips. Then, he blew out the match as she inhaled. He could visibly see the nerves settling in her face, and she coughed. While trying to maintain her breathing, she instinctively held the joint before him. Without a second thought, he pressed his lips to it and embraced the haze.

The faint glow of the lit tip appeared from the smoke and shadows. Looking at the joint again, June snapped his fingers. "That's it!"

"What's it?" Michaela asked, finally settling her coughing spell.

"The only way to break through fog is with *light*. So, if Baudelaire wants to be the man for Rochelle, he needs to bring light to her. Because if he can guide someone through existence, that means he's not lost."

"And with light comes clarity and comfort, exactly what Rochelle needs to continue her rediscovery!"

Michaela's red pen swayed back and forth as she sewed the letters into sentences. She scooted closer to him, presenting the script. How quickly the space between them shrunk. "How about this instead?"

June read the correction and grinned. "You truly are a wordsmith."

"You might be too. These are *your emotions entangled with my expression*. Just don't expect any writing credits."

"Wouldn't dream of stealing your shine," he laughed.

"Ready to keep it rolling?" Michaela asked.

"Ready for anything!" And so the bedroom walls became overgrown with cherry blossoms and fog, welcoming the two to the illusion once again.

More branches danced as Gi continued his pruning. By now, he'd cleared out about half the garden, and the day was steadily drifting into a drunken twilight. Over his shoulder sat the artist and the muse.

"The words...I can't explain where they came from. They felt comforting but distant. Like I was staring at my home in a thick fog," Rochelle admitted.

"Then allow me to be the spark of light that guides you to the origin," Baudelaire said while thrusting the chisel. A section of the black material fell off the side, completing the brow above the polished eyes.

Rochelle raised her chin. "Baudelaire?"

"Yes, Rochelle?"

"Why did you *choose me*?"

The abrupt question caught the artist off guard, nearly costing the bust a nostril. He stopped carving and pondered for a moment by scanning his immediate environment. Then, the artist approached his muse, striking a match for his rolled cigarette.

"I am a man ruled by intuition and expression, so I am unafraid of sharing this truth with you. I cannot explain the nature of the connection, nor would I attempt to put it into words; there aren't enough. But *I do not need to understand a thing to know it is real.*"

"Am I real?"

"How could you not be? Only the real can cause a re-action in me, and in that instant when our eyes met for the first time, I experienced a feeling more authentic than anything I've experienced in the last decade. And feelings cannot be fabricated."

"But how can you say that? You don't even know me, and..." her hair fell, shielding her face again. "I don't even know myself."

Baudelaire knelt before her, with the scent of spices still lingering in his mouth. She felt his callous-covered palms tickle the side of her neck. "Rochelle, don't you see? You have been blessed."

"Blessed? How is amnesia a blessing?"

"You may think that your lack of memory is a hindrance, but it is an opportunity."

"To do what?"

"*To become whoever you want to be.* To start fresh and stake your claim on a new existence," proclaimed Baude-laire.

"I...I only want to be...what you want me to be."

"Nonsense! I am here to help you discover what you have lost or define what you wish to gain. The opportunity to aid your evolution is worth more than my entire existence."

"Is that why you asked me to pose?"

"Indeed. I am compelled to construct your image because I recognize you as one worth immortalizing."

Baudelaire stroked his hand through her hair, and Ro-chelle responded by bringing the chisel to her palm. The blade nicked her hand, and a droplet of shimmering liquid weaved through the wound.

"You're so talented, Baudelaire. The world deserves you. But why are you here in Ingilaef?"

"It is because the world craves me that I arrived here. I admit I was lost. I no longer found any personal value in my creative endeavors, as they were all inherently linked to producing capital to pay for a lifestyle I truly abhorred. The soirees overrun by substances, the galleries filled with mindless drones, and the baseless questions about my artwork. A true hell. To rebel against the order, I halted all creative endeavors as a remedy, yet I became purposeless without my passion. So, I discarded my name and abandoned my studio to seek a spark of inspiration. And that inspiration was discovered in a rumor regarding an alchemist capable of concocting an otherworldly elixir."

"And that alchemist is here in Ingilaef?"

"I believe so, but Gi says otherwise. I think the gardener is hiding something. Alas, now, I have discovered something greater than this mythical potion."

"What's that?" Rochelle asked.

"*You.* It is you who have reminded me of who I am, you who have renewed my sense of life. So, I thank you, Rochelle. *You have restored me.*"

His cigarette burned in the corner of his lip as Rochelle brought her face over the water. Instead of being graced with a blank frame, she saw the fragments of something materializing in the ripples.

"When I was singing, I could only see one face amidst the others—your face. The lanterns and smoke concealed everything but your eyes. I don't know why, but I feel real with you, Baudelaire."

"Fate desired us to share this connection, and what we share will define our destinies."

"I concur, and because of that, *I trust you, Baudelaire.* I know with your aid I will come to know the best version of myself because you see me..."

"...for who I am."

June gasped as Michaela's lips pressed against his. The initial contact was forceful, shocking both, but the moisture quelled their apprehension. Sparks of microscopic electrons scurried out as his tongue came upon hers. Although his eyes were closed, he could see Michaela's honey-colored aura.

This...this is actually happening.

"I'm sorry...I got...too into it," said Michaela, pulling her face away to breathe.

"No, I want this. I want...you."

"Then, let me do it again."

Kisses were exchanged as Michaela tackled June to the bed, knocking over the ashtray. Locs fell from her undone ponytail, the strands covering his face. One tickled his nose, and he desperately fought the urge to sneeze as their lips connected again. He continued to paint her skin with his palm, each placed without regard to location. Cheek. Nose. Neck. Collarbone. Palm.

Michaela's shirt flew onto the floor, where June's mismatched socks landed. She lunged for the back of his head and brought his face into her breasts. "*Touch me here, please,*" she whispered, guiding hands elsewhere. His face rose from her chest, and he glanced at the wet stain on her panties. Thoughts tried to formulate into grips and pets and rubs, but she charged June's hand with another task as his arm was pulled lower and lower.

Michaela commanded June to stand while she fondled his belt. In a rush, he slipped out of his trousers and boxers. Both were nude. Exposed. *Vulnerable.* The college students ceased their ravenous clawing and remained immobile as if time had taken a lesson from the reflection pool. Only the rhythm of their beating hearts measured the passing moments.

"Tonight, I want...I want...to be seen. To be felt...to be desired," panted Michaela.

"You have me," responded June.

Michaela reached into the small drawer next to her table and removed a condom given out by Campus Health. June undid the packaging and placed the protection over his member. The scripts scattered on the floor, and the two were nestled in the comforter. June felt the cooling sweat of Michaela's skin against his own. He leaned into her moist thighs, and her hands tightened into fists that cut circulation in each of his fingers. Their hips rocked with a natural rhythm as a gushing was shared between their groins.

This is really happening!

Baudelaire returned to his artwork with Rochelle's scent laced around him. Now, his motions were more decisive—an etch there, a scrape here, pausing to appreciate the smooth, natural surfaces. Although he was working with force, his movements were still graceful. It was as if his body was controlled by some source higher than his mind and synchronized with hers.

Shards of blackened wood flew into the reflection pool as Baudelaire continued to develop his masterpiece. Each stroke removed more of the block, the chisel giving way to a new creation. Sweat poured along his brow, and he grinned from the exertion of passion. Rochelle sniffed a blossom that landed in her hand; the pink matter made her blush as it dissolved from her touch. She then repositioned her posture against the bank, granting Baudelaire a fresh angle to explore.

"Rochelle, it may be forward of me to confess this, but I desire only you. From this moment, I can continue my existence without hesitation, knowing there is someone as phenomenal as you," said Baudelaire.

Using the tools available to him, he dealt the sculpture a series of well-timed blows, each coming closer to the core of the bust. He alternated between swift strokes and deep trims, always remembering to remain visually connected with his subject. Baudelaire's chisel raised and lowered and raised and lowered, establishing a metronomic cadence. He wiped his forehead and observed the progress of his totem.

"When I came to Ingilaef, I was uncertain what to expect. It wasn't until our introduction I decided to return. And here now, after being reunited, I ask this of you: Will you allow the flames of our furnaces to crystalize the connection we share? Will you combat the forces of nature that oppose our limitless adoration for liberty? Will you love me even when the inevitable darkness extinguishes the world's divine light? I ask this only of you, for there is no other, living or dead, that can entreat my innermost wants as you have. Even my armory of golems does not ignite my heart like the melodies you produced."

Rochelle rose from the bank's edge and held Baudelaire's hand. "I accept, so long as you let me be a reflection of the realness I have realized within you." She allowed him to lead her from the bank to the stool. He instructed her to close eyes and wait patiently, building anticipation for the climax. And then, he granted her sight once more, revealing the product of his passion.

Sunlight reflected off the chiseled contours, and the black sculpture was warm when Rochelle touched it. "What is...that?" she asked.

"Totems are powerful charms that can link spirits to the real world. If you are indeed a fragment of reality, then this will be your foundation. Although small, it is proof you are real."

"And this totem is..."

"This is who I wanted you to meet. This is *you*."

The carved sculpture's face was like a winter horizon, with sharp crests for cheeks. A lake of frost surrounded the pupils' peaks, and the creation's mouth summoned a chilled valley where the wind echoed the most magnificent of voices. Upon seeing the sight, Rochelle fell into Baudelaire's arms. It was her, but it was so much more; it was Rochelle in the eyes of another. It was a foothold in a world that was once forgotten to her. He showed her she was more than a shade adrift on the endless shores.

A tear left her eye and trickled down her cheek. Baudelaire wiped it away with his finger and waited for Rochelle's response. However, instead of complimenting him, she returned to the bank's edge and peered into the water. There, forming in the stillness, was a faint image of the songstress.

Across the garden, the petal tucked in Gi's ear wilted to a dim violet. Noticing this, he scanned the orchard for any changes. His eyes landed on the couple and then on the reflection pool. Gi immediately dropped the basket of branches and raced to them.

"What have you done? No! Stop! This must stop immediately!"

He swatted Rochelle away from the water with his shears. Baudelaire gripped her close, shielding her from the dancing blade. The gardener's aggravated flailing led to the blade scratching Baudelaire's arm. Blood droplets flew on the ground and into the reflection pool.

"Gi, what is the meaning of this hysteria?"

"You...she...this," he pointed at the totem, "this is forbidden. Only the living are allowed to bear a form and reflection; those lost are merely *mirrorless mirages*. Why do you think there are no mirrors, glass, or shimmering surfaces here?"

"Who has instituted such a poor law?" inquired Baudelaire.

"It is the fabric of Ingilaef," said Gi. "I must correct this before it's too late. Rochelle, because you signed, it is your fate to be forever unbound. I will speak to the Tavern Master regarding your punishment. As for you, Baudelaire. You would knowingly tempt the fates with your actions, cognizant that your presence here is a gift?"

"Your initial warning failed to mention sculpting," he responded. "I will take my art and depart for the day. I suspect that this will not prohibit my entry into Ingilaef?"

"Alas, I cannot rescind the invitation, but this transgression must be dealt with accordingly," said Gi. "Give me the sculpture."

Surprised, Baudelaire pulled it close to his chest. "I will not. It is not yours to behold."

"Give it to me now!" The garden shears poked Baudelaire in the chest. A malevolent air surrounded the elderly man, bloodlust beginning to leak from the white overalls. Still, the sculptor held to his totem tighter than he held the chisel.

"I will not ask again. Give it to me, "threatened Gi.

"Baudelaire, just do as he asks. Don't ruin your chances of coming back."

Reluctantly, he released the carving, which Gi immediately threw upon the ground. Rochelle watched the gardener bring the hedge scissors across the totem's face. Then, another, and another, the blows chipping and cracking at the bust. Finally, the hardened blade sliced a gash from the left eye to the jawline, effectively scarring the masterpiece. Baudelaire screamed out at the destruction of his art. And then, Rochelle's reflection disappeared from the surface of the blood-diluted pool.

The Art of Creation

"That really happened..." Michaela whispered as June retracted his limp member from between her legs. A silent deadlock existed between them, their frames forming a foundation, and yet, each was unaware of the future. Michaela brought her hand to his cheek, caressing him. She peered into his pupils, catching a glimpse of her reflection, hair fanning like a portrait of Ophelia. Then, the rubber contraceptive slid off June's flaccid penis, returning them to reality.

"Gross!" Michaela shouted as the condom landed on her belly. June giggled and scooped up the used rubber, noting not to spill any contents on her bed. While he excused himself to the bathroom, Michaela reached for his sock and wiped the juices from her stomach. Her eyes adjusted to her surroundings as if, during the passionate sex, all her furniture was replaced with near-identical imitations. The floor was covered in their clothes, and pages of the script had slipped off the bed in the heat of the moment.

"Hand me my t-shirt, please?" Michaela asked once June returned.

After finding his boxers, he dropped to the floor and threw the black shirt onto the bed. Once dressed, she went to the restroom and relieved herself. Michaela peeked through the crack in her door. As he waited for her, June collected and sorted the pages of the script. "This should be in order," he stated.

"And yet, why does everything else feel so chaotic?" Michaela muttered to the mirror. "How did any of this happen? I never expected my weekend to end like this...but what now? Where do we go from here?" She took a moment to fix her hair and rubbed away the bags underneath her eyes. "Okay, Michaela, let's figure this out."

The bathroom door opened, and Michaela took a seat on the edge. She lit the rest of the weed, and smoke gathered around her head. Like a newly adopted puppy, June was perched with wide eyes at the foot of the bed.

"Before you say anything, I want to clarify something: *I don't do this,*" she said.

"What do you mean this?"

"Don't play dumb with me, June. I know how you artsy guys are. Using all that poetry and charisma and charm."

"Wait..."

"I'm not some desperate hoe who sleeps with her actors."

"I really wasn't expecting that to happen, honest," he said. "All I wanted to do was rehearse and maybe spend some time getting to know you."

"And why do you want to know me, June?"

"I want to know you because you are unique, talented, smart, and cute too. I haven't honestly met anybody like you on this campus, someone who sees me for who I am."

The heat inside the room elevated as Michaela started to piece the facts together. "You should know personal and professional is trouble. So, I'll ask again: why do you want to know me?"

"It's the truth, Michaela. I'm drawn to you, but that's because you're gravitating."

"Gravitating? Now, who's using clunky dialogue? Fine, June, I'll believe you for now. I just don't want you to get the wrong impression."

"Wrong impression? How so? Everything you've shown me has been authentic. Also, have you seen my pants?"

"We just met on Friday! How could you know anything about me? Do you even know my last name?"

June stopped his search and made eye contact with the flustered young woman. "Ummm...Peterson?"

"It's Patterson! Michaela Patterson!"

"*Please, God, help me find my pants,*" he whispered.

She stopped thumbing through the pages and palmed her forehead. "Did I just have a one-night stand with a stranger?"

"That's not entirely true. I mean, we know a few things about each other."

"Like what?"

"I know you are one of the best writers I've ever met. I know you're an appreciator of unique literature and prefer experimental pieces to the conventional; I know you based the story off Xavier's poetry collection." She waited for him to finish his confession before addressing his claims. "And I know you're struggling with a title."

"I'm struggling with a title? That's a bold statement," she said.

"Then, why does this production still not have a name?"

"Because naming a thing gives it power, and I'm worried the title won't match the energy."

June stretched his hand close to her. "I'd just call it *Edge of Existence* or something like that. It fits and sounds pretty catchy."

"How much closer to George R. R. Martin do you want me to get? I want something with more intrigue and allure. More importantly, why do you know these things? I don't know *shit* about you, except you're everywhere I am, just late. You take CP time to another level."

"I have my reasons for being tardy. As for why I know these things...didn't you say a writer's life is reflected in their work? So, I know these things because I've read your work. And I am *a big fan*." Michaela blushed at the admission. "It's embarrassing, but do you know how often I've run through this script?"

"Too many times if you're making these statements."

"You're not wrong. But because I've paid attention, I can confidently say that you share traits with your characters."

"Break that down," she said.

"You don't think it's ironic that Baudelaire doesn't title his work either? Exactly."

Michaela sat dumbfounded; had he read right through her? "June, you're quite intuitive, even if you don't belong here."

His head popped over the edge of the bed. "Just connecting the dots. Have you seen my pants anywhere? Like, I can't find them at all. So, if you help me find my pants, I'll be out of your hair in no time."

A sly grin appeared on her face. "Or I could kick you out now. Have an encore for your walk of fame?"

"Whoa! Let's not be hasty; it's like twelve degrees outside."

"I've heard that the cold causes a shrinkage problem," she teased.

"It certainly does, so I'd like to be dressed if I must depart."

If you must depart? Does he...want to stay with me? Michaela thought as she scrubbed underneath her side of the bed.

They continued to look for another two minutes in silence until she paused to soak in his expression. June was hanging onto the idea of something, waiting for an unconscious notion to become real. "Whatever it's worth," he began, "I'm not like other guys."

"Total cliché line," Michaela scoffed.

"But there's truth in clichés. I'm not sure what kind of experience you may have had before me, but because you've seen me for who I am, *I will see you for who you are.* Not what you can do for my career or my body. Although I can admit this was great, and I mean, if we're honest and hope we can be, *you started it.*"

"I did no such thing. How?"

"You kissed me first," June said.

"And you think the kiss was the first move? No, that was like the signing of the deal."

"What about all that flirting when we first met?"

"What flirting?" she asked.

"You're telling me you use those erotic innuendos in daily conversation?" There was a hint of playfulness in his tone, but she found the compliment underneath the teasing.

"Hey, my conversations aren't erotic."

He stopped and stared at her. "C'mon, really? Delivering diction? Receiving him well? *I need you?*"

"What's wrong with my words?"

"They're about as horny as a rabbit on molly."

"And yet, did you not reciprocate my energy? Admit it, you were curious because my words are wondrous. You should take a few notes, June. It's not just about the diction or delivery but also *the definition*."

Shadows seeped through the window and snuck their way into the bedroom. The darkness was so intense that when Michaela looked over the bed, she could only see the digital clock. The two gave up searching for his pants, and she retreated to the bed. June stood above her, his face half-concealed but full of inquiry.

"What do you want, June?"

"Michaela, can I stay here tonight? Actually, *I want to stay with you*. We don't have to do anything, as we've already done all we could. But I don't want our time together to end yet...so can I be here with you?"

The same idea had been inscribed on her tongue since he entered the establishment, but a statement such as this required courage to speak. Michaela lacked the courage to admit it, but he had the power to say what she thought.

June knelt before her; the light accented his masculine facial features. "If I'm a complete stranger, let me begin with this: Hi, my name is Daniel Elliott Junior, but..."

"The streets call you June, right?" She joked.

Embarrassment washed over his face as a laugh escaped her lips. "Still holding onto that?"

"*Writers have a flawless memory*; you would do well to remember that."

Michaela invited him back to the bed by brushing away a few ashes from her tray. She welcomed his presence with a snuggle and even started playing with the fine hairs on his bare shoulder as he fixed the covers. Although sensitive and moody, June was gentle, and he listened. Perhaps that's why she'd opened up to him in the moment. Maybe this mentorship wasn't to determine his acting ability but to determine if he could thrive in her space. Somehow, lying here with this stranger made her feel as if she were in *his* presence again, a presence that could soothe her chaotic mind long enough to bask in peace.

Propping her head on her palm, Michaela leaned closer. "Okay, question: Why June? Why not go by Daniel or Dan or Danny?"

"...I'm named after my dad, who goes by Dan. Now that I think about it, my dad doesn't like to be called Daniel, either.

"Wait, neither of you likes the name you were given? See, this is what I meant when I said names have power."

"Okay, you might be onto something. So anyway, when I was a kid, and we'd be at church, everybody would call me Lil Dan. But when I turned ten, I decided to switch things up and start going by Danny."

"But Lil Dan is cute."

"Yeah, for a six-year-old with crooked teeth and a binder full of holographic trading cards. Not for an actor."

"So that explains Lil Dan to Danny, but now you're June? How'd that one happen?"

June brought his hands together and slowly started rubbing his neck. "See, what had happened was...I had an identity crisis. And when I look back on it now, it's dumb as hell, but you couldn't tell that to the past me. This starts back in high school."

"Ooh, teenage angst!" Michaela smiled as she readjusted herself. Her head came to rest on his chest, and she threw one leg over him, enjoying the weight of another human.

"As you can see, I'm Black." Michaela almost chuckled at the apparent remark. "But I grew up around a lot of White people. Like a whole lot. Like middle-class suburbia with homeowners' associations, travel soccer teams, and book clubs full of Xanax-popping housewives. And yet, I was deeply rooted in my Blackness, thanks to my parents. They took me to a Black church, Black barbecues, and Black barber shops. Extremely thankful for that because you know *they* don't always know what to do with our hair."

Michaela dug her hands into the small afro, "Big facts."

He continued, "I never knew the struggle so many of us face until I went to public high school. I...I got called the 'smart' Black kid, as they used to say. But there was another word they loved to call me..."

"A name associated with a pretty gross cookie created by Nabisco?" He nodded. "Oooh yeah, I know how that goes. My older brother also had to deal with that particular problem."

"That's where the bullying always begins. Names and their power, right?"

"Told ya so," she said.

"*The Oreo*. It became my social brand. Oreo is too smart for sports, Oreo is too good to sit with us at the cafe, and Oreo can't dance, so why should we invite him to the party? I dealt with this every day from all types of people. The Black kids didn't want me because of my personality, and the Whites thought my Blackness was an issue to be corrected. So I joined theater because I figured, on stage, I could be *anybody but me*."

"Leave it to trauma to push us into creativity," said Michaela.

"Acting was my escape, and even though I wasn't the best at it, I loved it. I still love it...but that love was almost taken from me last year during *The Nightmare Before Christmas* production."

"The whole stage fright thing? Eh, it happens, though. A lot of newbies get nervous."

"I wish it were just that. Yes, I admit I get nervous and sometimes stutter or ramble, but that wasn't it. No, you see, I became Mr. Stagefright because my girlfriend at the time was in the audience."

"Did you not expect to see her there? Sounds like she surprised you."

"That she did, surprised me by breaking up with me right before the final show. It was horrible."

"Shit...she dumped you right before going on stage? That's mad disrespectful."

"I thought so, too. But she said she couldn't wait any longer, that she'd been hanging onto the decision for awhile, and there was no better time than now."

"I'm sorry to hear that. A break-up is never easy, but to be left right before a big event? Heartless."

"That's not the worst part about this shit, though. Afterward, we got into a big argument that caused a scene. Even Mr. Ray had to interject; it was bad. A lot was said, including something that screwed with my head."

"What'd she say if you feel like sharing?" Michaela asked.

June held his breath. Michaela caressed his cheek, and he exhaled. "She told me my performance confirmed I was a shitty actor and how she thinks I should give up on my dreams. And then...she called me Mr. Stagefright."

"Damn, are you serious? So, she came up with the name?"

He nodded, "Unfortunately, Oscar happened to be nearby and heard it. And that's how it spread."

"That's brutal. How long were you two together?"

"Since the end of junior year of high school. Relationship struggled a lot after coming to school here; she kept saying how she felt like I was holding her back. That our relationship wasn't shining like it did when we were younger."

"Sounds like an excuse."

"It was because not a week later, I ran into her being tongued down in the cafeteria. But that's a whole nother story."

"Sheesh, a quick rebound. Anyway, enough about your shitty ex. What happened next?"

"Later that night, after the production officially wrapped, I returned to the Thompson Theater. Once inside, I set my plan into motion." He tilted his head to show her the neck, and Michaela's fingers traced the rough patch. "See that? Turns out the threads of fate Gris talked about leave a hell of a burn."

"June, don't tell me you..." she pulled him close.

"I threw one of the rope props over the stage lights. Don't remember much, just the feeling of the texture against my skin."

"You tried to kill yourself?! But why? Because she broke up with you? She's obviously not worth it!"

"No, because she nearly ruined the one thing I held sacred: Acting. If I didn't have the stage, then I had nothing. And I was in a vulnerable state at the time. My first full year of college was hard, but the end of the year kicked my ass. The pressure from exams, the intense production schedule, no sleep, jacked on energy drinks, eating nothing but sugar and carbs, and stress from not having solidified summer plans. I couldn't handle it all; that conversation was the tipping point. So when she killed my dreams, I decided to die with them."

"But what about your parents, your friends, or the people you were going to leave behind? Did you not think about them?"

"I couldn't think about anybody else because I couldn't even think about myself."

"Life is precious. Once it's gone, *it's gone.*" Her grip on his arm was tighter than ever. Noticing it, she loosened her fingers, allowing his skin to breathe again.

"I know that now," he responded.

"June, you have a right to be here. If you ever need a reminder that you deserve to exist, *call me!* Seriously, don't do something like that ever again!"

"I...I'll keep that in mind, but I don't plan on hitting that low point again. Get this; it seems like this Oreo was double stuffed because the railing came crashing down."

"No way! Ha, so you're the reason the theater has brand-new lights?"

"You're welcome," he bowed his head.

"I guess there's a benefit to a breakdown after all. So how does this origin story end?"

"After I regained my senses, I stared at the broken glass on the ground, and, at that moment, everything became clear to me."

"What did you discover?"

"I saw myself for the first time as I am—shattered and fragile. But I also saw a mosaic—a *fragment of the future.*" He paused, bewildered by the word choice.

"After surviving that, I decided to discard the persona who tried to please others rather than himself. I vowed to embrace myself, flaws and all, which led to embracing this new name and identity. But I didn't want to create a brand new persona, so I borrowed from what existed. Back in high school, I had a music teacher who called me June, and, I don't know, I thought it was cool. So I went with that. Thus, June was born. The end," he said.

Michaela held her breath, reflecting on the entirety of the confession. "You think this trauma dumping will make me forgive you for almost spilling semen on me?" June's puppy eyes wagged up and down. "You're right; it will. Thank you for sharing."

Michaela's hand pressed against June's neck, and a kiss came to his cheek. They were investing. Connecting. Bonding. *Becoming.* He kissed her forehead, and Michaela's body suddenly stiffened like a corpse. Her right hand started to move, tap, and shake as if she were inscribing something on the comforter. The strange movements persisted for another minute, Michaela's pupils rapidly rotating behind the eyelids.

"Michaela, Michaela! Are you okay? Hey, hey! Talk to me!" June shouted.

Michaela broke from the shock and shook her hands free of the impulses. "Uh...about that, sorry," she apologized.

"Well, I'm officially freaked out. Can I ask what that was?"

"I guess it's fine since we're exposing our worst attributes. Sometimes, if I'm overstimulated, I will respond like that. It's not a seizure, but it's not normal, either. Most of the time, I can channel the energy into something productive like automatic writing."

"Automatic writing?" June asked.

"It's gonna sound weird, but I'm kind of like my own ghostwriter because of this weird flex."

"Can you control what you write? Or when it happens?" he asked.

"It's weird; the words are words I would choose, but I technically don't choose them. The body does that on its own. Could be a response to some negative childhood incident. Lord knows I've got a few heavy hitters in the vault."

"Oh yeah? Like what?"

"*A dead brother...*" she exhaled. "But that's classified information."

Although she could tell he wanted to dive further into the presented topic, June reoriented the conversation. "So, this is why you're having trouble? *Another you* wrote this script, and you now have to decipher what's being said. No wonder everything sounds the way it does," June stated.

"We've already established the dialogue needs work."

"Not just that. The whole story feels like being inside a dream. Your dream. Somewhat chaotic and unexpected, yet vivid and full of meaning. It doesn't follow typical plot lines, and some details feel too unbelievable to be based on realism, yet it relates to all individuals. It is an illusion...*Illusions of Ingilaef.* Hm, it could be a title?"

"A bit on the melodramatic side, but not bad. Also, if you want to keep that half of the bed you've already earned, don't tell anyone about this. As a matter of fact, *don't tell anybody about us.* I couldn't stand what kind of rumors people might start."

"Does this mean I'm not a stranger anymore?"

"No, you're a stranger—but not a complete one. We both shared something personal; I think that's called intimacy. Or trauma bonding?" Michaela bared a wry smile and tapped the pillow twice. Her eyes glanced over to the clock. "Shit!

It's already midnight. I'm acting like I don't have to be up in six hours."

"Oh, hell no. You're taking a 7 AM class?"

"Nah, I'm meeting my new biology tutor tomorrow. Long story, but I need some help in the class. So, I'll be waking up promptly at six tomorrow morning. Which means you will be up and out of here at the same time I am. Best to get the rest now."

Michaela pulled a satin bonnet behind her pillow and tucked in her locs. "Do you have an extra one of those? Or a du-rag?" asked June. She reached into the drawer and removed a secondary scarf. June whipped it around his head and tied a knot. Weirdly, they were a cute couple, preparing to sleep with their complementary scarves on. But she'd navigated enough intimacy for one night.

Michaela turned around and brought her finger close to his face. "Stick to your side, stranger."

"Wait...you don't want to cuddle?" He retracted his arms with childlike disappointment.

"No, I don't like being touched when sleeping. Look, I can admit that we had sex. And I can accept that it was, surprisingly, good sex, but that doesn't give you free access to my body. No cuddling and no kissing and no sex. "

"But I love cuddling," June whined.

"Do you love it enough to risk your chances at playing Baudelaire? Or anybody in the theater, for that matter?"

"Nope, I'm hip to the game. No touching. Understood." June tucked himself in while Michaela doused the lamp next to her bed. She lay awake, reminiscing on the moments she felt safe with her brother. How quickly the time had passed since they were together.

The curtains of sleep were about to fall over them when a blaring shriek came out of the darkness. June shot up and scratched his ears. The familiar noises caused his flesh to goosebump. "Do you hear that?" he asked.

"Are you serious? Of course, I hear it. It's the loudest thing in three miles. Is that...elevator music?" asked Michaela. The cheerful canto of Caribbean drums and samba sounds echoed in the room.

"That's my ringtone. Wait...my cell phone!" June threw off the sheets and found an object crumbling into a formless mass at the edge of the mattress. "Yes!" he shouted as he lifted the wrinkled khakis. "Look, my pants!"

She rubbed her eyes and let out a noticeably loud groan. "Damn it, Michaela. Why did you give him a chance?" June unlocked his device, glanced at the screen, and then fell silent. "So, who was it? Someone looking for the late-night date, mate?" She teased in a Cockney accent.

"No...it was my roommate. It's been a wild weekend for us, and he's got a lot to talk about..."

"Uh huh, your roommate? Okay, keep your secrets," said Michaela.

Enshrouded by suspicious shadows, June exposed a smile that would have served as a nightlight. "Michaela, I..."

"Enough. A good writer knows when to close a chapter. And we've reached the end of this tale. Goodnight, *Sleeper Agent.*" Michaela concluded the conversation with a kiss and a pinched arm.

As she turned around to fall asleep, June stared at the ceiling, contemplating a thought: Maybe his life was worth living; perhaps he was the protagonist of this journey, a master of his destiny. But he could only entertain such thoughts for so long before the contents of the text message invaded his mind.

"Heed the call! Heed the call! Heed the call! To seek enlightenment, you must heed the call of *the Hierophant!*"

Awaken, My Love!

As dawn loomed over the spires of the Lion's Den, an orb glimmered in the heavenly canvas. Leaving an extended tail of shimmering dust was Yol's Comet. The comet had soared around the solar system countless times since the celestial planet known as Earth was a molten core. Yet, it remained unaware of what existed on the surface for all the millennia it'd observed. All the hurtling mass knew was the depths of space as it had traveled beyond the farthest reaches of the uncharted Void. However, Yol's Comet was more than a cosmic phenomenon; it was the last grain in the hourglass, marking the moments before the alarm. When the comet's presence materialized, *the Hierophant awoke.*

The guardian of the Lemurian Order knew not how long its slumber lasted but knew it had been sleeping. And it could no longer return to that state of suspension because there was *a scent to track.* When had it first tasted the scent? Years? Days? Centuries ago? Regardless, the source of the smell had been close, like it was on the opposite side of the shimmering metal and cut stone.

The chain attached to it clinked as the guardian shook off the atrophy. From the gaped mouth drooled a caustic liquid that congealed when exposed to the atmosphere, and the nostrils snarled and hissed as it exhaled its first conscious breaths.

Like an infant, the Hierophant slacked its jaws to proclaim a mighty bellow that would rattle the spirits of any being within its acoustic range. But only a weak gasp escaped, and it collapsed under its weight. Not yet. The pallid creature whimpered and tried calling again, flexing the swollen laryngeal muscles. Again, a husky, harrowing whimper. Not yet. Lungs erupted with each exhale, set ablaze with each failed attempt. It hunched, igniting every synaptic cell in the sluggish body, from the cranial nexus to the ganglia scattered down its extended coccyx. Its next shout caught traction and started to form an intonation, but the fatigue from slumber silenced it. The binding chains slapped the wall as the laboring figure crashed against the damp floor covered in lavender fungal caps. *Not yet!*

It glanced around the Den, noting the environmental elements, including a burning torch. The azure fire flickered and licked at the wall, and the Hierophant coiled away from the torch. Unable to access its full strength, the sacred guardian of the Lemurian Order instead prepared for its exodus by humming. This ancient artist did not consider their audience nor the response they would provide upon hearing the tune; all the Hierophant desired was to sing a song beckoning its liberation. The somber requiem lulled through the Den and exited via the thousands of pores around the Oracle Chamber, echoing soft notes from the Lion's Den into the ears of every student, faculty, and staff member who resided on the cursed grounds of Morrison Straight University.

About the Author

Image by Jillian Clark

Johnny Lee Chapman III is an artist from Fuquay-Varina, North Carolina. Chapman started writing as a "Tumblr poet" during his first year at the University of North Carolina at Chapel Hill. In 2014, after graduating with a *B.S. in Dental Hygiene*, he leaped from page to the stage, beginning his career as a spoken word artist. Since then, he has performed regionally and nationally and is an active voice within his Carolina community. Over the years, his professional range of activities have grown to include movement and musical performances, workshop facilitation for all ages, event hosting, creative consultation, and artist mentorship. Chapman embraces the title of *storyteller,* the one in charge of relaying information by *inspiring imagination.* Offstage, he can be found cleaning the teeth of his community as a Registered Dental Hygienist, traveling with cameras to various places, playing guitar on the porch, or taking a voyage into the wilderness.

"Never let your ink run dry."

Website: www.3rdPlaceArts.com
Email: JohnnyLeeChapmanIII@gmail.com
Facebook: Johnny Lee Chapman III
Instagram: @TheGoldenMoments